LANDSLIDE

DESMOND BAGLEY was born in 1923 in England's Lake District and emigrated to Africa after the war. He held a number of jobs in Nairobi, Rhodesia and South Africa, and then became a journalist there. In 1962 he began to write a novel, *The Golden Keel*; after its successful publication in 1963 he and his wife returned to England, and he has been a full-time novelist ever since. He now lives in Guernsey.

Desmond Bagley has now written eleven highly-praised novels, each more successful than the last: all have been bestsellers in England and America, and they have now been translated into nineteen foreign languages. William Collins published his most recent book, *The Enemy*, in 1977.

D1136768

Available in Fontana by the same author

The Spoilers
The Vivero Letter
High Citadel
Wyatt's Hurricane
The Golden Keel
The Freedom Trap
Running Blind
The Snow Tiger
The Tightrope Men

DESMOND BAGLEY

Landslide

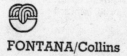
FONTANA/Collins

First published in 1967 by William Collins Sons & Co Ltd
First issued in Fontana Books 1969
Nineteenth Impression May 1978

© 1967 by Desmond Bagley

Made and printed in Great Britain by
William Collins Sons & Co Ltd Glasgow

FOR PHILIP JOSEPH
AND ALL GOOD BOOKSELLERS

I was tired when I got off the bus at Fort Farrell. No matter how soft the suspension of the bus and how comfortable the seat you still feel as though you've been sitting on a sack of rocks for a few hours, so I was tired and not very impressed by my first view of Fort Farrell—*The Biggest Little City in the North-Eastern Interior*—or so the sign said at the city limits. Someone must have forgotten Dawson Creek.

This was the end of the line for the bus and it didn't stay long. I got off, nobody got on, and it turned and wheeled away back towards the Peace River and Fort St. John, back towards civilization. The population of Fort Farrell had been increased by one—temporarily.

It was mid-afternoon and I had time to do the one bit of business that would decide if I stayed in this backwoods metropolis, so instead of looking for a hotel I checked my bag at the depot and asked where I could find the Matterson Building. The little fat guy who appeared to be the factotum around the depot looked at me with a twinkle in his eye and tittered. "You must be a stranger round here."

"Seeing I just got off the bus it may be possible," I conceded. I wanted to get information, not to give it.

He grunted and the twinkle disappeared. "It's on King Street; you can't miss it unless you're blind," he said curtly. He was another of those cracker-barrel characters who think they've got the franchise on wisecracks—small towns are full of them. To hell with him! I was in no mood for making friends, although I would have to try to influence people pretty soon.

High Street was the main drag, running as straight as though it had been drawn by a rule. Not only was it the main street but it was practically the only street of Fort Farrell—pop. 1,806 plus one. There was the usual line of false-fronted buildings trying to look bigger than they were and holding the commercial enterprises by which the locals tried to make an honest dollar—the gas stations and auto dealers, a grocery that called itself a supermarket, a barber's shop, "Paris

Modes" selling women's fripperies, a store selling fishing tackle and hunting gear. I noticed that the name of Matterson came up with monotonous regularity and concluded that Matterson was a big pumpkin in Fort Farrell.

Ahead was surely the only real, honest-to-God building in the town: an eight-storeyed giant which, I was sure, must be the Matterson Building. Feeling hopeful for the first time, I quickened my pace, but slowed again as High Street widened into a small square, green with cropped lawns and shady with trees. In the middle of the square was a bronze statue of a man in uniform, which at first I thought was the war memorial; but it turned out to be the founding father of the city—one William J. Farrell, a lieutenant of the Royal Corps of Engineers. *Pioneers, O Pioneers*—the guy was long since dead and the sightless eyes of his effigy stared blindly down false-fronted High Street while the irreverent birds made messes in his uniform cap.

Then I stared unbelievingly at the name of the square while an icy shudder crawled down my spine. Trinavant Park stood on the intersection of High Street and Farrell Street and the name, dredged out from a forgotten past, hit me like a blow in the belly. I was still shaken when I reached the Matterson Building.

Howard Matterson was a hard man to see. I smoked three cigarettes in his outer office while I studied the pneumatic charms of his secretary and thought about the name of Trinavant. It was not so common a name that it cropped up in my life with any regularity; in fact, I had come across it only once before and in circumstances I preferred not to remember. You might say that a Trinavant had changed my life, but whether he had changed it for better or worse there was no means of knowing. Once again I debated the advisability of staying in Fort Farrell, but a thin wallet and an empty belly can put up a powerful argument so I decided to stick around and see what Matterson had to offer.

Suddenly and without warning Matterson's secretary said, "Mr. Matterson will see you now." There had been no telephone call or ring of bell and I smiled sourly. So he was one of those, was he? One of the guys who exercised his power by saying, "Keep Boyd waiting for half an hour, Miss So-

and-so, then send him in," with the private thought—"That'll show the guy who is boss around here." But maybe I was misjudging him—maybe he really was busy.

He was a big, fleshy man with a florid face and, to my surprise, not any older than me—say, about thirty-three. Going by the extensive use of his name in Fort Farrell, I had expected an older man; a young man doesn't usually have time to build an empire, even a small one. He was broad and beefy but tending to run to fat, judging by the heaviness of his jowls and the folds about his neck, yet big as he was I topped him by a couple of inches. I'm not exactly a midget.

He stood up behind his desk and extended his hand. "Glad to meet you, Mr. Boyd. Don Halsbach has said a lot of nice things about you."

So he ought, I thought; *considering I found him a fortune*. Then I was busy coping with Matterson's knuckle-cracking grip. I mashed his fingers together hard to prove I was as big a he-man as he was and he grinned at me. "Okay, take a seat," he said, releasing my hand. "I'll fill you in on the deal. It's pretty routine."

I sat down and accepted a cigarette from the box he pushed across the desk. "There's just one thing," I said. "I wouldn't want to fool you, Mr. Matterson. This hasn't got to be a long job. I want to get clear of it by the spring thaw."

He nodded. "I know. Don told me about that—he said you want to get back to the North-West Territories for the summer. Do you think you'll make any money at that kind of geology?"

"Other people have," I said. "There have been lots of good strikes made. I think there's more metal in the ground up there than we dream of and all we have to do is to find it."

He grinned at me. "*We* meaning you." Then he shook his head. "You're in advance of your time, Boyd. The North-West isn't ready for development yet. What's the use of making a big strike in the middle of a wilderness when it would cost millions in development?"

I shrugged. "If the strike is big enough the money will be there."

"Maybe," Matterson said noncommittally. "Anyway, from what Don told me, you want a short-term job so you can get a grubstake together in order to go back. Is that it?"

"Just about."

"All right, we're your boys. This is the situation. The Matterson Corporation has a lot of faith in the potentialities of this section of British Columbia and we're in development up to our necks. We run a lot of interlinked operations—logging-centred mostly—like pulp for paper, plywood, manufactured lumber and so on. We're going to build a newsprint plant and we're making extensions to our plywood plants. But there's one thing we're short of and that's power—specifically electrical power."

He leaned back in his chair. "Now we could run a pipeline to the natural gas fields around Dawson Creek, pipe in the gas and use it to fuel a power station, but it would cost a lot of money and we'd be paying for the gas for evermore. If we did that the gas suppliers would have a hammerlock on us and would want to muscle in with their surplus money to buy a slice of what we've got—and they'd be able to do it, too, because they'd control our power." He stared at me. "We don't want to give away slices—we want the whole goddam pie—and this is how we do it."

He waved at a map on the wall. "British Columbia is rich in water power but for the most part it's undeveloped—we get 1,500,000 kilowatts out of a possible 22,000,000. Up here in the North-East there are a possible 5,000,000 kilowatts without a single generating set to make the juice. That's a hell of a lot of power going to waste."

I said, "They're building the Portage Mountain Dam on the Peace River."

Matterson snorted. "That'll take years and we can't wait for the Government to build a billion-dollar dam—we need the power now. So that is what we do. We're going to build our own dam—not a big one but big enough for us and for any likely expansion in the foreseeable future. We have a site staked out and we have Government blessing. What we want you to do is to see we don't make one of those mistakes for which we'll kick ourselves afterwards. We don't want to flood twenty square miles of valley only to find we've buried the richest copper strike in Canada under a hundred feet of water. This area has never been really checked over by a geologist and we want you to give it a thorough going-over before we build the dam. Can you do it?"

8

"Seems easy enough from where I'm sitting," I said. "I'd like to see it on a map."

Matterson gave a satisfied nod and picked up the telephone. "Bring in the maps of the Kinoxi area, Fred." He turned to me. "We're not in the mining business but we'd hate to pass up a chance." He rubbed his chin reflectively. "I've been thinking for some time we ought to do a geological survey of our holdings—it could pay off. If you do a good job here you might be in line for the contract."

"I'll think about it," I said coolly. I never liked to be tied down.

A man came in carrying a roll of maps. He looked more like a banker than J. P. Morgan—correctly dressed and natty in a conservative business suit. His face was thin and expressionless and his eyes were a cold, pale blue. Matterson said, "Thanks, Fred," as he took the maps. "This is Mr. Boyd, the geologist we're thinking of hiring. Fred Donner, one of our executives."

"Pleased to meet you," I said. Donner nodded curtly and turned to Matterson who was unrolling the maps. "National Concrete want to talk turkey about a contract."

"Stall them," said Matterson. "We don't sign a thing until Boyd has done his job." He looked up at me. "Here it is. The Kinoxi is a tributary of the Kwadacha which flows into the Finlay and so into the Peace River. Here, there's an escarpment and the Kinoxi goes over in a series of rapids and riffles, and just behind the escarpment is a valley." His hand chopped down on the map. "We put the dam here to flood the valley and get a good and permanent head of water and we put the power-house at the bottom of the escarpment— that gives us a good fall. The survey teams tells us that the water will back up the valley for about ten miles, with an average width of two miles. That'll be a new lake—Lake Matterson."

"That's a lot of water," I observed.

"It won't be very deep," said Matterson. "So we figure we can get away with a low cost dam." He stabbed his finger down. "It's up to you to tell us if we're losing out on anything in those twenty square miles."

I examined the map for a while, then said, "I can do that. Where exactly is this valley?"

9

"About forty miles from here. We'll be driving a road in when we begin to build the dam, but that won't help you. It's pretty isolated."

"Not so much as the North-West Territories," I said. "I'll make out."

"I guess you will at that," said Matterson with a grin. "But it won't be as bad as all that. We'll fly you in and out in the Corporation helicopter."

I was pleased about that; it would save me a bit of shoe-leather. I said, "I might want to sink some trial boreholes—depending on what I find. You can hire a drilling rig and I might want two of your men to do the donkey work."

Donner said, "That's going to an extreme length, isn't it? I doubt if it's justified. And I think your contract should specify that you do any necessary work yourself."

I said evenly, "Mr. Donner, I don't get paid for drilling holes in the ground. I'm paid for using my brains in interpreting the cores that come out of those holes. Now, if you want me to do the whole job single-handed that's all right with me, but it will take six times as long and you'll be charged *my* rate for the job—and I don't come cheap. I'm just trying to save you money."

Matterson waved his hand. "Cut it out, Fred; it may never happen. You'll only want to drill if you come across anything definite—isn't that right, Boyd?"

"That's it."

Donner looked down at Matterson with his cold eyes. "Another thing," he said. "You'd better not have Boyd survey the northern end. It's not . . ."

"I know what it's not, Fred," cut in Matterson irritably. "I'll get Clare straightened out on that."

"You'd better," said Donner. "Or the whole scheme might collapse."

That exchange meant nothing to me but it was enough to give me the definite idea that these two were having a private fight and I'd better not get in the way. That wanted clearing up, so I butted in and said, "I'd like to know who my boss is on this survey. Who do I take my orders from—you, Mr. Matterson? Or Mr. Donner here?"

Matterson stared at me. "You take them from me," he said

10

flatly. "My name is Matterson and this is the Matterson Cor
poration." He flicked his gaze up at Donner as though defy
ing him to make an issue of it, but Donner backed down after
a long moment by giving a sharp nod.

"Just as long as I know," I said easily.

Afterwards we got down to dickering about the terms of
my contract. Donner was a penny-pincher and, as he had
made me mad by trying to skinflint on the possible boring
operations, I set my price higher than I would have done
normally. Although it seemed to be a straightforward job and
I did need the money, there were undercurrents that I didn't
like. There was also the name of Trinavant that had come
up, although that seemed to have no particular relevance.
But the terms I finally screwed out of Donner were so good
that I knew I would have to take the job—the money would
set me up in business for a year in the North-West.

Matterson was no help to Donner. He just sat on the side-
lines and grinned while I gouged him. It was certainly a hell
of a way to run a corporation! After the business details had
been settled Matterson said, "I'll reserve a room for you at
the Matterson House. It doesn't compare with the Hilton, but
I think you'll be comfortable enough. When can you start on
the job?"

"As soon as I get my equipment from Edmonton."

"Fly it in," said Matterson. "We'll pay the freight."

Donner snorted and walked out of the room like a man
who knows when he isn't wanted.

2

The Matterson House Hotel proved to be incorporated into
the Matterson Building so I hadn't far to go when I left
Matterson's office. I also noticed a string of company offices
all bearing the name of Matterson and there was the Matterson Bank on the corner of the block. It seemed that Fort
Farrell was a real old-fashioned company town, and when
Matterson built his dam there would be the Matterson Power
Company to add to his list. He was getting a real stranglehold
on this neck of the woods.

I arranged with the desk clerk to have my bag brought up from the bus depot, then said, "Do you have a newspaper here?"

"Comes out Friday."

"Where's the office?"

"Trinavant Park—north side."

I walked out into the fading afternoon light and back down High Street until I came to the square. Lieutenant Farrell was staring sightlessly into the low sun which illuminated his verdigris-green face blotched with white where the birds had made free with him. I wondered what he would have thought if he knew how his settlement had turned out. Judging by the expression on his face he *did* know—and he didn't think much of it.

The office of the *Fort Farrell Recorder* seemed to be more concerned with jobbing printing than with the production of a newspaper, but my first question was answered satisfactorily by the young girl who was the whole of the staff—at least, all of it that was in sight.

"Sure we keep back copies. How far do you want to go back?"

"About ten years."

She grimaced. "You'll want the bound copies, then. You'll have to come into the back office." I followed her into a dusty room. "What was the exact date?"

I had no trouble in remembering that—everyone knows his own birthday. "Tuesday, September 4th, 1956."

She looked up at a shelf and said helplessly, "That's the one up there. I don't think I can reach it."

"Allow me," I said, and reached for it. It was a volume the size and weight of a dozen Bibles and it gave me a lot less trouble than it would have given her! I supposed it weighed pretty near as much as she did.

She said, "You'll have to read it in here; and you mustn't cut the pages—that's our record copy."

"I won't," I promised, and put it on a deal table. "Can I have a light, please?"

"Sure." She switched on the light as she went out.

I pulled up a chair and opened the heavy cover of the book. It contained two years' issues of the *Fort Farrell Recorder*— one hundred and four reports on the health and sickness of a community; a record of births and deaths, joys and sorrows, much crime and yet not a lot, all things considered, and a little goodness—there should have been more but goodness doesn't make the headlines. A typical country newspaper.

I turned to the issue of September 7th—the week-end after the accident—half afraid of what I would find, half afraid I wouldn't find anything. But it was there and it had made the front page headlines, too. It screamed at me in heavy black letters splashed across the yellowing sheet: JOHN TRINAVANT DIES IN AUTO SMASH.

Although I knew the story by heart, I read the newspaper account with care and it did tell me a couple of things I hadn't known before. It was a simple story, regrettably not uncommon, but one which did not normally make headlines as it had done here. As I remembered, it rated a quarter-column at the bottom of the second page of the Vancouver *Sun* and a paragraph filler in Toronto.

The difference was that John Trinavant had been a power in Fort Farrell as being senior partner in the firm of Trinavant and Matterson. God the Father had suddenly died and Fort Farrell had mourned. Mourned publicly and profusely in black print on white paper.

John Trinavant (aged 56) had been travelling from Dawson Creek to Edmonton with his wife, Anne (no age given), and his son, Frank (aged 22). They had been travelling in Mr. Trinavant's new car, a Cadillac, but the shiny new toy had never reached Edmonton. Instead, it had been found at the bottom of a two-hundred-foot cliff not far off the road. Skid marks and slashes in the bark of trees had shown how the accident happened. "Perhaps," said the coroner, "it may be that the car was moving too fast for the driver to be in proper control. That, however, is something no one will know for certain."

The Cadillac was a burnt-out hulk, smashed beyond repair. Smashed beyond repair were also the three Trinavants, all found dead. A curious aspect of the accident, however, was the presence of a fourth passenger, a young man now identified as Robert Grant, who had been found alive, but only just so, and who was now in the City Hospital suffering from third-degree burns, a badly fractured skull and several other assorted broken bones. Mr. Grant, it was tentatively agreed,

13

must have been a hitch-hiker whom Mr. Trinavant, in his benevolence, had picked up somewhere on the way between Dawson Creek and the scene of the accident. Mr. Grant was not expected to live. Too bad for Mr. Grant.

All Fort Farrell and, indeed, all Canada (said the leader writer) should mourn the era which had ended with the passing of John Trinavant. The Trinavants had been connected with the city since the heroic days of Lieutenant Farrell and it was a grief (to the leader writer personally) that the name of Trinavant was now extinguished in the male line. There was, however, a niece, Miss C. T. Trinavant, at present at school in Lausanne, Switzerland. It was to be hoped that this tragedy, the death of her beloved uncle, would not be permitted to interrupt the education he had so earnestly desired to give her.

I sat back and looked at the paper before me. So Trinavant had been a partner of Matterson—but not the Matterson I had met that day because he was too young. At the time of the smash he would have been in his early twenties—say about the age of young Frank Trinavant who was killed, or about my age at that time. So there must be another Matterson— Howard Matterson's father, presumably—which made Howard the Crown Prince of the Matterson empire. Unless, of course, he had already succeeded.

I sighed as I wondered what devil of coincidence had brought me to Fort Farrell; then I turned to the next issue and found—nothing! There was no follow on to the story in that issue or the next. I searched further and found that for the next year the name of Trinavant was not mentioned once —no follow-up, no obituary, no reminiscences from readers— nothing at all. As far as the *Fort Farrell Recorder* was concerned, it was as though John Trinavant had never existed— he had been *unpersonned*.

I checked again. It was very odd that in Trinavant's home town—the town where he was virtually king—the local newspaper had not coined a few extra cents out of his death. That was a hell of a way to run a newspaper!

I paused. That was the second time in one day that I had made the same observation—the first time in relation to Howard Matterson and the way he ran the Matterson Corporation. I wondered about that and that led me to something else—who owned the *Fort Farrell Recorder*?

The little office girl popped her head round the door. "You'll have to go now; we're closing up."

I grinned at her. "I thought newspaper offices never closed."

"This isn't the Vancouver *Sun*," she said. "Or the Montreal *Star*."

It sure as hell isn't, I thought.

"Did you find what you were looking for?" she asked.

I followed her into the front office. "I found some answers, yes; and a lot of questions." She looked at me uncomprehendingly. I said, "Is there anywhere a man can get a cup of coffee round here?"

"There's the Greek place right across the square."

"What about joining me?" I thought that maybe I could get some answers out of her.

She smiled. "My mother told me not to go out with strange men. Besides, I'm meeting my boy."

I looked at all the alive eighteen years of her and wished I were young again—as before the accident. "Some other time, perhaps," I said.

"Perhaps."

I left her inexpertly dabbing powder on her nose and headed across the square with the thought that I'd get picked up for kidnapping if I wasn't careful. I don't know why it is, but in any place that can support a cheap eatery—and a lot that can't—you'll find a Greek running the local coffee-and-doughnut joint. He expands with the community and brings in his cousins from the old country and pretty soon, in an average-size town, the Greeks are running the catering racket, splitting it with the Italians who tend to operate on a more sophisticated level. This wasn't the first Greek place I'd eaten in and it certainly wouldn't be the last—not while I was a poverty-stricken geologist chancing his luck.

I ordered coffee and pie and took it over to a vacant table intending to settle down to do some hard thinking, but I didn't get much chance of that because someone came up to the table and said, "Mind if I join you?"

He was old, maybe as much as seventy, with a walnut-brown face and a scrawny neck where age had dried the juices

15

out of him. His hair, though white, was plentiful and inqui-sitive blue eyes peered from beneath shaggy brows. I re-garded him speculatively for a long time, and at last he said, "I'm McDougall—chief reporter for the local scandal sheet."

I waved him to a chair. "Be my guest."

He put down the cup of coffee he was holding and grunted softly as he sat down. "I'm also the chief compositor," he said. "And the only copy-boy. I'm the rewrite man, too. The whole works."

"Editor, too?"

He snorted derisively. "Do I look like a newspaper editor?"

"Not much."

He sipped his coffee and looked at me from beneath the tangle of his brows. "Did you find what you were looking for, Mr. Boyd?"

"You're well-informed," I commented. "I've not been in town two hours and already I can see I'm going to be reported in the *Recorder*. How do you do it?"

He smiled. "This is a small town and I know every man, woman and child in it. I've just come from the Matterson Building and I know all about you, Mr. Boyd."

This McDougall looked like a sharp old devil. I said, "I'll bet you know the terms of my contract, too."

"I might." He grinned at me and his face took on the look of a mischievous small boy. "Donner wasn't too pleased." He put down his cup. "Did you find out what you wanted to know about John Trinavant?"

I stubbed out my cigarette. "You have a funny way of running a newspaper, Mr. McDougall. I've never seen such a silence in print in my life."

The smile left his face and he looked exactly what he was— a tired old man. He was silent for a moment, then he said unexpectedly, "Do you like good whisky, Mr. Boyd?"

"I've never been known to refuse."

He jerked his head in the direction of the newspaper office. "I have an apartment over the shop and a bottle in the apart-ment. Will you join me? I suddenly feel like getting drunk."

For an answer I rose from the table and paid the tab for both of us. While walking across the park McDougall said, "I get the apartment free. In return I'm on call twenty-four hours a day. I don't know who gets the better of the bargain."

"Maybe you ought to negotiate a new deal with your editor."

"With Jimson? That's a laugh—he's just a rubber stamp used by the owner."

"And the owner is Matterson," I said, risking a shaft at random.

McDougall looked at me out of the corner of his eye. "So you've got that far, have you? You interest me, Mr. Boyd; you really do."

"You are beginning to interest me," I said.

We climbed the stairs to his apartment, which was sparsely but comfortably furnished. McDougall opened a cupboard and produced a bottle. "There are two sorts of Scotch," he said. "There's the kind which is produced by the million gallons: a straight-run neutral grain spirit blended with good malt whisky to give it flavour, burnt caramel added to give it colour, and kept for seven years to protect the sacred name of Scotch whisky." He held up the bottle. "And then there's the real stuff—fifteen-year-old unblended malt lovingly made and lovingly drunk. This is from Islay—the best there is."

He poured two hefty snorts of the light straw-coloured liquid and passed one to me. I said, "Here's to you, Mr. McDougall. What brand of McDougall are you, anyway?"

I would swear he blushed. "I've a good Scots name and you'd think that would be enough for any man, but my father had to compound it and call me Hamish. You'd better call me Mac like everyone else and that way we'll avoid a fight." He chuckled. "Lord, the fights I got into when I was a kid."

I said, "I'm Bob Boyd."

He nodded. "And what interests you in the Trinavants?"

"Am I interested in them?"

He sighed. "Bob, I'm an old-time newspaperman so give me credit for knowing how to do my job. I do a run-down on everyone who checks the back files; you'd be surprised how often it pays off in a story. I've been waiting for someone to consult that particular issue for ten years."

"Why should the *Recorder* be interested in the Trinavants now?" I asked. "The Trinivants are dead and the *Recorder* killed them deader. You wouldn't think it possible to assassinate a memory, would you?"

17

"The Russians are good at it; they can kill a man and still leave him alive—the walking dead," said McDougall. "Look at what they did to Khrushchev. It's just that Matterson hit on the idea, too."

"You haven't answered my question," I said tartly. "Quit fencing around, Mac."

"The *Recorder* isn't interested in the Trinavants," he said. "If I put in a story about any of them—if I even mentioned the name—I'd be out on my can. This is a *personal* interest, and if Bull Matterson knew I was even talking about the Trinavants I'd be in big trouble." He stabbed his finger at me. "So keep your mouth shut, you understand." He poured out another drink and I could see his hand shaking. "Now, what's your story?"

I said, "Mac, until you tell me more about the Trinavants I'm not going to tell *you* anything. And don't ask me why because you won't get an answer."

He looked at me thoughtfully for a long time, then said, "But you'll tell me eventually?"

"I might."

That stuck in his gullet but he swallowed it. "All right; it looks as though I've no option. I'll tell you about the Trinavants." He pushed the bottle across. "Fill up, son."

The Trinavants were an old Canadian family founded by a Jacques Trinavant who came from Brittany to settle in Quebec back in the seventeen-hundreds. But the Trinavants were not natural settlers nor were they merchants—not in those days. Their feet were itchy and they headed west. John Trinavant's great-great-grandfather was a *voyageur* of note; other Trinavants were trappers and there was an unsubstantiated story that a Trinavant crossed the continent and saw the Pacific before Alexander Mackenzie.

John Trinavant's grandfather was a scout for Lieutenant Farrell, and when Farrell built the fort he decided to stay and put down roots in British Columbia. It was good country, he liked the look of it and saw the great possibilities. But just because the Trinavants ceased to be on the move did not mean they had lost their steam. Three generations of Trinavants in Fort Farrell built a logging and lumber empire, small but sound.

"It was John Trinavant who really made it go," said McDougall. "He was a man of the twentieth-century—born in 1900—and he took over the business young. He was only twenty-three when his father died. British Columbia in those days was pretty undeveloped still, and it's men like John Trinavant who have made it what it is to-day."

He looked at his glass reflectively. "I suppose that, from a purely business point of view, one of the best things that Trinavant ever did was to join up with Bull Matterson."

"That's the second time you've mentioned him," I said. "He can't be the man I met at the Matterson Building."

"Hell, no; that's Howard—he's just a punk kid," said McDougall contemptuously. "I'm talking about the old man —Howard's father. He was a few years older than Trinavant and they hooked on to each other in 1925. John Trinavant had the brains and directed the policy of the combination while Matterson supplied the energy and drive, and things really started to hum around here. One or the other of them had a finger in every goddam pie; they consolidated the logging industry and they were the first to see that raw logs are no damn' use unless you can do something with them, preferably on the spot. They built pulping plants and plywood plants and they made a lot of money, especially during the war. By the end of the war the folks around here used to get a lot of fun out of sitting around of an evening just trying to figure out how much Trinavant and Matterson were worth."

He leaned over and took the bottle. "Of course, it wasn't all logging—they diversified early. They owned gas stations, ran a bus service until they sold out to Greyhound, owned grocery stores and dry goods stores—everyone in this area paid them tribute in one way or another." He paused, then said broodingly, "I don't know if that's a good thing for a community. I don't like paternalism, even with the best intentions. But that's the way it worked out."

I said, "They also owned a newspaper."

McDougall's face took on a wry look. "It's the only one of Matterson's operations that doesn't give him a cash return. It doesn't pay. This town isn't really big enough to support a newspaper, but John Trinavant started it as a public service, as a sideline to the print shop. He said the townsfolk had a

19

right to know what was going on, and he never interfered with editorial policy. Matterson runs it for a different reason."

"What's that?"

"To control public opinion. He daren't close it down because Fort Farrell is growing and someone else might start an *honest* newspaper which he doesn't control. As long as he holds on to the *Recorder* he's safe because as sure as hell there's not room for two newspapers."

I nodded. "So Trinavant and Matterson each made a fortune. What then?"

"Then nothing," said McDougall. "Trinavant was killed and Matterson took over the whole shooting-match—lock, stock and barrel. You see, there weren't any Trinavants left."

I thought about that. "Wasn't there one left? The editorial in the *Recorder* mentioned a Miss Trinavant, a niece of John."

"You mean Clare," said McDougall. "She wasn't really a niece, just a vague connection from the East. The Trinavants were a strong stock a couple of hundred years ago but the Eastern branch withered on the vine. As far as I know Clare Trinavant is the last Trinavant in Canada. John came across her by accident when he was on a trip to Montreal. She was an orphan. He reckoned she must be related to the family somehow, so he took her in and treated her like his own daughter."

"Then she wasn't his heir?"

McDougall shook his head. "Not his natural heir. He didn't adopt her legally and it seems there's never been any way to prove the family connection, so she lost out as far as that goes."

"Then who *did* get Trinavant's money? And how did Matterson grab Trinavant's share of the business?"

McDougall gave me a twisted grin. "The answers to those two questions are interlocked. John's will established a trust fund for his wife and son, the whole of the capital to revert to young Frank at the age of thirty. All the proper safeguards were built in and it was a good will. Of course, provision had to be made in case John outlived everybody concerned and in that case the proceeds of the trust were to be devoted to the establishment of a department of lumber technology at a Canadian university."

"Was that done?"

"It was. The trust is doing good work—but not as well as it might, and for the answer to that one you have to go back to 1929. It was then that Trinavant and Matterson realised they were in the empire-building business. Neither of them wanted the death of the other to put a stop to it, so they drew up an agreement that on the death of either of them the survivor would have the option of buying the other's share at book value. And that's what Matterson did."

"So the trust was left with Trinavant's holdings but the trustees were legally obliged to sell to Matterson if he chose to exercise his option. I don't see much wrong with that."

McDougall clicked his tongue in annoyance. "Don't be naïve, Boyd." He ticked off points on his fingers. "The option was to be exercised at book value and by the time Donner had finished juggling the books my guess is that the book value had slumped in some weird way. That's one angle. Secondly, the Chairman of the Board of Trustees is William Justus Sloane, and W.J. practically lives in Bull Matterson's pocket these days. The Board of Trustees promptly reinvested what little they got from Matterson right back into the newly organised Matterson Corporation, and if anyone *controls* that dough now it's old Bull. Thirdly, it took the Board of Trustees an awful long time to get off its collective fanny to do anything about ratifying the terms of the trust. It took no less than four years to get that Department of Lumber Technology going, and it was a pretty half-hearted effort at that. From what I hear the department is awfully short of funds. Fourthly, the terms of the sale of Trinavant's holdings to Bull were never made public. I reckon he should have cut up for something between seven and ten million dollars but the Board of Trustees only invested two million in the Matterson Corporation and in *non-voting* stock, by God, which was just ducky for Bull Matterson. Fifthly . . . aaah . . . what am I wasting my time for?"

"So you reckon Bull Matterson practically stole the Trinavant money."

"There's no *practically* about it," McDougall snapped.

"Bad luck for Miss Clare," I said.

"Oh, she did all right. There was a special codicil in the will that took care of her. John left her half a million dollars

21

and a big slice of land. That's something Bull hasn't been able to get his hooks on—not that he hasn't tried."

I thought of the tone of the leader in which the recommendation had been made that Miss Trinavant's education should not be interrupted. "How old was she when Trinavant was killed?"

"She was a kid of seventeen. Old John had sent her to Switzerland to complete her education."

"And who wrote the leader on September 7th, 1956?"

McDougall smiled tightly. "So you caught that? You're a smart boy, after all. The leader was written by Jimson but I bet Matterson dictated it. It's a debatable point whether or not that option agreement could have been broken, especially since Clare wasn't legally of John's family, but he wasn't taking any chances. He flew out to Switzerland himself and persuaded her to stay, and he put that leader under her nose as an indication that the people of Fort Farrell thought likewise. She knew the *Recorder* was an honest newspaper; what she didn't know was that Matterson corrupted it the week Trinavant died. She was a girl of seventeen who knew nothing about business."

"So who looked after her half million bucks until she came of age?"

"The Public Trustee," said McDougall. "It's pretty automatic in cases like hers. Bull tried to horn in on it, of course, but he never got anywhere."

I went over the whole unsavoury story in my mind, then shook my head. "What I don't understand is why Matterson clamped down on the name of Trinavant. What did he have to hide?"

"I don't know," confessed McDougall. "I was hoping that the man who consulted that issue of the *Recorder* after ten years would be able to tell *me*. But from that day to this the name of Trinavant has been blotted out in this town. The Trinavant Bank was renamed the Matterson Bank, and every company that held the name was rebaptized. He even tried to change the name of Trinavant Square but he couldn't get it past Mrs. Davenant—she's the old battle-axe who runs the Fort Farrell Historical Society."

I said, "Yes, if it hadn't been for that I wouldn't have known this was Trinavant's town."

22

"Would it have made any difference?" When I made no answer McDougall said, "He couldn't rename Clare Trinavant either. It's my guess he's been praying to God she gets married. She lives in the district, you know—and she hates his guts."

"So the old man's still alive."

"He sure is. Must be seventy-five now, and he wears his age well—he's still full of piss and vinegar, but he always was a rumbustious old stallion. John Trinavant was the brake on him, but when John went then old Bull really broke loose. He organised the Matterson Corporation as a holding company and really went to town on money-making, and he wasn't particular how he made it—he still isn't, for that matter. And the amount of forest land he owns . . ."

I broke in. "I thought all forest land was Crown land."

"In British Columbia ninety-five per cent *is* Crown land, but five per cent—say, seven million acres—is under private ownership. Bull owns no less than one million acres, and he has felling franchises on another two million acres of Crown land. He cuts sixty million cubic feet of lumber a year. He's always on the edge of getting into trouble because of overcutting—the Government doesn't like that—but he's always weaselled his way out. Now he's starting his own hydroelectric plant, and when he has that he'll really have this part of the country by the throat."

I said, "Young Matterson told me the hydro plant was to supply power to the Matterson Corporation's own operations."

McDougall's lip quirked satirically. "And what do you think Fort Farrell is but a Matterson operation? We have a two-bit generating plant here that's never up to voltage and always breaking down, so now the Matterson Electricity Company moves in. And Matterson operations have a way of spreading wider. I believe the old Bull has a vision of the Matterson Corporation controlling a slice of British Columbia from Fort St. John to Kispiox, from Prince George clear to the Yukon—a private kingdom to run as he likes."

"Where does Donner come into all this?" I asked curiously.

"He's a money man—an accountant. He thinks in nothing but dollars and cents and he'll squeeze a dollar until it cries uncle. Now there's a really ruthless, conniving bastard for you. He figures out the schemes and Bull Matterson makes

23

them work. But Bull has put himself upstairs as Chairman of the Board—he leaves the day-to-day running of things to young Howard—and Donner is now riding herd on Howard to prevent him running hog-wild."

"He's not doing too good a job," I said, and told him of the episode in Howard's office.

McDougall snorted. "Donner can handle that young punk with one hand tied behind his back. He'll give way on things that don't matter much, but on anything important Howard definitely comes last. Young Howard puts up a good front and may look like a man, but he's soft inside. He's not a tenth of the man his father is."

I sat and digested all that for a long time, and finally said, "All right, Mac; you said you had a personal interest in all this. What is it?"

He stared me straight in the eye and said, "It may come as a surprise to you to find that even newspapermen have a sense of honour. John Trinavant was my friend; he used to come up here quite often and drink my whisky and have a yarn. I was sick to my stomach at what the *Recorder* did to him and his family when they died, but I stood by and let it happen. Jimson is an incompetent fool and I could have put such a story on the front page of this newspaper that John Trinavant would never have been forgotten in Fort Farrell. But I didn't, and you know why? Because I was a coward; because I was scared of Bull Matterson; because I was frightened of losing my job."

His voice broke a little. "Son, when John Trinavant was killed I was rising sixty, already an elderly man. I've always been a free-spender and I had no money, and it's always been in my mind that I come from a long-lived family. I reckoned I had many years ahead of me, but what can an old man of sixty do when he loses his job?" His voice strengthened. "Now I'm seventy-one and still working for Matterson. I do a good job for him—that's why he keeps me on here. It's not charity because Matterson doesn't even know the meaning of the word. But in the last ten years I've saved a bit and now that I don't have so many years ahead of me I'd like to do something for my friend, John Trinavant. I'm not running scared any more."

I said, "What would you propose to do?"

He took a deep breath. "You can tell *me*. A man doesn't walk in off the street and read a ten-year-old issue of a newspaper without a reason. I want to know that reason."

"No, Mac," I said. "Not yet. I don't know if I have a reason or not. I don't know if I have a right to interfere. I came to Fort Farrell purely by chance and I don't know if this is any of my business."

He puffed out his cheeks and blew out his breath explosively. "I don't get it," he said. "I just don't get it." He wore a baffled look. "Are you telling me that you read that ten-year-old issue just for kicks—or just because you like browsing through crummy country newspapers? Maybe you wanted to check which good housewife won the pumpkin pie baking competition that week. Is that it?"

"No dice, Mac," I said. "You won't get it out of me until I'm ready, and I'm a long way off yet."

"All right," he said quietly. "I've told you a lot—enough to get my head chopped off if Matterson hears about it. I've put my neck right on the block."

"You're safe with me, Mac."

He grunted. "I sure as hell hope so. I'd hate to be fired now with no good coming of it." He got up and took a file from a shelf. "I might as well give you a bit more. It struck me that if Matterson wanted to erase the name of Trinavant the reason might be connected with the way Trinavant died." He took a photograph from the file and passed it to me. "Know who that is?"

I looked at the fresh young face and nodded. I had seen a copy of the same photograph before but I didn't tell McDougall. "Yes, it's Robert Grant." I laid it on the table.

"The fourth passenger in the car," said McDougall, tapping the photograph with his fingernail. "That young man lived. Nobody expected him to live, but he did. Six months after Trinavant died I had a vacation coming, so I used it to do some quiet checking out of reach of old Bull. I went over to Edmonton and visited the hospital. Robert Grant had been transferred to Quebec; he was in a private clinic and he was incommunicado. From then on I lost track of him—and it's a hard task to hide from an old newspaperman with a bee in his bonnet. I sent copies of this photograph to a few of my friends—newspapermen scattered all over Canada—and not a thing has come up in ten years. Robert Grant has disappeared off the face of the earth."

"So?"

"Son, have you seen this man?"

I looked down at the photograph again. Grant looked to be only a boy, barely in his twenties and with a fine full life ahead of him. I said slowly, "To my best knowledge I've never seen that face."

"Well, it was a try," said McDougall. "I had thought you might be a friend of his come to see how the land lies."

"I'm sorry, Mac," I said. "I've never met this man. But why would he want to come here, anyway? Isn't Grant an irrelevancy?"

"Maybe," said McDougall thoughtfully. "And maybe not. I just wanted to talk to him, that's all." He shrugged. "Let's have another drink, for God's sake!"

That night I had the Dream. It was at least five years since I had had it last and, as usual, it frightened hell out of me. There was a mountain covered with snow and with jagged black rocks sticking out of the snow like snaggle teeth. I wasn't climbing the mountain or descending—I was merely standing there as though rooted. When I tried to move my feet it was as though the snow was sticky like an adhesive and I felt like a fly trapped on flypaper.

The snow was falling all the time; drifts were building up and presently the snow was knee-high and then at mid-thigh. I knew that if I didn't move I would be buried so I struggled again and bent down and pushed at the snow with my bare hands.

It was then that I found that the snow was not cold, but red hot in temperature, even though it was perfectly white in my dreams. I cried in agony and jerked my hands away and waited helplessly as the snow imperceptibly built up around my body. It touched my hands and then my face and I screamed as the hot, hot snow closed about me burning, burning, burning . . .

I woke up covered in sweat in that anonymous hotel room and wished I could have a jolt of Mac's fine Islay whisky.

The first thing I can ever remember in my life is pain. It is not given to many men to experience their birth-pangs and I don't recommend it. Not that any commendation of mine, for or against, can have any effect—none of us chooses to be born and the manner of our birth is beyond our control.

I felt the pain as a deep-seated agony all over my body. It became worse as time passed by, a red-hot fire consuming me. I fought against it with all my heart and seemed to prevail, though they tell me that the damping of the pain was due to the use of drugs. The pain went away and I became unconscious.

At the time of my birth I was twenty-three years old, or so I am reliably informed.

I am also told that I spent the next few weeks in a coma, hovering on that thin marginal line between life and death. I am inclined to think of this as a mercy because if I had been conscious enough to undergo the pain I doubt if I would have lived and my life would indeed have been short.

When I recovered consciousness again the pain, though still crouched in my body, had eased considerably and I found it bearable. Less bearable was the predicament in which I found myself. I was spreadeagled—tied by ankles and wrists—lying on my back and apparently immersed in liquid. I had very little to go on because when I tried to open my eyes I found that I couldn't. There was a tightness about my face and I became very much afraid and began to struggle.

A voice said urgently, "You must be quiet. You must not move. You must *not* move."

It was a good voice, soft and kind, so I relaxed and descended into that merciful coma again.

A number of weeks passed during which time I was conscious more frequently. I don't remember much of this period except that the pain became less obtrusive and I became stronger. They began to feed me through a tube pushed between my lips, and I sucked in the soups and the fruit juices and became even stronger. Three times I was aware that I had been taken to an operating theatre; I learned this not from my own knowledge but by listening to the chatter of nurses. But for the most part I was in a happy state of thoughtlessness. It never occurred to me to wonder what I was doing there or how I had got there, any more than a new-born baby in a cot thinks of those things. As a baby, I was content to let things go their own way so long as I was comfortable and comforted.

The time came when they cut the bandage from my face and eyes. A voice, a man's voice I had heard before, said, "Now, take it easy. Keep your eyes closed until I tell you to open them."

Obediently I closed my eyes tightly and heard the snip of the scissors as they clipped through the gauze. Fingers touched my eyelids and there was a whispered, "*Seems* to be all right." Someone was breathing into my face. The voice said, "All right; you can open them now."

I opened my eyes to a darkened room. In front of me was the dim outline of a man. He said, "How many fingers am I holding up?"

A white object swam into vision. I said, "Two."

"And how many now?"

"Four."

He gave a long, gusty sigh. "It looks as though you are going to have unimpaired vision after all. You're a very lucky young man, Mr. Grant."

"Grant?"

The man paused. "Your name is Grant, isn't it?"

I thought about it for a long time and the man assumed I wasn't going to answer him. He said, "Come now; if you are not Grant, then who are you?"

It is then they tell me that I screamed and they had to administer more drugs. I don't remember screaming. All I remember is the awful blank feeling when I realised that I didn't know who I was.

I have given the story of my rebirth in some detail. It is really astonishing that I lived those many weeks, conscious for a large part of the time, without ever worrying about my personal identity. But all that was explained afterwards by Susskind.

Dr. Matthews, the skin specialist, was one of the team which was cobbling me together, and he was the first to realise that there was something more wrong with me than mere physical disability, so Susskind was added to the team. I never called him anything other than Susskind—that's how he introduced himself—and he was never anything else than a good friend. I guess that's what makes a good psychiatrist. When I was on my feet and moving around outside hospitals we used to go out and drink beer together. I don't know if that's a normal form of psychiatric treatment—I thought head-shrinkers stuck pretty firmly to the little padded seat at the head of the couch—but Susskind had his own ways and he turned out to be a good friend.

He came into the darkened room and looked at me. "I'm Susskind," he said abruptly. He looked about the room. "Dr. Matthews says you can have more light. I think it's a good idea." He walked to the window and drew the curtains. "Darkness is bad for the soul."

He came back to the bed and stood looking down at me. He had a strong face with a firm jaw and a beak of a nose, but his eyes were incongruously soft and brown, like those of an intelligent ape. He made a curiously disarming gesture, and said, "Mind if I sit down?"

I shook my head so he hooked his foot on a chair and drew it closer. He sat down in a casual manner, his left ankle resting on his right knee, showing a large expanse of sock patterned jazzily and two inches of hairy leg. "How are you feeling?"

I shook my head.

"What's the matter? Cat got your tongue?" When I made no answer he said, "Look, boy; you seem to be in trouble. Now, I can't help you if you don't talk to me."

I'd had a bad night, the worst in my life. For hours I had struggled with the problem—*who am I?*—and I was no nearer to finding out than when I started. I was worn out and frightened and in no mood to talk to anyone.

Susskind began to talk in a soft voice. I don't remember everything he said that first time but he returned to the theme many times afterwards. It went something like this:

"Everyone comes up against this problem some time in his life; he asks himself the fundamentally awkward question: 'Who am I?' There are many related questions, too, such as,

'Why am I?' and 'Why am I *here*?' To the uncaring the questioning comes late, perhaps only on the death-bed. To the thinking man this self-questioning comes sooner and has to be resolved in the agony of personal mental sweat.

"Out of such self-questioning have come a lot of good things—and some not so good. Some of the people who have asked these questions of themselves have gone mad, others have become saints, but most of us come to a compromise. Out of these questions have arisen great religions. Philosophers have written too many books about them, books containing a lot of undiluted crap and a few grains of sense. Scientists have looked for the answers in the movement of atoms and the working of drugs. This is the problem which exercises all of us, every member of the human race, and if it doesn't happen to an individual then that individual cannot be considered to be human.

"Now, you've bumped up against this problem of personal identity head-on and in an acute form. You think that just because you can't remember your name you're a nothing. You're wrong. The self does not exist in a name. A name is just a word, a form of description which we give ourselves— a mere matter of convenience. The self—that awareness in the midst of your being which you call *I*—is still there. If it weren't, you'd be dead.

"You also think that just because you can't remember incidents in your past life your personal world has come to an end. Why should it? You're still breathing; you're still alive. Pretty soon you'll be out of this hospital—a thinking, questioning man, eager to get on with what he has to do. Maybe we can do some reconstructions; the odds are that you'll have all your memories back within days or weeks. Maybe it will take a bit longer. But I'm here to help you do it. Will you let me?"

I looked up at that stern face with the absurdly gentle eyes and whispered, "Thanks." Then, because I was very tired, I fell asleep and when I woke up again Susskind had gone.

But he came back next day. "Feeling better?"

"Some."

He sat down. "Mind if I smoke?" He lit a cigarette, then

30

looked at it distastefully. "I smoke too many of these damn' things." He extended the pack. "Have one?"

"I don't use them."

"How do you know?"

I thought about that for fully five minutes while Susskind waited patiently without saying a word. "No," I said. "No, I don't smoke. I *know* it."

"Well, that's a good start," he said with fierce satisfaction. "You know *something* about yourself. Now, what's the first thing you remember?"

I said immediately, "Pain. Pain and floating. I was tied up, too."

Susskind went into that in detail and when he had finished I thought I caught a hint of doubt in his expression, but I could have been wrong. He said, "Have you any idea how you got into this hospital?"

"No," I said. "I was *born* here."

He smiled. "At your age?"

"I don't know how old I am."

"To the best of our knowledge you're twenty-three. You were involved in an auto accident. Have you any ideas about that?"

"No."

"You know what an automobile is, though."

"Of course." I paused. "Where was the accident?"

"On the road between Dawson Creek and Edmonton. You know where those places are?"

"I know."

Susskind stubbed out his cigarette. "These ash-trays are too damn' small," he grumbled. He lit another cigarette. "Would you like to know a little more about yourself? It will be hearsay, not of your own personal knowledge, but it might help. Your name, for instance."

I said, "Dr. Matthews called me by the name of Grant."

Susskind said carefully, "To the best of our knowledge that is your name. More fully, it is Robert Boyd Grant. Want to know anything else?"

"Yes," I said. "What was I doing? What was my job?"

"You were a college student studying at the University of British Columbia in Vancouver. Remember anything about that?"

31

I shook my head.

He said suddenly, "What's a mofette?"

"It's an opening in the ground from which carbon dioxide is emitted—volcanic in origin." I stared at him. "How did I know that?"

"You were majoring in geology," he said drily. "What was your father's given name?"

"I don't know," I said blankly. "You said 'was'. Is he dead?"

"Yes," said Susskind quickly. "Supposing you went to Irving House, New Westminster—what would you expect to find?"

"A museum."

"Have you any brothers or sisters?"

"I don't know."

"Which—if any—political party do you favour?"

I thought about it, then shrugged. "I don't know—but I don't know if I took any interest in politics at all."

There were dozens of questions and Susskind shot them at me fast, expecting fast answers. At last he stopped and lit another cigarette. "I'll give it to you straight, Bob, because I don't believe in hiding unpleasant facts from my customers and because I think you can take it. Your loss of memory is entirely personal, relating solely to yourself. Any knowledge which does not directly impinge on the ego, things like the facts of geology, geographical locations, car driving know-how—all that knowledge has been retained whole and entire."

He flicked ash carelessly in the direction of the ash-tray. "The more personal things concerning yourself and your relationships with others are gone. Not only has your family been blotted out but you can't remember another single person—not your geology tutor or even your best buddy at college. It's as though something inside you decided to wipe the slate clean."

I felt hopelessly lost. What was there left for a man of my age with no personal contacts—no family, no friends? My God, I didn't even have any enemies, and it's a poor man who can say that.

Susskind poked me gently with a thick forefinger. "Don't give up now, bud; we haven't even started. Look at it this way—there's many a man who would give his soul to be able

32

to start again with a clean slate. Let me explain a few things to you. The unconscious mind is a funny animal with its own operating logic. This logic may appear to be very odd to the conscious mind but it's still a valid logic working strictly in accordance within certain rules, and what we have to do is to figure out the rules. I'm going to give you some psychological tests and then maybe I'll know better what makes you tick. I'm also going to do some digging into your background and maybe we can come up with something there."

I said, "Susskind, what chance is there?"

"I won't fool you," he said. "Due to various circumstances which I won't go into right now, yours is not entirely a straightforward case of loss of memory. Your case is one for the books—and I'll probably write the book. Look, Bob; a guy gets a knock on the head and he loses his memory—but not for long; within a couple of days, a couple of weeks at the most, he's normal again. That's the common course of events. Sometimes it's worse than that. I've just had a case of an old man of eighty who was knocked down in the street. He came round in hospital the next day and found he'd lost a year of his life—he couldn't remember a damn' thing of the year previous to the accident and, in my opinion, he never will."

He waved his cigarette under my nose. "That's general loss of memory. A *selective* loss of memory like yours isn't common at all. Sure, it's happened before and it'll happen again, but not often. And, like the general loss, recovery is variable. The trouble is that selective loss happens so infrequently that we don't have much on it. I could give you a line that you'll have your memory back next week, but I won't because I don't know. The only thing we can do is to work on it. Now, my advice to you is to quit worrying about it and to concentrate on other things. As soon as you can use your eyes for reading I'll bring in some textbooks and you can get back to work. By then the bandages will be off your hands and you can do some writing, too. You have an examination to pass, bud, in twelve months' time."

Susskind drove me to work and ripped into me when I lagged. His tongue could get a vicious edge to it when he thought it would do me good, and as soon as the bandages were off he pushed my nose down to the textbooks. He gave me a lot of tests—intelligence, personality, vocational—and seemed pleased at the results.

"You're no dope," he announced, waving a sheaf of papers. "You scored a hundred and thirty-three on the Wechsler-Bellevue—you have intelligence, so use it."

My body was dreadfully scarred, especially on the chest. My hands were unnaturally pink with new skin and when I touched my face I could feel crinkled scar tissue. And that led to something else. One day Matthews came to see me with Susskind in attendance. "We've got something to talk about, Bob," he said.

Susskind chuckled and jerked his head at Matthews. "A serious guy, this—very portentous."

"It is serious," said Matthews. "Bob, there's a decision you have to make. I've done all I can do for you in this hospital. Your eyes are as good as new but the rest of you is a bit battered and that's something I can't improve on. I'm no genius—I'm just an ordinary hospital surgeon specialising in skin." He paused and I could see he was selecting his words. "Have you ever wondered why you've never seen a mirror?"

I shook my head, and Susskind chipped in, "Our Robert Boyd Grant is a very undemanding guy. Would you like to see yourself, Bob?"

I put my fingers to my cheeks and felt the roughness. "I don't know that I would," I said, and found myself shaking.

"You'd better," Susskind advised. "It'll be brutal, but it'll help you make up your mind in the next big decision."

"Okay," I said.

Susskind snapped his fingers and the nurse left the room to return almost immediately with a large mirror which she laid face down on the table. Then she went out again and closed the door behind her. I looked at the mirror but made no attempt to pick it up. "Go ahead," said Susskind, so I picked it up reluctantly and turned it over.

"My God!" I said, and quickly closed my eyes, feeling the sour taste of vomit in my throat. After a while I looked again. It was a monstrously ugly face, pink and seamed with white lines in arbitrary places. It looked like a child's first clumsy attempt to depict the human face in wax. There was no character there, no imprint of dawning maturity as there should have been in someone of my age—there was just a blankness.

Matthews said quietly, "That's why you have a private room here."

I began to laugh. "It's funny; it's really damn' funny. Not only have I lost myself, but I've lost my face."

Susskind put his hand on my arm. "A face is just a face. No man can choose his own face—it's something that's given to him. Just listen to Dr. Matthews for a minute."

Matthews said, "I'm no plastic surgeon." He gestured at the mirror which I still held. "You can see that. You weren't in any shape for the extensive surgery you needed when you came in here—you'd have died if we had tried to pull any tricks like that. But now you're in good enough shape for the next step—if you want to take it."

"And that is?"

"More surgery—by a good man in Montreal. The top man in the field in Canada, and maybe in the Western Hemisphere. You can have a face again, and new hands, too."

"More surgery!" I didn't like that; I'd had enough of it.

"You have a few days to make up your mind," said Matthews.

"Do you mind, Matt?" said Susskind. "I'll take over from here."

"Of course," said Matthews. "I'll leave you to it. I'll be seeing you, Bob."

He left the room, closing the door gently. Susskind lit a cigarette and threw the pack on the table. He said quietly, "You'd better do it, bud. You can't walk round with a face like that—not unless you intend taking up a career in the horror movies."

"Right!" I said tightly. I knew it was something that had to be done. I swung on Susskind. "Now tell me something—who is paying for all this? Who is paying for this private room? Who is paying for the best plastic surgeon in Canada?"

Susskind clicked his tongue. "That's a mystery. Someone loves you for sure. Every month an envelope comes addressed to Dr. Matthews. It contains a thousand dollars in hundred-dollar bills and one of these." He fished in his pocket and threw a scrap of paper across the table.

I smoothed it out. There was but one line of typescript on it: FOR THE CARE OF ROBERT BOYD GRANT.

I looked at him suspiciously. "You're not doing this, are you?"

"Good Christ!" he said. "Show me a hospital head-shrinker who can afford to give away twelve thousand bucks a year. I couldn't afford to give you twelve thousand cents." He grinned. "But thanks for the compliment."

I pushed the paper with my finger. "Perhaps this is a clue to who I am."

"No, it's not," said Susskind flatly. He looked unhappy. "Maybe you've noticed I've not told you much about yourself. I did promise to dig into your background."

"I was going to ask you about that."

"I did some digging," he said. "And what I've been debating is not what I should tell you, but if I should tell you at all. You know, Bob, people get my profession all wrong. In a case like yours they think I should help you to get back your memory come hell or high water. I take a different view. I'm like the psychiatrist who said that his job was to help men of genius keep their neuroses. I'm not interested in keeping a man normal—I want to keep him happy. It's a symptom of the sick world we live in that the two terms are not synonymous."

"And where do I come in on this?"

He said solemnly, "My advice to you is to let it go. Don't dig into your past. Make a new life for yourself and forget everything that happened before you came here. I'm not going to help you recover your memory."

I stared at him. "Susskind, you can't say that and expect me just to leave it there."

"Won't you take my word for it?" he asked gently.

"No!" I said. "Would you if you were in my place?"

"I guess not," he said, and sighed. "I suppose I'll be bending a few professional ethics, but here goes. I'm going to make

36

it short and sharp. Now, take a hold of yourself, listen to me and shut up until I've finished."

He took a deep breath. "Your father deserted your mother soon after you were born, and no one knows if he's alive or dead. Your mother died when you were ten and, from what I can gather, she was no great loss. She was, to put it frankly, nothing but a cheap chippy and, incidentally, she wasn't married to your father. That left you an orphan and you went into an institution. It seems you were a young hellion and quite uncontrollable so you soon achieved the official status of delinquent. Had enough?"

"Go on," I whispered.

"You started your police record by the theft of a car, so you wound up in reform school for that episode. It seems it wasn't a good reform school; all you learned there was how to make crime pay. You ran away and for six months you existed by petty crime until you were caught. Fortunately you weren't sent back to the same reform school and you found a Warden who knew how to handle you and you began to straighten out. On leaving reform school you were put in a hostel under the care of a probation officer and you did pretty well at high school. Your good intelligence earned you good marks so you went to college. Right then it looked as though you were all right."

Susskind's voice took on a savage edge. "But you slipped. You couldn't seem to do anything the straight way. The cops pulled you in for smoking marijuana—another bad mark on the police blotter. Then there was an episode when a girl died in the hands of a quack abortionist—a name was named but nothing could be proved, so maybe we ought to leave that one off the tab. Want any more?"

"There's more?"

Susskind nodded sadly. "There's more."

"Let me have it," I said flatly.

"Okay. Again you were pulled in for drug addiction; this time you were mainlining on heroin. You just about hit the bottom there. There was some evidence that you were pushing drugs to get the dough to feed the habit, but not enough to nail you. However, now the cops were laying for you. Then came the clincher. You knew the Dean of Men was considering throwing you out of college and, God knows, he had

37

enough reason. Your only hope was to promise to reform but you had to back it up with something—such as brilliant work. But drugs and brilliant work don't go hand in hand so you were stupid enough to break into an office and try to doctor your examination marks."

"And I was caught at it," I said dully.

"It would have been better if you were," said Susskind. "No, you weren't caught red-handed but it was done in such a ham-fisted way that the Principal sent a senior student to find you. He found you all right. He found you hopped up on dope. You beat this guy half to death and lit out for places unknown. God knows where you thought you were going to take refuge—the North Pole, maybe. Anyway, a nice guy called Trinavant gave you a lift and the next thing was—Bingo!—Trinavant was dead, his wife was dead, his son was dead, and you were seven-eighths dead." He rubbed his eyes. "That just about wraps it up," he said tiredly.

I was cold all over. "You think I killed this man, Trinavant, and his family?"

"I think it was an accident, nothing more," said Susskind. "Now listen carefully, Bob; I told you the unconscious mind has its own brand of peculiar logic. I found something very peculiar going on. When you were pulled in on the heroin charge you were given a psychiatric examination, and I've seen the documents. One of the tests was a Bernreuter Personality Inventory and you may remember that I also gave you that test."

"I remember."

Susskind leaned back in his chair. "I compared the two profiles and they didn't check out at all; they could have been two different guys. And I'll tell you something, Bob: the guy that was tested by the police psychiatrist I wouldn't trust with a bent nickel, but I'd trust *you* with my life."

"Someone's made a mistake," I said.

He shook his head vigorously. "No mistake. Do you remember the man I brought in here who sat in on some of your tests? He's an authority on an uncommon condition of the human psyche—multiple personality. Did you ever read a book called *The Three Faces of Eve*?"

"I saw the movie—Joanne Woodward was in it."

"That's it. Then perhaps you can see what I'm getting at.

Not that you have anything like she had. Tell me, what do you think of the past life of this guy called Robert Boyd Grant?"

"It made me sick to my stomach," I said. "I can't believe I did that."

"*You* didn't," said Susskind sharply. "This is what happened, to the best of my professional belief. This man, Robert Boyd Grant, was a pretty crummy character, and he knew it himself. My guess is that he was tired of living with himself and he wanted to escape from himself—hence the drugs. But marijuana and heroin are only temporary forms of escape, and like everyone else he was locked in the prison of his own body. Perhaps he sickened himself but there was nothing he could do about it—a conscious and voluntary change of basic personality is practically an impossibility.

"But as I said, the unconscious has its own logic and we, in this hospital, accidentally gave it the data it needed. You had third-degree burns over sixty per cent of your body when you were brought in here. We couldn't put you in a bed in that condition, so you were suspended in a bath of saline solution which, to your unconscious, was a pretty good substitute for amniotic fluid. Do you know what that is?"

"A return to the womb?"

Susskind snapped his fingers. "You're with it. Now I'm speaking in impossibly untechnical terms, so don't go quoting me, especially to other psychiatrists. I think this condition was tailor-made for your unconscious mind. Here was a chance for rebirth which was grabbed at. Whether the second personality was lying there, ready to be used, or whether it was constructed during the time you were in that bath, we shall never know—and it doesn't matter. That there is a second personality—a better personality—is a fact, and it's something I'd swear to in a court of law, which I might have to do yet. You're one of the few people who can really call yourself a new man."

It was a lot to take in at once—too much. I said, "God! You've handed me something to think about."

"I had to do it," said Susskind. "I had to explain why you mustn't probe into the past. When I told you what a man called Robert Grant had done it was like listening to an account of the actions of someone else, wasn't it? Let me

39

give you an analogy: when you go to the movies and see a lion jumping at you, well—that's just the movies and there's no harm done; but if you go to Africa and a lion jumps at you, that's hard reality and you're dead. If you insist on digging into the past and succeed in *remembering as personal memories* the experiences of this other guy, then you'll split yourself down the middle. So leave it alone. You're someone with no past and a great future."

I said, "What chance is there that this other—bad—personality might take over again spontaneously?"

"I'd say there's very little chance of that," said Susskind slowly. "You rate as a strong-willed individual; the other guy had a weak will—strong-willed people generally don't go for drugs, you know. We all of us have a devil lurking inside us; we all have to suppress the old Adam. You're no different from anyone else."

I picked up the mirror and studied the reflected caricature. "What did I . . . what did *he* look like?"

Susskind took out his wallet and extracted a photograph. "I don't see the point in showing you this, but if you want to see it, here it is."

Robert Boyd Grant was a fresh-faced youngster with a smooth, unlined face. There was no trace of dissipation such as one might have expected—he could have been any college student attending any college on the North American continent. He wasn't bad-looking, either, in an immature way, and I doubted if he'd had any trouble finding a girl-friend to put in the family way.

"I'd forget about that face," advised Susskind. "Don't go back into the past. Roberts, the plastic surgeon, is a sculptor in flesh; he'll fix you up with a face good enough to play romantic lead with Elizabeth Taylor."

I said, "I'll miss you, Susskind."

He chuckled fatly. "Miss me? You're not going to miss me, bud; I'm not going to let you get away—I'm going to write the book on you, remember." He blew out a plume of smoke. "I'm getting out of hospital work and going into private practice. I've been offered a partnership—guess where? Right —Montreal!"

Suddenly I felt much better now I knew Susskind was still going to be around. I looked at the photograph again and said,

"Perhaps I'd better go the whole way. New man . . . new face . . . why not new name?"

"A sound idea," agreed Susskind. "Any ideas on that?"

I gave him the photograph. "That's Robert Grant," I said. "I'm Bob Boyd. It's not too bad a name."

3

I had three operations in Montreal covering the space of a year. I spent many weeks with my left arm strapped up against my right cheek in a skin grafting operation and, no sooner was that done, than my right arm was up against my left cheek.

Roberts was a genius. He measured my head meticulously and then made a plaster model which he brought to my room. "What kind of a face would you like, Bob?" he asked.

It took a lot of figuring out because this was playing for keeps—I'd be stuck with this face for the rest of my life. We took a long time working on it with Roberts shaping modelling clay on to the plaster base. There were limitations, of course; some of my suggestions were impossible. "We have only a limited amount of flesh to work with," said Roberts. "Most plastic surgery deals mainly with the removal of flesh; nose-bobbing, for instance. This is a more ticklish job and all we can do is a limited amount of redistribution."

I guess it was fun in a macabre sort of way. It isn't everyone who gets the chance to choose his own face even if the options are limited. The operations weren't so funny but I sweated it out, and what gradually emerged was a somewhat tough and battered face, the face of a man much older than twenty-four. It was lined and seamed as though by much experience, and it was a face that looked much wiser than I really was.

"Don't worry," said Roberts. "It's a face you'll grow into. No matter how carefully one does this there are the inevitable scars, so I've hidden those in folds of flesh, folds which usually come only with age." He smiled. "With a face like this I don't think you'll have much competition from people your own age; they'll walk stiff-legged around you without even knowing why. You'd better take some advice from Susskind on how to handle situations like that."

41

Matthews had handed over to Susskind the administration of the thousand dollars a month from my unknown benefactor. Susskind interpreted FOR THE CARE OF ROBERT BOYD GRANT in a wide sense; he kept me hard at my studies and, since I could not go to college, he brought in private tutors. "You haven't much time," he warned. "You were born not a year ago and if you flub your education now you'll wind up washing dishes for the rest of your life."

I worked hard—it kept my mind off my troubles. I found I liked geology and, since I had a skull apparently stuffed full of geological facts it wasn't too difficult to carry on. Susskind made arrangements with a college and I wrote my examinations between the second and third operations with my head and arm still in bandages. I don't know what I would have done without him.

After the examinations I took the opportunity of visiting a public library and, in spite of what Susskind had said, I dug out the newspaper reports of the auto smash. There wasn't much to read apart from the fact that Trinavant was a big wheel in some jerkwater town in British Columbia. It was just another auto accident that didn't make much of a splash. Just after that I started to have bad dreams and that scared me, so I didn't do any more investigations.

Then suddenly it was over. The last operation had been done and the bandages were off. In the same week the examination results came out and I found myself a B.Sc. and a newly fledged geologist with no job. Susskind invited me to his apartment to celebrate. We settled down with some beer, and he asked, "What are you going to do now? Go for your doctorate—"

I shook my head. "I don't think so—not just yet. I want to get some field experience."

He nodded approvingly. "Got any ideas about that?"

I said, "I don't think I want to be a company man; I'd rather work for myself. I reckon the North-West Territories are bursting with opportunities for a freelance geologist."

Susskind was doubtful. "I don't know if that's a good thing." He looked across at me and smiled. "A mite self-conscious about your face, are you? And you want to get away from people—go into the desert—is that it?"

"There's a little of that in it," I said unwillingly. "But I meant what I said. I think I'll make out in the north."

"You've been in hospitals for a year and a half," said Susskind. "And you don't know many people. What you should do is to go out, get drunk, make friends—maybe get yourself a wife."

"Good God!" I said. "I couldn't get married."

He waved his tankard. "Why not? You find yourself a really good girl and tell her the whole story. It won't make any difference to her if she loves you."

"So you're turning into a marriage counsellor," I said. "Why have you never got married?"

"Who'd marry a cantankerous bastard like me?" He moved restlessly and spilled ash down his shirt-front. "I've been holding out on you, bud. You've been a pretty expensive proposition, you know. You don't think a thousand bucks a month has paid for what you've had? Roberts doesn't come cheap and there were the tutors, too—not to mention my own ludicrously expensive services."

I said, "What are you getting at, Susskind?"

"When the *first* envelope came with its cargo of a thousand dollars, this was in it."

He handed me a slip of paper. There was the line of typing: FOR THE CARE OF ROBERT BOYD GRANT. Underneath was another sentence: IN THE EVENT OF THESE FUNDS BEING INSUFFICIENT, PLEASE INSERT THE FOLLOWING AD IN THE PERSONAL COLUMN OF THE VANCOUVER SUN—R.B.G. WANTS MORE.

Susskind said, "When you came up to Montreal I decided it was time for more money so I put the ad. in the paper. Whoever is printing this money doubled the ante. In the last year and a half you've had thirty-six thousand dollars; there are nearly four thousand bucks left in the kitty—what do you want to do with it?"

"Give it to some charity," I said.

"Don't be a fool," said Susskind. "You'll need a stake if you're setting off into the wide blue yonder. Pocket your pride and take it."

"I'll think about it," I said.

"I don't see what else you can do but take it," he observed. "You haven't a cent otherwise."

I fingered the note. "Who do you think this is? And why is he doing it?"

"It's no one out of your past, that's for sure," said Susskind. "The gang that Grant was running with could hardly scratch up ten dollars between them. All hospitals get these anonymous donations. They're not usually as big as this nor so specific, but the money comes in. It's probably some eccentric millionaire who read about you in the paper and decided to do something about it." He shrugged. "There are two thousand bucks a month still coming in. What do we do about that?"

I scribbled on the note and tossed it back to him. He read it and laughed. " 'R.B.G. SAYS STOP.' I'll put it in the personal column and see what happens." He poured us more beer. "When are you taking off for the icy wastes?"

I said, "I guess I will use the balance of the money. I'll leave as soon as I can get some equipment together."

Susskind said, "It's been nice having you around, Bob. You're quite a nice guy. Remember to keep it that way, do you hear? No poking and prying—keep your face to the future and forget the past and you'll make out all right. If you don't you're liable to explode like a bomb. And I'd like to hear how you're getting on from time to time."

Two weeks later I left Montreal and headed north-west. I suppose if anyone was my father it was Susskind, the man with the tough, ruthless, kindly mind. He gave me a taste for tobacco in the form of cigarettes, although I never got around to smoking as many as he did. He also gave me my life and sanity.

His full name was Abraham Isaac Susskind.

I always called him Susskind.

III

The helicopter hovered just above treetop height and I
shouted to the pilot, "That'll do it; just over there in the
clearing by the lake."

He nodded, and the machine moved sideways slowly and
settled by the lakeside, the downdraught sending ripples
bouncing over the quiet water. There was the usual soggy
feeling on touchdown as the weight came on to the hydraulic
suspension and then all was still save for the engine vibrations as the rotor slowly flapped around.

The pilot didn't switch off. I slammed the door open and
began to pitch out my gear—the unbreakable stuff that would
survive the slight fall. Then I climbed down and began to
take out the cases of instruments. The pilot didn't help at all;
he just sat in the driving seat and watched me work. I suppose
it was against his union rules to lug baggage.

When I had got everything out I shouted to him, "You'll be
back a week to-morrow?"

"Okay," he said. "About eleven in the morning."

I stood back and watched him take off and the helicopter
disappeared over the trees like a big ungainly grasshopper.
Then I set about making camp. I wasn't going to do anything
more that day except make camp and, maybe, do a little
fishing. That might sound as though I was cheating the
Matterson Corporation out of the best part of a day's work,
but I've always found that it pays not to run headlong into a
job.

A lot of men—especially city men—live like pigs when
they're camping. They stop shaving, they don't dig a proper
latrine, and they live exclusively on a diet of beans. I like to
make myself comfortable, and that takes time. Another thing
is that you can do an awful lot of work when just loafing
around camp. When you're waiting for the fish to bite your
eye is taking in the lie of the land and that can tell an
experienced field geologist a hell of a lot. You don't have to
eat all of an egg to know it's rotten and you don't have to

pound every foot of land to know what you'll find in it and what you won't find.

So I made camp. I dug the latrine and used it because I needed to. I got some dry driftwood from the shore and built a fire, then dug out the coffee-pot and set some water to boil. By the time I'd gathered enough spruce boughs to make a bed it was time to have coffee, so I sat with my back against a rock and looked over the lake speculatively.

From what I could see the lake lay slap-bang on a discontinuity. This side of the lake was almost certainly mesozoic, a mixture of sedimentary and volcanic rocks—good prospecting country. The other side, by the lie of the land and what I'd seen from the air, was probably palaeozoic, mostly sedimentary. I doubted if I'd find much over there, but I had to go and look.

I took a sip of the scalding coffee and scooped up a handful of pebbles to examine them. Idly I let them fall from my hand one at a time, then threw the last one into the lake where it made a small "plop" and sent out a widening circle of ripples. The lake itself was a product of the last ice age. The ice had pushed its way all over the land, the tongues of glaciers carving valleys through solid rock. It lay on the land for a long time and then, as quickly as it had come, so it departed.

Speed is a relative term. To a watching man a glacier moves slowly but it's the equivalent of a hundred yards' sprint when compared to other geological processes. Anyway, the glaciers retreated, dropping the rock fragments they had fractured and splintered from the bedrock. When that happened a rock wall was formed called a moraine, a natural dam behind which a lake or pond can form. Canada is full of them, and a large part of Canadian geology is trying to think like a piece of ice, trying to figure which way the ice moved so many thousands of years ago so that you can account for the rocks which are otherwise unaccountably out of place.

This lake was more of a large pond. It wasn't more than a mile long and was fed by a biggish stream which came in from the north. I'd seen the moraine from the air and traced the stream flowing south from the lake to where it tumbled over the escarpment and where the Matterson Corporation was going to build a dam.

46

I threw out the dregs of coffee and washed the pot and the enamel cup, then set to and built a windbreak. I don't like tents—they're no warmer inside than out and they tend to leak if you don't coddle them. In good weather all a man needs is a windbreak, which is easily assembled from materials at hand which don't have to be back-packed like a tent, and in bad weather you can make a waterproof roof if you have the know-how. But it took me quite a long time in the North-West Territories to get that know-how.

By mid-afternoon I had the camp ship-shape. Everything was where I wanted it and where I could get at it quickly if I needed it. It was a standard set-up I'd worked out over the years. The Polar Eskimos have carried *that* principle to a fine art; a stranger can drop into an unknown igloo, put out his hand in the dark and be certain of finding the oil-lamp or the bone fish-hooks. Armies use it, too; a man transferred to a strange camp still knows where to find the paymaster without half trying. I suppose it can be defined as good house-keeping.

The plop of a fish in the lake made me realise I was hungry, so I decided to find out how good the trout were. Fish is no good for a sustained diet in a cold climate—for that you need good fat meat—but I'd had all the meat I needed in Fort Farrell and the idea of lake trout sizzling in a skillet felt good. But next day I'd see if I could get me some venison, if I didn't have to go too far out of my way for it.

That evening, lying on the springy spruce and looking up at a sky full of diamonds, I thought about the Trinavants. I'd deliberately put the thing out of my mind because I was a little scared of monkeying around with it in view of what Susskind had said, but I found I couldn't leave it alone. It was like when you accidentally bite the inside of your cheek and you find you can't stop tongueing the sore place.

It certainly was a strange story. Why in hell should Matterson want to erase the name and memory of John Trinavant? I drew on a cigarette thoughtfully and watched the dull red eye of the dying embers on the fire. I was more and more certain that whatever was going on was centred on that auto accident. But three of the participants were dead, and the fourth couldn't remember anything about it, and what's more, didn't want to. So that seemed a dead end.

Who profited from the Trinavants' death? Certainly Bull Matterson had profited. With that option agreement he had the whole commercial empire in his fist—and all to himself. A motive for murder? Certainly Bull Matterson ran his business hard on cruel lines if McDougall was to be believed. But not every tight-fisted businessman was a murderer.

Item: Where was Bull Matterson at the time of the accident?

Who else profited? Obviously Clare Trinavant. And where was she at the time of the accident? In Switzerland, you damn' fool, and she was a chit of a schoolgirl at that. Delete Clare Trinavant.

Who else?

Apparently no one else profited—not in money, anyway. Could there be a way to profit other than in money? I didn't know enough about the personalities involved even to speculate, so that was another dead end—for the time being.

I jerked myself from the doze. What the hell was I thinking of? I wasn't going to get mixed up in this thing. It was too dangerous for me personally.

I was even more sure of that when I woke up at two o'clock in the morning drenched with sweat and quivering with nerves. I had had the Dream again.

2

Things seemed brighter in the light of the dawn, but then they always do. I cooked breakfast—beans, bacon and fried eggs—and wolfed it down hungrily, then picked up the pack I had assembled the night before. A backwoods geologist on the move resembles a perambulating Christmas tree more than anything else, but I'm a bigger man than most and it doesn't show much on me. However, it still makes a sizeable load to tote, so you can see why I don't like tents.

I made certain that the big yellow circle on the back of the pack was clearly visible. That's something I consider really important. Anywhere you walk in the woods on the North American continent you're likely to find fool hunters who'll let loose a 30.30 at anything that moves. That big yellow circle was just to make them pause before they squeezed the trigger, just time enough for them to figure that there are no yellow-spotted animals haunting the woods. For the same reason I wore a yellow-and-red checkered mackinaw that a drunken Indian wouldn't be seen dead in, and a woollen cap with a big red bobble on the top. I was a real colourful character.

I checked the breech of my rifle to make sure there wasn't one up the spout, slipped on the safety-catch and set off, heading south along the lake shore. I had established my base and I was ready to do the southern end of the survey. In one week the helicopter would pick me up and take me north, ready to cover the northern end. This valley was going to get a thorough going-over.

At the end of the first day I checked my findings against the Government geological map which was, to say the best of it, sketchy; in fact, in parts it was downright blank. People sometimes ask me: "Why doesn't the Government do a *real* geological survey and get the job done once and for all?" All I can say is that those people don't understand anything about the problems. It would take an army of geologists a hundred years to check every square mile of Canada, and then they'd have to do it again because some joker would have invented a gadget to see metals five hundred feet underground; or, maybe, someone else would find a need for some esoteric metal hitherto useless. Alumina ores were pretty useless in 1900 and you couldn't give away uranium in the 1930s. There'll still be jobs for a guy like me for many years to come.

What little was on the Government map checked with what I had, but I had it in more detail. A few traces of molybdenum and a little zinc and lead, but nothing to get the Matterson Corporation in an uproar about. When a geologist speaks of a trace, he means just that.

I carried on the next day, and the day after that, and by the end of the week I'd made pretty certain that the Matterson Corporation wasn't going to get rich mining the southern end of the Kinoxi Valley. I had everything packed back at the camp and was sitting twiddling my thumbs when the helicopter arrived, and I must say he was dead on time.

This time he dropped me in the northern area by a stream,

and again I spent the day making camp. The next day I was off once more in the usual routine, just putting one foot in front of the other and keeping my eyes open.

On the third day I realised I was being watched. There wasn't much to show that this was so, but there was enough; a scrap of wool caught on a twig near the camp which hadn't been there twelve hours earlier, a fresh scrape on the bark of a tree which I hadn't made and, once only, a wink of light from a distant hillside to show that someone had incautiously exposed binoculars to direct sunlight.

Now, in the north woods it's downright discourteous to come within spitting distance of a man's camp and not make yourself known, and anyone who hadn't secrecy on his mind wouldn't do it. I don't particularly mind a man having his secrets—I've got some of my own—but if a man's secrets involve me then I don't like it and I'm apt to go off pop. Still, there wasn't much I could do about it except carry on and hope to surprise this snoopy character somehow.

On the fifth day I had just the far northern part of the valley to inspect, so I decided to go right as far as I had to and make an overnight camp at the top of the valley. I was walking by the stream, trudging along, when a voice behind me said, "Where do you think you're going?"

I froze, then turned round carefully. A tall man in a red mackinaw was standing just off the trail casually holding a hunting rifle. The rifle wasn't pointing right at me; on the other hand, it wasn't pointing very far away. In fact, it was a moot point whether I was being held up at gun-point or not. Since this guy had just stepped out from behind a tree he had deliberately ambushed me, so I didn't care to make an issue of it right then—it wouldn't have been the right time. I just said, "Hi! Where did you spring from?"

His jaw tightened and I saw he wasn't very old, maybe in his early twenties. He said, "You haven't answered my question."

I didn't like that tightening jaw and I hoped his trigger finger wasn't tightening too. Young fellows his age can go off at half-cock awfully easily. I shifted the pack on my back. "Just going up to the head of the valley."

"Doing what?"

I said evenly, "I don't know what business it is of yours,

buster, but I'm doing a survey for the Matterson Corporation."

"No, you're not," he said. "Not on this land." He jerked his head down the valley. "See that marker?"

I looked in the direction he indicated and saw a small cairn of stones, much overgrown, which is why I hadn't spotted it before. It would have been pretty invisible from the other side. I looked at my young friend. "So?"

"So that's where Matterson land stops." He grinned, but there was no humour in him. "I was hoping you'd come this way—the marker makes explanations easier."

I walked back and looked at the cairn, then glanced at him to find he had followed me with the rifle still held easily in his hands. We had the cairn between us, so I said, "It's all right if I stand here?"

"Sure," he said airily. "You can stand there. No law against it."

"And you don't mind me taking off my pack?"

"Not so long as you don't put it this side of the marker." He grinned and I could see he was enjoying himself. I was prepared to let him—for the moment—so I said nothing, swung the pack to the ground and flexed my shoulders. He didn't like that—he could see how big I was, and the rifle swung towards me, so there was no question now about being held up.

I pulled the maps out of a side pocket of the pack and consulted them. "There's nothing here about this," I said mildly.

"There wouldn't be," he said. "Not on Matterson maps. But this is Trinavant land."

"Oh! Would that be Clare Trinavant?"

"Yeah, that's right." He shifted the rifle impatiently.

I said, "Is she available? I'd like to see her."

"She's around, but you won't see her—not unless she wants to see *you*." He laughed abruptly. "I wouldn't stick around waiting for her; you might take root."

I jerked my head down the valley. "I'll be camped in that clearing. You push off, sonny, and tell Miss Trinavant that I know where the bodies are buried." I don't know why I said it but it seemed a good thing to say at the time.

His head came up. "Huh!"

"Run away and tell Miss Trinavant just that," I said.

"You're just an errand boy, you know." I stooped, picked up the pack, and turned away, leaving him standing there with his mouth open. By the time I reached the clearing and looked back he had gone.

The fire was going and the coffee was bubbling when I heard voices from up the valley. My friend, the young gunman, came into sight but he'd left his artillery home this time. Behind him came a woman, trimly dressed in jeans, an open-necked shirt and a mackinaw. Some women can wear jeans but not many; Ogden Nash once observed that before a woman wears pants she should see herself walking away. Miss Trinavant definitely had the kind of figure that would look well in anything, even an old burlap sack.

And she looked beautiful even when she was as mad as a hornet. She came striding over to me in a determined sort of way, and demanded, "What is all this? Who are you?"

"My name's Boyd," I said. "I'm a geologist working on contract for the Matterson Corporation. I'm . . ."

She held up her hand and looked at me with frosty eyes. I'd never seen green frost before. "That's enough. This is as far up valley as you go, Mr. Boyd. See to it, Jimmy."

"That's what I told him, Miss Trinavant, but he didn't want to believe me."

I turned my head and looked at him. "Stay out of this, Jimmy boy: Miss Trinavant is on Matterson land by invitation—you're not, so buzz off. And don't point a gun at me again or I'll wrap it round your neck."

"Miss Trinavant, that's a lie," he yelled. "I never——"

I whirled and hit him. It's a neat trick if you can get in the right position—you straighten your arm out stiff and pivot from the hips—your hand picks up a hell of a velocity by the time it makes contact. The back of my hand caught him under the jaw and damn' near lifted him a foot off the ground. He landed flat on his back, flopped around a couple of times like a newly landed trout, and then lay still.

Miss Trinavant was looking at me open-mouthed—I could see her lovely tonsils quite plainly. I rubbed the back of my hand and said mildly, "I don't like liars."

"He wasn't lying," she said passionately. "He had no gun."

"I know when I'm being looked at by a 30.30," I said, and stabbed my finger at the prostrate figure in the pine needles.

"That character has been snooping after me for the last three days: I don't like that, either. He just got what was coming to him."

By the way she bared her teeth she was getting set to bite me. "You didn't give him a chance, you big barbarian."

I let that one go. I've been in too many brawls to be witless enough to give the other guy a chance—I leave that to the sporting fighters who earn a living by having their brains beaten out.

She knelt down, and said, "Jimmy, Jimmy, are you all right?" Then she looked up. "You must have broken his jaw."

"No," I said. "I didn't hit him hard enough. He'll just be sore in body and spirit for the next few days." I took a pannikin and filled it with water from the stream and dumped it on Jimmy's face. He stirred and groaned. "He'll be fit to walk in a few minutes. You'd better get him back to wherever you have your camp. And you can tell him that if he comes after me with a gun again I'll kill him."

She breathed hard but said nothing, concentrating on arousing Jimmy. Presently he was conscious enough to stand up on groggy feet and he looked at me with undisguised hatred. I said, "When you've got him bedded down I'll be glad to see you again, Miss Trinavant. I'll still be camped here."

She turned a startled face towards me. "What makes you think I ever want to see you again?" she flared.

"Because I know where the bodies are buried," I said pleasantly. "And don't be afraid; I've never been known to hit a woman yet."

I would have sworn she used some words I'd heard only in logging camps, but I couldn't be certain because she muttered them under her breath. Then she turned to give Jimmy a hand and I watched them go past the marker and out of sight. The coffee was pretty nigh ruined by this time so I tossed it out and set about making more, and a glance at the sun decided me to think about bedding down for the night.

It was dusk when I saw her coming back, a glimmering figure among the trees. I had made myself comfortable and was sitting with my back to a tree tending the fat duck which was roasting on a spit before the fire. She came up and stood over me. "What do you *really* want?" she asked abruptly.

I looked up. "You hungry?" She stirred impatiently, so I said, "Roast duck, fresh bread, wild celery, hot coffee—how does that sound?"

She dropped down to my level. "I told Jimmy to watch out for you," she said. "I knew you were coming. But I didn't tell him to go on Matterson land—and I didn't say anything about a gun."

"Perhaps you should have," I observed. "Perhaps you should have said, 'No gun'."

"I know Jimmy's a bit wild," she said. "But that's no excuse for what you did."

I took a flat cake of bread out of the clay oven and slapped it on a platter. "Have you ever looked down the muzzle of a gun?" I asked. "It's a mighty unsettling sensation, and I tend to get violent when I'm nervous." I handed her the platter. "What about some duck?"

Her nostrils quivered as the fragrance rose from the spitted bird and she laughed. "You've sold me. It smells so good."

I began to carve the duck. "Jimmy's not much hurt except in what he considers to be his pride. If he goes around pointing guns at people, one of these days there's going to be a bang and he'll hang as high as Haman. Maybe I've saved his life. Who is he?"

"One of my men."

"So you knew I was coming," I said thoughtfully. "News gets around these parts fast, considering it's so underpopulated."

She selected a slice of breast from her platter and popped it into her mouth. "Anything that concerns me I get to know about. Say, this is good!"

"I'm not such a good cook," I said. "It's the open air that does it. How do I concern you?"

"You work for Matterson; you were on my land. That concerns me."

I said, "When I contracted to do this job Howard Matterson had a bit of an argument with a man called Donner. Matterson said he'd straighten out the matter with someone called Clare—presumably you. Did he?"

54

"I haven't seen Howard Matterson in a month—and I don't care if I never see him again."

"You can't blame me for not knowing the score," I said. "I thought the job was above board. Matterson has a strange way of running his business."

She picked up a drumstick and gnawed on it delicately. "Not strange—just crooked. Of course, it all depends on which Matterson you're talking about. Bull Matterson is the crooked one; Howard is just plain sloppy."

"You mean he *forgot* to talk to you about it?" I said unbelievingly.

"Something like that." She pointed the drumstick at me. "What's all this about bodies?"

I grinned. "Oh, I just wanted to talk to you. I knew that would bring you running."

She stared at me. "Why should it?"

"It did—didn't it?" I pointed out. "It's a variation of the old story of the practical joker who sent a cable to a dozen of his friends: FLY—ALL IS DISCOVERED. Nine of them hastily left town. Everyone has a skeleton in some cupboard of their lives."

"You were just pining for company," she said sardonically.

"Would I pass up the chance of dining with a beautiful woman in the backwoods?"

"I don't believe you," she said flatly. "You can cut out the flattery. For all you knew I might have been an old hag of ninety, unless, of course, you'd been asking questions around beforehand. Which you obviously have. What are you up to, Boyd?"

"Okay," I said. "How's this for a starter? Did you ever get around to investigating that Trinavant-Matterson partnership agreement, together with the deal Matterson made with the trustees of the estate? It seems to me that particular business transaction could bear looking into. Why doesn't someone do something about it?"

She stared at me wide-eyed. "Wow! If you've been asking questions like that around Fort Farrell you're going to be in trouble as soon as the old Bull finds out."

"Yes," I said. "I understand he'd rather forget the Trinavants ever existed. But don't worry; he won't get to hear of it. My source of information is strictly private."

"I wasn't worrying," she said coldly. "But perhaps you think you can handle the Mattersons the same way you handled Jimmy. I wouldn't bank on it."

"I didn't think you cared—and I was right," I said with a grin. "But why doesn't someone investigate that smelly deal? You, for instance."

"Why should I?" she said offhandedly. "It has nothing to do with me how much Bull Matterson gyps the trustees. Tangling with the Mattersons wouldn't put money in my pocket."

"You mean you don't care that John Trinavant's intentions have been warped and twisted to put money in Matterson's pocket?" I asked softly.

I thought she was going to throw the platter at me. Her face whitened and pink spots appeared in her cheeks. "Damn you!" she said hotly. Slowly she simmered down. "I did try once," she admitted. "And I got nowhere. Donner has the books of the Matterson Corporation in such a goddam tangle it would take a team of high-priced lawyers ten years to unsnarl everything. Even I couldn't afford that and my attorney advised me not to try. Why are you so interested anyway?"

I watched her sop up gravy with a piece of bread; I like a girl with a healthy appetite. "I don't know that I am interested. It's just another point to wonder about. Like why does Matterson want to bury the Trinavants—permanently?"

"You stick your neck out, you'll get it chopped off," she warned. "Matterson doesn't like questions like that." She put down her platter, stood up and went down to the stream to wash her hands. When she came back she was wiping them on a man-sized handkerchief.

I poured her a cup of coffee. "I'm not asking Matterson—I'm asking a Trinavant. Isn't it something a Trinavant wonders about from time to time?"

"Sure! And like everyone else we get no answers." She looked at me closely. "What are you after, Boyd? And who the hell are you?"

"Just a beat-up freelance geologist. Doesn't Matterson ever worry you?"

She sipped the hot coffee. "Not much. I spend very little

time here. I come back for a few months every year to annoy him, that's all."

"And you still don't know what he has against the Trinavants?"

"No."

I looked into the fire and said pensively, "Someone was saying that he wished you'd get married. The implication was that there'd be no one around with the name of Trinavant any more."

She flared hotly. "Has Howard been——?" Then she stopped and bit her lip.

"Has Howard been . . . what?"

She rose to her feet and dusted herself down. "I don't think I like you, Mr. Boyd. *You* ask too many questions, and *I* get no answers. I don't know who you are or what you want. If you want to tangle with Matterson that's your affair; my disinterested advice would be 'Don't!' because he'll chop you up into little pieces. Still, why should I care? But let me tell you one thing—don't interfere with me."

"What would you do to me that Matterson wouldn't?"

"The name of Trinavant isn't quite forgotten," she said. "I have some good friends."

"They'd better be better than Jimmy," I said caustically. Then I wondered why I was fighting with her; it didn't make sense. I scrambled to my feet. "Look, I have no fight with you and I've no cause to interfere in your life, either. I'm a pretty harmless guy except when someone pokes a gun in my direction. I'll just go back and report to Howard Matterson that you wouldn't let me on your land. There's no grief in it for me."

"You do that," she said. There was puzzlement in her voice as she added, "You're a funny one, Boyd. You come here as a stranger and you dig up a ten-year-old mystery everyone has forgotten. Where did you get it from?"

"I don't think my informant would care to be named."

"I bet he wouldn't," she said with contempt. "I thought everyone in Fort Farrell had developed a conveniently bad memory as well as a yellow streak."

"Maybe you have friends in Fort Farrell, too," I said softly.

She zipped up her mackinaw against the chill of the night air. "I'm not going to stick around here bandying mysteries with you, Boyd," she said. "Just remember one thing. Don't come on my land—ever."

She turned to go away, and I said, "Wait! There are ghosties and ghoulies and beasties, and things that go bump in the night; I wouldn't want you to walk into a bear. I'll escort you back to your camp."

"My God, a backwoods cavalier!" she said in disgust, but she stayed around to watch me kick earth over the embers of the fire. While I checked my rifle she looked around at my gear, dimly illuminated in the moonlight. "You make a neat camp."

"Comes of experience," I said. "Shall we go?" She fell into step beside me and, as we passed the marker, I said, "Thanks for letting me on your land, Miss Trinavant."

"I'm a sucker for sweet talk," she said, and pointed. "We go that way."

3

Her "camp" was quite a surprise. After we had walked for over half an hour up a slope that tested the calf muscles there came the unexpected dark loom of a building. The hunting beam of the flashlamp she produced disclosed walls of fieldstone and logs and the gleam of large windows. She pushed open an unlocked door, then said a little irritably, "Well, aren't you coming in?"

The interior was even more of a surprise. It was warm with central heating and it was *big*. She flicked a switch and a small pool of light appeared, and the room was so large that it retreated away into shadows. One entire wall was windowed and there was a magnificent view down the valley. Away in the distance I could see the moonglow on the lake I had prospected around.

She flicked more switches and more lights came on, revealing the polished wooden floor carpeted with skins, the modern furniture, the wall brightly lined with books and a scattering of phonograph records on the floor grouped around a built-in hi-fi outfit as though someone had been interrupted.

This was a millionaire's version of a log cabin. I looked about, probably with my mouth hanging open, then said, "If this were in the States, a guy could get to be President just by being born here."

"I don't need any wisecracks," she said. "If you want a drink, help yourself; it's over there. And you might do something about the fire; it isn't really necessary but I like to see flames."

She disappeared, closing a door behind her, and I laid down my rifle. There was a massive fieldstone chimney with a fireplace big enough to roast a moose in which a few red embers glowed faintly, so I replenished it from the pile of logs stacked handily and waited until the flames came and I was sure the fire had caught hold. Then I did a tour of the room, hoping she wouldn't be back too soon. You can find out a lot about a person just by looking at a room as it's lived in.

The books were an eclectic lot; many modern novels but very little of the avant-garde, way-out stuff; a solid wedge of English and French classics, a shelf of biographies and a sprinkling of histories, mostly of Canada and, what was surprising, a scad of books on archæology, mostly Middle-Eastern. It looked as though Clare Trinavant had a mind of her own.

I left the books and drifted around the room, noting the odd pieces of pottery and statuary, most of which looked older than Methuselah; the animal photographs on the walls, mainly of Canadian animals, and the rack of rifles and shotguns in a glassed-in case. I peered at these curiously through the glass and saw that, although the guns appeared to be well kept, there was a film of dust on them. Then I looked at a photograph of a big brute of a brown bear and decided that, even with a telephoto lens, whoever had taken that shot had been too damn' close.

She said from close behind me, "Looks a bit like you, don't you think?"

I turned. "I'm not that big. He'd make six of me."

She had changed her shirt and was wearing a well-cut pair of slacks that certainly hadn't been bought off any shelf. She said, "I've just been in to see Jimmy. I think he'll be all right."

"I didn't hit him harder than necessary," I said. "Just enough to teach him manners." I waved my arm about the room. "Some shack!"

"Boyd, you make me sick," she said coldly. "And you can get the hell out of here. You have a dirty mind if you think I'm shacked up with Jimmy Waystrand."

"Hey!" I said. "You jump to an awful fast conclusion, Trinavant. All I meant was that this is a hell of a place you have here. I didn't expect to find *this* in the woods, that's all."

Slowly the pink spots in her cheeks died away, and she said, "I'm sorry if I took you the wrong way. Maybe I'm a little jumpy right now, and if I am, you're responsible, Boyd."

"No apology necessary, Trinavant."

She began to giggle and it developed into a full-throated laugh. I joined in and we had an hysterical thirty seconds. At last she controlled herself. "No," she said, shaking her head. "That won't do. You can't call me Trinavant—you'd better make it Clare."

"I'm Bob," I said. "Hello, Clare."

"Hello, Bob."

"You know, I didn't really mean to imply that Jimmy was anything to you," I said. "He isn't man enough for you."

She stopped smiling and, folding her arms, she regarded me for a long time. "Bob Boyd, I've never known another man who makes my hackles rise the way you do. If you think I judge a man by the way he behaves in a fight you're dead wrong. The trouble with you is that you've got logopædia— every time you open your mouth you put your foot in it. Now, for God's sake, keep your mouth shut and get me a drink."

I moved towards what looked like the drinks cabinet. "You shouldn't steal yo wisecracks from the Duke of Edinburgh," I said. "That's verging on *lèse majesté*. What will you have?"

"Scotch and water—fifty-fifty. You'll find a good Scotch in there."

Indeed it was a good Scotch! I lifted out the bottle of *Islay Mist* reverently and wondered how long ago it was since Hamish McDougall had seen Clare Trinavant. But I said nothing about that. Instead, I kept my big mouth shut as she had advised and poured the drinks.

60

As I handed her the glass she said, "How long have you been in the woods this trip?"

"Nearly two weeks."

"How would you like a hot bath?"

"Clare, for that you can have my soul," I said fervently. Lake water is damned cold and a man doesn't bathe as often as he should when in the field.

She pointed. "Through that door—second door on the left. I've put towels out for you."

I picked up my glass. "Mind if I take my drink?"

"Not at all."

The bathroom was a wonder to behold. Tiled in white and dark blue, you could have held a convention in there—if that was the kind of convention you had in mind. The bath was sunk into the floor and seemed as big as a swimming-pool, and the water poured steaming out of the faucet. And there was a plenitude of bath towels, each about an acre in extent.

As I lay soaking I thought about a number of things. I thought of the possible reason why Clare Trinavant should bring up the name of Howard Matterson when I brought up the subject of her marriage. I thought of the design of the labels of Scotch, especially on those from the island of Islay. I thought of the curve of Clare Trinavant's neck as it rose from the collar of her shirt. I thought of a man I had never seen—Bull Matterson—and wondered what he was like in appearance. I thought of the tendril of hair behind Clare Trinavant's ear.

None of these thoughts got me anywhere in particular, so I got out of the bath and finished the Scotch while I dried myself. As I dressed I became aware of music drifting through the cabin—some cabin!—which drowned out the distant throbbing of a diesel generator, and when I got back to Clare I found her sitting on the floor listening to the last movement of Sibelius's First Symphony.

She waved me to the drinks cabinet and held up an empty glass, so I gave us both a refill and we sat quietly until the music came to an end. She shivered slightly and pointed to the moonlit view down the valley. "I always think the music is describing this."

"Finland has pretty much the same scenery as Canada," I said. "Woods and lakes."

One eyebrow lifted. "Not only a backwoods cavalier, but an educated one."

I grinned at her. "I've had a college education, too."

She coloured a little and said quietly, "I'm sorry. I shouldn't have said that. It was bitchy, wasn't it?"

"That's all right." I waved my hand. "What made you build here?"

"As your mysterious informant has probably told you, I was brought up around here. Uncle John left me this land. I love it, so I built here." She paused. "And, since you're so well informed, you probably know that he wasn't really my uncle."

"Yes," I said. "I have only one criticism. Your rifles and shotguns need cleaning more often."

"I don't use them now," she said. "I've lost the taste for killing animals just for fun. I do my shooting with a camera now."

I indicated the close-up of the snapping jaws of the brown bear. "Such as that?" She nodded, and I said, "I hope you had your rifle handy when you took that shot."

"I was in no danger," she said. We fell into a companionable silence, looking into the fire. After a few minutes, she said, "How long will you be working for Matterson, Bob?"

"Not long. I've just about got the job cleaned up now—with the exception of the Trinavant land." I smiled. "I think I'll give that a miss—the owner is a shade tetchy."

"And then?" Clare questioned.

"And then back to the North-West Territories."

"Who do you work for up there?"

"Myself." I told her a little of what I was doing. "I hadn't been going for more than eighteen months when I made a strike. It brought me in enough to keep me going for the next five years and in that time I didn't find a thing that was worth anything. That's why I'm here working for Matterson—getting a stake together again."

She was thoughtful. "Looking for the pot of gold at the end of the rainbow?"

"Something like that," I admitted. "And you? What do you do?"

"I'm an archæologist," she said unexpectedly.

"Oh!" I said, rather inadequately.

She roused herself and turned to look at me. "I'm not a dilettante, Bob. I'm not a rich bitch playing around with a hobby until I can find a husband. I really work at it—you should read the papers I've written."

"Don't be so damned defensive," I said. "I believe you. Where do you do your prospecting?"

She laughed at that. "Mostly in the Middle East, although I've done one dig in Crete." She pointed to a small statuette of a woman bare to the waist and in a flounced skirt. "That came from Crete—the Greek government let me bring it out."

I picked it up. "I wonder if this is Ariadne?"

"I've had that thought." She looked across at the window. "Every year I try to come back here. The Mediterranean lands are so bare and treeless—I have to come back to my own place."

"I know what you mean."

We talked for a long time while the fire died. I don't remember now exactly what we talked about—it was just about the trivialities that went to make up our respective lives. At last, she said, "My God, but I'm suddenly sleepy. What time is it?"

"Two a.m."

She laughed. "No wonder, then." She paused. "There's a spare bed if you'd like to stay. It's pretty late to be going back to your camp." She looked at me sternly. "But remember— no passes. One pass and you're out on your ear."

"All right, Clare. No passes," I promised.

I was back in Fort Farrell two days later and, as soon as I got to my room at the Matterson House hotel, I filled the bathtub and got down to my favourite pastime of soaking, drinking and thinking deep thoughts.

I had left Clare early on the morning following our encounter and was surprised to find her reserved and somewhat distant. True, she cooked a good man-sized breakfast, but that was something a good housewife would do for her worst enemy by reflex action. I thought that perhaps she was regretting her fraternization with the enemy—after all, I *was* working for Matterson—or maybe she was miffed because I *hadn't* made a pass at her. You never know with women.

Anyway, she was pretty curt in her leave-taking. When I

commented that her cabin would be on the edge of a new lake as soon as Matterson had built the dam, she said violently, "Matterson isn't going to drown *my* land. You can tell him from me that I'm going to fight him."

"Okay, I'll tell him."

"You'd better go, Boyd. I'm sure you have a lot to do."

"Yes, I have," I said. "But I won't do it on your land." I picked up my rifle. "Keep smiling, Trinavant."

So I went, and half-way down the trail I turned to look back at the house, but all I could see was the figure of Jimmy Waystrand standing straddle-legged like a Hollywood cowboy at the top of the rise, making sure I left.

It didn't take long to check the rest of the Matterson patch and I was back at my main camp early and loafed about for a day until the helicopter came for me. An hour later I was back in Fort Farrell and wallowing in the bathtub.

Languidly I splashed hot water and figured out my schedule. The telephone in the bedroom rang but I ignored it and pretty soon it got tired and stopped. I had to see Howard Matterson, then I wanted to check with McDougall to confirm a suspicion. All that remained after that was to write a report, collect my dough and catch the next bus out of town. There was nothing for me in Fort Farrell beyond a lot of personal grief.

The telephone began to ring again so I splashed out of the tub and walked into the bedroom. It was Howard Matterson and he seemed to be impatient at being kept waiting. "I heard you were back," he said. "I've been expecting you up here."

"I'm ironing out the kinks in a bathtub," I said. "I'll be up to see you when I'm ready."

There was a silence while he digested that—I guess he wasn't used to waiting on other people. Finally, he said, "Okay, make it quick. Have a good trip?"

"Moderately so," I said. "I'll tell you about it when I come up. I'll pack in a nutshell what you want to know—there's no sound geological reason for any mining operations in the Kinoxi Valley. I'll fill in the details later."

"Ah! That's what I wanted to know." He rang off.

I dressed leisurely, then went up to his office. I was kept waiting even longer this time—forty minutes. Maybe Howard figured I rated a wait for the way I answered telephones. But

64

he was pleasant enough when I finally got past his secretary. "Glad to see you," he said. "Have any trouble?"

I lifted an eyebrow. "Was I expected to have any trouble?"

The smile hovered on his face as though uncertain whether to depart or not, but it finally settled back into place again. "Not at all," he said heartily. "I knew I'd picked a competent man."

"Thanks," I said drily. "I had to put a crimp in someone's style, though. You'd better know about it because you might be getting a complaint. Know a man called Jimmy Way-strand?"

Matterson busied himself in lighting a cigar. "At the north end?" he asked, not looking at me.

"That's right. It came to fisticuffs, but I managed all right," I said modestly.

Matterson looked pleased. "Then you did the *whole* survey."

"No, I didn't."

He tried to look stern. "Oh! Why not?"

"Because I don't slug women," I said urgently. "Miss Trinavant was most insistent that I did not survey her land on behalf of the Matterson Corporation." I leaned forward. "I believe you told Mr. Donner that you would straighten out that little matter with Miss Trinavant. Apparently you didn't."

"I tried to get hold of her, but she must have been away," he said. He drummed his fingers on the desk. "A pity about that, but it can't be helped, I suppose."

I thought he was lying, but it wouldn't help to say so. I said, "As far as the rest of the area goes, there's nothing worth digging up as far as I can see."

"No trace of oil or gas?"

"Nothing like that. I'll give you a full report. Maybe I can borrow a girl from your typing pool; you'll get it quicker that way." And I'd get out of town quicker, too.

"Sure," he said. "I'll arrange that. Let me have it as soon as you can."

"Right," I said, and got up to go. At the door I paused. "Oh, there's just one thing. By the lake in the valley I found traces of quick clay—it's not uncommon in sedimentary deposits in these parts. It's worth doing a further check; it could cause you trouble."

"Sure, sure," he said. "Put it in your report."

As I went down to the street I wondered if Matterson knew what I was talking about. Still, he'd get a full explanation in the report.

I walked down to Trinavant Park and saw that Lieutenant Farrell was still on guard duty policing the pigeons, then I went into the Greek joint and ordered a cup of coffee substitute and sat at a table. If McDougall was half the newspaperman he said he was, I could expect him any moment. Sure enough, he walked in stiffly within fifteen minutes and sat down next to me wordlessly.

I watched him stir his coffee. "What's the matter, Mac? Lost your tongue?"

He smiled. "I was waiting for you to tell me something. I'm a good listener."

I said deliberately, "There's nothing to stop Matterson building his dam—except Clare Trinavant. Why didn't you tell me she was up there?"

"I thought you'd do better making the discovery for yourself. Did you run into trouble son?"

"Not much! Who is this character, Jimmy Waystrand?"

McDougall laughed. "Son of the caretaker at Clare's place —a spunky young pup."

"He's seen too many Hollywood westerns," I said, and described what had happened.

McDougall looked grave. "The boy wants talking to. He had no right trailing people on Matterson land—and as for the rifle . . ." He shook his head. "His father ought to rip the hide off him."

"I think I put him on the right way." I glanced at him. "When did you last see Clare Trinavant?"

"When she came through town, about a month ago."

"And she's been up at the cabin ever since?"

"So far as I know. She never moves far from it."

I thought it wouldn't be too much trouble for Howard Matterson to climb into that helicopter of his for the fifty-mile flight from Fort Farrell. Then why hadn't he done so? Perhaps it was as Clare had said, that he was a sloppy businessman. I said, "What's between Clare and Howard Matterson?"

McDougall smiled grimly. "He wants to marry her."

I gaped, then burst out laughing. "He hasn't a snowball's hope. You ought to hear the things she says about the Mattersons—father and son."

"Howard has a pretty thick skin," said McDougall. "He hopes to wear her down."

"He won't do that by keeping away from her," I said. "Or by flooding her land. By the way, what's her legal position on that?"

"Tricky. You know that most of the hydro-electric resources of British Columbia are government-controlled through B.C. Electric. There are exceptions—the Aluminium Company of Canada built its own plant at Kitimat and that's the precedent that governs Matterson's project here. He's been lobbying the Government and has things pretty well lined up. If a land resources tribunal decides this is in the public interest, then Clare loses out."

He smiled sadly, "Jimson and the *Fort Farrell Recorder* are working on that angle right now, but he knows better than to ask me to write any of that crap, so he keeps me on nice safe topics like weddings and funerals. According to the editorial he was writing when I left the office, the Matterson Corporation is the pure knight guarding the public interest."

"He must have got the word from Howard," I said. "I gave him the results not long ago. I'm sorry about that, Mac."

"It isn't your fault; you were just doing your job." He looked at me out of the corner of his eye. "Have you decided what you are going to do?"

"About what?"

"About this whole stinking set-up. I thought you'd taken time off to decide when you were out in the woods."

"Mac, I'm no shining knight, either. There isn't anything I could do that would be any use, and I don't know anything that could help."

"I don't believe you," McDougall said bluntly.

"You can believe what you damn' well like," I said. I was getting tired of his prodding and pushing, and maybe I was feeling a mite guilty—although why I should feel guilty I wouldn't know. "I'm going to write a report, collect my pay and climb on to a bus heading out of here. Any mess you have in Fort Farrell is none of my business."

He stood up. "I should have known," he said wearily. "I

thought you were the man. I thought you'd have had the guts to put the Mattersons back where they belong, but I guess I was wrong." He pointed a shaky finger at me. "You know something. I *know* you know something. Whatever your lousy reasons for keeping it to yourself, I hope you choke on them. You're a gutless, spineless imitation of a man and I'm glad you're leaving Fort Farrell because I'd hate to vomit in the street every time I saw you."

He turned and walked into the street shakily and I watched him aim blindly across the square. I felt very sorry for him but I could do nothing for him. The man who had the information he needed was not Bob Boyd but Robert Grant, and Robert Grant was ten years dead.

I had one last brush with Howard Matterson when I turned in the report. He took the papers and maps and tossed them on to his desk. "I hear you had a cosy chat with Clare Trinavant."

"I stood her a dinner," I said. "Who wouldn't?"

"And you went up to her cabin."

"That's right," I said easily. "I thought it was in your interest. I thought that perhaps I could talk her round to a more reasonable frame of mind."

His voice was like ice. "And was it in my interest that you stayed all night?"

That gave me pause. By God, the man was jealous! But where could he have got his information? Clare certainly wouldn't have told him, so I was pretty certain it must have been young Jimmy Waystrand. The young punk was hitting back at me by tattling to Matterson. It must have been pretty common knowledge in Fort Farrell that Howard was hot for Clare and getting nowhere.

I smiled pleasantly at Matterson. "No, that was in *my* interest."

His face went a dull red and he lumbered to his feet. "That's not funny," he said in a voice like gravel. "We think a lot of Miss Trinavant round here—and a lot about her reputation." He started to move around the desk, flexing his shoulders, and I knew he was getting ready to take me.

It was unbelievable—the guy hadn't grown up. He was behaving like any callow teen-ager whose brains are still in his fists, or like a deer in the rutting season ready to take on all comers in defence of his harem. A clear case of retarded development.

I said, "Matterson, Clare Trinavant is quite capable of taking care of herself *and* her reputation. And you won't do her reputation any good by brawling—I happen to know her views on that subject. And she'd certainly get to know about it because if you lay a finger on me I'll toss you out of the nearest window and it'll be a matter for public concern."

He kept on coming, then thought better of it, and stopped. I said, "Clare Trinavant offered me a bath and a bed for the night—and it wasn't her bed. And if that's what you think of her, no wonder you're not making the grade. Now, I'd like my pay."

In a low, suppressed voice he said, "There's an envelope on the desk. Take it and get out."

I stretched out my hand and took the envelope, ripped it open and took out the slip of paper. It was a cheque drawn on the Matterson Bank for the full and exact amount agreed on. I turned and walked out of his office boiling with rage, but not so blindly that I didn't go immediately to the Matterson Bank to turn the cheque into money before Howard stopped it.

With a wad of bills in my wallet I felt better. I went to my room, packed my bag and checked out within half an hour. Going down King Street, I paid my last respects to Lieutenant Farrell, the hollow man of Trinavant Park, and walked on past the Greek place towards the bus depot. There was a bus leaving and I was glad to be on it and rid of Fort Farrell.

It wasn't much of a town.

IV

I did another freelance job during the winter down in the Okanagan valley near the U.S. border and before the spring thaw I was all set to go back to the North-West Territories as soon as the snows melted. There's not a great deal of joy for a geologist in a snow-covered landscape—he has to be able to see what he's looking for. It was only during the brief summer that I had a chance, and so I had to wait a while.

During this time, in my correspondence with Susskind, I told him of what had happened in Fort Farrell. His answer reassured me that I had done the right thing.

"I think you were well advised to cut loose from Fort Farrell; that kind of prying would not do you any good at all. If you stay away your bad dreams should tail off in a few weeks providing you don't deliberately think about the episode.

"Speaking as a psychiatrist, I find the ambivalent behaviour of Howard Matterson to be an almost classic example of what, to use the only expression conveniently available, is called a 'love-hate' relationship. I don't like this phrase because it has been chewed to death by the *litterateurs* (why must writers seize on our specialised vocabulary and twist meanings out of all recognition?) but it describes the symptoms, if only inadequately. He wants her, he hates her; he must destroy her and have her simultaneously. In other words, Mr. Matterson wants to eat his cake and have it, too. Taken all in all, Matterson seems to be a classic case of emotional immaturity—at least, he has all the symptoms. You're well away from him; such men are dangerous. You have only to look at Hitler to see what I mean.

"But I must say that your Trinavant sounds quite a dish!

"I've just remembered something I should have told you about years ago. Just about the time you left Montreal a private enquiry agent was snooping about asking questions about you, or rather, about Robert Grant. I gave him no joy and sent him away with a flea in his ear and my boot up his rump. I didn't tell you about it at the time because, in my opinion, you were then in no fit state to be the recipient of news of that sort; and subsequently I forgot about it.

"At the time I wondered what it was about and I still have not come to any firm conclusion. It certainly was nothing to do with the Vancouver police because, as you know, I straightened them out about you, and a hell of a task it was. Most laymen are thick-headed about psychiatry, but police and legal laymen have heads of almost impenetrable oak. They seem to think that the McNaughten Rules are a psychiatric dictum and not a mere legal formalism, and it was no

70

mean feat getting them to see sense and getting Bob Boyd off the hook for what Robert Grant had done. But I did it.

"So who could have employed this private eye? I did a check and I came up with nothing—it is not my field. Anyway, it is many years ago and probably means nothing now, but I thought I might as well tell you that someone, other than your mysterious benefactor, was interested in you."

That was interesting news but many years out of date. I chewed it over for some time, but, like Susskind, I could come to no conclusion, so I let it lie.

In the spring I headed north to the MacKenzie District where I fossicked about all summer somewhere between the Great Slave Lake and Coronation Gulf. It's a lonely life—there are not many people up there—but one meets the occasional trapper and there are always the wandering Eskimos in the far north. Again, it was a bad year and I thought briefly of giving it up as a bad job and settling for a salaried existence as a company wage slave. But I knew I wouldn't do that; I'd tasted too much freedom to be nailed down and I'd make a bad company man. But if I were to continue I'd have to go south again to assemble a stake for the next summer, so I humped my pack for civilisation.

I suppose I was all sorts of a fool to go back to British Columbia. I wanted to follow Susskind's advice and forget all about Fort Farrell, but the mind is not as easily controlled as all that. During the lonely days, and more especially the lonelier nights, I had thought about the odd fate of the Trinavants. I felt a certain responsibility because I had certainly been in that Cadillac when it crashed, and I felt an odd guilt about what might have caused it. I also felt guilty about running away from Fort Farrell—McDougall's last words still stuck in my craw—even though I had Susskind's assurance that I had done the right thing.

I thought a lot about Clare Trinavant, too—more than was good for a lone man in the middle of the wilderness.

Anyway, I went back and did a winter job around Kamloops in British Columbia, working for an academic team investigating earth tremors. I say "academic" but the tab was picked up by the United States Government because this work could lead to a better means of detecting underground atomic tests, so perhaps it was not so academic, after all. The pay

71

wasn't too good and the work and general atmosphere a bit too long-haired for me, but I worked through the winter and saved as much as I could.

As spring approached I began to get restless, but I knew I had not saved up enough to go back north for another summer's exploration. It really began to look as though this was the end of the line and I would have to settle down to the company grind. As it turned out I got the money in another way, but I would rather have worked twenty years for a company than gain the money the way I did.

I received a letter from Susskind's partner, a man called Jarvis. He wrote to tell me that Susskind had unexpectedly died of a heart attack and, as executor of the estate, he informed me that Susskind had left me $5,000.

"I know that you and Dr. Susskind had a very special relationship, deeper than that normal to doctor and patient," wrote Jarvis. "Please accept my deepest regrets, and you will know, of course, that I stand ready to help you in my professional capacity at any time you may need me."

I felt a deep sense of loss. Susskind was the only father I ever had or knew; he had been my only anchor in a world that had unexpectedly taken away three-quarters of my life. Even though we met but infrequently, our letters kept us close, and now there would be no more letters, no more gruff, irreverent, shrewd Susskind.

I suppose the news knocked me off my bearings for a while. At any rate, I began to think of the geological structure of the North-East Interior of British Columbia, and to wonder if it was at all necessary to go back to the far north that summer. I decided to go back to Fort Farrell.

Thinking of it in hindsight, I now know the reason. While I had Susskind I had a line back to my beginnings. Without Susskind there was no line and again I had to fight for my personal identity; and the only way to do it was to find my past, harrowing though the experience might be. And the way to the past lay through Fort Farrell, in the death of the Trinavant family and the birth of the Matterson logging empire.

At the time, of course, I didn't think that way. I just did things without thinking at all. I turned in the job, packed my bags and was on my way to Fort Farrell within the month,

The place hadn't changed any.

I got off the bus at the depot and there was the same fat little guy who looked me up and down. "Welcome back," he said.

I grinned at him. "I don't need to know where the Matterson Building is this time. But you can tell me one thing—is McDougall still around?"

"He was up to last week—I haven't seen him since."

"You'd be good in a witness-box," I said. "You know how to make a careful statement."

I went up King Street and into Trinavant Park and saw that there had been a change, after all. The Greek place now had a name—a garish neon sign proclaimed it to be the Hellenic Café. Lieutenant Farrell was still the same, though; he hadn't moved a muscle. I checked into the Matterson House Hotel and wondered how long I'd be staying there. Once I started lifting stones to see what nasty things lay underneath I could see that innkeeper Matterson might not want to have me around as part of his clientele. But this was for the future; now I might as well see how the land lay with Howard.

I took the elevator up to his office. He had a new secretary and I asked her to tell the boss that Mr. Boyd wanted to see him. I got into Howard's office in the record-breaking time of two minutes. Howard must have been very curious to know why I was back in Fort Farrell.

He hadn't changed, either, although there was no real reason why he should. He was still the same bull-necked, beefy guy, running to fat, but I thought I detected a shade more fat this time. "Well, well," he said. "I'm certainly surprised to see you again."

"I don't know why you should be," I said innocently. "Considering that you offered me a job."

He goggled at me incredulously. *"What?"*

"You offered me a job. You said you wanted a geological survey of all the Matterson holdings, and you offered the job to me. Don't you remember?"

He remembered that his mouth was open after a while and snapped it shut. "By Christ, but you've got a nerve! Do you think that . . ." He stopped and chuckled fatly. "No, Mr.

73

Boyd. I'm afraid we've changed our minds about that project."

"That's a pity," I said. "I find myself unable to go north this year."

He grinned maliciously. "What's the matter? Couldn't you find anyone to stake you?"

"Something like that," I said, and let a worried look appear on my face.

"It's tough all round," he said, enjoying himself, "but I'm sorry to tell you that I don't think there's a job going anywhere in this territory for a man in your line. In fact, I'll go further: I don't think there's *any* job around here that you could hold down. The employment situation is terrible in Fort Farrell this year." A thought struck him. "Of course, I might be able to find you a job as a bell-hop in the hotel. I have influence there, you understand. I hope you're strong enough to carry bags?"

I wasn't worried about letting him have his fun. "I don't think I'm down to that yet," I said, and stood up.

That didn't suit Howard; he wasn't through with grinding my face in the mud. "Sit down," he said genially. "Let's talk about old times."

"Okay," I said, and sat down again. "Seen anything of Clare Trinavant lately?"

That one really harpooned him. "We'll keep her name out of this," he snapped.

"I only wanted to know if she was around," I said reasonably. "She's a real nice woman—I'd like to meet her again some time."

He looked like someone who'd just swallowed his gum. The idea had just sunk in that I was really interested in Clare Trinavant—and he wasn't far wrong, at that. It looked as though my tenure of the hotel room would be even shorter than I thought. He recovered. "She's out of town," he said with satisfaction. "She's out of the country. In fact, she's even out of the hemisphere, and she won't be back for a long time. I'm sorry about that—really I am."

That was a pity; I'd been looking forward to exchanging insults with her again. Still, she wasn't the main reason I was back in Fort Farrell, even though she was a possibly ally I had lost.

I stood up again. "You're right," I said regretfully. "It's

74

tough all round." This time he didn't try to stop me; perhaps he didn't like my brand of chatty conversation. I made for the door, and said, "I'll be seeing you."

"Are you going to stick around here?" he demanded.

I laughed at him. "That depends if the employment situation is as bad as you say." I closed the door on him and grinned at his secretary. "A mighty fine boss you've got there. Yes, sir!" She looked at me as though I were mad, so I winked at her and carried on.

Baiting Howard Matterson was childish and pretty pointless, but I felt the better for it; it gave a boost to my flagging morale. I hadn't had much to do with him personally, and beyond the comments of Clare Trinavant and McDougall, I knew nothing about him. But now I knew he was a brave boy indeed; nothing suited Howard better than to put the boot to a man who was down. His little exhibition of sadism made me feel better and gave added enjoyment to the task of cutting him down to size.

As I walked along King Street I glanced at my watch and quickened my pace. If McDougall still kept to his usual schedule he'd be having his afternoon coffee at the Greek place—the Hellenic Café. Sure enough, there he was, brooding over an empty cup. I went to the counter and bought two cups of coffee which came to me via a chromium-plated monster which squirted steam from every joint and sounded like the first stage of an Atlas missile taking off.

I took the coffee over to the table and dumped a cup in front of Mac. If he was surprised to see me he didn't show it. His eyelids just flickered and he said, "What do *you* want?"

I sat down next to him. "I had a change of heart, Mac."

He said nothing, but the droop of his shoulders altered to a new erectness. I indicated the Espresso machine. "When did that sign of prosperity come in?"

"A couple of months ago—and the coffee's godawful," he said sourly. "Glad to see you, son."

I said, "I'll make this quick because I have an idea that it would be better all round if we aren't seen together too often. Howard Matterson knows I'm in town and I suspect he's mad at me."

"Why should he be?"

75

"I had a barney with him just before I left—eighteen months ago." I told Mac what had happened between us and of my suspicions of young Jimmy Waystrand.

Mac clicked his tongue. "The bastard!" he exclaimed. "You know what Howard did? He told Clare you'd boasted to him about spending the night in her cabin. She went flaming wild and cursed you up hill and down dale. You're not her favourite house guest any more."

"And she believed him?"

"Why wouldn't she? Who else could have told Howard? No one thought of Jimmy." He grunted suddenly. "So that's how he got a good job up at the dam. He's working for the Matterson Corporation now."

"So they're constructing the dam," I said.

"Yeah. Public opinion was well moulded and Matterson rammed it through over Clare's objections. They began building last summer and they're working as though Matterson ordered it finished for yesterday. They couldn't pour concrete in winter, of course, but they're pouring it now in a round-the-clock operation. In three months there'll be a ten-mile lake in that valley. They've already started to rip out the trees—but not Clare's trees, though. She says she'd rather see her trees drowned than go to a Matterson mill."

"I've got something to tell you," I said. "But it's too long and complicated to go into here. I'll come up to your apartment to-night."

His face crinkled into a smile, "Clare left some *Islay Mist* for me when she went. You know she's not here?"

"Howard took great pleasure in informing me," I said drily.

"Um," he said, and suddenly drained his cup of coffee. "I've just remembered there's something I have to do. I'll see you to-night—about seven." He rose stiffly. "My bones are getting older," he said wryly, and headed for the street.

I finished my coffee more leisurely and then went back to the hotel. My pace was quicker than that of McDougall and I'd almost caught up with him on High Street when he turned off and disappeared into the telegraph office. I carried on. There wasn't any more I wanted to say to him that couldn't wait until evening and, as I had told him, the less we were seen together the better. In a few days I wouldn't be too

76

popular around Fort Farrell and any Matterson employee who was seen to be too friendly with me wouldn't be too safe in his job. I'd hate to get McDougall fired.

I had not been evicted from my room yet—but that was a problem I had to bring up with Mac. Probably Howard didn't think I'd have the brazen nerve to stay at the Matterson House and it wouldn't have entered his mind to check—but as soon as I started to make a nuisance of myself he'd find out and I'd be out on my ear. I would ask Mac about alternative accommodation.

I lounged about until just before seven and then went over to Mac's apartment and found him taking his ease before a log fire. He pointed wordlessly to the bottle on the table and I poured myself a drink and joined him.

For a while I looked at the dancing flames, then said, "What I'm going to tell you I'm not sure you're going to believe, Mac."

"You can't surprise a newspaperman my age," he said. "We're like priests and doctors—we hear a lot of stories that we don't tell. You'd be surprised at the amount of news that's not fit to print, one way or another."

"Okay," I said. "But I still think it's going to surprise you —and it's something I haven't told another living soul—the only other people who know about it are a few doctors."

I launched forth on the story and told him everything—the waking up in hospital, Susskind's treatment, the plastic surgery—everything, including the mysterious $36,000 and the investigation by the private detective. I finished up by saying, "That's why I told you that I didn't *know* anything that could help. I wasn't lying, Mac."

"God, I feel sorry about that now," he mumbled. "I said things to you that no man should say to another."

"You weren't to know," I said. "No apologies needed."

He got up and found the file he had shown me before and dug out the photograph of Robert Grant. He looked at me closely and then his eyes switched to the photograph and then back to me again. "It's incredible," he breathed. "It's goddam incredible. There's no resemblance at all."

"I took Susskind's advice," I said. "Roberts, the surgeon, had a copy of that and used it as an example of what *not* to do."

77

"Robert Grant—Robert *B*. Grant," he murmured. "Why in hell didn't I have the sense to find out what that initial stood for? A fine reporter I am!" He put the photograph back in the file. "I don't know, Bob. You've put a lot of doubt in my mind. I don't know whether we should go through with this thing now."

"Why not? Nothing has changed. The Trinavants are still dead and Matterson is still screwing the lid down. Why shouldn't you want to go ahead?"

"From what you've told me, you stand in some personal risk," he said slowly. "Once you start monkeying about with your mind anything could happen. You could go nuts." He shook his head. "I don't like it."

I stood up and paced the floor. "I've *got* to find out, Mac—no matter what Susskind said. While he was alive I was all right; I leaned on him a lot. But now I have to find out *who I am*. It's killing me not to know." I halted behind his chair. "I'm not doing this for you, Mac; I'm doing it for me. I was in that car when it crashed, and it seems to me that this whole mystery stems from that crash."

"But what can you do?" asked Mac helplessly. "You don't *remember* anything."

I sat down again. "I'm going to stir things up. Matterson doesn't want the Trinavants talked about. Well, I'm going to do a lot of talking in the next few days. Something will break sooner or later. But first I want to get some ammunition, and you can supply that."

"You're really intent on going through with this?" asked Mac.

"I am."

He sighed. "All right, Bob. What do you want to know?"

"One thing I'd give a lot to know is where old man Matterson was when the crash happened."

Mac grimaced wryly. "I got there ahead of you. I had that nasty suspicion, too. But there's no joy there. Guess who's his alibi?"

"I wouldn't know."

"Me, goddam it!" said Mac disgustedly. "He was in the office of the *Recorder* for most of that day. I wish I couldn't vouch for it, but I can."

"What time of day did the crash happen?"

"It's no good," said Mac. "I thought of that, too. I've juggled the time factors and there's absolutely no way in which Bull Matterson can be placed at the scene of the accident."

"He stood to gain a lot," I said. "He was the only gainer—everyone else lost. I'm convinced he had something to do with it."

"For God's sake, when did you hear of one millionaire killing another?" Mac suddenly went very still. "Personally, that is," he said softly.

"You mean he could have hired someone to do it?"

Mac looked tired and old. "He could—and if he did we haven't a hope in hell of proving it. The killer is probably living it up in Australia on a fat bank-roll. It's nearly twelve years ago, Bob; how in hell can we prove anything now?"

"We'll find a way," I said stubbornly. "That partnership agreement—was it really on the level?"

He nodded. "Seemed so. John Trinavant was a damn' fool not to have revoked it when he got married and started a family."

"No possibility of forgery?"

"There's a thought," said Mac, but shook his head. "Not a chance. Old Bull dug up a living witness to the signatures." He got up to put another log on the fire, then turned and said despondently, "I don't see a single thing we can do."

"Matterson has a weak point," I said. "He's tried to lose the name of Trinavant and he must have had a good reason for it. Well, I'm going to get the name of Trinavant talked about in Fort Farrell. He must react to that in some way."

"Then what?"

"Then we play it as the chips fall." I hesitated. "If necessary, I'll come right into the open. I'll announce that I'm Robert Grant, the guy who was in the Trinavants' car. That should cause a tremor."

"*If* there was any jiggery-pokery about that car crash, and *if* Matterson had anything to do with it, the roof will fall in on your head," warned Mac. "If Matterson did kill the Trinavants you'll be in trouble. A three-time murderer won't hesitate at another."

"I can look after myself," I said—and hoped it was true. "That's another thing. I won't be able to stay at the Matterson

House once I start stirring the mud. Can you recommend alternative accommodation?"

"I've built a cabin on a piece of land just outside town," said Mac. "You can move in there."

"Hell, I can't do that. Matterson will tie you in with me and *your* head will be on the block."

"It's about time I retired," said Mac equably. "I was going to quit at the end of summer, anyway; and it doesn't matter if it's a mite sooner. I'm an old man, Bob—rising seventy-two; it's about time I rested the old bones. I'll be able to get in the fishing I've been promising myself."

"All right," I said. "But batten down the hurricane hatches. Matterson will raise a big wind."

"I'm not scared of Matterson," he said. "I never have been and he knows it. He'll just fire me and that will be that. Hell, I'm keeping a future Pulitzer prizewinner out of a job, anyway. It's time I packed up. There's just one story I want to write and it'll hit headlines all over Canada. I'm depending on you to give it to me."

"I'll do my best," I said.

Lying in bed that evening, I had a thought that made my blood run cold. McDougall had suggested that Matterson could have hired someone to do his dirty work and the terrifying possibility came to me that the someone could have been an unscrupulous bastard called Robert Grant.

Supposing Grant had boobed on the job and become involved in the accident himself by mischance. Supposing that Robert Boyd Grant was a triple murderer—what did that make me, Bob Boyd?

I broke into a cold sweat. Maybe Susskind had been right. Perhaps I'd discover in my past enough to drive me out of my mind.

I tossed and turned for most of the night and tried to get a grip on myself. I thought about every angle in an attempt to prove Grant's innocence. From what Susskind had told me, Grant had been on the run when the accident happened; the police were after him for an assault on a college student. Was it likely, then, that he would deliberately murder just because someone asked him?

He might—if his total getaway could thereby be financed.

But how would Bull Matterson know that Grant was the man he wanted? You don't walk up to the average college student and say, "I've got a family of three I want knocked off—what about it?" That would be ridiculous.

I began to think that the whole structure McDougall and I had built up was nonsensical, plausible though it might appear. How could one accuse a respectable, if ruthless, millionaire of murder? It was laughable.

Then I thought of my mysterious benefactor and the $36,000. Was this the pay-off to Grant? And what about that damned private detective? Where did he fit into the picture?

I dropped into an uneasy sleep and had the Dream, slipping into the hot snow and watching my flesh blister and blacken. And there was something else this time. I heard noises—the sharp crackle of flames from somewhere, and there was a dancing red light on the snow which sizzled and melted into rivulets of blood.

2

I was in no good mood when I went down to the street next morning. I was tired and depressed and I ached all over as though I had been beaten. The bright sunshine didn't help, either, because my eyes were gritty, and I felt as though there were many grains of sand under my eyelids. Altogether I wasn't in any good shape.

Over a cup of strong black coffee I began to feel better. *You knew you were going to have a tough time*, I argued with myself. *Are you going to chicken out now? Hell, you haven't even started yet—it's going to get tougher than this.*

That's what I'm afraid of, I told myself.

Think what a wallop you're going to give Matterson, I answered back. *Forget yourself and think of that bastard.*

By the time I finished the coffee I had argued myself back into condition and felt hungry, so I ordered breakfast, which helped a lot more. It's surprising how many psychological problems can be traced to an empty gut. I went out into King Street and looked up and down. There was a new car dealer a little way down the street and a used car lot up the street. The big place was owned by Matterson and, since I didn't want to put any money in his pocket, I strolled up to the used car lot.

I looked at the junk that was lying round and a thin-faced man popped out of a hut at the front of the lot. "Anything I can do for you? Got some good stuff here going cheap. Best autos in town."

"I'm looking for a small truck—four by four."

"Like a jeep?"

"If you have one."

He shook his head. "Got a Land-Rover, though. How about that? Better than the jeep, I think."

"Where is it?"

He pointed to a tired piece of scrap iron on four wheels. "There she is. You won't do better than that. British made, you know. Better than any Detroit iron."

"Don't push so hard, bud," I said, and walked over to have a look at the Land-Rover. Someone had used it hard; the paint had worn and there were dents in every conceivable place and in some which weren't so conceivable. The interior of the cab was well worn, too, and looked pretty rough, but a Land-Rover isn't a luxury limousine in the first place. The tyres were good.

I stepped back. "Can I look under the hood?"

"Sure." He released the catch and lifted the hood, chattering as he did so. "This is a good buy—only had one owner."

"Sure," I said. "A little old lady who only used it to go to church every Sunday."

"Don't get me wrong," he said. "I really mean that. It belonged to Jim Cooper; he runs a truck farm just outside town. He turned this in and got himself a new one. But this crate still runs real good."

I looked at the engine and halfway began to believe him. It was spotless and there were no telltale oil drips. But what the transmission was like was another story, so I said, "Can I take her out for half an hour?"

"Help yourself," he said. "You'll find the key in the lock."

I wheeled out the Land-Rover and headed north to where I knew I could find a bad road. It was also in the direction of where McDougall had his cabin and I thought I might as well check on its exact position in case I had to find it in a

82

hurry. I found a nice corrugated stretch of road and accelerated to find out what the springing was like. It seemed to be all right, although there were some nasty sounds coming from the battered body that I didn't care for.

I found the turn-off for Mac's place without much trouble and found a really bad road, a hummocky trail rising and dipping with the fall of the land and with several bad patches of mud. Here I experimented with the variety of gears which constitute the charm of the Land-Rover, and I also tried out the front-wheel drive and found everything in reasonable condition.

Mac's cabin was small but beautifully positioned on a rise overlooking a stretch of woodland, and just behind it was a stream which looked as though it might hold some good fish. I spent five minutes looking the place over, then I headed back to town to do a deal with the friendly small-town car dealer.

We dickered a bit and then finally settled on a price—a shade more than I had intended to pay and a shade less than he had intended to get, which made both of us moderately unhappy. I paid him the money and decided I might as well start here as anywhere else. "Do you remember a man called Trinavant—John Trinavant?"

He scratched his head. "Say, yes; of *course* I remember old John. Funny—I haven't thought of him in years. Was he a friend of yours?"

"Can't say I remember meeting him," I said. "Did he live round here?"

"Live round here? Mister, he *was* Fort Farrell!"

"I thought that was Matterson."

A gobbet of spit just missed my foot. "Matterson!" The tone of voice told me what he thought of that.

I said, "I hear he was killed in an auto accident. Is that right?"

"Yeah. And his son and wife both. On the road to Edmonton. Must be over ten years ago now. A mighty nasty thing, that was."

"What kind of a car was he driving?"

He looked at me with speculative eyes. "You got any special interest, Mister . . .?"

"The name's Boyd," I said. "Bob Boyd. Someone asked me

83

to check if I was in these parts. It seems as though Trinavant did my friend a good turn years ago—there was some money involved, I believe."

"I can believe that of John Trinavant; he was a pretty good guy. My name's Summerskill."

I grinned at him. "Glad to meet you, Mr. Summerskill. Did Trinavant buy his car from you?"

Summerskill laughed uproariously, "Hell, no! I don't have that class. Old John was a Cadillac man, and, anyway, he owned his own place up the road a piece—Fort Farrell Motors. It belongs to Matterson now."

I looked up the street. "Must make pretty tough competition for you," I said.

"Some," he agreed. "But I do all right, Mr. Boyd."

"Come to think of it," I said, "I've seen nothing else but the name of Matterson since I've been here, Mr. Summerskill. The Matterson Bank, Matterson House Hotel—and I believe there's a Matterson Corporation. What did he do—buy out Trinavant?"

Summerskill grimaced. "What you've seen is the tip of the iceberg. Matterson pretty near owns this part of the country —logging operations, sawmills, pulp mills. He's bigger than old John ever was—in power, that is. But not in heart, no, sir! No one had a bigger heart than John Trinavant. As for Matterson buying out Mr. Trinavant—well, I could tell you a thing or two about that. But it's an old story and better forgotten."

"Looks as though I came too late."

"Yeah, you tell your friend he was ten years too late. If he owed old John any dough it's too late to pay it back now."

"I don't think it was the money," I said. "My friend just wanted to make contact again."

Summerskill nodded. "Yeah, it's like that. I was born in Hazelton and I went away just as soon as I could, but of course I had a hankering to go back, so I did after five years. And you know what? The first two guys I went to see had died—the first two guys on my list. Things change around a place, they certainly do."

I stuck my hand out. "Well, it's been nice doing business with you, Mr. Summerskill."

"Any time, Mr. Boyd." We shook hands. "You want any spares, you come right back."

I climbed up into the cab and leaned out of the window. "If the engine drops out of this heap in the next couple of days you'll be seeing me soon enough," I promised, softening it with a grin.

He laughed and waved me away, and as I drove down King Street I thought that the memory of John Trinavant had been replanted in at least one mind. With a bit of luck Summerskill would mention it to his wife and a couple of his buddies. *You know what? Me and a stranger had a chat about a guy I haven't thought of in years.* You *must remember old John Trinavant. Remember when he started the* Recorder *and everyone thought it would go bust?*

So it would go, I hoped; and the ripples would go wider and wider, especially if I dropped some more rocks into this stagnant pool. Sooner or later the ripples would reach the ferocious old pike who ruled the pool, and I hoped he would take action.

I pulled up in front of the Forestry Service office and went inside. The Forestry Officer was called Tanner and he was cordial if not hopeful. I told him I was passing through and that I was interested in tree-farm licences.

"Not a chance, Mr. Boyd," he said. "The Matterson Corporation has licensed nearly all the Crown lands round here. There are one or two pockets left but they're so small you could spit across them."

I scratched my jaw. "Perhaps if I could see a map?" I suggested.

"Sure," he said promptly, and quickly produced a large-scale map of the area which he spread on his desk. "There you have it in a nutshell." His finger traced a wide sweep. "All this is the holding of the Matterson Corporation—privately owned. And this here . . ." a much larger sweep this time . . . "is Crown land franchised to the Matterson Corporation under tree-farm licences."

I looked closely at the map, which made very interesting viewing. To divert Tanner from what I was really after, I said, "What about public sustained-yield units?" Those were areas where the Forestry Service did all the work but let the felling franchises out on short-term contracts.

"None of those round here, Mr. Boyd. We're too far off the beaten track for the Forestry Service to run tree farms. Most of the sustained-yield units are down south."

"It certainly looks like a closed shop," I commented. "Any truth in what I hear that the Matterson Corporation got into trouble for over-felling?"

Tanner looked at me warily. Over-felling is the most heinous crime in the Forestry Service book. "I couldn't say about that," he said stiffly.

I wondered if he had been bought by Matterson, but on second thoughts I didn't think so. Buying a forestry officer in British Columbia would be like buying a Cardinal of the Church—just about impossible. Fifty per cent of the province's revenue comes from timber and conservation is the great god. To come out against conservation is like coming out against motherhood.

I checked the map again. "Thanks for your trouble, Mr. Tanner," I said. "You've been very obliging, but there seems precious little for me here. Any of these tree-farm licences likely to fall vacant?"

"Not for a long time, Mr. Boyd. The Matterson Corporation has put in a lot of capital in sawmills and pulp mills; they insisted on long-term licences."

I nodded. "Very wise; I'd want the same. Well, thanks again, Mr. Tanner."

I left him without satisfying the wondering look in his eye and drove down to the depot where I picked up a lot of geological gear that I had sent in advance. The fat depot superintendent helped me load the Land-Rover, and said, "You figuring on staying?"

"For a while," I said. "Just for a while. You can call me Trinavant's last hope."

A salacious leer spread over his face. "Clare Trinavant? You want to watch out for Howard Matterson."

I suppressed the desire to push his face in. "Not Clare Trinavant," I said gently. "John Trinavant. And I can take care of Howard Matterson, too, if he interferes. Have you got a phone anywhere?"

He still wore the surprised look as he said abstractedly, "In the hall."

I strode past him and he came pattering after me. "Hey,

mister; John Trinavant is dead—he's been dead for over ten years."

I stopped. "I know he's dead. That's the point. Don't you get it? Now beat it. This is a private telephone call."

He turned away with a baffled shrug and a muttered, "Aw, nuts!" I smiled because another rock had been thrown into the pool and another set of ripples started to affright the hungry pike.

Did you hear about that crazy man that just blew into town? Said he was Trinavant's last hope. I thought he meant Clare; you know, Clare Trinavant, but he said he meant John. Can you beat that, with old John been dead for ten—no, twelve—years! This guy was here a couple of years back and had words with Howard Matterson about Clare Trinavant. How do I know? Because Maggie Hope told me—she was Howard's secretary then. I warned her not to shoot her mouth off but it was no good. Howard fired her. But this guy is crazy, for sure. I mean, John Trinavant—he's dead.

I phoned the *Recorder* office and got hold of Mac. "Do you know of a good lawyer?" I asked.

"I might," he said cautiously. "What do you want a lawyer for?"

"I want a lawyer who isn't afraid of bucking Matterson. I know the land laws but I want a lawyer who can give legal punch to what I know—dress the stuff up in that scary legal language."

"There's old Fraser—he's retired now but he's a friend of mine and he doesn't like Matterson one little bit. Would he do?"

"He'll do," I said. "As long as he's not too old to go into court if necessary."

"Oh, Fraser can go into court. What are you up to, Bob?"

I grinned. "I'm going prospecting on Matterson land. My guess is that Matterson isn't going to like it."

There was a muffled noise in the receiver and I put the phone down gently.

They had driven a new road up to the Kinoxi Valley to take care of the stream of construction trucks carrying materials for the dam and the logging trucks bringing the lumber from the valley. It was a rough road, not too well graded and being chewed to pieces by the heavy traffic. Where there was mud they had corduroyed it with ten-inch logs which made your teeth rattle, and in places they had cut through the soil down to bedrock to provide a firmer footing.

No one took any notice of me; I was merely another man driving a battered truck which looked as though it had a right to be there. The road led to the bottom of the low escarpment where they were building the generator house, a squat structure rafted on a sea of churned-up mud in which a gang of construction workers sweated and swore. Up the escarpment, by the side of the brown-running stream, ran the flume, a 36-inch pipe to bring the water to the power-house. The road took off on the other side of the stream and clung to a hillside, zig-zagging its way to the top and towards the dam.

I was surprised to see how far they had got with the construction. McDougall was right: the Kinoxi Valley would be under water in three months. I pulled off the road and watched them pour concrete for a few minutes and noted the smooth way in which the sand and gravel trucks were handled. This was an efficient operation.

A big logging truck passed, going downhill like a juggernaut, and the Land-Rover rocked on its springs in the wind of its passing. There was not likely to be another close behind it so I pressed on up the road, past the dam and into the valley where I ran the Land-Rover off the road and behind trees where it was not likely to be seen. Then I went on foot away from the road, taking a slanting, climbing course across the hillside until I was high enough to get a good view of the valley.

It was a scene of desolation. The quiet valley I had known, where the fish jumped in the stream and the deer browsed in the woodlands, had been destroyed. In its place was a wilderness of jagged stumps and a tangle of felled brushwood on a ground of mud criss-crossed by the track marks of the trucks. Away up the valley, near the little lake, there was still the green of trees, but I could hear, even at that distance, the harsh scream of the power saws biting into living wood.

British Columbia is very conservation-minded where its lumber resources are concerned. Out of every dollar earned in the province fifty cents comes ultimately from the logging industry and the Government wants that happy state of affairs to continue. So the Forestry Service polices the woodlands and controls the cutting. There are an awful lot of men who get a kick out of murdering a big tree and there are a few money-greedy bastards who are willing to let them get their kicks because of the number of board-feet of manufactured lumber that the tree will provide at the sawmill. So the Forestry Service has its work cut out.

The idea is that the amount of lumber cut, expressed in cubic feet, should not exceed the natural annual growth. Now, when you start talking in cubic footage of lumber in British Columbia you sound like an astronomer calculating the distance in miles to a pretty far star. The forest lands cover 220,000 square miles, say, four times the size of England, and the annual growth is estimated at two and a half billion cubic feet. So the annual cutting rate is limited to a little over two billion cubic feet and the result is an increasing, instead of a wasting, asset.

That is why I looked down into the Kinoxi Valley with shocked eyes. Normally, in a logging operation, only the mature trees are cut; but here they were taking *everything*. I suppose it was logical. If you are going to flood a valley there is no point in leaving the trees, but this sight offended me. This was a rape of the land, something that had not been since the bad old days before the First World War when the conservation laws came in.

I looked up the valley and did a quick calculation. The new Matterson Lake was going to cover twenty square miles, of which five square miles in the north belonged to Clare Trinavant. That meant that Matterson was cutting a solid fifteen square miles of trees and the Forestry Service was letting him do it because of the dam. That amount of lumber was enough to pay for the dam with a hell of a lot left over.

It seemed to me that Matterson was a pretty sharp guy, but he was too damned ruthless for my taste.

I went back to the Land-Rover and drove back down the road and past the dam. Halfway down the escarpment I stopped and again drove off the road but I didn't bother to hide the vehicle this time. I *wanted* to be seen. I rummaged about in my gear and found what I wanted—something to confound the ignorant—and then, in full view of the road I started to act in a suspicious manner. I took my hammer and chipped at rocks, I dug at the ground like a gopher scrabbling a hole, I looked at pebbles through a magnifying-glass and I paced out large areas gazing intently at the dial of an instrument which I held in my hand.

It was nearly an hour before I was noticed. A jeep rocketed up the hill and slammed to a stop and two men got out. As they walked over I slipped off my wrist-watch and palmed it, then stooped to pick up a large rock. Booted feet crunched nearer and I turned. The bigger of the men said, "What are you doing here?"

"Prospecting," I said nonchalantly.

"The hell you are! This is private land."

"I don't think so," I said.

The other man pointed. "What's that you got there?"

"This? It's a geiger counter." I moved it near to the rock I held—and nearer to the luminous dial of my watch—and it buzzed like a demented mosquito. "Interesting," I said.

The big man leaned forward. "What is it?"

"Maybe uranium," I said. "But I doubt it. Could be thorium." I looked at the rock closely, then tossed it away casually. "That's stuff not payable, but it's an indication. It's an interesting geological structure round here."

They looked at each other, a little startled; then the big man said, "That may be, but you're still on private land."

I said pleasantly, "You can't stop me prospecting here."

"Oh no?" he said belligerently.

"Why don't you check with your boss? Might be better that way."

The smaller man said, "Yeah, Novak, let's check with Waystrand. I mean, *uranium*—or this other stuff—it sounds important."

The big man hesitated, then said in a heavy tone, "Have you got a name, mister?"

"The name's Boyd," I said. "Bob Boyd."

"Okay, Boyd. I'll see the boss. But I still think you're not going to stay round here."

I watched them go away and smiled, slipping the watch back on my wrist. So Waystrand was some kind of a boss up here. McDougall had said he'd been given a good job at the dam. I had a score to settle with him. I glanced up at the telephone line which followed the road. The big man would tell Waystrand and Waystrand would get on the telephone to Fort Farrell and Howard Matterson's reaction was predictable —he'd blow up.

It wasn't ten minutes before the jeep came back followed by another. I recognized Waystrand—he'd filled out a lot in the last eighteen months; his chest was broader, he looked harder and he wasn't so much the kid still wet behind he ears. But he still wasn't as big as I was, and I reckoned I could take him on if I had to, although I'd have to make it quick before the other two characters could get started. Odds of three to one were not too good.

Waystrand smiled wickedly as he came up. "So it's you. I wondered about that when I heard the name. Mr. Matterson's compliments and will you get the hell out of here."

"Which Mr. Matterson?"

"Howard Matterson."

"So you're still running and telling tales to him, Jimmy," I said caustically.

He balled his fists. "Mr. Matterson said I was to get you off this land nice and easy, with no trouble." He was holding himself in with an effort. "I owe you something, Boyd; and it wouldn't take much for me to give it to you. Mr. Matterson said if you *wouldn't* go quietly I had to see that you went anyway. Now, get off this land and back to Fort Farrell. It's up to you if you go under your own power or if you're carried off."

I said, "I have every right to be here."

Waystrand made a quick sign. "Okay, boys. Take him."

"Wait a minute," I said quickly. "I've had my say—I'll go." It would be pointless to get beaten up at this stage, although

I would dearly have loved to wipe the contemptuous grin off Waystrand's face.

"You're not so brave, Boyd; not when you're facing a man expecting a fight."

"I'll take you on any time," I said. "When you haven't got a gun."

He didn't like that, but he did nothing. They watched me pick up my gear and stow it in the Land-Rover and then Waystrand climbed into his jeep and drove slowly down the hill. I followed in the Land-Rover and the other jeep came after me. They were taking no chances of my slipping away.

We got down to the bottom of the escarpment and Waystrand slowed, waving me to a stop. He wheeled round in the jeep and came alongside. "Wait here, Boyd; and don't try anything funny," he said, then he shot off and waved down a logging truck that had just come down the hill. He spoke to the driver for a couple of minutes and then came back. "Okay, big man; on your way—and don't come back, although I'd sure like it if you did."

"I'll be seeing you, Jimmy," I said. "That's for sure." I slammed in the gear-lever and drove on down the road, following the loaded logging truck which had gone on ahead.

It wasn't very long before I caught up with it. It was going very slowly and I couldn't pass because this was in one of those places where the road builders had made a cutting right down to bedrock and there were steep banks of earth on either side. I couldn't understand why this guy was crawling, but I certainly didn't want to take the chance of passing and being squeezed to a pulp by twenty tons of lumber and metal.

The truck slowed even more and I crawled behind at less than walking pace, fuming at the delay. You put an ordinary nice guy in an automobile and he loses all the common decency he ever had. A guy who'll politely open a door for an old lady will damn' near kill the same old lady by cutting across her bows at sixty miles an hour just to beat a stop light, and he'll think nothing of it. This guy in front probably had his troubles and must have had a good and sound reason for going so slowly. I was in no particular hurry to get back to Fort Farrell but still I sat there and cursed—such is the relationship between a man and his auto.

I glanced into the mirror and was startled. The guy in front certainly had good reasons for going slowly, for coming behind at a hell of a lick was another logging truck, an eighteen-wheeler—twenty or more tons moving at thirty miles an hour. He got so close before he slammed on anchors that I heard the piercing hiss of his air-brakes and he slowed to our crawl with the ugly square front of his truck not a foot from the rear of the Land-Rover.

I was the filling in the nasty sandwich. I could see the driver behind laughing fit to bust and I knew that if I wasn't careful there'd be some red stuff in the sandwich which wouldn't be ketchup. The Land-Rover lurched a little as the heavy fender of the truck rammed into the rear, and there was a crunching noise. I trod delicately on the gas pedal and inched nearer to the truck in front—I couldn't move much nearer or else I'd have a thirty-inch log coming through the windshield. I remembered this cutting from the way in: it was a mile long and right now we were about a quarter way through. The next three-quarters of a mile was going to be tricky.

The truck behind blared its horn and a gap opened up in front as the guy ahead put on speed. I pressed on the gas but not fast enough, because the rear truck rammed me again, harder this time. This was going to be trickier than I thought; it looked as though we were going to do a speed run, and that could be goddam dangerous.

We came to a dip and the speed increased and we zoomed down at forty miles an hour, the truck behind trying to climb up the exhaust pipe of the guy in front and not worrying too much about me, caught in the middle. My hands were sweating and were slippery on the wheel, and I had to do some tricky work with gas pedal, clutch and brake. One mistake on my part—or on theirs—and the Land-Rover would be mashed into scrap-iron and I'd have the engine in my lap.

Three more times I was rammed from behind and I hated to think what was happening to my gear. And once I was nipped, caught between the heavy steel fenders of the two trucks for a fraction of a second. I felt the compression on the chassis and I swear the Land-Rover was momentarily lifted from the ground. There was a log rubbing on the windshield and the glass starred and smashed into a misty opacity and I couldn't see a damned thing ahead.

Fortunately the pressure released and I was running free again with my head stuck out of the side and I saw we were at the end of the cutting. One of the logs on the left side of the front truck seemed to be loaded a little higher than the others, and I judged it was high enough to clear the cab. I had to get out of this squeeze. There was very little room to manœuvre and those sadistic bastards could hold me there until we got to the sawmill if I couldn't figure a way out.

So I spun the wheel and chanced it and found I was wrong. The log didn't clear the top of the cab—not by a quarter of an inch—and I heard the rending tear of sheet metal. But I couldn't stop then; I fed gas to the engine frantically and tore free to find myself bucketing over the rough ground and heading straight for a big Douglas fir. I hauled on the wheel and swerved again and again, weaving among the trees and driving roughly parallel with the road.

I passed the front truck and saw my chance, so I rammed down hard on the gas pedal and shot ahead of it and fled down the road with that eighteen-wheel monster pounding after me, blaring its horn. I knew better than to stop and fight it out with those guys; they wouldn't stop on the road just because I did and me and the Land-Rover would be a total loss. I had the legs of them and scooted away in front, passing the turn-off to the sawmill and not stopping until I was a full mile the other side.

Then I stopped and held up my hands. They were shaking uncontrollably and, when I moved, my shirt was clammy against my skin because it was soaked in sweat. I lit a cigarette and waited until the shakes went away before I climbed out to survey the damage. The front wasn't too bad, although a steady drip of water indicated a busted radiator. The windshield was a total write-off and the top of the cab looked as though someone had used a blunt can-opener on it. The rear end was smashed up pretty badly—it looked like the front end of any normal auto crash. I looked in the back and saw the shattered wooden case and a clutter of broken bottles from my field testing kit. There was the acrid stink of chemicals from the reagents swimming about on the bottom and I hastily lifted the geiger counter out of the liquid—free acids don't do delicate instruments any good.

I stepped back and estimated the cost of the damage. Two bloody noses for two truckers; maybe a broken back for Jimmy Waystrand; and a brand-new Land-Rover from Mr. Howard Matterson. I was inclined to be a bit lenient on Howard; I didn't think he'd given any orders to squeeze me like that. But Jimmy Waystrand certainly had, and he was going to pay the hard way.

After a while I drove into Fort Farrell, eliciting curious glances from passers-by in King Street. I pulled into Summerskill's used car lot and he looked up and said in alarm, "Hey, I'm not responsible for that—it happened after you bought the crate."

I climbed out. "I know," I said soothingly. "Just get the thing going again. I think she'll want a new radiator—and get a rear lamp working somehow."

He walked round the Land-Rover in a full circle, then came back and stared at me hard. "What did you do—get into a fight with a tank?"

"Something like that," I agreed.

He waved. "That rear fender is twisted like a pretzel. How did that happen to a *rear* fender?"

"Maybe it got hot and melted into that shape," I suggested. "Cut the wonder. How long will it take?"

"You just want to get the thing moving again? A jury-rig job?"

"That'll do."

He scratched his head. "I have an old Land-Rover radiator back of the shed, so you're lucky there. Say a couple of hours."

"Okay," I said. "I'll be back in an hour and give you a hand." I left him and walked up the street to the Matterson Building. Maybe I just might have the beginnings of a quarrel with Howard.

I breezed into his outer office and said, without breaking stride, "I'm going to see Matterson."

"But—but he's busy," his secretary said agitatedly.

"Sure," I said, not stopping. "Howard is a busy, busy man." I threw open the door of his office and walked inside to find Howard in conference with Donner. "Hello, Howard," I said. "Don't you want to see me?"

"What do you mean by busting in like that?" he demanded. "Can't you see I'm busy." He thumbed a switch. "Miss Kerr, what do you mean by letting people into——"

I reached over and lifted his hand away from the intercom, breaking the connection. "She didn't let me," I said softly. "She couldn't stop me—so don't blame her. Now, I'll ask you a like-minded question. What do you mean by having Waystrand throw me out?"

"That's a silly question," he snarled. He looked at Donner. "Tell him."

Donner cracked his knuckles and said precisely, "Any geological exploration of Matterson land we'll organize for ourselves. We don't need you to do it for us, Boyd. You'll stay clear in future, I trust."

"You bet he'll stay clear," said Matterson.

I said, "Howard, you've held tree-farm licences for so long that you think you own the goddam land. Give you another few years and you'll think you own the whole province of British Columbia. Your head's getting swelled, Howard."

"Don't call me Howard," he snapped. "Come to the point."

"All right," I said. "I wasn't on Matterson land—I was on Crown land. Anyone with a prospector's licence can fossick on Crown land. Just because you have a licence to grow and cut lumber doesn't mean you can stop me. And if you think you can, I'll slap a court order on you so fast that it'll make your ears spin."

It took some time to sink in but it finally did and he looked at Donner in a helpless way. I grinned at Donner and mimicked Matterson. "Tell him."

Donner said, "*If* you were on Crown land—and that is a matter of question—then perhaps you are right."

I said, "There's no perhaps about it; you *know* I'm right."

Matterson said suddenly, "I don't think you were on Crown land."

"Check your maps," I said helpfully. "I bet you haven't looked at them for years. You're too accustomed to regarding the whole goddam country as your own."

Matterson twitched a finger at Donner, who left the room. He looked at me with hard eyes. "What are you up to, Boyd?"

"Just trying to make a living," I said easily. "There's a lot

96

of good prospecting country round here—it's just as good a place to explore as up north, and a lot warmer, too."

"You might find it too warm," he said acidly. "You're not going about things in a friendly way."

I raised my eyebrows. "*I'm* not! You ought to have been out on the road to Kinoxi this morning. I'd sooner be friendly with a grizzly bear than with some of your truckers. Anyway, I didn't come here to enter a popularity contest."

"Why did you come here?"

"Maybe you'll find out one day—if you're smart enough, Howard."

"I told you not to call me Howard," he said irritatedly.

Donner came in with a map, and I saw it was a copy of the one I had inspected in Tanner's office. Howard spread it on his desk and I said, "You'll find that the Kinoxi Valley is split between you and Clare Trinavant—she in the north and you in the south with the lion's share. *But* Matterson land stops just short of the escarpment—everything south of that is Crown land. And *that* means that the dam at the top of the escarpment and the power-house at the bottom is on Crown land, and I can go fossicking round there any time I like. Any comment?"

Matterson looked up at Donner, who nodded his head slightly. "It seems that Mr. Boyd is correct," he said.

"You're damn' right I'm correct." I pointed at Matterson. "Now there's something else I want to bring up—a matter of a wrecked Land-Rover."

He glared at me. "I'm not responsible for the way you drive."

The way he said it I was certain he knew what had happened. "All right," I said. "I'll be using the Kinoxi road pretty often in the near future. Tell your truckers to keep away from me, or someone will get killed in a road accident—and it won't be me."

He just showed me his teeth, and said, "I understand you *were* staying at the Matterson House." He leaned so heavily on the past tense that the sentence nearly busted in the middle.

"I get the message," I said. "Enemies to the death, eh, Howard?" I walked out without saying another word and went down to the Matterson House Hotel.

The desk clerk moved fast but I got in first. "I understand I've checked out," I said sourly.

"Er . . . yes, Mr. Boyd. I've prepared your bill."

I paid it, then went up and packed my case and lugged it across the road to Summerskill's car lot. He climbed out from under the Land-Rover and looked at me in a puzzled manner. "Not ready yet, Mr. Boyd."

"That's all right. I have to get something to eat."

He scrambled to his feet. "Hey, Mr. Boyd; you know, something funny has happened. I just checked the chassis and it has *bulged*."

"What do you mean—bulged?"

Summerskill held his hands about a foot apart with curled fingers like a man holding a short length of four-by-two, and brought them together slowly. "This damn' chassis has been *squoze*." He wore a baffled look.

"Will that make any difference to its running?"

He shrugged. "Not much—if you don't expect much."

"Then leave well alone," I advised. "I'll be back as soon as I've had a bite to eat."

I ate at the Hellenic Café, expecting to see McDougall but he didn't show up. I didn't want to see him at the *Recorder* office so I drifted round town for a while, keeping my eyes open. When after nearly an hour I hadn't seen him, I went back to Summerskill to find that he'd nearly finished the job.

"That'll be forty-five dollars, Mr. Boyd," he said. "And I'm letting it go cheap."

I dumped some groceries I had bought into the back of the Land-Rover and took out my wallet, mentally adding it to the account that Matterson was going to pay some day. As I counted out the bills, Summerskill said, "I wasn't able to do much with the top of the cab. I bashed the metal back into place and put some canvas on top; that'll keep the rain out."

"Thanks," I said. "If I have another accident—and that's not unlikely—you shall have my trade."

He pulled a sour face. "You have another accident like that and there'll be nothing left to repair."

I drove out of town to McDougall's cabin and parked the Land-Rover out of sight after I had unloaded everything. I stripped and changed and heated some water. A little went to make coffee and I washed my shirt and pants in the rest. I stacked the groceries in the pantry and began to get my gear in order, checking to see exactly what was ruined. I was grieving over a busted scintillometer when I heard the noise of a car, and when I ducked my head to look out of the window I saw a battered old Chevvy pulling up outside. McDougall got out.

"I thought I'd find you here," he said. "They told me at the hotel you'd checked out."

"Howard arranged it," I said.

"I had a telephone call from God not half an hour ago," said Mac. "The old Bull is getting stirred up. He wants to know who you are, where you're from, what your intentions are and how long you're going to stay around Fort Farrell." He smiled. "He gave me the job of finding out, naturally enough."

"No comment," I said.

Mac raised his eyebrows. "What do you mean?"

"I mean that I'm exercising my God-given right to keep my mouth shut. You tell old Matterson that I refuse to speak to the Press. I want to keep him guessing—I want him to come to me."

"Good enough," said Mac. "But he's lost you. No one knows you're here."

"We can't keep that a secret for long," I said. "Not in a town as small as Fort Farrell." I smiled. "So we finally goosed the old boy into moving. I wonder what did it."

"It could have been anything, from the talk I've heard round town," said Mac. "Ben Parker, for instance, thinks you're crazy."

"Who is Ben Parker?"

"The guy at the bus depot. Clarry Summerskill, on the other hand, holds you in great respect."

"*What* kind of Summerskill?"

Mac gave me a twisted grin. "His name is Clarence, and he doesn't like it. He doesn't think it's a suitable moniker for a used car dealer. He once asked me how in hell he could put up a sign saying, 'Honest Clarence', and not get laughed at. Anyway, he told me that any man who could do in three short

99

hours what you did to a Land-Rover must be the toughest guy in Canada. He based that on the fact that you didn't have a scratch on you. What *did* happen, anyway?"

"I'll put some water on for coffee," I said. "The Land-Rover's out back. Take a look at it."

Mac went out to look at the damage and came back wearing a wry face. "Drop over a cliff?" he asked.

I told him and he grew grave. "The boys play rough," he said.

"That's nothing. Just clean fun and games, that's all. It was a private idea of Jimmy Waystrand's; I don't think the Mattersons had anything to do with it. *They* haven't started yet."

The kettle boiled. "I'd rather have tea," said Mac. "Too much coffee makes me feel nervous and strung up, and we don't want that to happen, do we?" So he made strong black tea which tasted like stewed pennies. He said, "Why did you go up to the dam, anyway?"

"I wanted to get Howard stirred up," I said. "I wanted to get noticed."

"You did," Mac said drily.

"How much is that dam costing?" I asked.

Mac pondered. "Taking everything in—the dam, the power-house and the transmission lines—it'll run to six million dollars. Not as big as the Peace River Project, but not small potatoes."

"I've been doing some figuring," I said. "I reckon that Matterson is taking over ten million dollars' worth of lumber out of the Kinoxi Valley. He's taking *everything* out, remember, not the less-than-one-per-cent cut that the Forestry Service usually allows. That leaves him with four million bucks."

"Nice going," said Mac.

"It gets better. He doesn't really want that four million dollars—he'd only have to pay tax on it; but the electricity plant does need maintenance and there's depreciation to take into account, so he invests three million dollars and that takes care of it. He makes one million bucks net, and he has free power for the Matterson enterprises for as far into the future as I can see."

"Not to mention the dough he makes on the power he sells," said Mac. "That's pure cream."

"It's like having a private entrance to Fort Knox," I said.

Mac grunted. "This smells of Donner. I've never known such a guy for seeing money where no one else can see it. And it's legal, too."

I said, "I think Clare Trinavant is a sentimental fool. She's letting emotion take the place of thinking. The Kinoxi Valley is going to be flooded and there is nothing she can do to stop it."

"So?"

"So she has five square miles of woodland up there that's going to be wasted, and she's passing up three million dollars just because she has a grudge against the Mattersons. Isn't she aware of that?"

Mac shook his head. "She's not a businesswoman—takes no interest in it. Her financial affairs are managed by a bank in Vancouver. I doubt if she's given it a thought."

I said, "Doesn't the Forestry Service have anything to say about it? It seems silly to waste all that lumber."

"The Forestry Service has never been known to prosecute anyone for *not* cutting," he pointed out. "The problem has never come up before."

"With three million bucks coming in for sure she could build her own sawmill," I said forcefully. "If she doesn't want the Mattersons in on it."

"Bit late for that, isn't it?" Mac asked.

"That's the pity of it." I brooded over it. "She's more like Howard Matterson than she thinks; he is also an emotional type, although a bit more predictable." I smiled. "I reckon I can make Howard jump through hoops."

"Don't think you can treat the old man like that," said Mac warningly. "He's tougher and more devious. He'll save up his Sunday punch and sneak it in from an unexpected direction." He switched the subject. "What's the next move?"

"More of the same. Old Matterson reacted fast so we must have hit a sore spot. I stir up talk about the Trinavants and I root about up near the dam."

"Why go near the dam? What's that got to do with it?"

I scratched my head. "I don't really know; I just have a hunch that there's an answer up there somewhere. We're not really sure that it wasn't my prowling around there that attracted Bull Matterson's interest. Another thing—I'd like to go up to Clare's cabin. How do I get there without crossing Matterson land? That might be a bit unwise now."

"There's a road in from the back," said Mac. He didn't ask me why I wanted to go up there, but instead dug out a tattered old map. I studied it and sighed. It was a hell of a long way round and I'd have given my soul for the Matterson Corporation helicopter.

2

The next day I spent in Fort Farrell, spreading the good word and really laying it on thick. Up to then I'd mentioned the name of Trinavant to only two people, but this time I covered a good cross-section of the Fort Farrell population, feeling something like a cross between a private detective and a Gallup pollster. That evening, in the cabin, I trotted up the results in approved pollster fashion and sorted out my findings.

One of the things that stood out was the incredible ease with which a man's name could be erased from the public memory. Of the people who had moved into Fort Farrell in the last ten years fully eighty-five per cent of them had never heard of John Trinavant; and the same applied to those young people who had grown to maturity since his death.

The other, older people remembered him with a bit of nudging, and, almost always, with kindness. I came to the conclusion that Shakespeare was dead right: "The evil that men do lives after them; the good is oft interred with their bones." Still, the same analogy applies throughout our world. Any murderer can get his name in the newspapers, but if a decent man wishes to announce to the world that he's lived happily with his wife for twenty-five or fifty years he has to pay for it, by God!

There was also a fairly widespread resentment of the Mattersons, tinged somewhat with fear. The Matterson Corporation had got such a grip on the economic life of the community that it could put the squeeze on anybody, indirectly if not directly. Nearly everyone in Fort Farrell had a relative on the Matterson payroll, so there was a strong resistance to answering awkward questions.

Reactions to the name of John Trinavant were surer. Folks seemed amazed at themselves that they had allowed him to be forgotten. *I don't know why, but I haven't thought of old John in years.* I knew why. When the only source of public information in a town closes tight on a subject, when letters to the Editor about a dead man just don't get published, when a powerful man quietly discourages talk, then there is no particular call to remember. The living have their own bustling and multitudinous affairs and the dead slide into oblivion.

There had been talk of a John Trinavant Memorial to face the statue of Lieutenant Farrell in Trinavant Park. *I don't know why, but it never seemed to get off the ground; maybe there wasn't enough money for it—but, sure as hell, John Trinavant pumped enough money into this town. You'd think people would be ashamed of themselves, but they're not— they've just forgotten what he did for Fort Farrell.*

I got tired of hearing the refrain—*I don't know why.* The depressing part of it was that they really didn't know why, they didn't know that Bull Matterson had screwed the lid down tight on the name of Trinavant. He could have given the Hitlers and Stalins a pointer or two on thought control, and more and more I was impressed at the effort which he must have put into this operation, although I still had no idea as to why he had done it.

"Where are the Trinavants buried?" I asked Mac.

"Edmonton," he said briefly. "Bull saw to it."

The Trinavants did not even have a resting-place in the town they had built.

After a day's intensive poking and prying into the Trinavant mystery I decided to give Fort Farrell a miss next day. If two conversations had caused Bull Matterson to react, then that day's work must be giving him conniptions, and acting on sound psychological principles, I wanted to be hard to find— I wanted to give him time to come really to the boil.

That cut out investigating the site of the dam, so I decided to go up to Clare Trinavant's cabin. Why I wanted to go there I didn't know, but it was as good a place as any to keep out of Matterson's way and maybe I could get in a day of deep thought with some fishing thrown in,

It was a hundred and twenty miles on rutted, jolting roads

—a wide swing round the Matterson holdings—and when I reached the cabin I was sore and aching. It was even bigger than I remembered, a long low sprawling structure with a warm red cedar shingle roof. Standing apart from it was another cabin, smaller and simpler, and there was smoke curling from the grey stone chimney. A man emerged carrying a shot-gun which he stood leaning against the wall not too far from his hand.

"Mr. Waystrand?" I called.

"That's me."

"I have a letter for you from McDougall of Fort Farrell."

McDougall had insisted on that because this was Jimmy Waystrand's father, whose allegiance to Clare Trinavant was firm and whose attitude to Bob Boyd was likely to be violent. "You cut his son and you insulted Clare—or so he thinks," said Mac. "You'd better let me straighten him out. I'll give you a letter."

Waystrand was a man of about fifty with a deeply grooved face as brown as a nut. He read the letter slowly, his lips moving with the words, then gave me a swift glance with hard blue eyes and read it again very carefully to see if he'd got it right first time. Then he said a little hesitantly, "Old Mac says you're all right."

I let out my breath slowly. "I wouldn't know about that—it's not my place to say. But I'd trust his judgment on most things; wouldn't you?"

Waystrand's face crinkled into a reluctant smile. "I reckon I would. What can I do for you?"

"Not much," I said. "A place to pitch a camp—and if you could spare a steelhead from the creek there, I'd be obliged."

"You're welcome to the trout," he said. "But there's no need to camp. There's a bed inside—if you want it. My son's away." His eyes held mine in an unwinking stare.

"Thanks," I said. "That's very kind of you, Mr. Waystrand."

I didn't have to go fishing for my dinner, after all, because Waystrand cooked up a tasty hash and we shared it. He was a slow-moving, taciturn man whose thought processes moved in low gear, but that didn't mean he was stupid—he just took a little longer to reach the right conclusion, that's all. After we had eaten I tried to draw him out. "Been with Miss Trinavant long?"

He drew on his pipe and expelled a plume of pale blue smoke. "Quite a time," he said uninformatively. I sat and said nothing, just waiting for the wheels to go round. He smoked contemplatively for a few minutes, then said, "I was with the old man."

"John Trinavant?"

He nodded. "I started working for John Trinavant when I was a nipper just left school. I've been with the Trinavants ever since."

"They tell me he was a good man," I said.

"Just about the best." He relapsed into contemplation of the glowing coal in the bowl of his pipe.

I said, "Pity about the accident."

"Accident?"

"Yes—the auto crash."

There was another long silence before he took the pipe from his mouth. "Some folks would call it an accident, I suppose."

I held my breath. "But you don't?"

"Mr. Trinavant was a good driver," he said. "He wouldn't drive too fast on an icy road."

"It's not certain he was driving. His wife might have been at the wheel—or his son."

"Not on that car," said Waystrand positively. "It was a brand-new Cadillac two weeks old. Mr. Trinavant wouldn't let anyone drive that car except himself until the engine got broken in."

"Then what do you think happened?"

"Lots of funny things going on about that time," he said obscurely.

"Such as?" I prompted.

He tapped the dottle from his pipe on the heel of his boot. "You're asking a lot of questions, Boyd; and I don't see why I should answer 'em, except that old Mac said I should. I ain't got too much love for you, Boyd, and I want to find out one thing for sure. Are you going to bring up anything that'll hurt Miss Trinavant?"

I held his eye. "No, Mr. Waystrand. I'm not."

He stared at me for a moment longer, then waved his arm largely. "All these woodlands, hundreds of thousands of acres —Bull Matterson got 'em all, 'cept this tract that John left to

Miss Trinavant. He got the sawmills, the pulp mills—just about everything that John Trinavant built up. Don't you think the accident came at the right time?"

I felt depressed. All Waystrand had were the same unformulated suspicions that plagued Mac and myself. I said, "Have you any evidence that it *wasn't* an accident? Anything at all?"

He shook his head heavily. "Nothing to show."

"What did Cl . . . Miss Trinavant think about it? I don't mean when it happened, but afterwards."

"I ain't talked to her about it—it ain't my place—and she's said nothing to me." He shook the dottle from his pipe into the fire and put the pipe on the mantel. "I'm going to bed," he said brusquely.

I stayed up for a while, chasing the thing round in circles, and then went to bed myself, to the sparely furnished room that had been Jimmy Waystrand's. It had a bleak aspect because it was as anonymous as any hotel room; just a bed, a primitive wash-stand, a cupboard and a few bare shelves. It looked as though young Jimmy had cleared out for good, leaving nothing of his youth behind him, and I felt sorry for old Waystrand.

The next day I fished a little and chopped some logs because the log pile looked depleted. Waystrand came out at the sound of the axe and watched me. I had stripped off my shirt because the exercise made me sweat and swinging that axe was hard work. Waystrand regarded me for a while, then said, "You're a strong man, but you're misusing your strength. That's not the way to use an axe."

I leaned on the axe and grinned at him. "Know a better way?"

"Sure; give it to me." He took the axe and stood poised in front of the log, then swung it down casually. A chip flew and then another—and another. "See," he said. "It's in the turn of the wrists." He demonstrated in slow motion, then handed back the axe. "Try it that way."

I chopped in the way he had shown me, rather inexpertly, and sure enough the work went easier. I said, "You're experienced with an axe."

"I used to be a logger for Mr. Trinavant—but that was

before the accident. I got pinned under a ten-inch log and hurt my back." He smiled slowly. "That's why I'm letting you get on with the chopping—it don't do my back no good."

I chopped for a while, then said, "Know anything about the value of lumber?"

"Some. I was boss of a section—I picked up something about values."

"Matterson is clearing out his part of the Kinoxi," I said. "He's taking everything—not just the normal Forestry Service allowable cut. What do you think the value per square mile is?"

He pondered for a while and said finally, "Not much under seven hundred thousand dollars."

I said, "Don't you think Miss Trinavant should do something about this end? She'll lose an awful lot of money if those trees are drowned."

He nodded. "You know, this land hasn't ever been cut over since John Trinavant died. The trees have been putting on weight in the last twelve years, and there's a lot of mature timber which should have been taken out already. I reckon, if you made a solid cut, this land would run to a million dollars a square mile."

I whistled. I'd underestimated her loss. Five million bucks was a lot of dough. "Haven't you talked to her about it?"

"She's not been here to be talked to." He shrugged rather sheepishly. "And I'm no great hand with a pen."

"Maybe I'd better write to her?" I suggested. "What's her address?"

Waystrand hesitated. "You write to the bank in Vancouver; they pass it on." He gave me the address of her bank.

I stayed around until late afternoon, chopping a hell of a lot of logs for Waystrand and cursing young Jimmy with every stroke. That young whelp had no right to leave his old man alone. It was evident that there was no Mrs. Waystrand and it wasn't good for a man to be alone, especially one suffering from back trouble.

When I left, Waystrand said, "If you see my boy, tell him he can come back any time." He smiled grimly. "That is, if you can get near enough to talk without him taking a swing at you."

I didn't tell him that I'd already encountered Jimmy. "I'll pass on the message when I see him—and I *will* be seeing him."

"You did right when you straight-armed him that time," said Waystrand. "I didn't think so then, but from what Miss Trinavant said afterwards I saw he had it coming." He put out his hand. "No hard feelings, Mr. Boyd."

"No hard feelings," I said, and we shook on it. I put the Land-Rover into gear and bumped down the track, leaving Waystrand looking after me, a diminishing and rather sad figure.

I made good time on the way back to Fort Farrell but it was dark by the time I was on the narrow track to McDougall's cottage. Halfway along, on a narrow corner, I was obstructed by a car stuck in the mud and only just managed to squeeze through. It was a Lincoln Continental, a big dream-boat the size of a battleship and certainly not the auto for a road like this; the overhangs fore and aft were much too long and it would scrape its fanny on every dip of the road. The trunk top looked big enough to land a helicopter on.

I pushed on to the cabin and saw a light inside. Mac's beat-up Chevvy wasn't around so I wondered who the visitor was. Being of a cautious nature and not knowing what trouble might have stirred up in my absence, I coasted the Land-Rover to a halt very quietly and sneaked across to look through the window before I went in.

A woman was sitting quietly before the fire reading a book. A woman I had never seen before.

VI

I pushed open the door and she looked up. "Mr. Boyd?"

I regarded her. She looked as out of place in Fort Farrell as a *Vogue* model. She was tall and thin with the emaciated thinness which seems to be fashionable, God knows why. She looked as though she lived on a diet of lettuce with thin brown bread—no butter; to sit down to steak and potatoes would no doubt have killed her by overtaxing an unused digestive system. From head to foot she reflected a world of which the good people of Fort Farrell know little—the jazzed-up, with-it world of the sixties—from the lank straight hair to the mini-skirt and the kinky patent-leather boots. It wasn't a world I particularly liked, but I may be old-fashioned. Anyway, the little-girl style certainly didn't suit this woman, who was probably in her thirties.

"Yes, I'm Boyd."

She stood up. "I'm Mrs. Atherton," she said. "I apologize for just barging in, but everyone does round here, you know."

I placed her as a Canadian aping a British accent. I said, "What can I do for you, Mrs. Atherton?"

"Oh, it isn't what you can do for me—it's what I can do for you. I heard you were staying here and dropped in to see if I could help. Just being neighbourly, you know."

She looked as neighbourly as Brigitte Bardot. "Kind of you to take the trouble," I said. "But I doubt if it's necessary. I'm a grown boy, Mrs. Atherton."

She looked up at me. "I'll say you are," she said admiringly. "My, but you are big."

I noticed she'd helped herself to Mac's Scotch. "Have *another* drink," I said ironically.

"Thanks—I believe I will," she said nonchalantly. "Will you join me?"

I began to think that to get rid of her was going to be quite a job; there's nothing you can do with an uninsultable woman short of tossing her out on her can, and that's not my style. I said, "No, I don't think I will."

"Suit yourself," she said easily, and poured herself a healthy slug of Mac's jealously conserved *Islay Mist*. "Are you going to stay in Fort Farrell long, Mr. Boyd?"

I sat down. "Why do you ask?"

"Oh, you don't know how I look forward to seeing a fresh face in this dump. I don't know why I stay here—I really don't."

I said cautiously, "Does Mr. Atherton work in Fort Farrell?"

She laughed. "Oh, there's no Mr. Atherton—not any more."

"I'm sorry."

"No need to be sorry, my dear man; he's not dead—just divorced." She crossed her legs and gave me a good look at her thigh; those mini-skirts don't hide much, but to me a female knee is an anatomical joint and not a public entertainment, so she was wasting her time. "Who are you working for?" she asked.

"I'm a freelance," I said. "A geologist."

"Oh dear—a technical man. Well, don't talk to me about it —I'm sure it would be way over my head."

I began to wonder about the neighbourly bit. Mac's cabin was well off the beaten track and it would be a very good Samaritan who would drive into the woods outside Fort Farrell to bring comfort and charity, especially if it meant ditching a Lincoln Continental. Mrs. Atherton didn't seem to fit the part.

She said, "What are you looking for—uranium?"

"Could be. Anything that's payable." I wondered what had put uranium into her mind. Something went "twang" in my head and a warning bell rang.

"I have been told that the ground has been pretty well picked over round here. You may be wasting your time." She laughed trillingly and flashed me a brilliant smile. "But I wouldn't know anything about such technical matters. I only know what I'm told."

I smiled at her engagingly. "Well, Mrs. Atherton, I prefer to believe my own eyes. I'm not inexperienced, you know."

She gave me an unbelievably coy look. "I'll bet you're not." She downed the second third of her drink. "Are you interested in history, Mr. Boyd?"

I looked at her blankly, unprepared for the switch. "I haven't thought much about it. What kind of history?"

She swished the Scotch around in her glass. "One has to do *something* in Fort Farrell or one is sent perfectly crazy," she said. "I'm thinking of joining the Fort Farrell Historical Society. Mrs. Davenant is President—have you met her?"

"No, I haven't." For the life of me I couldn't see where this talk was leading, but if Mrs. Atherton was interested in history then I was a ring-tailed lemur.

"You wouldn't think it, but I'm really a shy person," she said. She was dead right—I wouldn't think it. "I wouldn't want to join the society by myself. I mean—a novice among all those really experienced people. But if someone would join with me to give me some support, that would be different."

"And you want *me* to join the historical society?"

"They tell me Fort Farrell has a very interesting history. Did you know it was founded by a Lieutenant Farrell way back in . . . oh . . . way back? And he was helped by a man called Trinavant, and the Trinavant family really built up this town."

"Is that so?" I said drily.

"It's a pity about the Trinavants," she said casually. "The whole family was wiped out not very long ago. Isn't it a pity that a family that built a whole town should disappear like that?"

Again there was a "twang" in my mind and this time the warning bell nearly deafened me. Mrs. Atherton was the first person who had broached the subject of the Trinavants of her own free will; all the others had had to be nudged into it. I thought back over what she had said earlier and realized she had tried to warn me off in a not very subtle way, and she had brought up the subject of uranium. I had conned the construction men up at the dam into thinking I was looking for uranium.

I said, "Surely the *whole* family wasn't wiped out. Isn't there a Miss Clare Trinavant?"

She seemed put out. "I believe there is," she said curtly. "But I hear she's not a *real* Trinavant."

"Did you know the Trinavants?" I asked.

"Oh, yes," she said eagerly—too eagerly. "I knew John Trinavant very well."

I decided to disappoint her, and stood up. "I'm sorry, Mrs. Atherton. I don't think I'm interested in local history. I'm strictly a technical man and it's not my line." I smiled. "It might be different if I were going to put my roots down in Fort Farrell—then I might work up an interest—but I'm a nomad, you know; I keep on the move."

She looked at me uncertainly. "Then you're not staying in Fort Farrell long?"

"That depends on what I find," I said. "From what you tell me I may not find much. I'm grateful to you for that information, negative though it is."

She seemed at a loss. "Then you won't join the historical society?" she said in a small voice. "You're not interested in Lieutenant Farrell and the Trinavants and , , , er . . . the others who made this place?"

"What possible interest could I have?" I asked heartily.

She stood up. "Of course. I understand. I should have known better than to ask. Well, Mr. Boyd; anything you want you just ask me and I'll try to help you."

"Where will I contact you?" I asked blandly.

"Oh . . . er . . . the desk clerk at the Matterson House will know where to find me."

"I'm sure I shall be calling on your help," I said, and picked up the fur coat which was draped over a chair. I helped her into the coat and caught sight of an envelope on the mantel. It was addressed to me.

I opened it and found a one-line message from McDougall: COME TO THE APARTMENT AS SOON AS YOU GET IN. MAC.

I said, "You'll need some help in getting your car on the road, Mrs. Atherton. I'll get my truck and give you a push."

She smiled. "It seems that you are helping me more than I am helping you, Mr. Boyd." She swayed on the teetering high heels of her boots and momentarily pressed against me.

I grinned at her. "Just being neighbourly, Mrs. Atherton; just being neighbourly."

2

I pulled up in front of the darkened *Recorder* office and saw lights in the upstairs apartment, and got a hell of a surprise when I walked in.

Clare Trinavant was sitting in the big chair facing the door, and the apartment was in a shambles with the contents of cupboards and drawers littering the floor. McDougall turned as I opened the door and stood holding a pile of shirts.

Clare looked at me with no expression. "Hello, Boyd."

I smiled at her. "Welcome home, Trinavant." I was surprised how glad I was to see her.

"Mac tells me I have an apology to make to you," she said.

I frowned. "I don't know what you have to apologize about."

"I said some pretty hard things about you when you left

Fort Farrell. I have just learned they were unjustified; that Howard Matterson and Jimmy Waystrand combined to cook up a bastardly story. I'm sorry about that."

I shrugged. "Doesn't matter to me. I'm sorry it happened for your sake."

She smiled crookedly. "You mean my reputation? I have no reputation in Fort Farrell. I'm the odd woman who goes abroad and digs up pots and would rather mix with the dirty Arabs than good Christian folk."

I looked at the mess on the floor. "What's going on here?"

"I've been canned," said McDougall matter-of-factly. "Jimson paid me off this afternoon and told me to get out of the apartment before morning. I'd like the use of the Land-Rover."

"Sure," I said. "I'm sorry about this, Mac."

"I'm not," he said. "You must have stung old Bull where it hurts."

I looked at Clare. "What brings you back? I was about to write you."

A *gamine* grin came to her face. "Do you remember the story you once told me? About the man who sent a cable to a dozen of his friends: 'Fly, all is discovered'?" She nodded towards Mac and dug into the pocket of her tweed skirt. "A pseudo-Scotsman called Hamish McDougall can also write an intriguing cable." She unfolded a paper, and read, "IF YOU VALUE YOUR PEACE OF MIND COME BACK QUICKLY. What do you think of that for an attention-getter?"

"It brought you back pretty fast," I said. "But it wasn't my idea."

"I know. Mac told me. I was in London, doing some reading in the British Museum. Mac knew where to get me. I took the first flight out." She waved her hand. "Sit down, Bob. We've got some serious talking to do."

As I pulled up a chair, Mac said, "I told her about you, son."

"Everything?"

He nodded. "She had to know. I reckon she had a right to know. John Trinavant was her nearest kin—and you *were* in the Cadillac when he died."

I didn't like that very much. I had told Mac the story in

confidence and I didn't like the idea of having it spread around. It wasn't the kind of life-story that a lot of people would understand.

Clare watched the expression on my face. "Don't worry; it will go no further. I've made that very clear to Mac. Now, first of all—what were you going to write me about?"

"About the lumber on your land in the north Kinoxi Valley. Do you know how much it's worth?"

"I hadn't thought about it much," she admitted. "I'm not interested in lumber. All I know is that Matterson isn't going to make a cent on it."

I said, "I checked with your Mr. Waystrand. I'd made an estimate and he confirmed it, or rather, he told me I was way out. If you don't cut those trees you'll lose five million bucks."

Her eyes widened. "Five million dollars!" she breathed. "Why, that's impossible."

"What's impossible about it?" asked Mac. "It's a total cut, Clare; every tree. Look, Bob told me a couple of things so I checked on the statistics. A normal Forestry Service controlled cutting operation is mighty selective. Only half of one per cent of the usable lumber is taken and that runs to about five thousand dollars a square mile. The Kinoxi is being stripped to the ground, like they used to do back at the turn of the century. Bob's right."

Pink spots glowed in her cheeks. "That penny-pinching son-ofabitch," she said vehemently.

"Who?"

"Donner. He offered me two hundred thousand dollars for the felling rights and I told him to go jump into Matterson Lake as soon as it was deep enough for him to drown in."

I looked at Mac, who shrugged. "That's Donner for you," he agreed.

"Wait a minute," I said. "Didn't he raise his price at all?"

She shook her head. "He didn't have time. I threw him out."

"Matterson isn't going to let those trees drown if he can help it," I said. "Not if he can make money out of them. I bet he'll make another offer before long. But don't take a penny under four million, Clare; he'll make enough profit on that."

"I don't know what to do," she said. "I hate putting money in Matterson's pocket."

114

"Don't be sentimental about it," I said. "Stick him for as much as you can, and then think of ways of harpooning him once you've got his money. A person who didn't like Matterson could do him a lot of damage with a few million bucks to play around with. You don't have to keep the dough if you consider it tainted."

She laughed. "You've got an original mind, Bob."

I was struck by a thought. "Do either of you know of a Mrs. Atherton?"

Mac's eyebrows crawled up his forehead like two white furry caterpillars until they met his hairline. "Lucy Atherton? Where in hell did you meet *her*?"

"In your cabin."

He was struck speechless for a moment and gobbled like a turkey-cock. I looked at Clare, who said, "Lucy Atherton is Howard's sister. She's a Matterson."

Comprehension didn't so much dawn as strike like lightning. "So that's what her game was. She was trying to find out how interested I was in the Trinavants. She didn't get very far."

I told them what had happened at our meeting, and when I'd finished Mac said, "Those Mattersons are smart. They knew I wouldn't be at the cabin because I had to get clear here—and they knew you wouldn't know who she was. Old Bull sent her out on a reconnaissance."

"Tell me more about her."

"She's in between husbands," said Mac. "Atherton was her second—I think—and she divorced him about six months ago. I'm surprised she's around here; she's usually busy on the social round—New York, Miami, Las Vegas. And from what I hear she could be a nympho."

"She's a man-hungry vixen," said Clare in a calm, level voice.

I thought about that. When getting the Continental out of the mud I'd had a devil of a job to prevent her raping me. Not that I'm sexless, but she was so goddam thin that a man could cut himself to death on her bones, and anyway I like to make a choice for myself once in a while.

"Now we *know* Bull is getting worried," said Mac in satisfaction. "The funny thing is that he doesn't seem to care if we know it. He must have guessed that you'd ask me about the Atherton woman."

"We'll figure that one out later," I said. "It's getting late and we have to get this stuff back to the cabin."

"You'd better come with us, Clare," said Mac. "You can have Bob's bed and the young bucko can sleep out in the woods to-night."

Clare poked me in the chest with her finger and I knew she was getting pretty smart at interpreting the expression on my face. "I'll look after my own reputation, Boyd. Did you think I was going to stay at the Matterson House?" she asked cuttingly.

3

I changed gear noisily as I drove up to the cabin and there was a rustle of leaves at the roadside and the sound of something heavy moving away. "That's funny," said Mac in perplexity. "There's been no deer round here before."

The headlights swung across the front of the cabin and I saw a figure dart away into cover. "That's no goddam deer," I said, and jumped clear before the Land-Rover stopped moving. I chased after the man but stopped as I heard a smash of glass from within the cabin and whirled to dive through the doorway. I collided with someone who struck out, but it takes a lot to stop a man my size and I drove him back by sheer weight and momentum.

He gave ground and vanished into the darkness of the cabin and I felt in my pocket for a match. But then I caught the acrid reek of kerosene choking in my throat so thickly that I realized the whole cabin must have been wet with it and that to strike a match would be like lighting up a cigar in a powder-magazine.

There was a movement in the darkness ahead of me and then I heard the crunch of Mac's footsteps coming to the cabin door. "Stay out of here, Mac," I yelled.

My eyes were getting accustomed to the interior darkness and I could see the light patch of a window at the back of the cabin. I dropped to one knee in a crouch and looked around slowly. Sure enough, the light patch was momentarily

116

eclipsed as someone moved across it and I had my man placed. He was moving from left to right, trying to get to the door unnoticed. I dived for where I thought his legs were and grabbed him, and he fell on top of me but didn't come to the ground.

Then I felt a sharp pain thumping in my shoulder and had to let go and there was a boot in my face before I could roll over out of the way. By the time I stumbled to the door there was just the sound of running footsteps disappearing in the distance, and I saw Clare bending over a prostrate figure.

It was Mac, and he got groggily to his feet as I walked up. "Are you all right?"

He held his belly. "He . . . just rammed . . . me," he whispered painfully. "Knocked the wind out of me."

"Take it easy," I said.

"We'd better get him into the cabin," said Clare.

"Stay away from there," I said harshly. "It's ready to go off like a bomb. There's a flashlamp in the Land-Rover; will you get it?"

She went away and I walked Mac a few steps to a stump he could sit on. He was wheezing like an old steam engine and I cursed the man who'd done that to him. Clare came back with the lamp and flashed it at me. "My God!" she exclaimed. "What happened to your face?"

"It got stepped on. Give me the torch." I went into the cabin and looked around. The stink of kerosene made me gag and I saw the reason why it should; the place was a mess —all the sheets and blankets had been ripped from the beds, and the mattresses had been knifed open to liberate the stuffing. All this had been piled in the middle of the floor and doused with kerosene. There must have been five gallons because the floor was swimming.

I collected a pressure lantern and some cans from the larder and joined the others. "We'll have to camp out to-night," I said. "The cabin's too dangerous to use until we clean it out. It's lucky I didn't unpack the truck—we still have blankets we can use."

Mac was better and breathing more easily. He said, "What's wrong with the cabin?" I told him and he cursed freely until he recollected that Clare was by his elbow. "Sorry," he mumbled. "I got carried away."

117

She gave a low laugh. "I haven't heard cussing like that since Uncle John died. Who do you think did this, Bob?"

"I don't know—I didn't see any faces. But the Mattersons move fast. Mrs. Atherton made her report and Matterson acted."

"We'd better report it to the police," she said.

Mac snorted. "A lot of good that will do," he said disgustedly. "We didn't see who it was and we have no evidence to connect it with the Mattersons. Anyway, I can't see the cops tackling Bull Matterson—he draws too much water to be bull-dozed by Sergeant Gibbons."

I said, "You mean that Gibbons has been bought just like everyone else?"

"I mean nothing of the kind," said Mac. "Gibbons is a good guy; but he'll need hard evidence before he as much as talks to Matterson—and what evidence have you got? None that Gibbons can use, that's for sure."

I said, "Let's make camp and talk about it then. And not too near the cabin, either."

We camped in a glade a quarter of a mile from the cabin and I lit the lantern and set about making a fire. My left shoulder hurt and when I put my hand to it, it came away sticky with blood. Clare said in alarm, "What's happened?"

I looked at the blood stupidly. "My God, I think I've been stabbed!"

4

I left Clare and Mac to clean out the cabin next morning and drove into Fort Farrell. The wound in my shoulder wasn't too bad; it was a clean cut in the flesh which Clare bound up without too much trouble. It was sore and stiff but it didn't trouble me much once the bleeding was staunched.

Mac said, "Where are you going?"

"To pay a call," I said shortly.

"Keep out of trouble—do you hear me?"

"There'll be no trouble for me," I promised.

The feed-pump was giving trouble, so I left the Land-Rover with Clarry Summerskill, then walked up the street to the police station to find that Sergeant Gibbons was absent from Fort Farrell. There was nothing unusual in that—an RCMP sergeant in the country districts has a big parish and Gibbons's was bigger than most.

The constable listened to what I had to tell him and his brow furrowed when I told him of the stab wound. "You didn't recognize these men?"

I shook my head. "It was too dark."

"Do you—or Mr. McDougall—have any enemies?"

I said carefully, "You might find that these men were employees of Matterson's."

The constable's face closed up as though a blind was drawn. He said warily, "You could say that for half the population of Fort Farrell. All right, Mr. Boyd; I'll look into it. If you would make a written statement for the record I'd be obliged."

"I'll send it to you," I said wearily. I saw I wouldn't get anywhere without hard evidence. "When is Sergeant Gibbons due back?"

"In a couple of days. I'll see he's informed of this."

I bet you will, I thought bitterly. This constable would be only too pleased to pass such a hot potato to the sergeant. The sergeant would read my statement, nose around and find nothing and drop the whole thing. Not that one could blame him in the circumstances.

I left the police station and crossed to the Matterson Building. The first person I saw in the foyer was Mrs. Atherton. "Hello there," she said gaily. "Where are you going?"

I looked her in the eye. "I'm going up to rip out your brother's guts."

She trilled her practised laughter. "I wouldn't, you know; he's got himself a bodyguard. You wouldn't get near him." She looked at me appraisingly. "So the old Scotsman has been talking about me."

"Nothing to your credit," I said.

"I really wouldn't go up to see Howard," she said as I pressed for the elevator. "It wouldn't do you any good to be bounced from the eighth floor. Besides, the old man wants to see you. That's why I'm here—I've been waiting for you."

"Bull Matterson wants to see me?"

"That's right. He sent me to get you."

"If he wants to see me, I'm around town often enough," I said. "He can find me when he wants me."

"Now is that a way to treat an old man?" she asked. "My father is seventy-seven, Mr. Boyd. He doesn't get around much these days."

I rubbed my chin. "He doesn't have to, does he? Not when he can get other people to do his running for him. All right, Mrs. Atherton. I'll come and see him."

She smiled sweetly. "I knew you'd see reason. I have my car just outside."

We climbed into the Continental and drove out of town to the south. At first, I thought we were heading for Lakeside, the nearest thing to an upper-class suburb Fort Farrell can afford—all the Matterson Corporation executives lived out there—but we by-passed it and headed farther south. Then I realized that Bull Matterson wasn't just an executive and he didn't consider himself as upper class. He was king and he'd built himself a palace appropriate to his station.

On the way Mrs. Atherton didn't say much—not after I'd choked her off rudely. I was in no mood for chit-chat from her and made it pretty clear. It didn't seem to worry her. She smoked one cigarette after the other and drove the car with one hand. A woman wearing a mini-skirt and driving a big car leaves little to the imagination, and that didn't worry her either. But she liked to think it worried me because she kept casting sly glances at me out of the corner of her eye.

Matterson's palace was a reproduction French château not much bigger than the Château Frontenac in Quebec, and it gave me an inkling of the type of man he was. It was a type I had thought had died out during the nineteenth century, a robber baron of the Jim Fisk era who would gut a railroad or a corporation and use the money to gut Europe of its treasures. It seemed incredible that such men could still exist in the middle of the twentieth century, but this overgrown castle was proof.

We went into a hall about as big as a medium-sized football field, littered with suits of armour and other bric-à-brac. Or were they fake? I didn't know, but it didn't really make any difference—fake or not, they illuminated Matterson's character. We ignored the huge sweep of staircase and took an elevator which was inconspicuously tucked away in one corner. It wasn't a very big one and Mrs. Atherton took the opportunity to make a pass at me during the ride. She pressed hard against me, and said, "You're not very nice to me, Mr. Boyd," in a reproachful tone.

"I'm not very sociable with rattlesnakes, either," I observed.

She slapped me, so I slapped her in return. I'm willing to play along with all this bull about the gentle sex as long as they stay gentle, but once they use violence, then all bets are off. They can't expect it both ways, can they? I didn't slap her hard—just enough to make her teeth rattle—but it was unexpected and she stared at me in consternation. In her world she'd been accustomed to slapping men around and they'd taken it like gentlemen, but now one of the poor hypnotized rabbits had stood up and bitten her.

The elevator door slid open silently. She ran out and pointed down the corridor. "In there, damn you," she said in a choked voice, and hurried in the opposite direction.

The door opened on to a study lined with books and quiet as a cemetery vault. A lot of good cows had been butchered to provide the bindings on those books and I wondered if they shone with that gentle brown glow because they were well used or because some flunkey brightened them up every day the same time he polished his master's shoes. Tall windows reached from floor to ceiling on the opposite wall and before the windows a big desk was placed; it had a green leather top, tooled in gold.

Behind the desk was a man—Bull Matterson.

I knew he was five years older than McDougall but he looked five years younger, a hale man with a bristling but trim military moustache the same colour as newly fractured cast iron, which matched his hair. He was a big man, broad of shoulder and thick in the trunk, and the muscle was still there, not yet gone to fat. I guessed he still took exercise. The only signs of advanced age were the brown liver spots on the backs of his hands and the rather faded look in his blue eyes.

He waved his hand. "Sit down, Mr. Boyd." The tone of voice was harsh and direct, a tone to be obeyed.

I looked at the low chair, smiled slightly and remained standing. The old man was up to all the psychological tricks. His head twitched impatiently. "Sit down, Boyd. That *is* your name, isn't it?"

"That's my name," I agreed. "And I'd rather stand. I don't anticipate staying long."

121

"As you wish," he said distantly. "I've asked you up here for a reason."

"I hope so," I said.

A glimmer of a smile broke the iron face. "It *was* a damn silly thing to say," he agreed. "But don't worry; I'm not senile yet. I want to know what you're doing in Fort Farrell."

"So does everyone else," I said. "I don't know what business it is of yours, Mr. Matterson."

"Don't you? A man comes fossicking on my land and you think it's not my business?"

"Crown land," I corrected.

He waved the distinction aside irritably. "What are you doing here, Boyd?"

"Just trying to make a living."

He regarded me thoughtfully. "You'll get nowhere blackmailing me, young man. Better men than you have tried it and I've broken them."

I lifted my eyebrows. "Blackmail! I haven't asked anything from you, Mr. Matterson, and I don't intend to. Where does the blackmail come in? You might have your secrets to hide, Matterson, but I'm not in the money market where they're concerned."

"What's your interest in John Trinavant?" he asked bluntly.

"Why should you care?"

He thumped his fist and the solid desk shivered. "Don't fence with me, you young whippersnapper."

I leaned over the desk. "Who, in God's name, do you think you are? And who do you think I am?" He suddenly sat very still. "I'm not one of the townsfolk of Fort Farrell whom you've whipped into silence. You think I'm going to stand by when you burn out an old man's home?"

His face purpled. "Are you accusing me of arson, young man?"

"Let's amend it to attempted arson," I said. "It didn't work."

He leaned back. "Whose house am I supposed to have attempted to burn?"

"Not content with firing McDougall just because you thought he was making friends with the wrong people, you——"

He held up his hand. "When was this so-called arson attempt made?"

"Last night."

He flicked a switch. "Send my daughter to me," he said brusquely to a hidden microphone. "Mr. Boyd, I assure you that I don't burn down houses. If I did, they'd get burned to the ground; there wouldn't be any half-assed attempts. Now, then: let us get back to the subject. What's your interest in John Trinavant?"

I said, "Maybe I'm interested in the background of the woman I'm going to marry." I said it on the spur of the moment, but on second thoughts it didn't seem a half bad idea.

He snorted. "Oh—a fortune-hunter."

I grinned at him. "If I were a fortune-hunter I'd set my sights on your daughter," I pointed out. "But it would take a stronger stomach than mine."

I didn't find out what he would have said to that because just then Lucy Atherton came into the room. Matterson swung round and looked at her. "An attempt was made to burn out McDougall's place last night," he said. "Who did it?"

"How should I know?" she said petulantly.

"Don't lie to me, Lucy," he said gratingly. "You've never been good at it."

She cast a look of dislike at me and shrugged. "I tell you I don't know."

"So you don't know," said Matterson. "All right: who gave the order—you or Howard? And don't worry about Boyd being here. You tell me the truth, d'you hear?"

"All right, I did," she burst out. "I thought it was a good idea at the time. I knew you wanted Boyd out of here."

Matterson looked at her incredulously. "And you thought you'd get him out by burning old Mac's cabin? I've fathered an imbecile. Of all the stupid things I ever heard!" He swung out his arm and pointed at me. "Take a look at this man. He's taken on the job of bucking the Matterson Corporation and already he's been running rings round Howard. Do you think that the burning of a cabin is going to make him just go away?"

She took a deep breath. "Father, this man hit me."

I grinned. "Not before she hit me."

Matterson ignored me. "You're not too old for *me* to give you a good lathering, Lucy. Maybe I should have done it sooner. Now get the hell out of here." He waited until she reached the door. "And remember—no more tricks. I'll do this my way."

The door slammed.

I said, "Your way is legal, of course."

He stared at me with suffused eyes. "Everything I do is legal." He simmered down and took a cheque-book from a drawer. "I'm sorry about McDougall's cabin—that's not my style. What's the damage?"

I reflected that I was the one who had lectured Clare on sentimentality. Besides, it was Mac's dough, anyway. I said, "A thousand bucks should cover it," and added, "There's also the question of a wrecked Land-Rover that belongs to me."

He looked up at me under grey eyebrows. "Don't try to shake me down," he said acidly. "What story is this?"

I told him what had happened on the Kinoxi road. "Howard told Waystrand to bounce me, and Waystrand did it the hard way," I said.

"I seem to have fathered a family of thugs," he muttered and scribbled out the cheque, which he tossed across the desk. It was for $3,000.

I said, "You've given your daughter a warning; what about doing the same for Howard? Any more tricks on his part and he'll lose his beauty—I'll see to that."

Matterson looked at me appraisingly. "You could take him at that—it wouldn't be too hard." There was contempt in his voice for his own son, and for a moment I was on the verge of feeling sorry for him. He picked up the telephone. "Get me Howard's office at the Matterson Building."

He put his hand over the mouthpiece. "I'm not doing this for Howard's sake, Boyd. I'm going to get rid of you, but when I do it'll be legal and there'll be no kickback."

A squawk came from the telephone. "Howard? Now get this. Leave Boyd alone. Don't do a damn' thing—I'll handle it. Sure, he'll go up to the dam—he's legally entitled to walk on that land—but what the hell can he do when he gets there? Just leave him alone, d'you hear? And, say, did you have anything to do with that business at McDougall's cabin last night. You don't know—well, ask your fool sister."

He slammed down the telephone and glared at me. "Does that satisfy you?"

"Sure," I said. "I'm not looking for trouble."

"You'll get it," he promised. "Unless you leave Fort Farrell. With your record it wouldn't be too much trouble to get you tossed in the can."

I leaned over the desk. "What record, Mr. Matterson?" I asked softly.

"I know who you are," he said in a voice like gravel. "Your new face doesn't fool me any, Grant. You have a police record as long as my arm—delinquency, theft, drug-peddling, assault—and if you step out of line just once while you're in Fort Farrell you'll be put away fast. Don't stir anything up here, Grant. Just leave things alone and you'll be safe."

I took a deep breath. "You lay it on the line, don't you?"

"That's always been my policy—and I warn a man only once," he said uncompromisingly.

"So you've bought Sergeant Gibbons."

"Don't be a fool," said Matterson. "I don't have to buy policemen—they're on my side anyway. Gibbons will go by the book and you are recorded on the wrong page."

I wondered how he knew I had been Grant, and then suddenly I knew who had employed a private investigator to check on me. But he wouldn't have done that unless he had been worried about something; he was still hiding something and that gave me the confidence to say, "To hell with you, Matterson. I'll go my own way."

"Then I feel sorry for you," he said grimly. "Look, boy: stay out of this. Don't trouble yourself with things that don't concern you." There was a strange tone in his voice; with any other man one might have thought he was pleading.

I said, "How do I get back to Fort Farrell? Your daughter brought me up here, but I doubt if she'll be willing to take me back."

Matterson chuckled coldly. "The exercise will do you good. It's only five miles."

I shrugged and walked out on him. I went down the stairs instead of taking the elevator and found the great hall deserted. Going outside the house was like being released from prison and I stood on the front step savouring the fresh air. There were too many tensions in the Matterson household for a man to be comfortable.

Lucy Atherton's Continental was still standing where she had left it, and I saw that the key was still in the ignition lock. I climbed in and drove back to Fort Farrell. The exercise would be even better for her.

5

I parked the Continental outside the Matterson Building, cashed the cheque in the Matterson Bank and walked across to pick up the Land-Rover. Clarry Summerskill said, "I've fixed the pump, Mr. Boyd, but that'll be another fifteen dollars. Look, it'll pay you better to get a new heap—this one is about shot. I've got a jeep just come in which should suit you. I'll take the Land-Rover as a trade-in."

I grinned. "How much will you give me on it?"

"Mr. Boyd, you've *ruined* it," he said earnestly. "All I want it for now are the spare parts, but I'll still give you a good price."

So we dickered and I ended up by driving back to Mac's cabin in a jeep. Clare and Mac had just about finished cleaning up, although the stink of kerosene still lay heavily on the air inside. I gave Mac a thousand dollars in folding money and he looked at it in surprise. "What's this?"

"Conscience money," I said, and told him what had happened.

He nodded. "Old Bull is a ruthless bastard," he said. "But he's never been caught in anything illegal. To tell you the truth, I was a mite surprised at what happened last night."

Clare said thoughtfully, "I wonder how he knew you were Grant."

"He hired a detective to find out—but that's not the point. What I want to know is *why* he thought it necessary to check up on me so many years ago. Another thing that puzzles me is the old man's character."

"What do you mean?"

I said, "Look at it this way. He strikes me as being an

126

honest man. He may be as ruthless as Genghis Khan and as tough as hickory, but I think he's straight. Everything he said gave that impression. Now, what could a man like that be hiding?"

"He *did* bring up the question of blackmail," said Clare tentatively. "So you want to know what he could be blackmailed for."

I said, "What's your impression of him, Mac?"

"Pretty much the same. I said he'd never been *caught* in anything illegal and he never has. You get talk around town that a man couldn't make the dough that he has by legal means, but that's only the talk of a lot of envious failures. Could be that he *is* straight."

"So what could he have done that makes him talk of blackmail?"

"I've been giving thought to that," said Mac. "You'd better sit down, son, because what I've got to tell you might knock you on your back. Clare, put the kettle on; it's about time we had tea, anyway."

Clare smiled and filled the kettle. Mac waited until she came back. "This has something to do with you, too," he said. "Now I want you both to listen carefully, because this is complicated."

He seemed to hunt a little, searching for a place to begin, then he said, "Folks are more different now than they used to be, especially young folks. Time was then you could tell a rich man from a poor man by the way he dressed, but not any more. And that goes in spades for teen-agers and college students.

"Now, in that Cadillac which crashed there were four people—John Trinavant, his wife and two young fellows—Frank Trinavant and Robert Boyd Grant, both college students. Frank was the son of a rich man and Robert was a bum—to say the best of him. But you couldn't tell the difference by the way they dressed. You know college kids: they dress in a kind of uniform. Both these boys were dressed in jeans and open-necked shirts and they'd taken off their jackets."

I said slowly, "What the hell are you getting at, Mac?"

"Okay, I'll come right out with it," he said. "How do you know you are Robert Boyd Grant?"

I opened my mouth to tell him—then shut it again.

He smiled sardonically. "Just because somebody told you, but not out of your own knowledge."

Clare said incredulously, "You think he might be *Frank Trinavant*?"

"He might," said Mac. "Look, I've never gone for all this psychiatric crap. Frank was a good boy—and so are you, Bob. I checked on Grant and decided I'd never come across a bigger sonofabitch in my life. It's never made sense to me that you should be Grant. Your psychiatrist, Susskind, explained it all away cleverly by this multiple personality stuff, but I don't give a good goddam for that. I think you're plain Frank Trinavant—still the same guy but you happen to have lost your memory."

I sat there stunned. After a while my brain got working again in a cranky sort of fashion, and I said, "Steady on, Mac. Susskind couldn't have made that kind of error."

"Why couldn't he?" Mac demanded. "Remember, he was told you were Grant. You've got to realize the way it was. *Matterson* made the identification of the bodies, he tagged the three dead people as Trinavants. Naturally there was no room for error in the case of John Trinavant and his wife, but the dead boy he named as Frank Trinavant." He snorted. "I've seen Highway Patrol photographs of that body and how in hell he was sure I'll never know."

"Surely there must have been some means of identification," said Clare.

Mac looked at her soberly. "I don't know if you've seen a really bad auto smash—one followed by a gasoline fire. Bob, here, was burnt beyond recognition—and he lived. The other boy was burnt and killed. The shoes were ripped from their feet and neither of them was wearing a wrist-watch when they were found. The shirts had been pretty near burnt off their backs and they wore identical jeans. They were both husky guys, much about the same size."

"This is ridiculous," I said. "How come I knew so much about geology unless I'd been taking a course like Grant?"

Mac nodded. "True." He leaned forward and tapped me on the knee. "But so was Frank Trinavant. He was majoring in geology too."

"For God's sake!" I said explosively. "You'll have me

believing in this crazy story. So they were both majoring in geology. Did they know each other?"

"I shouldn't think so," said Mac. "Grant went to the University of British Columbia; Trinavant to the University of Alberta. Tell me, Bob, before I go any further: is there anything in all that you know of that would blow this idea to hell? Can you find any sound proof to show that you are Grant and not Frank Trinavant?"

I thought about it until it hurt. Ever since Susskind took me in hand I *knew* I was Grant—but only because I was told so. To make a mean pun, I had taken it for granted. Now it came as a shock to find the matter in question. Yet try as I would, I couldn't think of any real proof to settle it one way or the other.

I shook my head. "No proof from where I'm standing."

Mac said gently, "This leads to an odd situation. If you *are* Frank Trinavant, then you inherit old John's estate which puts Bull Matterson in a hell of a jam. The whole question of the estate goes into the melting-pot again. Maybe he'd still be able to enforce that option agreement in the courts, but the trust fund would revert to you and the financial flapdoodle he's been pulling would come into the open."

My jaw dropped. "Wait a minute, Mac. Let's not take this thing too far."

"I'm just pointing out the logical consequences," he said. "If you are Frank Trinavant—and can prove it—you're a pretty rich guy. But you'll be taking the dough from Matterson, and he won't like it. And that's apart from the fact that he'll be branded as a crook and will be lucky to escape jail."

Clare said, "No wonder he doesn't want you around."

I rubbed my chin. "Mac, you say it all boils down to Matterson's identification of the bodies. Do you think he did it deliberately or was it a mistake? Or was there a mistake at all? I could still be Grant, for all I know and can prove."

"I think he *wanted* the Trinavants dead," said Mac flatly. "I think he took a chance. Remember, the survivor was in a bad way—you weren't expected to live another twelve hours. If Matterson's chance didn't come off—if you survived as Frank Trinavant—then it would have been a mistake on his part, understandable in the circumstances. Hell, maybe he didn't know himself which was which, but he took the chance and it paid off in a way that even he couldn't expect. You survived but without memory—and he'd tagged you as Grant."

"He talked about blackmail," I said. "And from what you've just handed me, he had every justification for believing I would blackmail him—*if I am Grant*. It's just the sort of thing a guy like Grant would do. But would Frank Trinavant blackmail him?"

"No," said Clare instantly. "He wasn't the type. Besides, it's not blackmail to demand your own rights."

"Hell, this thing is biting its own tail," said Mac disgustedly. "If you *are* Grant you can't blackmail him—you have no standing. So why is he talking about blackmail?" He stared at me speculatively. "I think, maybe, he committed one illegal act—a big one—to which you were a witness, and he's scared of it coming to light because it would knock the footing right out from under him."

"And this illegal act?"

"You know what I mean," snapped Mac. "Let's not be mealy-mouthed about it. Let's come right out and say murder."

We didn't talk too much about it after that. Mac's final statement was a bit too final, and we couldn't speculate on it without any firm proofs—not out loud, that is. Mac took refuge in chores about the house and refused to say another word, but I noticed he kept a bright eye on me until I got tired of his silent questioning and went out to sit by the stream. Clare took the jeep and went into town on the pretext of buying new blankets and mattresses for Mac.

Mac had handed me the biggest problem I had ever had in my life. I thought back to the days when I was reborn in the Edmonton hospital and searched for any mental clue to my identity—as though I had never done so before. Nothing I found led to any positive result and I found I now had two possible pasts. Of the two I much preferred Trinavant; I had heard enough of John to be proud to be his son. Of course, if I did turn out to be Frank Trinavant, then complications would set in between me and Clare.

I tossed a stone in the stream and idly wondered how close

the kinship was between Frank and Clare and could it possibly be a bar to marriage, but I assumed it wouldn't be.

That short and ugly word which had been Mac's final pronouncement had given us pause. We had discussed the possibility in vague terms and it had come to nothing as far as Matterson was concerned. He had his alibi—Mac himself.

I juggled the possibilities and probabilities around, thinking of Grant and Trinavant as two young men whom I might have known in the distant past but without any relationship to me. It was a technique Susskind had taught me to stop me getting too involved in Grant's troubles. I got nowhere, of course, and gave up when Clare came back.

I camped in the woodland glade again that night because Clare had still not gone up to the Kinoxi Valley and the cabin had only two rooms. Again I had the Dream and the hot snow ran in rivers of blood and there was a jangle of sound as though the earth itself was shattering, and I woke up breathless with the cold night air choking in my throat. After a while I built up the fire again and made coffee and drank it, looking towards the cabin where a gleam of light showed where someone was sitting up half the night.

I wondered if it was Clare.

VII

Nothing much happened just after that. I didn't make any move against Bull Matterson and McDougall didn't push me. I think he realized I had to have time to come to terms with the problem he had handed me.

Clare went up to her cabin in the Kinoxi Valley, and before she went I said, "Maybe you shouldn't have stopped me doing that survey on your land. I might have come across a big strike of manganese or something—enough to have stopped the flooding of the valley."

She said slowly, "Suppose you found something now—would it still make a difference?"

"It might—if it were a big enough find. The Government

might favour a mining settlement rather than a dam; it would employ more people."

"Then why don't you come and give the land a check?" She smiled. "A last-ditch effort."

"Okay," I said. "Give me a few days to get sorted out."

I went prospecting but nowhere near the dam. In spite of Matterson's assurance of safety, something might have stirred up, say, between me and Jimmy Waystrand—or those truckers, if I came across them—and I wanted no trouble until I had got things clear in my mind. So I fossicked about on the Crown lands to the west, not really looking for anything in particular and with my mind only half on the job.

After two weeks I went back to Fort Farrell, no more decided than I had been when I left. I was dreaming a lot of nights and that wasn't doing me any good, either. The dreams were changing in character and becoming frighteningly real —burnt bodies strewn about an icy landscape, the crackle of flames reddening the snow and a jangling sound that was cruel in its intensity. When I got back to Mac's cabin I was pretty washed-up.

He was concerned about me. "Sorry to have put this on you, son," he said. "Maybe I shouldn't have brought it up."

"You did right," I said heavily. "It's tough on me, Mac, but I can stand it. You know, it comes as quite a shock to discover you have a choice of pasts."

"I was a fool," Mac said bluntly. "Ten minutes' thought and ten cents' worth of understanding and I'd have known better. I've been kicking myself ever since I opened my big mouth."

"Forget it," I said.

"But *you* won't, though." He was silent for a while. "If you pulled out now and forgot the whole thing I wouldn't think any the worse of you for it, boy. There'd be no recriminations from me—not like last time."

"I won't do that," I said. "Too much has happened. Old Matterson has tried to scare me off, for one thing, and I don't push easy. There are other reasons, too."

He looked at me with a shrewd eye. "You haven't finished thinking about this yet. Why don't you give Clare's land the once-over, like you promised. You need more time."

He wasn't fitted to the role of Cupid, but he meant well and it really wasn't a bad idea, so a couple of days later I left for the North Kinoxi in the jeep. The road hadn't got any better since my last trip, and I was more tired when the big cabin came in sight than if I'd walked all the way.

Waystrand came to meet me with his stiff, slow walk, and I asked, "Is Miss Trinavant around, Mr. Waystrand?"

"Walking in the woods," he said briefly. "You staying?"

"For a while," I said. "Miss Trinavant wants me to do a survey." He nodded but said nothing. "I haven't seen your son yet, so I haven't been able to pass on your message."

He shrugged heavily. "Wouldn't make any difference, I suppose. You eaten?"

I shared some food with him and then did some more log-chopping while he looked on with approval at my improved handling of the axe. When I began to sweat I stripped off my shirt, and after a while he said, "Don't want to be nosy, but was you chawed by a bear?"

I looked down at the cicatrices and shiny skin on my chest. "More like a Stutz Bearcat," I said. "I was in an auto accident."

"Oh," was all he vouchsafed, but a puzzled frown came on to his face. Presently he went away and I continued chopping.

Clare came back from the woods towards sunset and appeared glad to see me. She wanted to know if the Mattersons had made any moves, but merely nodded when I said that no move had been made by either side.

We had dinner in the big cabin, during which she asked me about the survey, so after dinner I got out the Government map and indicated what I was going to do and how I was going to go about it. She said, "Is there much chance of finding anything?"

"Not much, I'm afraid—not from what I saw of the Matterson land in the south. Still, there's always a chance; strikes have been made in the most unlikely places." I talked about that for quite a while and then drifted into reminiscences of the North-West Territories.

Suddenly Clare said, "Why don't you go back, Bob? Why don't you leave Fort Farrell? It's not doing you any good."

"You're the third person who has asked me to quit," I said. "Matterson, McDougall and now you."

"My reasons might be the same as Mac's," she said. "But don't couple me with Matterson."

133

"I know, Clare," I said. "I'm sorry. But I'm not going to quit."

She knew finality when she heard it and didn't press it any more. Instead, she said, "Can I come with you when you do the survey?"

"Why not? It's your land," I said. "You can keep a close eye on me so I don't skip the hard bits."

We arranged to leave early, but in fact we didn't get away too soon the following morning. To begin with, I overslept which is something I hardly ever do. For the first time in nearly three weeks I slept soundly without dreaming and awoke refreshed but very late. Clare said she hadn't the heart to wake me and I didn't put up too much of a protest. That was why we were delayed long enough for unexpected, and unwelcome, visitors to drop from the sky.

I was in my room when I heard the helicopter and saw it settle lightly in the open space at the back. Howard Matterson and Donner got out and I saw Clare go forward to meet them. The rotor swished to a stop and the pilot dropped to the ground, so it looked as though Matterson intended to stay for longer than a few minutes.

There seemed to be an argument going on. Howard was jabbering nineteen to the dozen, with Donner putting in his two cents' worth from time to time, while Clare stood with a stony face and answered monosyllabically. Presently Howard waved at the cabin and Clare shrugged. All three of them moved out of sight and I heard them talking in the big main room.

I hesitated, then decided it was none of my business. Clare knew the score about the lumber on her land and I knew she wouldn't let Howard get away with anything. I continued to fill my pack.

I could hear the rumble of Howard's voice, with the lighter, colourless interjections of Donner. Clare appeared to be saying little, and I hoped most of it consisted of "No." Presently there was a tap on the door and she came in. "Won't you join us?" Her lips were compressed and the pink spots on her cheeks were danger signals I had seen before.

I followed her into the main room and Howard scowled

and reddened when he saw me. "What's he doing here?" he demanded.

"What's it to you?" Clare asked. She indicated Donner. "You've brought your tame accountant. This is *my* adviser." She turned to me. "They've doubled their offer," she said in an acid voice. "They're offering half a million dollars for the total felling rights on five square miles of my land."

"Have you put up a counter-offer?" I asked.

"Five million dollars."

I grinned at her. "Be reasonable, Clare: the Mattersons wouldn't make a profit out of that. Now, I'm not suggesting you split the difference, but I think that if you subtracted their offer from yours there might be a basis for a sale. Four and a half million bucks."

"Ridiculous," said Donner.

I swung on him. "What's ridiculous about it? You know you're trying to pull a fast one."

"You keep out of this." Howard was fuming.

"I'm here by invitation, Howard," I said. "Which is more than you are. Sorry to have spoiled your con game, but there it is. You know this land hasn't been cut over for twelve years and you know the amount of mature timber that's ready for the taking. Some of those big trees would go nicely in the mill, wouldn't they? I think it's a reasonable offer, and my advice to you is to take it or leave it."

"By God, we'll leave it," he said tightly. "Come on, Donner."

I laughed. "Your father isn't going to like that. He'll have your guts for garters, Howard. I doubt if he ever ruined a deal by being too greedy."

That stopped him. He glanced at Donner, then said, "Mind if we have a private conversation?"

"Go ahead," said Clare. "There's plenty of room outside." They went out, and Clare said, "I hope you're right."

"I'm right, but Howard might be obstinate. I think he's a man who sets himself on a course and doesn't deviate. He isn't flexible, and flexibility is very important to a businessman. I'm afraid he might make a fool of himself."

"What do you mean?"

I said, "He's so set on making a killing here that it might

blind him to a reasonable deal—and I don't think Donner can control him. That might bitch things up. Will you leave the dickering to me?"

She smiled. "You seem to know what you're doing."

"Maybe. But the biggest deals I've made so far have been with used car dealers—I may be out of my league here. I never dickered in millions before."

"Neither have I," she said. "But if what I hear about used car dealers is correct, they're as tricky to deal with as anyone else. Try to imagine Howard as Clarry Summerskill."

"That's an insult to Clarence," I said.

Howard and Donner came back. Howard said heartily, "Well, I think we can sort this thing out. I'll disregard the insults I've been offered so far by Boyd and make you a new offer. Clare, I'll double up again and make it a round million dollars—I can't say fairer than that."

She looked at him coldly. "Four and a half."

Donner said in his precise voice, "You're being too rigid, Miss Trinavant."

"And you're being too free and easy," I said. I grinned at Howard. "I have a proposition. Let's get Tanner, the Forestry Service man, up here to do an independent valuation. I'm sure Clare will abide by his figure if you will."

I hadn't any fear that Matterson would go for that, and he didn't. His voice sounded like the breaking of ice-floes. "There's no need to waste time on fooleries. The dam is nearly finished—we close the sluices in two weeks. In less than four months this land will be flooded and we have to get the lumber out before then. That's cutting things very fine and it'll take every man I've got to do it in time—even if we start now."

"So make a deal now," I said. "Come up with a sensible offer."

He gave me a look of intense dislike. "Can't we be reasonable, Clare?" he pleaded. "Can't we talk without this character butting in?"

"I think Bob's doing all right," she said.

Donner said quickly, "A million and a half."

"Four and a half," said Clare stolidly.

Howard made a noise expressive of disgust, and Donner

136

said, "We keep coming up, Miss Trinavant, but you make no effort to meet us."

"That's because I know the value of what I've got."

I said, "All right, Donner; we'll come down to meet you. Let's say four and a quarter. What's your counter-offer?"

"For Christ's sake!" said Howard. "Has he the right to negotiate on your behalf, Clare?"

She looked him in the eye. "Yes."

"To hell with that," he said. "I'm not dealing with a broken-down geologist who hasn't two cents to rub together."

"Then the deal's off," she said, and stood up. "If you'll excuse us, we have work to do." I never admired her more than I did then; she was putting all her faith in the negotiating ability of a man she hardly knew. But it sure made me sweat.

Donner cut in quickly, "Let's not be hasty." He nudged Howard. "Something can be worked out here. You asked me for my counter-offer, Boyd. Here it is: two million dollars flat—and not a cent more."

Donner appeared quite calm but Howard was ready to go off pop. He had come here expecting to get a five-million-dollar property for a mere half-million, and now it was his turn to be squeezed he didn't like it one little bit. But for a moment I wondered if I was making a mistake. My estimate was on my own assessment—which could be wrong because I wasn't a lumberman—and on the word of old Waystrand, a man who did chores around the house.

I felt sweat trickling down my back as I said, "Nothing doing."

Howard exploded. "All right," he shouted. "That's an end to it. Let's get the hell out of here, Donner. You've a fool for an adviser, Clare. Boyd couldn't advise a man lost in the desert how to take a drink of water. If you want to take up our final offer, you know where to find me."

He started to walk out. I glanced at Donner, who obviously didn't want to leave, and I knew I was right, after all. Donner was ready to carry on wheeling and dealing, so therefore he was ready to make another offer; but he'd lost control of Howard as I knew he would. Howard, lost in his rage, wouldn't let him continue, and what I had been afraid of was about to happen.

I said, "Now is the time to separate the men from the boys. Get old Waystrand in here, Clare."

She looked at me in surprise, but obediently went outside and I heard her calling for him. Howard also stopped and looked at me uncertainly, fidgeting on one leg; and Donner eyed me speculatively.

Clare came back, and I said, "I warned you, Howard, that your old man wouldn't like this. If you pass up a good deal in which you can make a damned good profit I don't think he'll let you stay as boss of the Matterson Corporation. What do you say, Donner?"

Donner smiled thinly. "What would you expect me to say?"

I said to Clare, "Get pen and paper. Write a formal letter to Bull Matterson offering him the felling rights for four and a quarter million. He'll beat you down to four and still make a cool million bucks profit. And tell him you'd rather deal with a man, not a boy. Waystrand can take the letter to-day."

Clare went to the writing-desk and sat down. I thought Howard was going to take a swing at me but Donner tugged at his coat and drew him back. They both retreated and Donner whispered urgently. I had a good idea of what he was saying, too. If that letter was ever delivered to old Bull it would be an admission on Howard's part that he'd fallen down on a big job. Already, from what I had seen, the old man held him in contempt and had even given him Donner as a nursemaid. Bull Matterson would never forgive his son for putting a million dollars in jeopardy.

Waystrand came in and Clare looked up. "I want you to take a letter into Fort Farrell, Matthew."

The whispering across the room rose to a sibilant crescendo and finally Howard shrugged. Donner said urgently, "Wait a minute, Miss Trinavant." He addressed me directly and there was no suggestion that I was not empowered to negotiate. "Did you mean that, Boyd—that you'd take four million dollars?"

"Miss Trinavant will," I said.

His lips tightened momentarily. "All right. I'm empowered to agree." He took a contract form from his pocket. "All we need to do is to fill in the amount and get Miss Trinavant's witnessed signature."

"I don't sign anything before my lawyer checks it," she said coolly. "You'll have to wait on that."

Donner nodded. He didn't expect anything else; he was a legalist himself and that was the way his own mind worked. "As soon as possible, please." He pulled out a pen and filled in a blank space in the middle of the contract, then pushed the pen into Howard's hand. Howard hesitated, and Donner said drily, "Sign—you'd better."

Howard's lips tightened, then he dashed off his signature. He straightened up and pointed a trembling finger at me. "Watch it, Boyd—just watch it, that's all. You'll never do this to me again—ever."

I smiled. "If it's any consolation, Howard, you never had a chance. We had you whipsawed from the beginning. First, we knew exactly what we had, and, second, I had quite a job talking Clare round into selling; she didn't care if she sold or not, and that's a hell of a bargaining advantage. But you wanted it—you *had* to have it. Your old man would never let you pass it up."

Donner said, "You all see that I witness Mr. Matterson's signature." He signed the contract and dropped it on the table. "I think that's all."

Howard swung on his heel and left without another word, and Donner followed him. Clare slowly tore into fragments the letter she had written, and looked up at Waystrand. "You won't have to go into Fort Farrell after all, Matthew."

Waystrand shuffled his feet and cracked a slow grin. "Looks like you're being looked after all right, Miss Clare." He gave me a friendly nod and left.

My legs felt weak so I sat down. Clare said practically, "You look as though you need a drink." She went over to the cabinet and brought back a slug of Scotch big enough to kill an elephant. "Thanks, Bob."

"I never thought we'd do it," I said. "I thought I was going to blow the whole thing. When Howard started to leave . . ." I shook my head.

"You blackmailed him," she said. "He's scared to death of his father and you used that to blackmail him."

"He had it coming—he tried to give you a hell of a raw deal. Old Bull will never know it, though; and he'll be happy with his million bucks." I looked up at her. "What are you going to do with your four million?"

She laughed. "I'll be able to organize my own digs now—I've never been able to afford it before. But first I want to take care of you. I didn't like Howard's crack about a broken-down geologist."

"Hey!" I said. "I didn't do that much."

"You did more than I could have done. I couldn't have faced Howard down like that. I'd hate to play poker with you, Bob Boyd. You certainly deserve a negotiator's fee."

I hadn't thought about that. Clare said, "Let's be business-like about it—you did the job and you get the pay. What about twenty per cent?"

"For God's sake, that's too much." I saw the glint in her eye. "Ten per cent."

"We'll split the difference," she said. "Fifteen per cent—and you'll take it."

I took a mouthful of whisky and nearly choked as I realized I had just made myself $600,000.

2

As I have said, we started off late that morning and didn't get far before we stopped for a bite to eat. The way Clare made a fire, I saw she knew her way around the woods—it was just big enough for its purpose and no bigger, and there was no danger of setting the woods alight. I said, "How come Waystrand works for you?"

"Matthew? He worked for Uncle John. He was a good logger but he had an accident."

"He told me about that," I said.

"He's had a lot of grief," said Clare. "His wife died just about the same time; it was cancer, I think. Anyway, he had the boy to bring up, so Uncle John asked him if he'd like to work around the house—the house in Lakeside. He couldn't work as a logger any more, you see."

I nodded. "And you took him over, more or less?"

"That's right. He looks after the cabin while I'm away." She frowned. "I'm sorry about young Jimmy, though; he's gone wild. He and his father had a dreadful quarrel about something, and Jimmy went to work for the Matterson Corporation."

I said, "I think that's what the quarrel was about. The job was a pay-off to Jimmy for blowing the gaff about me to Howard."

She coloured. "You mean about that night in the cabin?"

I said, "I owe Jimmy something for that—and for something else." I told her of the wild ride down the Kinoxi road sandwiched between the logging trucks.

"You could have been killed!" she said.

"True, but it would have been written off as an accident." I grinned. "Old Bull paid up like a gentleman, though. I've got a jeep now."

I got out the geological maps of the area and explained what I was going to do. She cottoned on fast, and said, "It's not so different from figuring out where to dig for archæological remains; it's just that the signs are different."

I nodded in agreement. "This area is called the Rocky Mountain Trench. It's a geological fault caused by large-scale continental movement. It doesn't move so as you'd notice, though; it's one of these long-term things. Anyway, in a trench things tend to get churned to the surface and we may find something, even though there was nothing on the Matterson land. I think we'll go right to the head of the valley."

It wasn't far, not more than ten miles, but we were bushed by the time we got there. I hadn't found anything on the way but I didn't expect to; we had struck in pretty much of a direct line and would do the main exploration going downhill on the way back, zig-zagging from one side of the valley to the other. It's easier that way.

By the time we made camp it was dark. There was no moon and the only light came from the fire which crackled cheerily and shed a pleasant glow. Beyond the fire was a big black nothing away down the valley which I knew was an ocean of trees—Douglas fir, spruce, hemlock, western red cedar—all commercially valuable. I said, "How much land have you got here?"

"Nearly ten thousand acres," said Clare. "Uncle John left it to me."

"It might pay you to set up your own small sawmill," I said. "You have a lot of ripe timber here which needs cutting out."

"I'd have to haul out the lumber across Matterson land," she said. "It's not economical to go the long way round. I'll think about it."

I let her attend to the cooking while I cut spruce boughs for the beds, one on each side of the fire. She ministered to the fire and the pans deftly with hardly a waste movement, and I could see I couldn't teach her anything about that department. Soon the savoury scent of hash floated up and she called, "Come and get it."

As she gave me a plateful of hash she smiled. "Not as good as the duck you served me."

"This is fine," I said. "Maybe we'll get some fresh meat to-morrow, though."

We ate and talked quietly, and had coffee. Clare felt in her pack and produced a flask. "Like a drink?"

I hesitated. I wasn't used to drinking when out in the woods; not out of any high principles, but the amount of liquor you can hump in a pack doesn't go very far, so I never bothered to carry any at all. Still, on a day when a guy can make $600,000 anything can happen, so I said, "One jigger would go down well."

It was a nice night. Even in summer you don't get many warm nights in the North-East Interior of British Columbia, but this was one of them—a soft and balmy night with the stars veiled in a haze of cloud. I sipped the whisky, and what with the smell of the wood-smoke and the peaty taste of the Scotch on my tongue I felt relaxed and at ease. Maybe the fact that I had a girl next to me had something to do with it, too; you don't meet many of those in the places I'd been accustomed to camping and when you did they had flat noses, broad cheekbones, blackened teeth and stank of rancid oil— delightful to other Eskimos but no attraction to me.

I undid a button of my shirt to let the air circulate, and stretched my legs. "I wouldn't have any other life than this," I said.

"You can do anything you want now," said Clare.

"Say, that's so, isn't it?" I hadn't thought much about the money; it hadn't yet sunk in that I was pretty rich.

"What are you going to do?" she asked.

I said dreamily, "I know of a place just north of the Great

Slave Lake where a man with a bit of dough—enough to finance a real exploration—would have a chance of striking it rich. It really needs a magnetometer survey and for that you need a plane, or better, a whirlybird—that's where the money comes in."

"But you *are* rich," she pointed out. "Or you will be as soon as the deal goes through. You'll have more than I inherited from Uncle John, and I never thought I was particularly poor."

I looked at her. "I said just now I wouldn't want any other life. You have your archæology—I have my geology. And you know damn' well we don't do those things just to pass the time."

She smiled. "I guess you're right." She peered at me closely. "That scar—there, on your chest. Is that . . .?"

"The accident? Yes, it is. They don't trouble much with plastic surgery where it doesn't usually show."

She put her hand out slowly and touched my chest with her fingertips. I said, "Clare, you *knew* Frank Trinavant. I know I haven't his face, but if I am Frank, then surely to God there must be something of him left in me. Can't you see anything of him?"

Her face was troubled. "I don't know," she said hesitatingly. "It was so long ago and I was so young. I left Canada when I was sixteen and Frank was twenty-two; he treated me as a kid sister and I never really *knew* him." She shook her head and said again, "I don't know."

Her fingertips traced the long length of the scar, and I put my arm round her shoulders and pulled her closer. I said, "Don't worry about it; it doesn't really matter."

She smiled and whispered, "You're so right. It doesn't matter—it doesn't matter at all. I don't care who you are or where you come from. All I know is that you're Bob Boyd."

Then we were kissing frantically and her arm was about me under my shirt and drawing me closer. There was a hiss and a sudden *wooof* as half a jigger of good Scotch got knocked into the fire, and a great yellow and blue flame soared to the sky.

Later that night I said drowsily, "You're a hard woman—you

made me gather twice as many spruce boughs as we needed."

She punched me in the ribs and snuggled closer, "You know what?" she said pensively.

"What?"

"You remember when you slept in the cabin that time—when I warned you about making passes?"

"Mmm—I remember."

"I *had* to warn you off. If I hadn't I'd have been a gone girl."

I opened one eye. "You *would*?"

"Even then," she said. "I still feel weak and mushy about it. Do you know you're quite a man, Bob Boyd? Maybe too much for me to handle. You'd better not radiate maleness so much around other women from now on."

I said, "Don't be silly,"

"I mean it."

A few minutes later she said, "Are you awake?"

"Uh-uh."

"You won't think I'm silly if I tell you something?"

"Depends what it is."

There was a silence, then she said, "You *earned* that negotiator's fee, you know—and never forget it. I was glad you earned it for another reason."

I said sleepily, "What reason?"

"You're too goddam proud," she said. "You might never have done anything about me if you'd thought about it too much. I thought you'd be scared off by my money, but now *you* have money, and it doesn't apply."

"Nonsense!" I said. "What's a mere six hundred thousand bucks? I want the lot. I pulled her closer. "I want everything you've got."

She gave a small cry and came to me again. Finally, just as the false dawn hesitated in the sky, she went to sleep, her head on my shoulder and one arm thrown across my chest.

3

The survey that should have taken four days stretched to two weeks. Maybe we were taking the honeymoon before we were married, but, then, so have lots of other folks—it's not the worst crime in the world. All I know is that it was the happiest time of my life.

We talked—my God, how we talked! For two people to really get to know each other takes a hell of a lot of words, in spite of the fact that the most important thing doesn't need words at all. By the time two weeks were up I knew a lot about archæology I didn't know before and she knew enough geology to know that the survey was a bust.

But neither of us worried about that. Three of the days towards the end were spent near a tiny lake we discovered hidden away in the folds of the hills. We pitched our camp near the edge and swam every morning and afternoon without worrying about costumes, and rubbed each other warm and dry when we came out shivering. At nights, in the hush of the forest, we talked in low tones, mostly about ourselves and about what we were going to do with the rest of our lives. Then we would make love.

But everything ends. One morning she said thoughtfully, "Matthew must be just about ready to send out a search-party. Do you realize how long we've been gone?"

I grinned. "Matthew has more sense. I think he's got around to trusting me." I rubbed my chin. "Still, we'd better get back, I suppose."

"Yes," she said glumly.

We cleaned up the camp and packed our gear in silence. I helped her on with her pack, then said, "Clare, you know we can't get married right away?"

Her voice was soft with surprise, "Why ever not?"

I kicked at a stone. "It wouldn't be fair. If I marry you and stay around here, things are going to bust loose and you might be hurt. If they're going to bust at all I want it to be before we're married."

She opened her mouth to argue—she was a great arguer—but I stopped her. "Susskind might be right," I said. "If I probe too deeply into my past I might very well go nuts. I wouldn't want that to happen to you."

She was silent for a while, then she said, "Supposing I accept that—what do you intend to do?"

"I'm going to break this thing wide open—*before* we're married. I've got something to fight for now, besides myself. If I come through the other side safely, then we'll get married.

If not—well, neither of us will have made an irrevocable mistake."

She said calmly, "You're the sanest man I know—I'm willing to take a chance on your sanity."

"Well, I'm not," I said. "You don't know what it's like, Clare: not having a past—or having two pasts, for that matter. It eats a man away from the inside. I've got to know, and I've got to take the chance of knowing. Susskind said it might break me in two and I don't want you too much involved."

"But I am too involved," she cried. "Already I am."

"Not as much as if we were married. Look, if we were married I'd hesitate when it's fatal to hesitate, I wouldn't push hard when pushing might win, I'd not take a chance when it was necessary to take a chance. I'd be thinking of you too damn' much. Give me a month, Clare; just one month."

Her voice was low. "All right, a month," she said. "Just one month."

We reached her cabin late at night, weary and out-of-sorts, neither of us having said much to the other during the day. Matthew Waystrand met us, smiled at Clare and gave me a hard look. "Got the fire lit," he said gruffly.

I went into my bedroom and shucked off my pack with relief, and when I'd changed into a fresh shirt and pants Clare was already luxuriating in a hot bath. I walked over to Matthew's place and found him smoking before a fire. I said, "I'm going pretty soon. Look after Miss Trinavant."

He looked at me glumly. "Think she needs it more'n usual?"

"She might," I said, and sat down. "Did you mail that letter she gave you?" I meant the Matterson contract going to her lawyer in Vancouver.

He nodded. "Got an answer, too." He cocked his head. "She's got it."

"Good." I waited for him to say something else and when he didn't I stood up and said, "I'm going now. I have to get back to Fort Farrell."

"Wait a minute," he said. "I've been thinking about what you said. You wanted to know if anything unusual happened about the time old John was killed. Well, I remember something, but I don't know if you'd call it unusual."

"What was that?"

"Old Bull bought himself a new car just the week after. It was a Buick."

"No," I said. "I wouldn't call it unusual."

Waystrand said, "Funny thing is that it was a replacement for a car he already had—a car he'd had just three months."

"Now that is funny," I said softly. "What was wrong with the old one?"

"Don't know," said Waystrand laconically. "But I hardly know what could have gone wrong in three months."

"What happened to it?"

"Don't know that, either. Just disappeared."

I thought about it. It would be a devil of a job trying to find out what had happened to a car twelve years earlier, especially a car that had "just disappeared". It didn't seem as though there would be much hope in following up such a tenuous lead as that, although who could tell? It might be worth a check in the licensing office. I said, "Thanks, Matthew—you don't mind me calling you Matthew?"

He frowned. "You took a long time on that survey of yours. How's Miss Trinavant?"

I grinned. "Never better—she assured me herself. Why don't you ask her?"

He grunted. "I don't reckon I will. Yeah, I don't mind you calling me by my given name. That's what it's for, ain't it?"

4

I left early next morning just after daybreak. I suppose you couldn't have called the few words Clare and I had an argument, but it left a certain amount of tension. She thought I was wrong and she wanted to get married right away, and I thought otherwise, and we had sulked like a couple of kids. Anyway, the tension dissolved in her bed that night; we were getting to be like a regular married couple.

We discussed the Matterson contract which her lawyer had thought not too larcenous, and she signed it and gave it to me.

I was to drop it in to Howard's office and get a duplicate signed by him. Just before I left, she said, "Don't stick your neck out too far, Bob. Old Bull wields a mean axe."

I reassured her and bumped up the track in the jeep and made Fort Farrell by late morning. McDougall was pottering about his cabin, and looked at me with a knowing eye. "You look pretty bushy-tailed," he said. "Made your fortune yet?"

"Just about," I said, and told him what had happened with Howard and Donner.

I thought he'd go into convulsions. He gasped and chortled and stamped his foot, and finally burst out with: "You mean you made six hundred thousand bucks just for insulting Howard Matterson? Where's my coat? I'm going down to the Matterson Building right away."

I laughed. "You're dead right." I gave him the contract. "See that gets to Howard—but don't part with it until you get a duplicate signed by him. And you'd better check it word for word."

"You're damned right I will," said Mac. "I wouldn't trust that bastard as far as I could throw a moose. What are you going to do?"

"I'm going up to the dam," I said. "It seems to worry Howard. What's been happening up there?"

"The dam itself is just about finished; they closed the sluices a couple of days ago and the lake has started to fill up." He chuckled. "They've had trouble bringing the generator armatures in; those things are big and heavy and they didn't find them too easy to manage. Got stuck in the mud right outside the power-house, so I hear."

"I'll have a look," I said. "Mac, when you're in town I want you to do something. I want you to spread the word that I'm the guy who survived the accident which killed the Trinavants."

He chuckled. "I get it—you're putting the pressure on. Okay, I'll spread the word. Everybody in Fort Farrell will know you are Grant by sundown."

"No," I said sharply. "You mention no names. Just say that I'm the guy who survived the accident, nothing more." He looked at me in bewilderment, so I said, "Mac, I don't know if I'm Grant and I don't know if I'm Frank Trinavant. Now,

Bull Matterson may think I'm Grant, but I want to keep the options open. There may come a time when I have to surprise him."

"That's tricky," said Mac admiringly. He eyed me shrewdly. "So you made up your mind, son."

"Yes, I made up my mind."

"Good," he said heartily. As an apparent afterthought, he said, "How's Clare?"

"She's fine."

"You must have given her place a good going-over."

"I did," I said smoothly. "I made absolutely sure there's nothing there worth the digging. Took two whole weeks on the job."

I could see he was going to pursue the subject a little further so I backed out. "I'm going up the dam," I said. "See you to-night—and do exactly what I said." I climbed into the jeep and left him to mull it over.

Mac had been right when he said the Matterson Corporation was having trouble with the generators. This was not a big hydro-electric scheme like the Peace River Project at Portage Mountain, but it was big enough to have generators that were mighty hard to handle when transporting them on country roads. They had been shipped up from the States and had got to the railhead quite easily, but from then on they must have been troublesome.

I nearly burst out laughing when I drove past the power-house at the bottom of the escarpment. A big logging truck loaded with an armature was bogged down in the mud, surrounded by a sweating, swearing gang shouting fit to bust a gut. Another gang was laying a corduroy road up to the power-house—a matter of nearly two hundred yards—and they were up to their knees in an ocean of mud.

I stopped and got out to watch the fun. I didn't envy those construction men one little bit; it was going to be one hell of a job getting that armature to the power-house in an intact condition. I looked into the sky and watched the clouds coming in from the west, from the Pacific, and thought it looked like rain. One good downpour and the trouble would be compounded tenfold.

A jeep came up the road and skidded to a halt in the mud and Jimmy Waystrand got out and stamped over. "What the hell are you doing here?"

I gestured to the stalled truck. "Just watching the fun."

His face darkened. "You're not welcome round here," he said harshly. "Beat it!"

"Have you checked with Bull Matterson lately?" I asked mildly. "Or hasn't Howard passed the word on."

"Oh, hell!" he said exasperatedly. I could see he was itching to toss me out but he was more afraid of old Bull than he was of me.

I said gently, "One wrong move from you, Jimmy, and a court order gets slapped on Bull Matterson. That'll cost him money and you can bet your last cent—if you're left with one —that it'll come out of your pay packet. Your best bet is to get on with your job and get that mess cleaned up before it rains again."

"Rains again!" he said savagely. "It hasn't rained yet."

"Oh? Then how come all the mud?"

"How in hell do I know?" he said. "It just came. It just . . ." He stopped and glared at me. "What the hell am I doing chewing the fat with you?" He turned and went back to his jeep. "Remember!" he shouted. "You make no trouble or you get whipped."

I watched him go, then looked down at the mud interestedly. It looked like ordinary mud. I bent down and took some in my hand and rubbed my fingers together. It felt slimy without any grittiness and was as smooth as soap. It would make a good grade of mud for lubricating an oil drill; maybe Matterson could make a few cents out of bottling and selling it. I tasted it with the tip of my tongue; there was no saltiness, but I didn't expect to find any because the human tongue is not a very reliable guide.

I watched the men slipping and sliding around for a while, then went to the back of the jeep and picked out two empty test-tubes. I picked my way into the middle of the mess, getting thoroughly dirty in the process, and stooped to fill them full of the greyish, slippery goo. Then I went back to the jeep, put the test-tubes away carefully, and drove on up the escarpment.

There was no mud anywhere on the escarpment nor on the

road which climbed it. They were still working on the dam, putting in the final touches, but the sluices were closed and the water was building up behind the concrete wall. Already the scene of desolation which I had grieved over was being covered by a clean sheet of water. Perhaps it was a merciful thing to do, to hide the evidence of greed. The new lake spread shallowly into the distance with the occasional spindly tree, too poor for even Bull Matterson to make a profit on, standing forlornly in the flood. Those trees would die as soon as the roots became water-logged, and they would fall and rot.

I looked back at the activity at the bottom of the escarpment. The men looked like ants I had seen—a crowd of ants trying to drag along the corpse of a big beetle they had found. But they weren't having as much success with the trucks as the ants did with the beetle.

I took one of the test-tubes and looked at it thoughtfully, then put it back in its nest of old newspaper. Ten minutes later I was batting it out on the road back to Fort Farrell.

I badly wanted to use a microscope.

VIII

I was still giving myself a headache at the microscope when Mac came back from town. He dumped a box full of groceries on the table which made the slide jiggle. "What you got there, Bob?"

"Trouble," I said, without looking up.

"For us?"

"For Matterson," I said. "If this is what I think it is, then that dam isn't worth two cents. I could be wrong, though."

Mac cackled with laughter. "Hey, that's the best news I've heard in years. What kind of trouble has he got?"

I stood up. "Take a look and tell me what you see."

He bent down and peered through the eyepiece. "Don't see much—just a few bits of rock—leastways, I think it's rock."

I said, "That's the stuff that goes to make up clay; it's rock, all right. What else can you tell me about it? Try to describe is as though you were telling a blind man."

He was silent for a while, then he said, "Well, this isn't my line. I can't tell you what kind of rock it is, but there are a few big round bits and a lot of smaller flat ones."

"Would you describe those flat bits as card-shaped?"

"Not so as you'd notice. They're just thin and flat." He straightened up and rubbed his eyes. "How big are those things?"

"The big roundish ones are grains of sand—they're pretty big. The little flat ones are about two microns across—they're the clay mineral. In this case I think it's montmorillonite."

Mac flapped his hand. "You lost me way back. What's a micron? It's a long time since I went to school and they've changed things pretty much since."

"A thousandth of a millimetre," I said.

"And this monty-what-d'you-call-it?"

"Montmorillonite—just a clay mineral. It's quite common." He shrugged. "I don't see anything to get excited about."

"Few people would," I said. "I warned Howard Matterson about this, but the damned fool didn't check. Anyone round here got a drilling-rig, Mac?"

He grinned. "Think you found an oil well?"

"I want something that'll go through not more than forty feet of soft clay."

He shook his head. "Not even that. Anyone who wants to bore for water hires Pete Burke from Fort St. John." He looked at me curiously. "You seem upset about this."

I said, "That dam is going to get smashed up if something isn't done about it fast. At least, I *think* it is."

"That wouldn't trouble me," said Mac decisively.

"It might trouble me," I said. "No dam—no Matterson Lake, and Clare loses four million dollars because the Forestry Service wouldn't allow the cut."

Mac stared at me open-mouthed. "You mean it's going to happen *now*?"

"It might happen to-night. It might not happen for six months. I might be wrong altogether and it might not happen at all."

He sat down. "All right, I give up. What can ruin a big chunk of concrete like that overnight?"

"Quick clay," I said. "It's pretty deadly stuff. It's killed a lot of people in its time. I haven't time to explain, Mac; I'm going to Fort St. John—I want access to a good laboratory."

I left quickly and, as I started the jeep, I looked across at the cabin and saw Mac scratch his head and bend down to look through the microscope. Then I was moving away from the window fast, the wheels spinning because I was accelerating too fast.

I didn't much like the two hundred miles of night driving, but I made good time and Fort St. John hadn't woken up when I arrived; it was dead except for the gas-refining plant on Taylor Flat which never sleeps. I was registered by a drowsy desk clerk at the Hotel Condil and then caught a couple of hours' sleep before breakfast.

Pete Burke was a disappointment. "Sorry, Mr. Boyd; not a chance. I've got three rigs and they're all out. I can't do anything for you for another month—I'm booked up solid."

That was bad. I said, "Not even for a bonus—a big one."

He spread his hands. "I'm sorry."

I looked from his office window into his yard. "There's a rig there," I said. "What about that?"

He chuckled. "Call that a rig! It's a museum piece."

"Will it go through forty feet of clay and bring back cores?" I asked.

"If that's all you want it to do, it might—with a bit of babying." He laughed. "I tell you, that's the first rig I had when I started this business, and it was dropping apart then."

"You've got a deal," I said. "If you throw in some two-inch coring bits."

"Think you can operate it? I can't spare you a man."

"I'll manage," I said, and we got down to the business of figuring out how much it was worth.

I left Burke loading the rig on to the jeep and went in search of a fellow geologist. I found one at the oil company headquarters and bummed the use of a laboratory for a couple of hours. One test-tube full of mud was enough to tell me what I wanted to know: the mineral content was largely montmorillonite as I had suspected, the salt content of the water was under four grams a litre—another bad sign—and half-an-hour's intensive reading of Grim's *Applied Clay Mineralogy* told me to expect the worst.

But inductive reasoning can only go so far and I had to drill to make sure. By early afternoon I was on my way back to

Fort Farrell with that drilling rig which looked as if it had been built from an illustration in Agricola's *De Re Metallica*,

2

Next morning, while inhaling the stack of hot-cakes Mac put before me, I said, "I want an assistant, Mac. Know any husky young guy who isn't scared of the Mattersons?"

"There's me."

I looked at his scrawny frame. "I want to haul a drilling-rig up the escarpment by the dam. You couldn't do it, Mac."

"I guess you're right," he said dejectedly. "But can I come along anyway?"

"No harm in that, if you think you're up to it. But I must have another man to help me."

"What about Clarry Summerskill—he doesn't like Matterson and he's taken a fancy to you?"

I said dubiously, "Clarry isn't exactly my idea of a husky young guy."

"He's pretty tough," said Mac. "Any guy called Clarence who survives to his age must be tough."

The idea improved with thinking. I could handle a drilling-rig but the stone-age contraption I'd saddled myself with might be troublesome and it would be handy to have a mechanic around. "All right," I said. "Put it to him. If he agrees, ask him to bring a tool kit—he might have to doctor a diseased engine."

"He'll come," said Mac cheerfully. "His bump of curiosity won't let him keep away."

By mid-morning we were driving past the power-house and heading up the escarpment road. Matterson's construction crew didn't seem to have made any progress in getting that armature towards its resting-place, and there was just as much mud, but more churned up than ever. We didn't stop to watch but headed up the hill, and I stopped about halfway up.

"This is it." I pointed across the escarpment. "I want to drill the first hole right in the middle, there."

Clarry looked up the escarpment at the sheer concrete wall of the dam. "Pretty big, isn't it? Must have cost every cent of what I heard." He looked back down the hill. "Those guys likely to make trouble, Mr. Boyd?"

"I don't think so," I said. "They've been warned off." Privately I wasn't too sure; walking around and prospecting was one thing, and operating a drilling-rig was something very different. "Let's get the gear out."

The heaviest part was the gasoline engine which drove the monster. Clarry and I manhandled it across the escarpment, staggering and slipping on the slope, and dumped it at the site I had selected, while Mac stayed by the jeep. After that it was pretty easy, though time-consuming, and it was nearly two hours before we were ready to go.

That rig was a perfect bastard, and if Clarry hadn't been along I doubt if I would ever have got it started. The main trouble was the engine, a cranky old two-stroke which refused to start, but Clarry cozened it, and after the first dozen refusals it burst into a noisy clatter. There was so much piston slap that I half expected the connecting-rod to bust clean out of the side of the engine, but it held together by good luck and some magic emanating from Clarry, so I spudded in and the job got under way.

As I expected, the noise brought someone running. A jeep came tearing up the road and halted just behind mine and my two friends of the first encounter came striding across. Novak yelled above the noise of the engine, "What the hell are you doing?"

I cupped my hand round my ear. "Can't hear you."

He came closer. "What are you doing with this thing?"

"Running a test hole."

"Turn the damned thing off," he roared.

I shook my head and waved him away downhill and we walked to a place where polite conversation wasn't so much of a strain on the eardrums. He said forcefully, "What do you mean—running a test hole?"

"Exactly what I say—making a hole in the ground to see what comes up."

"You can't do that here."

"Why not?"

"Because . . . because . . ."

"Because nothing," I snapped. "I'm legally entitled to drill on Crown land."

He was undecided. "We'll see about that," he said belligerently, and strode away back to his jeep. I watched him go, then went back to the drill to supervise the lifting of the first core.

Drilling through clay is a snap and we weren't going very deep, anyway. As the cores came up I numbered them in sequence and Mac took them and stowed them away in the jeep. We had finished the first hole before Jimmy Waystrand got round to paying us a visit.

Clarry was regretfully turning off the engine when Mac nudged me. "Here comes trouble."

I stood up to meet Waystrand. I could see he was having his own troubles down at the power-house by his appearance; he was plastered with mud to mid-thigh, splashed with mud everywhere else, and appeared to be in a short temper. "Do I have to have trouble with you again?" he demanded.

"Not if you don't want it," I said. "I'm not doing anything here to cause you trouble."

"No?" He pointed to the rig. "Does Mr. Matterson know about that?"

"Not unless someone told him," I said. "I didn't ask his permission—I don't have to."

Waystrand nearly blew his top. "You're sinking test holes between the Matterson dam and the Matterson power-house, and you don't think you need permission? You must be crazy."

"It's still Crown land," I said. "If Matterson wants to make this his private preserve he'll have to negotiate a treaty with the Government. I can fill this hillside as full of holes as a Swiss cheese, and he can't do anything about it. You might get on the telephone and tell him that. You can also tell him he didn't read my report and he's in big trouble."

Waystrand laughed. "He's in trouble?" he said incredulously.

"Sure," I said. "So are you, judging by the mud on your pants. It's the same trouble—and you tell Howard exactly that."

"I'll tell him," said Waystrand. "And I can guarantee you won't drill any more holes." He spat on the ground near my foot and walked away.

Mac said, "You're pushing it hard, Bob."

156

"Maybe," I said. "Let's get on with it. I want two more holes to-day. One on the far side and another back there by the road."

We hauled the rig across the hillside again and sank another hole to forty feet, and then laboriously hauled it all the way back to a point near the jeep and sank a third hole. Then we were through for the day and packed the rig in the back of the jeep. I wanted to do a lot more boring and normally I would have left the rig on the site but this was not a normal operation and I knew that if I left the rig it would look even more smashed up by morning.

We drove down the hill again and were stopped at the bottom by a car which skidded to a stop blocking the road. Howard Matterson got out and came close. "Boyd, I've had all I can stand from you," he said tightly.

I shrugged. "What have I done now?"

"Jimmy Waystrand says you've been drilling up there. That comes to a stop right now."

"It might," I agreed. "If I've found out what I want to know. I wouldn't have to drill, Howard, if you'd read my report. I told you to watch out for qui——"

"I'm not interested in your goddam report," he butted in. "I'm not even interested in your drilling. But what I am interested in is this story I hear about you being the guy who survived the crash in which old Trinavant was killed."

"Are people saying that?" I said innocently.

"You know goddam well they're saying it. And I want that stopped, too."

"How can *I* stop it?" I asked. "I'm not responsible for what folks say to each other. They can say what they like—it doesn't worry me. It seems to worry you, though." I grinned at him pleasantly. "Now, I wonder why it should."

Howard flushed darkly. "Look, Boyd—or Grant—or whatever else you call yourself—don't try to nose into things that don't concern you. This is the last warning you're going to get. My old man gave you a warning and now it's coming from me, too. I'm not as soft as my old man—he's getting foolish in his old age—and I'm telling you to get to hell out of here before you get pushed."

I pointed at his car. "How can I get out with that thing there?"

"Always the wisecracks," said Howard, but he went back and climbed into his car and opened a clear way. I eased forward and stopped alongside him. "Howard," I said. "I don't push so easily. And another thing—I wouldn't call your father soft. He might get to hear of it and then you'd find out personally how soft he is."

"I'll give you twenty-four hours," said Howard, and took off. His exit was spoiled by the mud on the road; his wheels failed to grip and he skidded sideways and the rear of his auto crunched against a rock. I grinned and waved at him and carried on to Fort Farrell.

Clarry Summerskill said thoughtfully, "I did hear something about that yesterday. Is it right, Mr. Boyd?"

"Is what right?"

"That you're this guy, Grant, who was smashed up with John Trinavant?"

I looked at him sideways, and said softly, "Couldn't I be anyone else besides Grant?"

Summerskill looked puzzled. "If you were in that crash I don't rightly see who else you could be. What sort of games are you playing, Mr. Boyd?"

"Don't think about it too much, Clarry," advised Mac. "You might sprain your brain. Boyd knows what he's doing. It's worrying the Mattersons, isn't it? So why should it worry you, too?"

"I don't know that it does," said Clarry, brightening a little. "It's just that I don't understand what's going on."

Mac chuckled. "Neither does anyone else," he said. "Neither does anyone else,—but we're getting there slowly." Clarry said, "You want to watch out for Howard Matterson, Mr. Boyd—he's got a low boiling-point. When he gets going he can be real wild. Sometimes I think he's a bit nuts."

I thought so, too, but I said, "I wouldn't worry too much about that, Clarry, I can handle him."

When we pulled up in front of Mac's cabin, Clarry said, "Say, isn't that Miss Trinavant's station wagon?"

"It is," said Mac. "And there *she* is."

Clare waved as she came to meet us. "I felt restless," she said. "I came over to find out what's going on,"

"Glad to have you," said Mac. He grinned at me. "You'll have to sleep out in the woods again."

Clarry said, "Your auto going all right, Miss Trinavant?"

"Perfectly," she assured him.

"That's great. Well, Mr. Boyd, I'll be getting along home—my wife will be wondering where I am. Will you need me again?"

"I might," I said. "Look, Clarry; Howard Matterson saw you with me. Will that make trouble for you? I'm not too popular right now."

"No trouble as far as I'm concerned—he's been trying to put me out of business for years and he ain't done it yet. You want me, you call on me, Mr. Boyd." He shook his head. "But I sure wish I knew what was going on."

Mac said, "You will, Clarry. As soon as we know ourselves."

Summerskill went home and Mac shepherded Clare and me into the cabin.

"Bob's being awfully mysterious about something," he said. "He's got some crack-brained idea that the dam is going to collapse. If it does, you'll be four million dollars to the bad, Clare."

She shot me a swift glance. "Are you serious?"

"I am. I'll be able to tell you more about it when I've looked at the cores I've got in the jeep. Let's unload them, Mac."

Pretty soon the table was filled with the lengths of two-inch cylindrical core. I arranged them in order and rejected those I didn't want. The cores I selected for inspection had a faint film of moisture on the surface and felt smooth and slick, and a check on the numberings told me that they'd come up from the thirty-foot level. I separated them in three heaps and said to Clare, "These came from three borings I made to-day on the escarpment between the dam and the power-house." I stroked one of them and looked at the moisture on my finger. "If you had as many sticks of dynamite you couldn't have anything more dangerous."

Mac moved away nervously and I smiled. "Oh, these are all right here; it's the stuff up at the escarpment I'm worried about. Do you know what 'thixotropic' means?"

Clare shook her head and Mac frowned. "I should know," he admitted. "But I'm damned if I do."

I walked over to a shelf and picked up a squeeze-tube. "This is the stickum I use on my hair; it's thixotropic gel." I uncapped the tube and squeezed some of the contents into the palm of my hand. "Thixotropic means 'to change by touch'. This stuff is almost solid, but when I rub it in my hands, like this, it liquefies. I brush it on to my hair—so—and each hair gets a coating of the liquid. Then I comb it and, after a while, it reverts to its near solid state, thus keeping the hair in place."

"Very interesting," said Mac. "Thinking of starting a beauty parlour, son?"

I made no comment. Instead I picked up one of the cores. "This is clay. It was laid down many thousands of years ago by the action of glaciers. The ice ground the rock to powder, and the powder was washed down rivers until it reached either the sea or a lake. I rather think that this was laid down in a fresh-water lake. I'll show you something. Got a sharp knife, Mac?"

He gave me a carving knife and I cut two four-inch lengths from the middle of the same core. One of the lengths I put on the table standing upright. "I've prepared for this," I said, "because people won't believe this unless they see it, and I'll probably have to demonstrate it to Bull Matterson to get it through his thick skull. I have some weights here. How many pounds do you suppose that cylinder of clay can support?"

"I wouldn't know," said Mac. "I suppose you *are* getting at something."

I said, "The cross-section is a bit over three square inches." I put a ten-pound weight on the cylinder and quickly added another. "Twenty pounds." A five-pound weight went on top of that. "Twenty-five pounds." I added more weights, building up a tower supported by the cylinder of clay. "Those are all the weights I have—twenty-nine pounds. So far we've proved that this clay will support a weight of about fifteen hundred pounds a square foot. Actually, it's much stronger."

"So what?" said Mac. "You've proved it's strong. Where has it got you?"

"Is it strong?" I asked softly. "Give me a jug and a kitchen spoon."

He grumbled a bit about conjuring tricks, but did what I asked. I winked at Clare and picked up the other clay cylinder. "Ladies and gentlemen, I assure you there is nothing up

160

my sleeve but my arm." I put the clay into the jug and stirred vigorously as though I were mixing cake dough. Mac looked at me unimpressed, but Clare was thoughtful.

I said, "This is the meaning of thixotropic," and poured the contents of the jug on to the table. A stream of thin mud splashed out and flowed in a widening pool of liquidity. It reached the edge of the table and started to drip on to the floor.

Mac let out a yelp. "Where did the water come from? You had water already in that jug," he accused.

"You know I didn't. You gave me the jug yourself." I pointed at the dark pool. "How much weight will that support, Mac?"

He looked dumbfounded. Clare stretched out her hand and dipped a finger into the mud. "But where *did* the water come from, Bob?"

"It was already in the clay." I pointed at the other cylinder still supporting its tower of weights. "This stuff is fifty per cent water."

"I still don't believe it," said Mac flatly. "Even though I've seen it."

"I'll do it again if you like," I offered.

He flapped his hand. "Don't bother. Just tell me how this clay can hold water like a sponge."

"Remember when you looked through the microscope—you saw a lot of little flat chips of rock?" He nodded. "Those chips are very small, each about five-hundredths of a millimetre, but there are millions of them in a cubic inch. And—this is the point—they're stacked up like a house of cards. Have you ever built up a house of cards, Clare?"

She smiled. "I've tried, but it's never got very high. Uncle John was an expert at it."

I said, "Then you know that a house of cards structure is mostly empty space." I tapped a core. "Those spaces are where the water is held."

Mac still looked a little bewildered, but he said, "Sounds feasible."

Clare said quietly, "There's more, isn't there? You haven't shown us this just as a party trick."

"No, I haven't," I said. "As I said, when this sediment was first laid down it was at the bottom of the sea or a lake. Any salts in the water tend to have an electrolytic action—they act as a kind of glue to stick the whole structure together. If, however, the salts leach out, or if there were very few salts in the first place, as would happen if the deposit were laid down in fresh water, then the glueing effect becomes less. Clare, what is the most characteristic thing about a house of cards?"

"It falls down easily."

"Right! It's a very unstable structure. I'd like to tell you a couple of stories to illustrate why this stuff is called quick clay. Deposits of quick clay are found wherever there has been much glaciation—mainly in Russia, Scandinavia and Canada. A few years ago, round about the middle fifties, something happened in Nicolet, Quebec. The rug was jerked from under the town. There was a slide which took away a school, a garage, quite a few houses and a bull-dozer. The school wound up jammed in a bridge over the river and caught fire. A hole was left six hundred feet long, four hundred feet wide and thirty feet deep."

I took a deep breath. "They never found out what triggered that one off. But here's another one. This happened in a place called Surte in Sweden, and Surte is quite a big town. Trouble was it slid into the Gota river. Over a hundred million cubic feet of topsoil went on the rampage and it took with it a railroad, a highway and the homes of three hundred people. *That* one left a hole half a mile long and a third of a mile wide. It was started by someone using a pile-driver on a new building foundation."

"A pile-driver!" Mac's mouth stayed open.

"It doesn't take much vibration to set quick clay on the move. I told you it was thixotropic, it changes by touch—and it doesn't need much of a touch if the conditions are right. And when it happens the whole of a wide area changes from solid to liquid and the topsoil starts to move—and it moves damn' fast. The Surte disaster took three minutes from start to finish. One house moved four hundred and fifty feet—how would you like to be in a house that took off at nearly twenty miles an hour?"

"I wouldn't," said Mac grimly.

I said, "Do you remember what happened to Anchorage?"

"Worst disaster Alaska ever had," said Mac. "But that was a proper earthquake."

"Oh, there *was* an earthquake, but it wasn't that that did the damage to Anchorage. It *did* trigger off a quick clay slide, though. Most of the town happened to be built on quick clay and Anchorage took off for the wide blue yonder, which happened to be in the direction of the Pacific Ocean."

"I didn't know that," said Mac.

"There are dozens of other examples," I said. "During the war British bombers attacking a chemical factory in Norway set off a slide over an area of fifty thousand square yards. And there was Aberfan in South Wales: that was an artificial situation—the slag heap of a coal mine—but the basic cause was the interaction of clay and water. It killed a schoolful of children."

Clare said, "And you think the dam is in danger?"

I gestured at the cores on the table. "I took three samples from across the escarpment, and they show quick clay right across. I don't know how far it extends up and down, but it's my guess that it's all the way. There's an awful lot of mud appeared down at the bottom. A quick clay slide can travel at twenty miles an hour on a slope of only one degree. The gradient of that escarpment must average fifteen degrees, so that when it goes, it'll go fast. That power plant will be buried under a hundred feet of mud and it'll probably jerk the foundations from under the dam, too. If that happens, then the whole of the new Matterson lake will follow the mud. I doubt if there'd be much left of the power plant."

"Or anyone in it," said Clare quietly.

"Or anyone in it," I agreed.

Mac hunched his shoulders and stared loweringly at the cores. "What I don't understand is why it hasn't gone before now. I can remember when they were logging on the escarpment and cutting big trees at that. A full grown Douglas fir hits the ground with a mighty big thump—harder than a pile-driver. The whole slope should have collapsed years ago."

I said, "I think the dam is responsible. I think the quick clay layer surfaces somewhere the other side of the dam. Everything was all right until the dam was built, but then they closed the sluices and the water started backing up and covering the quick clay outcropping. Now it's seeping down in the quick clay all under the escarpment."

Mac nodded. "That figures."

"What are you going to do about it?" asked Clare.

"I'll have to tell the Mattersons somehow," I said. "I tried to tell Howard this afternoon but he shut me up. In my report I even told him to watch out for quick clay, but I don't think he even read it. You're right, Clare: he's a sloppy business-man." I stretched. "But right now I want to find out more about these samples—the water content especially."

"How will you do that?" asked Mac interestedly.

"Easy. I cut a sample and weigh it, then cook the water out on that stove there, then weigh it again. It's just a sum in subtraction from then on."

"I'll make supper first," said Clare. "Right now you'd better clear up this mess you've made."

After supper I got down to finding the water content. The shear strength of quick clay depends on the mineral constitu-ents and the amount of water held—it was unfortunate that this particular clay was mainly montmorillonite and deficient in strength. That, combined with a water content of forty per cent, averaged out over three samples, gave it a shear strength of about one ton per square foot.

If I was right and water was seeping into the quick clay strata from the new lake, then conditions would rapidly become worse. Double the water percentage and the shear strength would drop to a mere 500 pounds a square foot, and a heavy-footed construction man could start the whole hillside sliding.

Clare said, "Is there anything that can be done about it—to save the dam, I mean?"

I sighed. "I don't know, Clare. They'll have to open the sluices again and get rid of the water in the lake, locate where the clay comes to the surface and then, maybe, they can seal it off. Put a layer of concrete over it, perhaps. But that still leaves the quick clay under the escarpment in a dangerous condition."

"So what do you do then?" asked Mac.

I grinned. "Pump some more water into it." I laughed out-right at the expression on his face. "I mean it, Mac; but we pump in a brine solution with plenty of dissolved salts. That will put in some glue to hold it together and it will cease to be thixotropic."

"Full of smart answers, aren't you?" said Mac caustically. "Well, answer this one. How do you propose getting the Matterson Corporation to listen to you in the first place? I can't see you popping into Howard's office to-morrow and getting him to open those sluices. He'd think you were nuts."

"I could tell him," said Clare.

Mac snorted in disgust. "From Howard's point of view, you and Bob have gypped him out of four million bucks that were rightly his. If you tried to get him to close down construction on the dam he'd think you were planning another fast killing. He wouldn't be able to figure how you're going to do it, but he'd be certain you were pulling a fast one."

I said, "What about old Bull? He might listen."

"He might," said Mac. "On the other hand, you asked me to spread that story around Fort Farrell and he might have got his dander up about it. I wouldn't bank on him listening to anything you have to say."

"Oh, hell!" I said. "Let's sleep on it. Maybe we'll come up with something to-morrow."

I bedded down in the clearing because Clare had my bed, and I stayed awake thinking of what I had done. Had I achieved anything at all? Fort Farrell had been a murky enough pool when I arrived, but now the waters were stirred up into muddiness and nothing at all could be seen. I was still butting my head against the mystery of the Trinavants and, so far, nothing had come of my needling the Mattersons.

I began to think about that and came up against something odd. Old Bull had known who I was right from the start and he had got stirred up pretty fast. From that I argued that there was something he had to hide with regard to the Mattersons—and perhaps I was right, because it was he who had clamped down on the name of Trinavant.

Howard, on the other hand, had been stirred up about other things—our argument about Clare, his defeat in the matter of my prospecting on Crown land, another defeat in the matter of the cutting of the lumber on Clare's land. But then I had asked Mac to spread around the story that I was the survivor of the Trinavant auto smash—and Howard had immediately blown his top and given me twenty-four hours to get out of town.

165

Now, that was very odd! Bull Matterson had known who I was but hadn't told his son—why not? Could it be there was something he didn't want Howard to know?

And Howard—where did he come into all this? Why was he so annoyed when he found who I was? Could he be trying to protect his father?

I heard a twig snap and sat up quickly. A slim shadow was moving through the trees towards me, then Clare said in a warm voice, "Did you think I was going to let you stay out here alone?"

I chuckled. "You'll scandalize Mac."

"He's asleep," she said, and lay down beside me. "Besides, it isn't easy to scandalize a newspaperman of his age. He's grown-up, you know."

3

Next morning, at breakfast, I said, "I'll have a crack at Howard—try to get him to see sense."

Mac grunted. "Do you think you can just walk into the Matterson Building?"

"I'll go up to the escarpment and put a hole in it," I said. "That'll bring Howard running to me. Will you ask Clarry if he'll join the party?"

"That'll bring Howard," Mac agreed.

"You could get into a fight up there," Clare warned.

"I'll chance that," I said, and stabbed at a hot-cake viciously. "It might be just what's needed to bring things into the open. I'm tired of this pussyfooting around. You stay home this time, Mac."

"You try to keep me away," Mac growled, and mimicked, "You can't stop *me* fossicking on Crown land." He rubbed his eyes. "Trouble is, I'm a mite tired."

"Didn't you sleep?"

He kept his eyes studiously on his plate. "Too much moving around during the night; folks tromping in and out at all hours—could have been Grand Central Station."

Clare dropped her eyes, and her throat and face flushed deep pink. I smiled amiably. "Maybe *you* ought to have slept out in the woods—it was right peaceful out there."

166

He pushed back his chair. "I'll go get Clarry."

I said, "Tell him there might be trouble, then it's up to him if he comes or not. It's not really his fight."

"Clarry won't mind a crack at Howard."

"It's not Howard I'm thinking of," I said. I had Jimmy Waystrand in mind, and those two bodyguards of his who ran his errands.

But Clarry came and we pushed off up the Kinoxi road. Clare wanted to come too, but I squashed that idea flat. I said, "When we come back we'll be hungry—and maybe a bit banged up. You have a good dinner waiting, and some bandages and the mercuro-chrome."

No one stopped us as we drove past the power-house and up the escarpment road. We drove nearly to the top before stopping because I wanted to sink a test hole just below the dam. It was essential to find out if the quick clay strata actually ran under the dam.

Clarry and I manhandled the gasoline engine across the escarpment and got the rig set up. No one paid us any attention although we were in plain sight. Down at the bottom of the hill they were still trying to get that generator armature into the power plant and had made a fair amount of progress, using enough logs on the ground to feed Matterson's sawmill for twenty-four hours. I could hear the shouting and cursing as orders were given, but that was drowned out as Clarry started the engine and the drilling began.

I was very careful with the cores as they came up from the thirty-foot level and held one of them out to Mac. "It's wetter here," I said.

Mac shifted his boots nervously. "Are we safe here? It couldn't go now, could it?"

"It could," I said. "But I don't think it will—not just yet." I grinned. "I'd hate to slide to the bottom, especially with the dam on top of me."

"You guys talk as though there's going to be an earthquake," said Clarry.

"Don't sprain your brain," said Mac. "I've told you before." He paused. "That's exactly what we are talking about."

"Huh!" Clarry looked about him. "How can you predict an earthquake?"

"There's one coming now," I said, and pointed. "Here comes Howard with storm signals flying."

He was coming across the hillside with Jimmy Waystrand close behind, and when he got closer I saw he was furious with rage. He shouted, "I warned you, Boyd; now you'll take the consequences."

I stood my ground as he came up, keeping a careful eye on Waystrand. I said, "Howard, you're a damn' fool—you didn't read my report. Look at all that mud down there."

I don't think he heard a word I said. He stabbed a finger at me. "You're leaving right now—we don't want you around."

"We! I suppose you mean you and your father." This was no good. There was no point in getting into a hassle with him when there were more important things to be discussed. I said, "Listen, Howard; and, for God's sake, simmer down. You remember I warned you about quick clay?"

He glared at me. "What's quick clay?"

"Then you didn't read the report—it was all set out in there."

"To hell with your report—all you keep yammering about is that goddam report. I paid for the damn' thing and whether I read it or not is my affair."

I said, "No, it isn't—not by a long chalk. There may be men ki——"

"Will you, for Christ's sake, shut up about it," he yelled.

Mac said sharply, "You'd better listen to him, Howard."

"You keep out of this, you old fool," commanded Howard. "And you too, Summerskill. You're both going to regret being mixed up with this man. I'll see you regret it—personally."

"Howard, lay off McDougall," I said. "Or I'll break your back."

Clarry Summerskill spat expertly and befouled Howard's boot. "You don't scare me none, Matterson."

Howard took a step forward and raised his fist. I said quickly, "Hold it! Your reinforcements are coming, Howard." I nodded across the hillside to where two men were coming across the rough ground—one a chauffeur in trim uniform supporting the other by the arm.

Bull Matterson had come out of his castle at last.

Clarry's jaw dropped as he stared at the old man and at the

big black Bentley parked on the road. "Well, I'm damned!" he said softly. "I haven't seen old Bull in years."

"Maybe he's come out to defend his bull-calf," said Mac sardonically.

Howard went to help the old man, the very picture of filial devotion, but Bull angrily shook away the offered hand. From the look of him, he was quite spry and able to get on by himself. Mac chuckled. "Why, the old guy is in better shape than I am."

I said, "I have a feeling that this is going to be the moment of truth."

Mac glanced at me slyly. "Don't they say that about bull-fighting when the matador poises his sword to kill the bull? You'll have to have a sharp sword to kill this one."

The old man finally reached us and looked around with a hard eye. To his chauffeur he said curtly, "Get back to the car." He cast an eye on the drilling-rig, then swung on Jimmy Waystrand. "Who are you?"

"Waystrand. I work down on the power plant."

Matterson lifted his eyebrows. "Do you? Then get back on your job."

Waystrand looked uncertainly at Howard, who gave a short nod.

Matterson stared at Clarry. "I don't think we need you, either," he said harshly. "Or you, McDougall."

I said quietly, "Go and wait by the jeep, Clarry," and then stared down the old man. "McDougall stays."

"That's up to him," said Matterson. "Well, McDougall?"

"I'd like to see a fair fight," said Mac cheerfully. "Two against two." He laughed. "Bob can take Howard and I reckon you and me are fairly matched for the Old Age Championship." He felt the top of the gasoline engine to see if it was still hot, then nonchalantly leaned his rump against it.

Matterson swivelled his head. "Very well. I don't mind a witness for what I'm going to say." He fixed me with a cold blue eye and I must have been nuts ever to think he had the faded eyes of age. "I gave you a warning, Grant, and you have chosen to ignore it."

Howard said, "Do you really think this guy is Grant—that he was in the crash?"

"Shut up," said Matterson icily and without turning his head. "I'll handle this. You've made enough mistakes already —you and your fool sister." He hadn't taken his eye off me. "Have you anything to say, Grant?"

"I've got a lot to say—but not about anything that might have happened to John Trinavant and his family. What I want to say is of more immediate impor——"

"I'm not interested in anything else," Matterson cut in flatly. "Now put up or shut up. Do you have anything to say? If not, you can get to hell out of here, and I'll see that you do it."

"Yes," I said deliberately. "I might have one or two things to say. But you won't like it."

"There have been a lot of things in my life I haven't liked," said Matterson stonily. "A few more won't make any difference." He bent forward a little and his chin jutted out. "But be very careful about any accusations you may make—they may backfire on you."

I saw Howard moving nervously. "Christ!" he said, looking at Mac. "Don't push things."

"I told you to shut up," said the old man. "I won't tell you again. All right, Grant: say your piece, but bear this in mind. My name is Matterson and I own this piece of country. I own it and everyone who lives in it. Those I don't own I can lean on—and they know it." A grim smile touched his lips. "I don't usually go about talking this way because it's not good politics—people don't like hearing that kind of truth. But it is the truth and you know it."

He squared his shoulders. "Now, do you think anyone is going to take your word against mine? Especially when I bring your record out. The word of a drug-pusher and a drug-addict against mine? Now, say your piece and be damned to you, Grant."

I looked at him thoughtfully. He evidently believed I had uncovered something and was openly challenging me to reveal it, depending upon Grant's police record to discredit me. It was a hell of a good manœuvre if I did know something, which I didn't—and if I were Grant.

I said, "You keep calling me Grant. I wonder why."

The planes of his iron face altered fractionally. "What do you mean by that?" he said harshly.

"You ought to know," I said. "You identified the bodies." I smiled grimly. "What if I'm Frank Trinavant?"

He didn't move but his face went a dirty grey. Then he swayed a little and tried to speak, and an indescribable choking sound burst from his lips. Before anyone could catch him he crashed to the ground like one of his own felled trees.

Howard rushed forward and stooped over him and I looked over his shoulder. The old man was still alive and breathing stertorously. Mac pulled at my sleeve and drew me away. "Heart-attack," he said. "I've seen it before. That's why he never moved from home much."

In the moment of truth my sword had been sharp enough —perhaps too sharp. But was it the moment of truth? I still didn't know. I still didn't know if I were Grant or Frank Trinavant. I was still a lost soul groping blindly in the past.

IX

It was touch and go.

Howard and I had a yelling match over Matterson's prostrate body. Howard did most of the yelling—I was trying to cool him off. The chauffeur came across from the Bentley at a dead run, and Mac pulled me away. He jerked his thumb at Howard. "He'll be too busy with his father to attend to you —but Jimmy Waystrand won't, if he comes up here. Howard will sick his boys on to you like dogs on to a rabbit. We'd better get out of here."

I hesitated. The old man looked bad and I wanted to stay to see that he was all right; but I saw the force of Mac's argument—this was no place to linger any more. "Come on," I said. "Let's move."

Clarry Summerskill met us and said, "What happened—did you hit the old guy?"

"For God's sake!" said Mac disgustedly. "He had a heart-attack. Get into the jeep."

"What about the rig?" asked Clarry.

"We leave it," I said. "We've done all we can here." I stared across the hillside at the small group below the dam. "Maybe we've done too much."

I drove the jeep down the hill prepared for trouble, but nothing happened as we passed the power-house and when we were on the road out I relaxed. Mac said speculatively, "It knocked the old bastard for six, didn't it? I wonder why?"

"I'm beginning to wonder about Bull Matterson," I said. "He doesn't seem too bad to me."

"After what he said to you?" Mac was outraged.

"Oh, sure; he's tough, and he's not too particular about his methods as long as they work—but I think he's essentially an honest man. If he had deliberately confused the identification in the auto crash he'd have *known* who I was. It wouldn't have come as such a surprise as to give him a heart-attack. He's just had a hell of a shock, Mac."

"That's true." He shook his head. "I don't get it."

"Neither do I," said Clarry. "Will someone tell me what's going on?"

I said, "You can do something for me, Clarry. Take a trip to the licensing office and check if Bull Matterson registered a new Buick round about the middle of September, 1956. I heard he did."

"So what?" said Mac.

"So what happened to the old one? Matthew Waystrand told me it was only three months old. You are in the used auto business, Clarry. Is it possible to find out what happened to that car?"

His voice rose. "After twelve years? I should say it was impossible." He scratched his head. "But I'll try."

He pulled up at Mac's cabin and Clarry went into Fort Farrell in his own car. Mac and I told Clare what had happened and she became gloomy. "I used to call him Uncle Bull," she said. Her head came up. "He wasn't a bad man, you know. It was only when that man Donner came into the business that the Matterson Corporation became really tight-fisted."

Mac was sceptical. "Donner isn't the man at the top; he's only a paid hand. It's Bull Matterson who is reaping the profits from the finagling that was done with the Trinavant Trust."

She smiled wanly. "I don't think he considered it to be cheating. I think Bull just thought of it as a smart business deal—nothing dishonest."

172

"But goddam immoral," observed Mac.

"I don't think considerations like that ever enter his head," she said. "He's just become a machine for making money. Is he really ill, Bob?"

"He didn't look too bright when I saw him last," I said. "Mac, what do we do now?"

"What about—the Trinavant business or the dam?" He shrugged. "I don't think it's up to you this time, Bob. The ball's in Howard's court and he might come after you."

"We must do something about the dam. Perhaps I can talk to Donner."

"You'd never get in to see him—Howard will prime him with a suitable story. All you can do is to sit tight and wait for the breaks—or you can leave town."

I said, "I wish to God I'd never heard of Fort Farrell." I looked up. "Sorry, Clare."

"Don't be a fool," said Mac. "Are you turning soft just because an old man has a heart-attack? Hell, I didn't think he had a heart in the first place. Keep fighting, Bob. Try to give them another slug while they're off balance."

I said slowly, "I could get out of town. I could go to Fort St. John and try to stir up some interest there. Someone, somewhere, might be intrigued at the idea of a dam collapsing."

"Might as well go there as anywhere else," said Mac. "Because one thing is certain—the Mattersons are mad as hornets right now, and no one in Fort Farrell is going to lift a finger to help you with Howard breathing down his neck. Old Bull was right—the Mattersons own this country and everyone knows it. Nobody will listen to you now, Bob. As for going into Fort St. John, you'll have to go through Fort Farrell to do it. My advice to you is to wait until after dark."

I stared at him. "Are you crazy? I'm no fugitive."

His face was serious. "I've been thinking about that. Now that Bull is out of the way there'll be no one to hold Howard down. Donner can't do it, that's for certain. And Jimmy Waystrand and some of Howard's goons could make an awful mess of you. Remember what happened a couple of years ago to Charley Burns, Clare? A broken leg, a broken arm, four busted ribs and his face kicked in. Those boys play rough—and I'll bet they're looking for you now, so don't go into Fort Farrell just yet."

Clare stood up. "There's nothing to stop *me* going into Fort Farrell."

Mac cocked an eye at her. "For what?"

"To see Gibbons," she said. "It's about time the police were brought into this."

He shrugged. "What can Gibbons do? One sergeant of the RCMP can't do a hell of a lot—not in this set-up."

"I don't care," she said. "I'm going to see him." She marched from the cabin and I heard her car start up. I said to Mac sardonically, "What was that you were saying a little earlier about giving them another slug while they're off balance?"

"Don't be nippy," said Mac. "I spoke a little too fast, that's all. I just hadn't got everything digested."

"Who was this guy, Burns?"

"Someone who got on the wrong side of Howard. He was beaten up—everyone knows why, but no one could pin anything on Howard. Burns left town and never came back. I'd forgotten about him—and he hadn't got in Howard's hair half as much as you have. I've never seen him so mad as I did this morning." He got up and looked into the stove. "I want some tea. I'm just going out to the woodpile."

He walked out and I just sat there thinking about what to do next. The trouble was that I had still got no further on the Trinavant mystery, and the man who could tell me about it was probably in hospital at that moment. I felt inclined to go into Fort Farrell, walk into the Matterson Building and bust Howard one in the snoot, which might not solve anything but it would do me a lot of good.

The door slammed open and I knew I wouldn't have to go into Fort Farrell. Howard stood on the threshold with a rifle in his hands, and the round hole in the muzzle looked as big as the bottomless pit. "Now, you sonofabitch," he said, breathing hard. "What's this about Frank Trinavant?"

He took two steps forward and the rifle didn't waver. Behind him Lucy Atherton slipped into the cabin and smiled maliciously at me. I started to get out of the chair and he said in a hard voice, "Sit down, buster; you're not going anywhere."

I flopped back. Why are you interested in Frank Trinavant?" I asked. "Hasn't he been dead a long time?" It was hard to keep my voice level. Facing a gun has a curious effect on the vocal chords.

"Scared, Boyd?" asked Lucy Atherton.

"Keep quiet," said Howard. He moistened his lips and came forward slowly and stared at me. "Are you Frank Trinavant?"

I laughed at him. I had to work at it, but I laughed.

"Damn you, answer me!" he shouted, and his voice cracked. He took a step forward and his face worked convulsively. I kept a wary eye on his right hand and hoped the rifle didn't have too light a trigger. I was hoping that he would come one step closer so I would have a fighting chance of knocking the barrel aside, but he stopped short. "Now you listen to me," he said in a trembling voice. "You're going to answer me and you're going to tell me the truth. Are you Frank Trinavant?"

"What does it matter?" I said. "I might be Grant—I might be Trinavant. Either way, I was in the car, wasn't I?"

"Yeah, that's right," he said. "You were in the car." He went dangerously calm and studied my face. "I knew Frank, and I've seen pictures of Grant. You look like neither. You had a lot of surgery. I see. It must have hurt a lot—I hope."

Lucy Atherton giggled.

"Yeah," he said. "You were in the car. It's only if you look real close you can see the scars, Lucy. They're just fine hairlines."

I said, "You seem interested, Howard."

"I wondered about that—you calling me Howard all the time. Frank used to do it. Are you Frank?"

"What's the difference?"

"Sure," he agreed. "What's the difference? What did you see in the car? Now you can tell me, or you're going to have to get some more surgery done on that pretty face."

"You tell me what I saw—and I'll tell you if you're right."

His face tightened in anger and he made a slight move, but not enough to bring him within range of my hands. It was awkward sitting down; it's not a position from which you can move quickly.

"Let's have no games," he said harshly. "Talk!"

A voice from the door said, "Lay that gun down, Howard, or I'll blow your spine out."

175

I flicked my eyes to the door and saw Mac holding a double-barrelled shotgun on Howard. Howard froze and turned slowly, pivoting on his hips. Mac said sharply, "The gun, Howard—lay it down. I won't tell you again."

"He's right," said Lucy quickly. "He's got a shotgun."

Howard lowered the rifle and I stood and took it as it slipped from his hands; if it dropped on the floor it might have gone off. I stepped back and looked at Mac, who smiled grimly. "I put the shotgun into the jeep this morning in case we needed it," he said. "Lucky I did. All right, Howard: walk over to that wall. You too, sister Lucy."

I examined Howard's rifle. The safety-catch was off, and as I worked the action, a round flew out of the breech. I hadn't been very far from having my head blown off. "Thanks, Mac," I said.

"No time for formalities," he said. "Howard, sit on the floor with your back to the wall. And you, Lucy. Don't be shy."

Howard's face was filled with hate. He said, "You're not going to get far with this kind of thing. My boys will nail you, Boyd."

"Boyd?" I said. "I thought it was Grant—or Trinavant. The thing that's eating you, Howard, is that you don't *know*, do you? You're not sure."

I turned to Mac. "What do we do now?"

He grinned. "You go and follow Clare. Make sure she brings Gibbons on the run. We can nail this sonofabitch for armed hold-up. I'll keep him here."

I looked at Howard dubiously. "Don't let him jump you."

"He'd be too scared." Mac patted the shotgun. "I've got buckshot in this baby; at this range it would blow him clean in two. Hear that, Howard?"

Matterson said nothing, and Mac added, "That goes for sister Lucy, too. You just sit there, Mrs. Atherton."

"Okay, Mac," I said. "I'll see you within the half-hour." I picked up Howard's rifle and unloaded it, tossing the bullets into a corner. As I ran for the jeep I threw the rifle into the undergrowth and within a minute I was on my way.

But not for long. There was a corner just before the turn-off to Fort Farrell and, as I spun the wheel and the jeep swung round, I saw a tree felled right across the track. There was hardly time to jam on the brakes and the jeep rammed it head-on. Fortunately I'd slowed for the corner but the impact didn't do the front end of the jeep any good, and I nearly rammed my head through the windshield.

The next thing I knew was that someone was trying to haul me out of the cab. There was a shrill whistle and a shout— "Here he is!"

Someone's hand was on my shirt, bunching it up and pulling at me. So I bent my head and bit it hard. He yelled and let go, which gave me a moment to collect my wits. I could only see the one man who was coming at me again, so I dived across the cab and out the other side. The front end of a jeep is too restricted for a big guy like me to fight comfortably.

I was still a bit dizzy from the crack on the head but not too dizzy to see the man coming round the rear of the jeep. He came a bit too fast for his own good and ran his kneecap into my boot, which just about ruined him. While he lay on the ground howling in pain I ran for the woods, conscious of the shouts behind and the thud of running boots as at least two men chased me.

I'm not much good for the hundred yards' sprint because I carry too much beef for it, but I can put up a pretty fair turn of speed when necessary. So could the guys behind and for the first five minutes there was nothing in it. But they tended to waste breath on shouting while I kept my big mouth shut, and soon they began to lag behind.

Presently I risked a look over my shoulder. There was no one in sight although I could hear them hollering, so I ducked behind a tree and got my breath back. The shouts came nearer and I heard the crackle of twigs. The first man plunged past and I let him go, stooping to pick up a rock which just fitted into my fist. I heard the second man coming and stepped out from behind the tree right in his path.

He didn't have time to stop—or to do anything at all. His mouth was open in surprise, so I closed it for him, putting all my muscle into a straight jolt to his jaw. It was the rock in my fist that did it, of course; I felt a slight crunch and his feet slid out from under him. He fell on his back and rolled over and he didn't make another move.

I listened for a while. The guy I had let go in front was out of sight but I could still hear him shouting. I also heard other shouts coming from the road, and I estimated there must be a dozen of them, so I took off again at right-angles to my original course, moving as fast as I could without making too much noise.

I didn't do too much thinking at this time, but I realized that these were Matterson's dogs that were set on me with probably Jimmy Waystrand leading the pack. My first job was to give them the slip and that wasn't going to be too easy. These were loggers, used to the woods, and probably they knew more about them than I did. They certainly knew the local country better, so I had to make sure I wasn't herded the way they wanted me to go. A better thing would be to lose them altogether.

The woodland this close to town held a spindly third growth of no commercial value and used mainly for cutting wood for the domestic fires of Fort Farrell. The trouble was that a man could see a long way through it and there was no place to hide, especially if you wore a red woollen shirt like I did. I thought I had got clear without being seen, but a shout went up and I knew I hadn't made it.

I abandoned the quietness bit and put on speed again, running uphill and feeling the strain in my lungs. On top of the rise I looked across the valley and saw the real woodlands with the big trees. Once over there I might have a chance of dodging them, and I went down into that valley lickety-split like a buck-rabbit being chased by a fox.

From the shouts behind I reckoned I was keeping my distance, but that was no consolation. Any dozen determined men can run down a loner in the long haul; they can spell and pace each other. But the loner has one advantage—the adrenalin jumped into his system by the knowledge of what will happen to him when he gets caught. I had no illusions about that; a dozen husky loggers don't put out a lot of energy in running cross-country just to play patty-cake at the end of it. If they caught me I'd probably be ruined for life. Once, up in the North-West Territories, I'd seen the results when a man was ganged-up on and booted around; the end-result could hardly be called human.

So I ran for my life because I knew I'd have no life worth living if I lagged. I ignored the muscular pains creeping into my legs, the harsh rasp of air in my throat and the coming stitch in my side. I just settled down for the long, long run across that valley. I didn't look back to see how close they were because that wastes time; not much—maybe fractions of a second every time you turn your head—but fractions of a second add up and could count in the end. I just pumped my legs and kept a watch on the ground ahead of me, choosing the easiest way but not deviating too much from the straight line.

But I kept my ears open and could hear the yells coming from behind, some loud and close and others fainter and farther back. The pack was stringing out with the fittest men to the front. If there had been only two men as before I'd have stopped and fought it out, but there was no chance against a dozen, so I plunged on and lengthened my stride, despite the increasing pain in my side.

The trees were closer now, tall trees reaching to the sky— Douglas fir, red cedar, spruce, hemlock—the big forest that spread north clear to the Yukon. Once lost in there I might have a fighting chance. There were trees big enough to hide a truck behind, let alone a man; there was a confusion of shadow as the sun struck through the leaves and branches creating dappled patterns; there were fallen trees to duck behind and holes to hide in and a thick layer of pine needles on which a man could move quietly if he looked where he was putting his feet. The forest was safety of a sort.

I reached the first big fir and risked a look back. The first man was two hundred yards away and the rest were strung out behind him in a long line. I sprinted for the next tree, changed course and headed for another. Here, at the edge, the trees weren't too crowded and there were large vistas where a man could be seen for quite a long way, but it was a damn' sight better than being caught in the open.

I was moving more slowly now, intent on quietness rather than speed as I dodged from tree to tree- zig-zagging each time and keeping an eye on the way back because I had to make sure I wasn't seen. It was no longer a race—it was a cat-and-mouse game, and I was the mouse.

Now that I was no longer operating on full steam I managed to get my breath back, but my heart still pumped violently until I thought it was going to burst its way through my chest. I managed a grin as I hoped the other guys weren't in better shape and dodged deeper into the forest. Behind, everything had gone quiet and for a moment I thought they had given up, but then I heard a shout from the left and an answering call from the right. They had spread out and had begun to comb the woods.

I pressed on, hoping they had no experienced trackers among them. It was unlikely they would have, but the possibility couldn't be ignored. It was a long time till sunset, nearly four hours to go, and I wondered if Matterson's boys would have enough incentive to go right through with it. I had to find a good hiding-place and let the search flow over me, so I kept my eyes open as I slipped deeper into the dappled green.

Ahead was a rock outcropping of tumbled boulders with plenty of cover in it. I ignored it—they wouldn't pass up a chance like that and they'd search every cranny. Still, that would take time—there's an awful lot of holes where a man *may* be hiding compared to the one he is using, and this was my one hope. I heard a shout from way back and judged they were making poorer time than I, wasting valuable minutes in poking and prying, deviating to look behind that fallen log or into that likely-looking hole where a tree had fallen and torn up its roots.

I didn't want to be driven too far into the forest. I was worried about Mac and how long he could hold Matterson and his sister. Clare had gone to see Gibbons, but there had been no particular urgency at that time and Gibbons might not move his butt fast enough. So I wanted to get back to the cabin somehow, and every yard I was driven into the forest meant another yard to go back.

The firs soared up all round, their massive trunks branchless for a full fifty feet. Yet I found what I was looking for— a young cedar with branches low enough for it to be climbed. I swarmed up into it and crawled out on one of the branches. The spreading boughs would hide me from the ground—I hoped—but as an added precaution I took off that revealing red shirt and wadded it into a bundle. Then I waited.

Nothing happened for over ten minutes, then they came so quietly that I saw the flicker of movement before I heard a sound. A man came into view at the edge of the clearing and looked about him, and I froze into immobility. He was not more than fifty yards away and he was very still as he stared into the woods across the clearing, his head swinging round as he gave the area a real thorough going-over with his eyes. Then he gestured and another man joined him and the two of them walked across the clearing light-footedly.

A man doesn't look up much. The bones of his skull project over his eyes just where his eyebrows are—that's to protect his eyes from the direct sun. And looking up much puts a strain on the neck muscles, too. I guess it's all been designed by nature to protect the delicate eye from glare. Anyway, it so happens that only an experienced searcher will scan the tops of trees—it's something that doesn't occur to the average man and there's a built-in resistance—partly psychological and partly physiological—to see that it doesn't.

These two were no exceptions. They walked across the clearing emulating Fenimore Cooper's heroes and stopped for a moment below the cedar. One of them said, "I think it's a bust."

The other cut him short with a chopping motion of his hand. "Quiet! He could be around here."

"Not a chance. Hell, he's probably five miles from here by now. Anyway, my feet hurt."

"More'n your feet'll hurt if Waystrand finds you falling down on the job."

"Huh, that young punk!"

"Can you whip him? You're welcome to try but I wouldn't put my money on you. Anyway, Matterson wants this guy found, so come on and stop moaning about it."

They moved away across the clearing but I stayed put. In the distance I heard a shout, but otherwise all was still. I waited a full fifteen minutes before I dropped from the tree and, although it was chilly, I had left my shirt up there and out of sight.

I didn't retrace my steps but cut across at an angle in the direction of Mac's cabin. If I could get back there and if Mac still had Howard cooped up he would make a valuable hostage, a passport to safety. I trod carefully, and viewed every open space suspiciously before venturing into it, and I penetrated right to the edge of the forest before I encountered anyone.

In any crowd of men there is always one like this—the man who doesn't pull his weight, the man who goofs off when there's a job to be done. He was sitting with his back to a tree and rolling a cigarette. He had evidently had foot trouble because, although he was wearing his boots, they were unlaced and he must have had them off.

He was a damned nuisance because, although he was goofing off, he was ideally placed at the edge of the forest to survey the scrubland I had to cross to get to Mac's cabin. In fact, if Waystrand had placed him there deliberately he couldn't have chosen a better position.

I retreated noiselessly and looked about for a weapon. This attack had to be sudden and quick; I didn't know how many other guys were within shouting distance and one squawk from him and I'd be on the run again. I selected a length of tree bough and cut the twigs from it with my knife. When I went back he was still there, had got his cigarette lit and was puffing it with enjoyment.

I circled and came up behind the tree very carefully and raised the cudgel as I edged round. He never knew what hit him. The wood caught him on the temple and he didn't even gasp as he fell sideways, the cigarette falling from his lax fingers. I dropped the club and stepped in front of him, automatically stepping on the glowing cigarette as it crisped the pine needles. Hastily I grabbed him under the arms and hauled him to a place where we weren't overlooked.

I had a moment of panic when I thought he was dead, but he groaned and his eyelids fluttered a little before he relapsed into unconsciousness. I had no compunction about hitting a man when he wasn't looking, but I didn't want to kill anybody—not because I didn't feel like it but because a man could get hanged that way. The law is pretty strict about dead bodies and I wanted Gibbons on my side.

He was wearing a dark grey shirt which was just what I wanted, so I stripped it from him and then searched him for good measure. He didn't have much in his pockets—a wallet containing three dollar-bills and some personal papers, a few coins, a box of matches and a pack of tobacco and a jack-knife. I took the matches and the knife and left him the rest, then I put on the shirt, that neutral, pleasantly inconspicuous shirt which was as good as a disguise.

I put him in a place where no one would stumble over him too easily, then walked boldly out of the forest, cutting across

182

the scrubland towards Mac's cabin which couldn't have been more than a mile away according to my calculations. I had gone halfway when someone hailed me. Fortunately he was a long way off, too far to see my face in the fading light. "Hey, you! What happened?"

I cupped my hands to my mouth. "We lost him."

"Everyone's wanted at McDougall's cabin," he shouted. "Matterson wants to talk to you."

I felt my heart give a sudden bump. What had happened to Mac? I waved, and shouted, "I'll be there."

He carried on in the opposite direction, and as he passed, I angled away and kept my face from him. As soon as he was out of sight I broke into a run until I saw lights in the gathering darkness, then I paused, wondering what to do next. I had to find out what had happened to Mac, so I circled the cabin to come at it from the other, unexpected side and as I drew nearer I heard the rumble of the voices of many men.

Someone had brought a pressure-lantern from the cabin and set it up on the stoop, and from where I was lying by the stream I could see there were about twenty men lounging about in front of the cabin. Counting the dozen who had chased me and who were still coming back from the forest, that made a force of at least thirty—maybe more. It looked as though Howard was gathering an army.

I stayed there for a long time, maybe an hour, and tried to figure out what was happening. There was no sign of Mac, nor of Clare and Gibbons. I saw Waystrand come into the group. He looked tired and worn, but then, so did I, and I didn't feel a bit sorry for him. He asked someone an obvious question and was waved to the cabin. I watched him enter and didn't have long to wait for an explanation of the gathering, because almost immediately he came out again followed by Howard.

Howard stood on the stoop and held up his hands and everything became quiet except for the croaking of frogs around me. "All right," said Howard loudly. "You know why you're here. You're going to look for a man—a man called Boyd. Most of you have seen him around Fort Farrell so you know what he looks like. And you know why we want him, don't you?"

A rumble came from the group of men. Howard said, "For those of you who came in late— this is it. This man Boyd beat up my father—he hit a man more than twice his age—an old man. My father is seventy-six years old. How old do you reckon Boyd is?"

My blood chilled at the audible reaction from the mob in front of the stoop. "Now you know why I want him," yelled Howard. He waved his arm. "You're all on full pay until he's found, and I'll give a hundred dollars to the man who spots him first."

A yell went up from the mob and Howard waved his arm violently to get silence. "What's more," he shouted, "I'll give a thousand dollars each to the men who catch him."

There was pandemonium for a while and Howard let it go on.

I could see the twisted grin on his face in the harsh light of the pressure-lantern. He held up his arms for silence again. "Now, we've lost him for the moment. He's in the woods out there. He has no food, and my betting is that he's scared. But watch it, because he's armed. I came here to beat the daylights out of him because of what he did to my old man, and he held me up at rifle-point. So watch it."

Waystrand whispered to him, and Howard said, "I may be wrong there, boys. Waystrand here says he didn't have a gun when he made for the woods, so that makes your job easier. I'm going to divide you up into teams and you can get going. When you catch him, keep him there and send a message back to me. Understand that—don't try to bring him back into Fort Farrell. This is a slippery guy and I don't want to give him a chance to get away. Keep him on the spot until I get there. Tie him up. If you don't have any rope then break his goddam leg. I won't cry if you rough him up a bit."

The laughter that broke out was savage. Howard said, "All right. I want Waystrand, Novak, Simpson and Henderson to head the teams. Come into the cabin, you guys, and I'll lay things out."

He went back into the cabin followed by Waystrand and three others. I stayed where I was for a couple of minutes, wishing I knew what was being said in the cabin, then I withdrew, slowly and carefully, and went back into the darkness.

If ever I had seen anyone working up a lynching party it

had been Howard. The bastard had set a mob thirsting for my blood and I wouldn't be safe anywhere around Fort Farrell—not with a thousand dollars on my head. Those loggers of his were tough boys and he'd filled them up with such a pack of goddam lies that it would be useless for me to try to explain anything.

I was struck by a sudden idea and wormed my way to the place where I had bedded down the previous night, and was deeply thankful that I had slept out and had been sloppy enough not to take my gear back to the cabin. My pack was still lying where I had left it, and I hastily replaced the few items I had taken out. Now I had at least the absolute minimum necessary for a prolonged stay in the woods—everything except food and a weapon.

There came a renewed burst of noise from the direction of the cabin and the sound of several engines starting up. Someone came blundering through the undergrowth and I withdrew away from the cabin, still undecided as to what to do next. In all my life I had never been in as tough a position as this, except when I woke up in hospital to find myself an erased blank. I tightened the pack straps and thought grimly that if a man could survive that experience he could survive this one.

Use your brains, I told myself. *Think of a safe place.*

The only safe place I could think of was the inside of a jail —just as an honoured guest, of course. An RCMP sergeant wouldn't—or shouldn't—let anyone tramp over him and I reckoned I'd be as safe in one of Gibbons's cells as anywhere else until this blew over and I could find someone sane enough to start explaining things to. So I headed for the town, circling around so as not to walk on the road. I wanted to head for Gibbons's place by the least populous route.

I should have known that Howard would have it staked out. The last thing in the world he wanted was for the cops to interfere, and if I got to Gibbons then maybe the jig would be up. Howard would never be able to hide the fact that I didn't hit old Matterson and the truth would inevitably come out, something he couldn't afford to happen. So even though he thought I was somewhere in the woods he had coppered his bet by staking out the police-station just in case I made a run for Gibbons.

Of course I didn't think of that at the time, although I was very careful as I walked the quiet streets of Fort Farrell. It was a linear town, long and thin, built around the one main street, and I had chosen a route which took me past very few houses on the way to the police-station. There was a moon, an unfortunate circumstance, and I tried to keep as much in the shadows as I could. I met nobody on the way and I began to think I would make it. I hoped to God that Gibbons was around.

I was within a hundred yards of the station when I was tackled. I suppose being so near had made me let my guard down. The first thing I knew was a burst of bright light in my eyes as someone shone a flashlight on me—then a cry: "That's him!"

I ducked and skidded to one side and felt something thump into my pack with a frightening force and the impact threw me off-balance so that I sprawled on the ground. The flash-lamp shone around searching, and as it found me I got a boot in my ribs. I rolled frantically away, knowing that if I didn't get up I could be kicked to death. Those loggers' boots are heavy and clinched with steel and a real good kick can smash a man's rib-cage and drive the bone into his lungs.

So I rolled faster and faster although impeded by the pack, trying to escape that damned flashlamp. A voice said hoarsely, "Get the bastard, Jack!" and a badly aimed boot crashed into the back of my right thigh. I put my hands on the ground and swung round with my legs, flailing them wildly, and tripped up someone who came crashing on top of me.

His head must have hit the ground because he went flaccid and I heaved him off and staggered to my feet just in time to meet a bull-like rush from another man. The guy with the flashlamp was standing well back, damn him, giving me no chance to get away into darkness, but at least it put me and my attackers on equal terms.

I had no odd ideas about fair play—that's a civilized idea and civilization stops when you set thirty men against one. Besides, I had learned my fighting in the North-West Terri-tories, and the Marquess of Queensberry's rules don't hold good north of the 60th Parallel. I swung my boot, sideways on, at the man's kneecap and scraped it forcibly down his shin to end up by stamping with my heel on his foot just above the instep. My left fist went for his guts and my right

186

hand for his chin, palm open so that the heel of my hand forced his head back and my fingertips were in his eyes.

He got in a couple of good body blows while I was doing that but thereafter was fully occupied with his own aches and pains. He howled in anguish as I raked his shin to the bone and his hands came up to protect his eyes. I gave him another thump in the belly and the breath came out of him in a great gasp and he started to crumple. I'm a big guy and pretty strong, so I just picked him up and threw him at my friend with the flashlamp.

He made contact and the flashlamp went out. I heard the glass break as it hit the ground. I didn't stick around to hear any more because there may have been more of the goons. I just picked up my feet and headed out of town.

2

By midnight I was well into the forest and pretty well tuckered out. I had been chased from town and nearly caught, too, and when I doubled back I nearly ran into another bunch of Matterson's men who must have been pulled in from the woods. So I gave it up and struck west, that being the direction I thought they would least expect me to go—into the wilderness.

I didn't expect to gain anything by going west, but at least it gave me a breathing-space and time to think out a plan of action. The moon was high in the sky and I found a quiet hole among some rocks and shucked off my pack with relief. I was tired. I had been on the run more or less continuously for ten hours and that tends to take the steam out of a man. I was hungry, too, but I couldn't do much about that except tighten up my belt.

I reckoned I was safe for the time being. Matterson couldn't possibly organize a proper search at night even if he knew the exact area in which I was hiding, and the only danger was in someone falling over me by accident. I needed rest and sleep and I had to have it, because next day was likely to be even livelier.

I took off my boots and changed my socks. My feet were going to be my best friends for the foreseeable future and I didn't want them going bad on me. Then I had a sip of water from the canteen attached to my pack. I was all right for water—I had filled the canteen when crossing a stream—but I still didn't waste it because I didn't know this country very well and maybe there wouldn't be a stream next time I wanted one.

I sat back flexing my toes luxuriously and thought of the events of the day. It was the first time I'd been able to put two thoughts together consecutively—all my efforts had been directed to sheer survival.

First, I thought of Clare and wondered what in hell had happened to her. She had gone to see Gibbons pretty early and should have arrived back at Mac's cabin, with or without the cop, long before sunset. Yet I had seen no sign of her during Howard Matterson's lynch-law speech. That left two possibilities—one, that she was in the cabin, which meant she was held under duress; and two, she wasn't in the cabin, in which case I didn't know where the devil she was.

Then there was Mac. Somehow Matterson had come from under Mac's shotgun safely, which meant that something must have happened to Mac. Let's say he was out of the game —and Clare, too—which left me the only one of us free and able to do anything at all. And so far all I had been able to do was to run like an Olympic marathon runner.

I thought of Howard's speech and the specific instructions he had issued and tried to figure out what he meant to do. I was to be held where I was captured until Howard caught up with me. And that added up to a nasty situation, because I couldn't see what he could do with me apart from killing me.

He certainly couldn't kill me openly; I doubted if his men would stand for that. But suppose I was "accidentally" killed; supposing Howard said that he had killed me in self-defence. There were many ways of arranging something like that Or I could "escape" from Howard, never to be seen again. In the deep woods there are places where a body might never be found for a century.

All of which led me to take a fresh look at Howard Matterson. Why would he want me dead? Answer: because it was *he* who had something to do with the crash—not old Bull. And what could he have to do with the crash? Answer: he had probably arranged it personally—he was probably an outright murderer.

I had checked on where Bull had been when the crash happened, but it had never occurred to me to check on Howard. One doesn't think of a kid of twenty-one as being a murderer when there's someone else at hand with all the motives and qualifications. I had slipped there. Where was Howard when the crash happened? Answer: I didn't know —but I could make a good guess.

After all, he could capture me and take me back to Fort Farrell, and then the whole story would blow up in his face. He *had* to get rid of me and the only way was by another killing.

I shivered slightly. I had led a pretty tough life but I had never been pursued with deadly intention before. This was quite a new experience and likely to be my last. Of course, it was still possible for me to quit. I could head farther west and then south-west to the coast, hitting it at Stewart or Prince Rupert; I could then get lost and never see Fort Farrell again. But I knew I wouldn't do that because of Mac and Clare— especially Clare.

I dug a blanket from my pack and wrapped it round me. I was dead beat and in no fit condition to make important decisions. It would be time enough in daylight to worry about what to do next. I dropped off to sleep with Mac's words echoing in my ears: *Keep fighting; give them another slug while they're off balance.*

It was very good advice whether they were off balance or not. I sleepily made up my mind about two things. The first was that I had to fight on ground of my own choosing, ground that I knew well. The only ground in this area that I knew well was the Kinoxi Valley, and I knew that very well because I had prospected it thoroughly, and I knew I could out-dodge anyone there.

The other vital thing was to make the chasing of Bob Boyd a very unprofitable undertaking. I had to make it unmistakably clear that to harry me in any way wasn't worth anything like a thousand dollars, and the only way these loggers could be taught a lesson like that was by violence. Three of them, perhaps, had already come to this conclusion; one had a busted kneecap, another a busted jaw, and the third a shin laid open to the bone. If stronger measures were necessary for discouragement then I would see they were administered.

I wanted to get Howard in the open from behind his screen of thugs and the only way to do that was to scare them off. It takes a hell of a lot to scare the average logger; it's a dangerous job of work in the first place and they don't scare easily. But it was something I had to do—I had to get them off my back—and I would have to do things so monstrously efficient in their execution that they would think twice about attempting to earn that thousand dollars.

X

I was on the move by sunrise next morning and heading north. I reckoned I was twelve miles west of Fort Farrell and so was moving parallel to the road that had been driven up to the Kinoxi Valley, but far enough away from it to be out of the net of Matterson's searchers—I hoped. Hunger was beginning to gnaw at my gut but not so much as to weaken—I could go, maybe, another day and a half before food became a real problem, and I might have to.

I plugged away hour after hour, keeping up a steady pace, travelling faster than I normally did when on the move. I reckon I was keeping up a steady speed of two and a half miles an hour over the ground, which wasn't at all bad across this kind of country. I kept looking back to check the landscape, not so much to see if I was being followed but to make sure I was travelling in a straight line. It's awfully easy to veer and most people do quite unconsciously. That's why, in bad conditions such as fog or thick snow, you find guys getting lost and wandering in circles. I've been told that it's due to differences in the length of your legs and the resulting slight difference in stride. Long ago I'd checked up on my own propensity to veer and figured I tended to swerve about 4° from the straight line and to the right; after I knew that it didn't take much practice to be able to correct it consciously.

But it's always a good idea to check on theory and I like to know what the landscape looks like behind me; such knowledge could be useful if I had to make a run for it. There was, of course, always the possibility of seeing someone else, and I had already figured that in country where the *average* population was one person to three square miles, then anyone I saw was unlikely to pop up accidentally and was therefore to be regarded with suspicion.

I was able to find food of a sort while still on the move. I picked up and pocketed maybe a couple of pounds of mushrooms. I knew they were good eating but I'd never eaten them raw and I wouldn't experiment. I doubted if they'd kill me but I didn't want to be put out of action with possible stomach cramps, so I just kept them by me although my mouth was drooling.

I rested up frequently but not for long each time—about five minutes in the hour. More than that would have tightened my leg muscles and I needed to keep limber. I didn't even stop for long at midday, just enough to change my socks, wash the others in a stream and pin them to the top of my pack to dry out while I was on the move. I filled my water canteen and pressed on north.

Two hours before sunset I began to look round for a place to camp—a nice secluded place—and found one on top of a rise where I had a good view into valleys on both sides. I shucked my pack and spent half an hour just looking, making sure there was no one around, then I undid the pack and produced from the bottom my own personal survival kit.

In the North-West Territories I had been in the wilderness for months at a time, and since rifle ammunition is heavy to carry, I had tended to conserve it and find other ways of getting fresh meat. The little kit which I carried in an old chocolate tin was the result of years of experience and it always lived in the bottom of my pack ready for use.

The jack-rabbits come out and play around just before sunset, so I selected three wire snares, carefully avoiding the fish-hooks in the tin. I once stuck a fish-hook in my finger just at the start of a season and ignored the wound. It festered and I had to come into a trading-post before the season was halfway through with a blood-poisoned finger the size of a banana. That little prick with a hook cost me over a thousand dollars and nearly cost me my right hand so I've been careful of fish-hooks ever since.

I had seen rabbit trails in plenty so I staked out the three snares, then collected some wood for a fire, selecting small dead larch twigs and making sure they were bone dry. I took them back to camp and arranged them so as to make a small fire, but did not put a match to it. It would be time for that after sunset when the smoke would not be noticeable, little though it would be. I found a small birch tree and cut a cylinder of bark with my hunting knife, and arranged it around the fire as a shield, propping it up with small stones so as to allow a bottom draught.

Half an hour after sunset I lit the fire and retreated a hundred yards to see the effect. I could see it because I knew it was there, but it would take a man as good as me or better to find it otherwise. Satisfied about that, I went back, poured some water into a pannikin and set the mushrooms to boil. While they were cooking I went to see if I had any luck with the snares. Two of them were empty but in one I had caught a half-grown doe rabbit. She didn't have more than a couple of mouthfuls of flesh on her but she'd have to satisfy me that night.

After supper I did a circuit of the camp, then came back and risked a cigarette. I reckoned I'd come nearly thirty miles heading due north. If I angled north-west from here I should strike the Kinoxi Valley in about fifteen miles, hitting it about a third of the way up just where Matterson's logging camp was. That could be dangerous but I had to start hitting back. Prowling around the edges of this thing was all very well but it would get me nowhere at all; I had to go smack into the centre and cause some trouble.

After a while I made sure the fire was out and went to sleep.

2

I topped a rise and looked over the Kinoxi Valley at just about two o'clock next afternoon. The new Matterson Lake had spread considerably since I had seen it last, and now covered about one-third of its designed extent, drowning out the wasteland caused by the logging. I was just about level with the northernmost point it had reached. The logged area extended considerably farther and stretched way up the valley, almost, I reckoned, to the Trinavant land. Matterson had just about stripped his land bare.

As the logging had proceeded the camp had been shifted up-valley and I couldn't see it from where I was standing, so I dipped behind the ridge again and headed north, keeping the ridge between me and the valley bottom. Possibly I was now on dangerous ground, but I didn't think so. All my activities so far had been centred on Fort Farrell and on the dam which was to the south at the bottom of the valley.

I put myself in Howard Matterson's place and tried to think his thoughts—a morbid exercise. Boyd had caused trouble in Fort Farrell, so watch it—we nearly caught him there and he might try for it again. Boyd was interested in the dam, he was drilling there—so watch it because he might go back. But Boyd had never shown much interest in the Kinoxi Valley itself, so why should he go there?

I knew what I was going to do there—I was going to raise hell! It was ground I had prospected and I knew all the twists and turns of the streams, all the draws and ravines, all the rises and falls of the land. I was going to stick to the thick forest in the north of the valley, draw in Howard's hunters and then punish them so much that they'd be afraid to push it further. I had to brake this deadlock and get Howard in the open.

And I thought the best place to start raising hell was the Matterson logging camp.

I went north for four miles and finally located the camp. It was situated on flat ground in the valley bottom and set right in the middle of the ruined forest. There was too much open ground around it for my liking but that couldn't be helped, and I saw that I could only move about down there at night. So I used the remaining hours of daylight in studying the problem.

There didn't seem to be much doing down there, nor could I hear any sounds of activity from farther up the valley where the loggers should have been felling. It looked as though Howard had pulled most of the men away from the job to look for me and I hoped they were still sitting on their butts around Fort Farrell. There was a plume of smoke rising from what I judged was the cookhouse and my belly rumbled at the thought of food. That was another good reason for going down to the camp.

I watched the camp steadily for the next three hours and didn't see more than six men. It was too far to judge really properly but I guessed these were old-timers, the cooks and bottle-washers employed around the camp who were too old or not fit enough to be of use, either in logging or in chasing Bob Boyd. I didn't see I'd have much trouble there.

I rubbed my chin as I thought of the consequences of Howard's action and the conclusions to be drawn from them. He'd pulled off his loggers at full pay to search for me, and that was wasting him an awful lot of time and money. If he didn't get them back on the job it might be too late to save the trees—unless he'd opened the sluices on the dam to prevent the lake encroaching any farther up the valley. But even then he'd be running into financial trouble; the sawmill must have been geared to this operation and the cutting off of the flow of raw lumber from the valley would have its repercussions there—if he didn't get his loggers back to work pretty soon the sawmill would have to close down.

It seemed to me that Howard wanted me very badly—this was another added brick in the structure of evidence I was building. It wasn't evidence in the legal sense, but it was good enough for me.

Towards dusk I made my preparations. I took the blankets from the pack and strapped them on the outside and, when it was dark enough, I began my descent to the valley floor. I knew of a reasonably easy way and it didn't take long before I was approaching the edge of the camp. There were lights burning in two of the prefabricated huts, but otherwise there was no sign of life beyond the wheezing of a badly played harmonica. I ghosted through the camp, treading easily, and headed for the cookhouse. I didn't see why I shouldn't stock up on supplies at Howard's expense.

The cookhouse had a light burning and the door was ajar. I peered through a window and saw there was no one in sight so I slipped through the doorway and closed the door behind me. A big cooking-pot was steaming on the stove and the smell of hash nearly sent me crazy, but I had no time for luxuries—what I wanted was the stock-room.

I found it at the end of the cookhouse; a small room, shelved all round and filled with canned goods. I began to load cans into my pack, taking great care not to knock them together. I used shirts to separate them in the pack and added a small sack of flour on top. I was about to emerge when someone came into the cookhouse and I closed the door again quickly.

There was only one door from the stock-room and that led into the cookhouse—a natural precaution against the healthy appetites of thieving loggers. For the same reason there was no window, so I had to stay in the stock-room until the cookhouse was vacated or I had to take violent action to get out . . .

I opened the door a crack and saw a man at the stove stirring the pot with a wooden spoon. He tasted, put the spoon back in the pot, and walked to a table to pick up a pack of salt. I saw that he was an elderly man who walked with a limp and knew that violence was out of the question. This man had never done me any harm nor had he set out to hurt me, and I couldn't see myself taking Howard's sins out on him.

He stayed in the cookhouse for an eternity—not more than twenty minutes in reality—and I thought he'd never go. He puttered around in a pestiferous way; he washed a couple of dishes, wrung out a dishrag and set it to dry near the stove, headed towards the stock-room as though he were going to get something, changed his mind in mid-limp just as I thought I'd have to hit him after all, and finally tasted the contents of his pot again, shrugged, and left the cookhouse.

I crept out, checked that all was clear outside, and slid from the cookhouse with my booty. Already an idea had occurred to me. I had decided to raise hell, and raise hell I would. The camp was lit by electricity and I had heard the deep throb of a diesel generator coming from the edge of the camp. It was no trick to find it, guided by the noise it made, and the only difficulty I had was in keeping to the shadows.

The generator chugged away in its own hut. For safety's sake, I explored around before I did anything desperate, and found that the next hut was the saw doctor's shop. In between the two huts was a thousand-gallon tank of diesel oil which, on inspection of the simple tube gauge, proved to be half full. To top it off, there was a felling axe conveniently to hand in the saw shop which, when swung hard against the oil tank, bit through the thin-gauge sheet metal quite easily.

It made quite a noise and I was glad to hear the splash of the oil as it spurted from the jagged hole. I was able to get in another couple of swings before I heard a shout of alarm and by that time I could feel the oil slippery underfoot. I retreated quickly and ignited the paper torch I had prepared and tossed it at the tank, then ran for the darkness.

At first I thought my torch must have gone out, but suddenly there came a great flare and flames shot skyward. I could see the figure of a man hovering uncertainly on the edge of the fire and then I went away, making the best speed I could in spite of my conviction that no one would follow me.

3

By dawn I was comfortably ensconced in the fork of a tree well into the thick forest of the north of the valley. I had eaten well, if coldly, of corned beef and beans and had had a few hours' sleep. The food did me a power of good and I felt ready for anything Matterson could throw at me. As I got myself ready for the day's mayhem I wondered how he would begin.

I soon found out, even before I left that tree. I heard the whirr of slow-moving blades and a helicopter passed overhead not far above treetop level. The downdraught of the rotor blew cold on my face and a few pine needles showered to the ground. The whirlybird departed north but I stayed where I was, and sure enough, it came back a few minutes later but a little to the west.

I dropped out of the tree, brushed myself down, and hoisted the pack. Howard had deduced what I wanted him to deduce and the helicopter reconnaissance was his first move. It was still too early for him to have moved any shock troops into the valley, but it wouldn't be long before they arrived and I speculated how to spend my time.

I could hear the helicopter bumbling down the valley and thought that pretty soon it would be on its way back on a second sweep, so I positioned myself in a good place to see it. It came back flying up the valley dead centre, and I strained my eyes and figured it contained only two men, the pilot and one passenger. I also figured that, if they saw me, they wouldn't come down because the pilot would have to stick with his craft and his passenger wouldn't care to tangle with me alone. That gave me some leeway.

It was a simple enough plan I evolved but it depended on psychology mostly and I wondered if my assessment of Howard's boys was good enough. The only way to find out was to try it and see. It also depended on some primitive technology and I would have to see if the wiles I had learned in the north would work as well on men as on animals.

I went through the forest for half a mile to a game trail I knew of, and there set about the construction of a deadfall. A snare may have been all right for catching a rabbit but you need something bigger for a deer—or a man. There was another thing, too; a deer has no idea of geometry or mechanics and wouldn't understand a deadfall even if you took the trouble to explain. All that was necessary was to avoid man scent and the deer would walk right into it. But a man would recognize a deadfall at first sight, so this one had to be very cleverly constructed.

There was a place where the trail skirted a bank about four feet high and on the other side was a six-foot drop. Anyone going along the trail would of necessity have to pass that point. I man-handled a two-foot boulder to the edge of the bank and checked it with small stones so that it teetered on the edge and would need only a slight touch to send it falling. Then I got out the survival kit and set a snare for a man's foot, using fishing-line run through forked twigs to connect to a single pebble which held the boulder.

The trap took me nearly half an hour to prepare and from time to time I heard the helicopter as it patrolled the other side of the valley. I camouflaged the snare and walked about the deadfall, making sure that it looked innocent to the eye. It was the best I could do, so I walked up the trail about four hundred yards to where it ran through a marshy area. Deliberately I ploughed through the marsh to the dry ground on the other side leaving much evidence of my passage—freshly broken grasses, footprints and gouts of wet mud on the dry land. I went still farther up the trail then struck off to the side and in a wide circle came back to my man-trap.

That was half of the plan. The second half consisted of going down the trail to a clearing through which ran a stream. I dumped my pack by the trail and figured out when the helicopter would be coming over again. I thought it would be coming over that clearing on to the next pass so I sauntered down to the stream and filled my canteen.

I was right, and it came over so unexpectedly it surprised even me. The tall firs muffled the sound until it was roaring overhead. I looked up in surprise and saw the white blob of a face looking down at me. Then I ran for cover as though the devil was at my heels. The 'copter wheeled in the air and made a second pass over the clearing, and then a wider circle and finally it headed down valley going fast. Matterson had found Boyd at last.

I went back to the clearing and regretfully ripped a piece of my shirt and stuck it on a thorn not far up the game trail. I'd see these guys did the right thing even if I had to lead them by the nose. I humped the pack to a convenient place from where I could get a good view of my trap and settled down to wait and used the time to whittle a club with my hunting knife.

By my figuring the helicopter would be back pretty soon. I didn't think it would have to go farther south than the dam, say, ten miles in eight minutes. Give them fifteen minutes to decide the right thing to do, and another eight minutes to get back, and that was a total of about a half-hour. It would come back loaded with men, but it couldn't carry more than four, apart from the pilot. Those it would drop and go back for another load—say, another twenty minutes.

So I had twenty minutes to dispose of four men. Not too long, but enough, I hoped.

It was nearer three-quarters of an hour before I heard it coming back, and by the lower note I knew it had landed in the clearing. Then it rose and began to circle and I wondered how long it was going to do that. If it didn't go away according to my schedule it would wreck everything. It was with relief that I heard it head south again and I kept my eye on the trail to the clearing, hoping that my bait had been taken.

Pretty soon I heard a faint shout which seemed to have a triumphant ring to it—the bait had been swallowed whole. I looked through the screen of leaves and saw them coming up the trail fast. Three of them were armed—two shotguns and one rifle—and I didn't like that much, but I reflected that it wouldn't make any difference because this particular operation depended on surprise.

They came up that trail almost at a run. They were young and fresh and, like a modern army, had been transported to the scene of operations in luxury. If I had to depend on out-running them I'd be caught in a mile, but that wasn't the intention. I had run the first time because I'd been caught by surprise but now everything had changed. These guys didn't know it but they weren't hunting me—they were victims.

They came along the trail two abreast but were forced into single file where the trail narrowed with the bank on one side and the drop on the other. I held my breath as they came to the trap. The first man avoided the snare and I cursed under my breath; but the second man put his foot right in it and tripped out the pebble. The boulder toppled on to number three catching him in the hip. In his surprise he grabbed hold of the guy in front and they both went over the drop followed by the boulder which weighed the best part of a hundred and fifty pounds.

There was a flurry of shouting and cursing and when all the excitement had died down one man was sitting on the ground looking stupidly at his broken leg and the other was yowling that his hip hurt like hell.

The leader was Novak, the big man I had had words with before. "Why don't you look where you're putting your big feet?"

"It just fell on me, Novak," the man with the hurt hip expostulated. "I didn't do a damn' thing."

I lay in the bushes not more than twenty feet away and grinned. It had not been a bad estimate that if a big rock pushes a man over a six-foot drop then he's liable to break a bone. The odds had dropped some—it was now three to one.

"I've got a busted leg," the man on the ground wailed.

Novak climbed down and examined it while I held my breath. If any trace of that snare remained they would know that this was no chance accident. I was lucky—either the fishing-line had broken or Novak didn't see the loop. He stood up and cursed. "Jesus! We're not here five minutes and there's a man out of action—maybe two. How's your hip?"

"Goddam sore. Maybe I fractured my pelvis."

Novak did some more grumbling, then said, "The others will be along soon. You'd better stay here with Banks—splint that leg if you can. Me and Scottie'll get on. Boyd is getting farther away every goddam minute."

He climbed up on the trail and after a few well-chosen remarks about Banks and his club-footed ancestry, he said, "Come on, Scottie," and moved off.

I had to do this fast. I watched them out of sight, then flicked my gaze to Banks. He was bending over the other man and looking at the broken leg and he had his back to me. I broke cover, ran the twenty feet at a crouch and clubbed him before he had time to turn.

He collapsed over the other man, who looked up with frightened eyes. Before he had time to yell I had grabbed a shotgun and was pushing the muzzle in his face. "One cheep and you'll get worse than a broken leg," I threatened.

He shut his mouth and his eyes crossed as they tried to focus on that big round iron hole. I said curtly, "Turn your head."

"Huh!"

"Turn your head, dammit! I haven't all day."

Reluctantly he turned his head away. I groped for the club I had dropped and hit him. I was soft, I guess; I didn't relish hitting a man with a broken leg, but I couldn't afford to have him start yelling. Anyway, I didn't hit him hard enough. He sagged a bit and shook his head dizzily and I had to hit him again a bit harder and he flopped out.

I hauled Banks off him and felt a bit dizzy myself. It occurred to me that if I kept thumping people on the skull, sooner or later I'd come across someone with thin bones and I'd kill him. Yet it was a risk I had to run. I had to impress these guys somehow and utter ruthlessness was one way to do it—the only way I could think of.

I took off Banks's belt and hog-tied him quickly, then took off with the shotgun after Novak and Scottie. I don't think more than four minutes had elapsed since they had left. I had to get to the place where the trail crossed the marsh before they did and, because the trail took a wide curve, I had only half the distance to go to get there. I ran like a hare through the trees and arrived breathless and panting just in time to hide behind the tall reeds by the marsh and at the edge of the trail.

I heard them coming, not moving as quickly as they had done at first. I suppose that four men hunting a fugitive have more confidence than two—even if they are armed. Anyway, Novak and Scottie were not coming too fast. Novak was in the lead and caught sight of the trail I had made in the marsh. "Hey, we're going right," he shouted. "Come on, Scottie."

He plunged past me into the marshy ground, his speed quickening, and Scottie followed a little more slowly, not having seen what all the excitement was about. He never did see, either, because I bounced the butt of the shotgun on the back of his head and he went flat on his face in the mud.

Novak heard him fall and whirled round, but I had already reversed the shotgun and held it on him. "Drop the rifle, Novak."

He hesitated. I patted the shotgun. "I don't know what's in here—birdshot or buckshot—but you're going to find out the hard way if you don't drop that rifle."

He opened his hands and the rifle fell into the mud. I stepped out of the reeds. "Okay, come here—real slow."

He stepped out of the mud on to dry land, his feet making sucking noises. I said, "Where's Waystrand?"

Novak grinned. "He's coming—he'll be along."

"I hope so," I said, and a puzzled look came over Novak's face. I jerked the gun, indicating the prostrate Scottie. "Pick him up—and don't put a finger near that shotgun lying there, or I'll blow your head off."

I stepped off the trail and watched him hoist Scottie on to his back. He was a big man, nearly as big as I am, and Scottie wasn't too much of a load. "Okay," I said. "Back the way you came, Novak."

I picked up the other shotgun and kept him going at a fast clip down the trail, harrying him unmercifully. By the time we reached the others he was very much out of breath, which was just the way I wanted him. Banks had recovered. He looked up, saw Novak and opened his mouth to yell. Then he saw me and had a shotgun pointing at him and shut his mouth with a snap. The guy with the broken leg was still unconscious.

I said, "Dump Scottie over the edge."

Novak turned and gave me a glare but did as I said. He wasn't too careful about it and Scottie would have a right to complain, but I supposed I'd be blamed for everything. I said, "Now you go over—and do it real slow."

He lowered himself over the edge and I told him to walk away and keep turned round with his back to me. It was awkward lowering myself but I managed it. Novak tried something, though; as he heard the thump of my heels he whirled round but subsided when he saw I still had him covered.

"All right," I said. "Now take off Scottie's belt and tie him —heels to ankles, hog fashion. But, first, take off your own belt and drop it."

He unbuckled his belt and withdrew it from the loops of his pants and for a moment I thought he was going to throw it at me, but a steadying of the shotgun on his belly made him think otherwise. "Now drop your pants."

He swore violently but again did as I said. A guy with his pants around his ankles is in no shape to start a rough-house; it's a very hampering position to be in, as a lot of guys have found out when surprised with other men's wives. But I will say that Novak was a game one—he tried.

He had just finished tying Scottie when he threw himself at my legs in an attempt to bring me down. He ought to have known better because I was trying to get into position to thump him from behind. His jaw ran into the butt of the shotgun just as it was descending on him and that put him out.

I examined Scottie's bonds and, sure enough, Novak had tried to pull a fast one there, too. I made sure of him, then fastened up Novak hurriedly. There wasn't a deal of time left and the helicopter would be coming back any moment. I took a shotgun and splintered the butt against a rock and then filled my pocket with shotgun shells for the other gun. On impulse I searched Novak's pockets and found a blackjack—a small, handy, leather-bound club, lead-weighted and with a wrist loop. I smiled. If I was going to go on skull-bashing I might as well do it with the proper implement.

I put it in my pocket, confiscated a pair of binoculars Scottie carried and grabbed the shotgun. In the distance I could hear the helicopter returning, later than I thought it would.

On impulse I pulled out a scrap of paper and scribbled a message which I left in Novak's open mouth. It read: IF

202

ANYONE WANTS THE SAME JUST KEEP ON FOLLOWING ME—
BOYD.

Then I took off for the high ground.

No one followed me. I got a reasonably safe distance away,
then lay in some bushes and watched the discovery through
the glasses. It was too far to hear what was being said, but
by the action I could guess at it. The helicopter landed out of
sight and presently another four men came up the trail and
stumbled across my little quartet. There was a great deal of
arm-waving and one guy ran back to stop the helicopter taking
off.

Novak was roused and sat up holding his jaw. He didn't
seem to be able to speak very well. He spat out the paper in
his mouth and someone picked it up and read it. He passed it
round the group and I saw one man look over his shoulder
nervously; they had made a count of the guns and knew I
was now armed.

After a lot of jabber they made a rough stretcher and carried the guy with the broken leg back to the clearing. No one
came back, and I didn't blame them. I had disposed of four
men in under the half-hour and that must have been unnerving
for the others; they didn't relish plunging into the forest with
the chance of receiving the same treatment—or worse.

Not that I was in danger of blowing myself up like a bull-
frog about what I had done. It had been a combination of
skill and luck and was probably unrepeatable. I don't go for
this bunk about "His arm was strong because his cause was
just." In my experience the bad guys of this world usually
have the strongest arms—look at Hitler, for instance. But
Napoleon did say that the moral is to the physical as three is
to one, and he was talking out of hard experience. If you can
take the other guys by surprise, get them off balance and
split them up, then you can get away with an awful lot.

I put away the glasses and looked at the shotgun, then broke
it open to see what would have happened to Novak's belly if
I'd pulled the trigger. My blood ran cold when I withdrew the
cartridges—these were worse than buckshot. A heavy buckshot load in a 12-gauge carries nine pellets which don't spread
too much at short range, but these cartridges held rifled slugs
—one to a cartridge.

Some hunting authorities don't allow deer-hunting with rifles, especially in the States, so the arms manufacturers came up with this solution for the shotgunner. You take a slug of soft lead nearly three-quarters of an inch in diameter to fit a 12-gauge barrel and grooved to give it spin in the smooth bore. The damn' thing weighs an ounce and enough powder is packed behind it to give it a muzzle velocity of 1600 feet per second. When a thing like that hits flesh it blows a hole out the other side big enough to put both your fists into. If I had twitched the trigger down at the marsh Novak's belly would have been spattered all over the Kinoxi Valley. No wonder he had dropped his rifle.

I looked at the slug cartridge with distaste and hunted through my booty until I found some small buckshot to reload the shotgun. Fired at not too close a range that would discourage a man without killing him, which was what I wanted. No matter what the other guys did, I had no intention of looking at a noose in a rope one dark morning.

I looked out at the empty landscape, then withdrew to head up valley.

4

For two days I dodged about the North Kinoxi Valley. Howard Matterson must have talked to his boys, putting some stuffing back into them, because they came looking for me again, but never, I noticed, in teams of less than six. I played tag with them for those two days, always edging over to the east when I could. They never caught sight of me, not even once, because while one man can move quietly, six men moving in a bunch make more than six times the racket. And they took care to move in a bunch. Novak must have told them exactly what happened and they were warned about splitting up.

I made half a dozen deadfalls during those two days but only one was sprung. Still, that resulted in a broken arm for someone, who was taken out by helicopter. Once I heard a barrage of shots from a little ravine I had just left and wondered what was happening. If you get a lot of men wandering about the woods armed with guns some fool is going to pull the trigger at the wrong time, but that's no excuse for the rest of them loosing off. I discovered afterwards that someone had to be taken out with a gunshot wound—someone had shot at him in error, he had shot back and the rest of the boys had let fly. Too bad for him.

The looted food supply was running out and I had to replenish. It was dangerous to go back to the logging camp—Matterson would have it sealed off tight—so I was heading east to Clare's cabin. I knew I could stock up there and I hoped to find Clare. I had to get news to Gibbons about what Howard was doing; he wouldn't look kindly on a manhunt in his territory and he'd move in fast. In any case, I wanted to find out what had happened to Clare.

Twice I made a break to the east, only to find a gang of Matterson's loggers in the way so that I had to fade back and try to circle them. The third time I was lucky and when I got to the cabin I was very tired but not too tired to approach with extreme caution. I had not had much sleep in the last forty-eight hours, mostly restricting myself to catnapping an hour at a time. That's when the loner comes off worst: he's always under pressure while the other guys can take it easy.

It was dusk when I came to the cabin and I lay on the hillside looking down at it for some time. Everything seemed to be quiet and I noted with disappointment that there were no lights in the big cabin, so evidently Clare was absent. Still, it seemed old Waystrand was around because a bright and welcome gleam shone from his place.

I came in to the cabin on a spiral, checking carefully, and was not too stupid to look through the window of Waystrand's cabin to make sure he was alone. He was sitting before the stove, the air about his head blue with pipe-smoke, so I went round to the door and tried to walk in. To my surprise it was locked, something very unusual.

Waystrand's voice rumbled, "Who's that?"

"Boyd."

I heard his footsteps on the wooden floor as he came to the door. "Who did you say?"

"Bob Boyd. Open up, Matthew."

The door opened a crack after bolts were drawn and a light shone on me. Then he flung the door wide open. "Come in. Come in, quick."

I stumbled over the threshold and he slammed the door behind me and shot the bolts. I turned to see him replace a shotgun on the rack on the wall. "Have they been bothering you, too, Matthew?"

He swung round and I saw his face. He had a shiner—the ripest black eye I've ever seen—and his face was cut about. "Yeah," he said heavily. "I've been bothered. What the hell's going on, Boyd?"

I said, "Howard Matterson's gone wild and he's after my blood. He's got his boys worked up, too—told them I hammered the daylights out of old Bull."

"Did you?"

I stared at him. "What would I want to hit an old man for? Right now I want to massacre Howard, but that's different. Old Bull had a heart-attack—I saw it and McDougall saw it. So did Howard, but he's lying about it."

Matthew nodded. "I believe you."

I said, "Who gave you the shiner, Matthew?"

He looked down at the floor. "I had a fight with my own son," he said. His hands curled up into fists. "He whipped me —I always thought I could handle him, but he whipped me."

I said, "I'll take care of Jimmy, Mr. Waystrand. He's second on my list. What happened?"

"He came up here with Howard three days ago," said Matthew. "In that 'copter. Wanted to know if you were around. I told him I hadn't seen you, and Howard said that if I did I was to let him know. Then Howard said he wanted to search Miss Trinavant's cabin, and I said he couldn't do that. He said that maybe you were hiding out in there, so I asked him if he was calling me a liar." Matthew shrugged. "One thing led to another and my boy hit me—and there was a fight."

He raised his head. "He whipped me, Mr. Boyd, but they didn't get into the cabin. I came right in here and took that shotgun and told them to get the hell off the place."

I watched him sink dejectedly into the chair before the stove and felt very sorry for him. "Did they go without any more trouble?"

He nodded. "Not much trouble. I thought at one time I'd have to shoot Jimmy. I'd have pulled the trigger, too, and he knew it." He looked up with grief in his eyes. "He's gone real bad. I knew it was happening but I never thought the time would come when I'd be ready to shoot my own son."

"I feel sorry about that," I said. "Did Howard cause any ructions?"

"No," said Matthew with contempt. "He just stood back and laughed like a hyena while the fight was going on—but he stopped laughing when I pointed the shotgun at his gut."

That sounded like Howard. I took off my pack and dumped it on the floor. "Seen anything of Cl—Miss Trinavant?"

"Not seen her for a week," he said.

I sighed and sat down. Clare hadn't been back to her cabin since this whole thing started and I wondered where she was and what she was doing.

Matthew looked at me in concern. "You look beat," he said. "I've been going on about my own troubles, but you sure got more."

I said, "I've been on the run for six days. These woods are crawling with guys hoping for a chance to beat my brains in. If you want to earn a thousand dollars, Matthew, all you have to do is to turn me in to Howard."

He grunted. "What would I do with a thousand bucks? You hungry?"

I smiled faintly. "I couldn't eat more than three moose—my appetite's given out on me."

"I got a stew that just needs heating up. Won't be more'n fifteen minutes. Why don't you get cleaned up." He took some keys looped on a string from a box, and tossed them to me. "Those will open the big cabin. Go get yourself a bath."

I tossed the keys in my hand. "You wouldn't let Howard have these."

"That's different," he said. "He ain't a friend of Miss Trinavant."

I had a hot bath and shaved off a week's growth of beard and then looked and felt more human. When I got back to Matthew's cabin he had a steaming plate of stew waiting for me which I got on the outside of at top speed and then asked for more. He smiled and said, "Outdoor life agrees with you."

"Not this kind of life," I said. I reached over to my coat and took from a pocket one of the rifle slug cartridges which I laid on the table. "They're loaded for bear, Matthew."

He picked up the cartridge and, for the first and last time in my experience, he swore profusely, "Good Christ in heaven!" he said. "The goddam sons of bitches—I wouldn't use one of those on a deer." He looked up. "Old Bull must have died."

I hadn't thought of that and felt a chill. "I hope not," I said sincerely. "I've been hoping he recovers. He's the only man who can get me out of this hole. He can stand up and tell those loggers that I didn't hammer him—that he had a heart-attack. He can get Howard off my back."

"Isn't it funny," said Matthew in a very unfunny and sad voice, "I've never liked Bull but he and I have a lot in common. Both our boys have gone bad."

I said nothing to that; there wasn't much I could say. I finished eating and had some coffee and felt a lot better after this first hot meal I'd had in days. Matthew said, "There's a bed for you all made up. You can sleep well to-night." He stood up and took down the shotgun. "I'll have a look around —we don't want your sleep disturbed."

I turned in to a soft bed and was asleep almost before my head hit the pillow and I slept right through until daybreak and only woke with the sun shining into my eyes. I got up and dressed then went into the main room. There was no sign of Matthew, but there was coffee steaming on the stove and a frypan already laid out with eggs and bacon near by waiting to be fried.

I had a cup of coffee and began to fry up half a dozen eggs. I had just got them ready when I heard someone running outside. I jumped to the window, one hand grabbing the shotgun, and saw Matthew making good time towards the cabin. He crashed open the door and said breathlessly, "A lot of guys . . . heading for here . . . not more'n ten minutes . . . behind me."

I took my coat, put it on, and hoisted my pack which felt heavy. "I put some grub in your pack," said Matthew. "Sorry it's all I could do."

I said quickly, "You can do something else. Get into Fort Farrell, get hold of Gibbons and tell him what's going on up here. And see if you can find out what's happened to McDougall and Clare. Will you do that?"

"I'll be on my way as soon as I can," he said. "But you'd better get out of here. Those boys were coming fast."

I stepped out of the cabin and made for the trees, slanting

my way up the hill to the place from which I had looked down the previous night. When I got there I unslung the glasses and looked down at the cabin.

There were at least six of them that I could see when I sorted out their comings and goings. They were walking in and out of Matthew's cabin as though they owned the place and had broken into Clare's cabin. I presumed they were searching it. I wondered how they had known I was there and concluded that they must have had a watcher staked out, and it was the lights in Clare's cabin when I had a bath that had been the tip-off.

I cursed myself for that piece of stupidity but it was too late for recriminations. When a man gets hungry and tired he begins to slip up like that, to make silly little mistakes he wouldn't make normally. It's by errors like that that a hunted man is usually nailed down, and I thought I'd better watch it in future.

I bit my lips as I focused the glasses on a man delving into the engine of Matthew's pick-up truck. He rooted around under the hood and pulled out a handful of spaghetti—most of the electrical wiring, judging by how much of it there was.

Matthew wouldn't be going to Fort Farrell—or anywhere else—for quite a while.

XI

The weather turned nasty. Clouds lowered overhead and it rained a lot, and then the clouds came right down to ground level and I walked in a mist. It was good and bad. The poor visibility meant that I couldn't be spotted as easily and the low clouds put that damned helicopter out of action. Twice it had spotted me and put the hounds on my trail, but now it was useless. On the other hand, I was wet all the time and daren't stop to light a fire and dry out. Living constantly in wet clothes, my skin started to whiten and wrinkle and it chafed where rubbed by folds of my shirt and pants. I also developed a bad cold, and a sneeze at the wrong time could be dangerous.

Howard's staffwork had improved. He had me pinned

down in a very small area, not more than three square miles, and had cordoned it off tightly. Now he was tightening the noose inexorably. God knows how many men he was using, but there were too many for me to handle. Three times I tried to bust out, using the mist as cover, and three times I failed. The boys weren't afraid to use their shotguns, either, and it was only by chance that I wasn't filled full of holes on my last attempt. As it was, I had heard the whistle of buckshot around me, and one slug grazed me in the thigh. I ducked out of there fast and retreated to a hidey-hole where I slapped a Band-Aid on the wound. The muscle in my leg was a bit stiff but it didn't slow me down much.

I was wet and cold and miserable, to say nothing of being hungry and tired, and I wondered if I'd come to the end of my tether. It wouldn't have taken much for me to have lain down and slept right on the spot and let them come and find me. But I knew what would happen if I did. I had no particular ambition to go through life crippled even if Howard let it go at that, so I dragged myself wearily to my feet and set off on the move again, prowling through the mist to find a way out of this contracting circle.

I nearly stumbled over the bear. It growled and reared up, towering a good eight feet, waving its forelegs with those cruel claws and showing its teeth. I retreated to a fair distance and considered it thoughtfully.

There's more nonsense talked about the grizzly than any other animal, barring the wolf. Grown men will look you straight in the eye and tell you of the hair-raising experiences they've had with grizzlies; how a grizzly will charge a man on sight, how they can outrun a horse, tear down a tree and create hell generally with no provocation. The truth is that a grizzly is like any other animal and has more sense than to tangle with a man without good reason. True, they're apt to be bad-tempered in the spring when they've just come out of hibernation, but a lot of people are like that when they've just got out of bed.

And they're hungry in the spring, too. The fat has gone from them and their hide hangs loose and they want to be left alone to eat in peace, just like most of us, I guess. And the females have their young in the spring and are touchy about interference, and quite justifiably so in my opinion. Most of the tall tales about grizzlies have been spun around camp fires to impress a tenderfoot or tourist and even more have been poured out of a bottle of rye whisky.

Now it was high summer—as high as summer gets in British Columbia—and this grizzly was fat and contented. He dropped back on to four legs and continued to do what he had been doing before I interrupted him—grubbing up a juicy root. He kept a wary eye on me, though, and growled once or twice to show he wasn't too scared of me.

I stepped back behind a tree so as not to cause him too much alarm while I figured out what to do about him. I could just go away, of course, but I had a better idea than that because the thought had occurred to me that an 800-pound bear could be a powerful ally if I could recruit him. There are not many men who will face a charging grizzly.

The nearest of Matterson's men were not more than a half-mile from this spot, as I knew to my cost, and were closing in slowly. The natural tendency of the bear would be to move away as they approached. I already knew they made a lot of noise when moving and the bear would soon hear them. The only reason he hadn't heard me was that I'd developed a trick of ghosting along quietly—it's one of the things you learn in a situation like I was in; you learn it or you're dead.

What I had to do was to make the bear ignore his natural inclination. Instead of moving away, he had to move towards the oncoming men, and how in hell could I make him do that? You don't shoo away a grizzly like you do a cow, and I had to come up with an answer fast.

After a moment's thought I took some shotgun shells from my pocket and began to dissect them with my hunting knife, throwing away the slugs but keeping the powder charges. In a little while I had a heap of powder grains wrapped up in a glove to keep them dry. I bent down to dig into the carpet of pine needles with the knife; pine needles have a felting effect when they get matted and shed water like the feathers on a duck, and I didn't have to dig very far to find dry, flammable material.

All the time I kept my eye on brother bear, who was

chomping contentedly on his roots while keeping an eye on me. He wasn't going to bother me if I didn't bother him—at least that was the theory I had, although I coppered my bet by choosing an easily climbable tree within sprinting distance. From one of the side pockets of the pack I extracted the folded Government geological map of the area and a notebook I kept in there. I tore up the map into small sheets and ripped pages from the book, crumpling them into spills.

I built a fire on that spot, laying down the paper spills, lacing them liberally with gunpowder and covering the lot with dry pine needles. From the fire I led a short trail of gunpowder for easy ignition, and right in the centre I embedded three shotgun shells.

After listening for a moment and hearing nothing, I circled around the bear about one-sixth of a circle, and built another fire in the same way—and yet another on the other side. He reared and growled when he saw me moving about but subsided when he saw I wasn't coming any closer. Any animal has its "safe" distance carefully measured out and takes action only if it feels its immediate territory infringed on. The action will then depend on the animal: a deer will run for it—a grizzly will attack.

The fires laid, I waited for Matterson's boys to make the next move, and the bear would give me warning when that was coming since he was between us. I just stood cradling the shotgun in my arms and waited patiently, never taking my eyes off the grizzly.

I didn't hear a thing—but he did. He stirred and turned his head, waving it from side to side like a cobra about to strike. He made snuffling noises, sniffing the wind, and suddenly he growled softly and turned away from me, looking in the other direction. I thanked the years of experience that had taught me how to keep matches dry by filling a full matchbox with melted candle wax so that the matches were embedded in a block of paraffin wax. I ripped three matches free from the block and got them ready to strike.

The bear was backing slowly towards me and away from whatever was coming towards him. He looked back at me uneasily, feeling he was trapped, and whenever a grizzly feels like that the best place to be is somewhere else. I stooped and struck the match and dropped it on the powder trail, which fizzed and flashed into fire. Then I ran like hell to the other fire, shooting into the air as I went.

The bear had lumbered into action as I broke cover and was covering the ground fast heading straight towards me, but the bang of the shotgun gave him pause and he skidded to a halt uncertainly. From behind the bear I heard an excited shout. Someone else had also heard the shot.

The bear turned his head uncertainly and started to move again, but just then one of the shotgun shells in the first fire exploded, just as I ignited the second fire. He didn't like that at all and turned away growling all the time, as I sprinted to the third fire and dropped a match on it.

Bruin didn't know what the hell to do! There was trouble —man trouble—coming up on one side and loud unnerving noises on the other. There were a couple more shouts from the other side of the bear and that almost decided him, but just then all hell broke loose. Two more shells exploded one after the other and half a second later it sounded as though a war had broken out.

The grizzly's nerve broke and he turned and bolted in the opposite direction. I added to the fun by stinging his rump with a charge of buckshot and then began to run, following close in his rear. He charged among the trees like a demon out of hell—nearly half a ton of frightful, ravening ferocity. Actually, he was not so much frightful as frightened, but it's then that the grizzly is at his most dangerous.

I saw three men looking up the slope, aghast at what was coming down on them. I suppose to them it was all teeth and claws and twice as large as life—and another tale would be told in a bar-room if they lived to tell it. They broke and scattered, but one was a little late and the bear gave him a flick in passing. The man screamed as he was slammed into the ground but luckily for him the bear didn't stop his rush to maul him.

I went past at a dead run, my boots skidding on the slippery ground. The bear was moving much faster than I could and was out-distancing me fast. From ahead there was another shout and a couple of shots and I spun round a tree to find a guy waving a shotgun at the departing bear. He turned and saw me coming down at him fast and took a sudden snapshot at me. The hammer of his shotgun fell on an empty chamber and by then I was on to him. I took him in the chest with my shoulder and the impact knocked the feet from under him and he went sprawling, aided by a clout behind the ear I gave him as I went on my way. I had learned something from that bear.

I didn't stop running for fifteen minutes, not until I was sure no one was chasing me. I reckoned they were too busy looking after their casualty—when a bear clouts you in passing there are steel-like claws in his fist. I saw my friend bounding down the hillside and became conscious that the mist was lifting. He slowed up and slowly ambled to a stop, looking behind him. I waved and took another direction because that was one bear I wouldn't like to meet for the next couple of days.

Almost as I had stumbled on the bear I came across the man staring into the haze and wondering what all the noise was about. I had no time for evasive action so I tackled him head on, first ramming the muzzle of the gun into his belly. By the time he had recovered from that I had my hunting knife at his throat.

He eased his head back to an unnatural angle trying to get away from the sharp point and a drool of spittle ran down from one corner of his mouth. I said, "Don't make a noise—you'll only get hurt."

He nodded, then stopped as the knife pricked his Adam's apple. I said gently, "Why are you hunting me?"

He gurgled, but didn't say a thing. I said again, "Why are you hunting me? I want an answer. A truthful answer."

It was forced out of him. "You beat up old Bull Matterson. That was a lousy thing to do."

"Who said I beat up the old man?"

"Howard was there—he says so. So does Jimmy Waystrand."

"What does Waystrand know about it? He wasn't there."

"He reckons he was and Howard doesn't say he wasn't."

"They're both liars," I said. "The old man had a heart-attack. What does he say about it?"

"He don't say nothing. He's sick—real sick." Hatred looked at me out of the man's eyes."

214

"In hospital? Or at home?"

"He's at home, so I heard." He managed a grin. "Mister, you've got it coming to you."

"Old Matterson had a heart-attack," I said patiently. "I didn't lay a finger on him. Would a little matter of a thousand dollars have anything to do with me being chased all over these woods?"

He looked at me with contempt. "That don't matter." he said. "We just don't like strangers beating up old men."

That was probably true. I doubt if these loggers would set out on a manhunt like this on a purely blood-money basis. They weren't bad guys, just fools who'd been whipped up into a frenzy by Howard's lies. The thousand dollars was merely icing on the cake. I said, "What's your name?"

"Charlie Blunt."

"Well, Charlie, I wish we could talk this out over a beer, but I regret it's impossible. Look, if I was such a bad guy as Howard makes out I could have knocked out your people like ducks at a shooting-gallery. People have been shooting at me but I haven't shot back. Does that make sense to you?"

A frown wrinkled his face and I could see he was thinking about it. I said, "Take Novak and those other guys—I could have slit their throats quite easily. Come to that, there's nothing to prevent me from slitting yours right now."

He tensed and I pricked him with the knife. "Take it easy, Charlie; I'm not going to. I wouldn't hurt a hair of your head. Do you think that makes sense, either?"

He gulped and shook his head hurriedly. "Well, think about it," I said. "Think about it and talk about it to those other guys back there. Tell them I said old Bull had a heart-attack and that Howard Matterson and Jimmy Waystrand have been feeding them a line. Talking about Jimmy, I don't think much of a guy who'd beat up his own father—do you?"

Blunt's head made a sideways movement. "Well, he did," I said. "All you have to do to prove I'm telling the truth is to ask Matthew Waystrand. His place isn't too far from here—not so far that a man couldn't walk over and get at the truth for once. Talk about that to the other guys, too. Let you and them decide who's telling the truth in this neck of the woods."

I eased up on the knife. "I'm going to let you go, Charlie.

I'm not even going to sap you or tie you up so you won't set the other guys on my trail again. I'm just going to let you go as you are, and if you want to raise a holler that's your privilege. But you can tell the other guys this—tell them I've had a bellyful of running and not hitting back too hard. Tell them I'm getting into a killing mood. Tell them that the next man I see on my trail is a dead man. I think you're very lucky, Charlie, that I picked you to take the message—don't you?"

He lay quiet and didn't say or do anything. I stood up and looked down at him. I said, "The killing starts with you, Charlie, if you try anything." I picked up the shotgun and walked away from him without glancing back. I could feel his eyes on my back and it gave me a prickly feeling, not knowing what he was doing. He could be aiming at my back with his gun right at that moment and it took all the will-power I had not to break into a run.

But I had to take a chance on the reasonableness of men some time. I had come to the conclusion that sheer raw violence wouldn't get me out of this jam—that it only produced counter-violence in its turn. I hoped I had put a maggot of doubt in one man's mind, the "reasonable doubt" that every jury is asked to consider.

I walked on up the hill until I knew I was out of range and the tension eased suddenly. At last I turned and looked back. Way down the hill Blunt was standing, a miniscule figure looking up at me. There was no gun in his hands and he had made no move for or against me. I waved at him and, after a long pause, he waved back. I went on—up and over the hill.

2

The weather cleared up again, and I had broken out of Howard's magic circle. I had no doubt that they would come after me again. To think that a man like Blunt could have any lasting restraint was to fool myself, but at least I had a temporary respite. When, after a whole day, I saw no one and heard no one, I took a chance and killed a deer, hoping there was no one there to hear the shot.

I gralloched it and, being hungry for meat, made a small fire to cook the liver, that being the quickest to cook and most easily digested. Then I quartered the beast and roasted strips of flesh before the fire and stuffed the half-raw pieces into my pack. I didn't stay long in that place but hid the rest of the carcase and moved on, afraid of being cornered. But no one came after me.

I bedded down that night by a stream, something I had never done since this whole chase had started. It was the natural thing to do and I had not done the natural thing ever, out of fear. But I was tired of being unnatural and I didn't care a damn about what happened. I suppose the strain was telling and that I had just about given up. All I wanted was a good night's sleep and I was determined to get it, even though I might be wakened by looking into a gun barrel in the middle of the night.

I cut spruce boughs for my bed, something I hadn't done because the traces could put men on my trail, and even built a fire, not caring whether I was seen or not. I didn't go to the extreme length of stripping before I turned in, but I did spread the blankets, and as I lay there before the fire, full of meat and with the coffee-pot to hand, everything looked cheerful just as most of my camps looked cheerful in better times.

I had made camp early, being wearied to the bone of moving continually, and by dusk I was on the point of falling asleep. Through my drowsiness I heard the throb of an engine and the whir of blades cutting through the air overhead and I jerked myself into wakefulness. It was the goddam helicopter still chasing me—and they must have seen the light of the fire. That blaze would stand out like a beacon in the blackness of the woods.

I think I groaned in despair but I moved my bones stubbornly and got to my feet as the sound died away suddenly in the north. I stretched, and looked round the camp. It was a pity to leave it and go on the run again but it looked as though I had to. Then I thought again. *Why* had I to run? Why shouldn't I stop right here and fight it out?

Still, there was no reason to be taken like a sitting bird, so I figured out a rough plan. It didn't take long to find a log nearly as tall as myself to put under the blankets, and by the time I had finished it looked very like a sleeping man. To add to the illusion I rigged a line to the log so I could move it from a distance to give the appearance of a man stirring in his sleep. I found a convenient place where I could lie down behind a stump and tested it. It would have fooled me if I didn't know the trick.

If anything was to happen that night I would need plenty of light, so I built up the fire again into a good blaze—and was almost caught by surprise. It was only by a snapping twig in the distance that I realized I had much less time than I thought. I ducked into my hiding-place and checked the shotgun, seeing that it was loaded and I had spare shells. I was quite near the fire so I rubbed some damp earth on the barrel so that it wouldn't gleam in the light and then pushed the gun forward so that it would handle more conveniently.

The suddenness of the impending attack meant one of two things. That the helicopter was scouting just ahead of a main party, or that it had dropped a single load of men—and that meant not more than four. They'd already found out what happened when they did stupid things like that and I wondered if they would try it again.

A twig cracked again in the forest much closer and I tensed, looking from side to side and trying to figure out from which side the attack would come. Just because a twig had cracked to the west didn't mean there wasn't a much smarter guy coming in from the east—or maybe the south. The hair on the nape of my neck prickled; I was to the south and maybe someone was standing right behind me ready to blow my brains out. It hadn't been too smart of me to lie flat on my belly—it's an awkward position to move from, but it was the only way I could stay close in to the camp and still not stick out like a sore thumb.

I was about to take a cautious glance behind me when I saw someone—or something—move out of the corner of my eye, and I froze rigid. The figure came into the firelight and I held my breath as I saw it was Howard Matterson. At last I had drawn the fox.

He came forward as though he were walking on eggshell and stooped over my pack. He wouldn't have any difficulty in identifying it because my name was stencilled on the back

218

Cautiously I gathered in the slack of my fishing-line and tugged. The log rolled over a little and Howard straightened quickly.

The next thing that happened was that he put the gun he was carrying to his shoulder and the dark night was split by the flash and roar as he put four shotgun shells into the blanket from a distance of less than eight feet as fast as he could operate the action.

I jumped and started sweating. I had all the evidence I needed that Howard wanted me out of the way in the worst way possible. He put his foot to the blanket and kicked it and stubbed his toe on the log. I yelled, "Howard, you bastard, I've got you covered. Put down tha——"

I didn't get it all out because Howard whirled and let rip again and the blast dazzled my eyes against the darkness of the wood. Someone yelled and gurgled horribly and a body crashed down and rolled forward. I had been right about a smarter guy coming in from behind me. Jimmy Waystrand must have been standing not six feet away from me and Howard had been too goddam quick on the trigger. Young Jimmy had got a bellyful.

I jumped to my feet and took a shot at Howard, but my eyes were still dazzled by the flash of his discharge and I missed. Howard looked at me incredulously and shot blindly in my direction, but he'd forgotten that his automatic shotgun held only five shells and all there was was the dry snap of the hammer.

I must say he moved fast. With one jump he had cleared the fire, going in an unexpected direction, and I heard the splashing as he forded the stream. I took another shot at him into the darkness and must have missed again because I heard him crashing away through the undergrowth on the other side, and gradually the noises became fainter.

I knelt down next to Jimmy. He was as dead as I've seen any man—and I've seen a few. Howard's shotgun must have been loaded with those damned rifled slugs and Jimmy had caught one dead centre in the navel. It had gone clean through and blown the spine out of his back and there was a mess of guts spilled out on the ground.

I rose unsteadily to my feet, walked two paces and vomited.

All the good meat I had eaten came up and spilled on the ground just like Jimmy Waystrand's guts. I shivered and shook for five minutes like a man with fever and then got myself under control. I took the shotgun and carefully reloaded with rifled slug shells because Howard deserved only the best. Then I went after him.

It was no trick to follow him. A brief on-and-off glimpse of the flashlamp showed me muddied footprints and broken grasses, but that set me thinking. He still had his gun and had presumably reloaded with another five shells. If the only way I could follow him was with a flashlamp I was about to get my head blown off. It didn't matter how much better I was in the woods on a night as dark as this. If I used a light all he had to do was to hole up, keep quiet and then let go as I conveniently illuminated his target for him. That was sure death.

I stopped short and started thinking again. I hadn't done any real thinking since Howard had pumped four shots into that log—everything had happened so fast. I cranked my brain into low gear and started it working again. There couldn't be anyone else other than Howard or I'd have been nailed back at the camp while I was puking and twitching over the body of Jimmy Waystrand. The two must have come from that helicopter which must be within reasonable walking distance.

I had heard the sound of the helicopter die away to the north quite suddenly and that must have been where it had come to earth. There was a place not far to the north where the soil was thin, a mere skin on the bedrock. No trees grew there and there was ample space to land that whirlybird. Howard had plunged away to the west and I reckoned he wasn't much good in the woods anyway, so there was a chance I could get to the helicopter first.

I abandoned his trail and moved fast unhampered by the pack. I had humped that pack continuously over miles of ground for nearly two weeks and its absence gave me an airy sense of freedom and lightness. By leaving the pack I was taking a chance because if I lost it I was done for—I couldn't hope to survive in the woods without the gear I had. But I had the reckless feeling that this was the make or break time: I would either come out on top this night or be defeated by Howard—and defeat meant a slug in the guts like Jimmy Waystrand because that was the only way he could stop me.

I moved fast and quietly, halting every now and then to listen. I didn't hear Howard but pretty soon I heard the swish of air driven by rotors and knew that not only was the helicopter where I thought it was but the pilot was nervous and ready for a quick take-off. I reckon he'd started his engine when he heard the shots back at my camp.

Acting on sound principles, I circled round to come on the helicopter from the opposite direction before coming out on to the open ground, and when I did come out of cover it was at the crouch. The noise was enough to make my approach silent and I came up behind the pilot who was standing and looking south, waiting for something to happen.

Something did happen. I pushed the muzzle of the shotgun in his ribs and he jumped a foot. "Calm down," I said. "This is Boyd. You know who I am?"

"Yeah," he said nervously.

"That's right," I said. "We've met before—nearly two years ago. You took me from the Kinoxi back to Fort Farrell on the last trip. Well, you're going to do it again." I bored the gun into his ribs with a stronger pressure. "Now, take six steps forward and don't turn round until I tell you. I think you know better than to try any tricks."

I watched him walk away and then come to a halt. He could have easily got away from me then because he was just a darker shadow in the darkness of that moonless cloudy night, but he must have been too scared. I think my reputation had spread around. I climbed up into the passenger seat and then said, "Okay, climb up here."

He clambered up and sat in the pilot's seat rigidly. I said conversationally, "Now, I can't fly this contraption but you can. You're going to fly it back to Fort Farrell and you're going to do it nice and easy with no tricks." I pulled out my hunting knife and held it out so the blade glinted in the dim light of the instrument panel. "You'll have this in your ribs all the way, so if you have any idea of crash-landing this thing just remember that you'll be just as dead as me. You can also take into account that I don't particularly care

221

whether I live or die right now—but you might have different ideas about that. Got it?"

He nodded. "Yeah, I've got it. I won't play tricks, Boyd."

Maliciously I said, "Mr. Boyd to you. Now, get into the air —and make sure you head in the right direction."

He pulled levers and flicked switches and the engine note deepened and the rotors moved faster. There was a flash from the edge of the clearing and a Perspex panel in the canopy disintegrated. I yelled, "You'd better make it damned quick before Howard Matterson blows your head off."

That helicopter suddenly took off like a frightened grasshopper. Howard took another shot and there was a *thunk* from somewhere back of me. The 'copter jinked around in the air and then we were away with the dark tide of firs streaming just below. I felt the pilot take a deep breath and relax in his seat. I felt a bit more relaxed myself as we gained more height and bored steadily south.

Air travel is wonderful. I had walked and run from Fort Farrell and been chased around the Kinoxi Valley for nearly two weeks, and in that wonderful machine we headed straight down the valley and were over the dam in just fifteen minutes with another forty miles—say, half an hour— to go to Fort Farrell. I felt the tension drain out of me but then deliberately tightened up again in case the frightened man next to me should get up his nerve enough to pull a fast one.

Pretty soon I saw the lights of Fort Farrell ahead. I said, "Bull Matterson should have a landing-strip at the house —does he?"

"Yeah; just next the house."

"You land there," I said.

We flew over Fort Farrell and the upper-crust community of Lakeside and suddenly we were over the dark bulk of Matterson's fantastic château and coming down next to it. The helicopter settled and I said, "Switch off."

The silence was remarkable when the rotors flopped to a stop. I said, "Does anyone usually come out to meet you?"

"Not at night."

That suited me. I said, "Now, you stay here. If you're not here when I come back then I'll be looking for you one day— and you'll know why, won't you?"

222

There was a tremble in the pilot's voice. "I'll stay here, Mr. Boyd." He wasn't much of a man.

I dropped to the ground, put away the knife and hefted the shotgun, then set off towards the house which loomed against the sky. There were a few lights showing, but not many and I reckoned most of the people would be asleep. I didn't know how many servants were needed to keep the place tidy but I thought there wouldn't be many around that time of night.

I intended to go in by the front door since it was the only way I knew and was coming to it when it opened and a light spilled on to the ground in front of the house. I ducked back into what proved to be the house garage, and listened intently to what was going on.

A man said, "Remember, he must be kept quiet."

"Yes, doctor," said a woman.

"If there's any change, ring me at once." A car door slammed. "I'll be home all night." A car engine started and headlights switched on. The car curved round and the headlights momentarily illuminated the interior of the garage, then it was gone down the drive. The front door of the house closed quietly and all was in darkness again.

I waited awhile to let the woman get settled and used the time to explore the garage. By the look of it, in the brief glimpses of my flashlamp, the Mattersons were a ten-car family. There was Mrs. Atherton's big Continental, Bull Matterson's Bentley, a couple of run-of-the-mill Pontiacs and a snazzy Aston Martin sports job. I flicked the light farther into the garage towards the back and held it on a Chevvy— it was McDougall's beat-up auto. And standing next to it was Clare's station-wagon!

I swallowed suddenly and wondered where Clare was—and old Mac.

I was wasting time here so I went out of the garage and walked boldly up to the front door and pushed it open. The big hall was dimly lit and I tiptoed up the great curving staircase on my way to the old man's study. I thought I might as well start there—it was the only room I knew in the house.

There was someone inside. The door was ajar and light flooded out into the dimly lit corridor. I peeked inside and saw Lucy Atherton pulling out drawers in Bull Matterson's desk. She tossed papers around with abandon and there was a drift of them on the floor like a bank of snow. She'd be a very suitable person to start with, so I pushed open the door and was across the room before she knew I was there.

I rounded the desk and got her from behind with her neck in the crook of my elbow, choking off her wind. "No noise," I said quietly, and dropped the shotgun on the soft carpet. She gurgled when she saw the keen blade of my knife before her eyes. "Where's the old man?"

I relaxed my grip to give her air enough to speak and she whispered through a bruised throat, "He's . . . sick."

I brought the point of the knife closer to her right eye—not more than an inch from the eyeball. "I won't ask you again."

"In . . . bedroom."

"Where's that? Never mind—show me." I slammed the knife into its sheath and dragged her down with me into a stoop as I picked up the shotgun. I said, "I'll kill you if you raise a noise, Lucy. I've had enough of your damn' family. Now, where's the room?"

I still kept the choke-hold on her and felt her thin body trembling against mine as I frog-marched her out of the study. Her arm waved wildly at a door, so I said, "Okay, put your hand on the knob and open it."

As soon as I saw her turn the knob I kicked the door open and pushed her through. She went down on her knees and sprawled on the thick carpet and I ducked in quickly and closed the door behind and lifted the shotgun in readiness for anything.

Anything proved to be a night nurse in a trim white uniform who looked up with wide eyes. I ignored her and glanced around the room; it was big and gloomy with dark drapes and there was a bed in a pool of shadow. Heaven help me, but it was a four-poster with drapes the same colour as those at the windows but drawn back.

The nurse was trembling but she was plucky. She stood up and demanded, "Who are you?"

"Where's Bull Matterson?" I asked.

Lucy Atherton was crawling to her feet so I put my boot on her rump and pushed her down again. The nurse trembled even more. "You can't disturb Mr. Matterson; he's a very sick man." Her voice dropped. "He's . . . he's *dying*."

A rasping voice from the darkened bed said, "Who's dying? I heard that, young woman, and you're talking nonsense."

The nurse half-turned away from me towards the bed. "You *must* be quiet, Mr. Matterson." Her head turned and her eyes pleaded with me. "*Please go.*"

Matterson said, "That you, Boyd?"

"I'm here."

His voice was sardonic. "I thought you'd be around. What kept you?" I was about to tell him when he said irritably, "Why am I kept in darkness? Young lady, switch on a light here."

"But, Mr. Matterson, the doct——"

"Do as I say, damn it. You get me excited and you know what'll happen. Switch on a light."

The nurse stepped to the bedside and clicked a switch. A bedside lamp lit up the shrunken figure in the big bed. Matterson said, "Come here, Boyd."

I hauled Lucy from the floor and pushed her forward. Matterson chuckled. "Well, well, if it isn't Lucy. Come to see your father at last, have you? Well, what's your story, Boyd? It's a mite late for blackmail."

I said to the nurse, "Now, see here: you don't make a move to leave this room—and you keep dead quiet."

"I'm not going to leave my patient," she said stiffly.

I smiled at her. "You'll do."

"What's all the whispering going on?" inquired Matterson.

I stepped up to the bedside keeping tight hold of Lucy. "Howard's going hog wild up in the Kinoxi," I said. "He's whipped up your loggers into a lynching-party—got them all steamed up with a story of how I beat you up. They've had me on the run for nearly two weeks. And that's not all. Howard's killed a man. He's for the eight o'clock walk."

Matterson looked at me expressionlessly. He'd aged ten years in two weeks; his cheeks were sunken and the bones of his skull were sharply outlined by the drawn and waxy skin, his lips were bluish and the flesh round his neck had sagged. But there was still a keen intelligence in his eyes. He said tonelessly, "Who did he kill?"

"A man called Jimmy Waystrand. He didn't intend to kill Waystrand—he thought he was shooting at me."

"Is that the guy I saw up at the dam?"

"He's the one." I dropped a shotgun shell on Matterson's chest. "He was shot with one of these."

Matterson scrabbled with a dessicated hand and I edged the shell into his fingers. He lifted it before his eyes and said softly, "Yes, a very efficient way of killing." The shell dropped from his fingers. "I knew his father. Matthew's a good man—I haven't seen him in years." He closed his eyes and I saw a tear squeeze under the eyelid and on to his cheek. "So Howard's done it again. Aaah, I might have known it would happen."

"*Again!*" I said urgently. "Mr. Matterson, did Howard kill John Trinavant and his family?"

He opened his eyes and looked up at me. "Who are you, son? Are you Grant—or are you John Trinavant's boy? I must know."

I shook my head soberly. "I don't know, Mr. Matterson. I really don't know. I lost my memory in the crash."

He nodded weakly. "I thought you'd got it back again." He paused, and the breath rattled in his throat. "They were so burned—black flesh and raw meat . . . I didn't know, God help me!" His eyes stared into the vast distances of the past at the horrors of the crash on the Edmonton road. "I took a chance on the identification—it was for the best," he said.

Whose best? I thought bitterly, but I let no bitterness come into my voice as I asked evenly, "Who killed John Trinavant, Mr. Matterson?"

Slowly he lifted a wasted hand and pointed a shaking finger at Lucy Atherton. "She did—she and her hellion brother."

XII

Lucy Atherton tore her arm from my grasp and ran across the room towards the door. Old Bull, ill though he was, put all his energy into a whipcrack command. "*Lucy!*"

She stopped dead in the middle of the room. Matterson said coldly, "What load have you got in the gun?"

I said, "Rifled slugs."

His voice was even colder. "You have my permission to put one through her if she takes another step. Hear that, Lucy? I should have done it myself twelve years ago."

I said, "I found her in your study going through the desk. I think she was looking for your will."

"It figures," said the old man sardonically. "I sired a brood of devils." He raised his hand. "Young woman, plug that telephone in this socket here."

The nurse started at being addressed directly. All that had been going on was too much for her. I said, "Do it—and do it fast." She brought over the telephone and plugged it in by the bedside. As she passed on her way back I asked, "Have you anything to write with?"

"A pen? Yes, I've got one."

"You'd better take notes of what's said here. You might have to repeat it in court."

Matterson fumbled with the telephone and gave up. He said, "Get Gibbons at the police-station." He gave me the number and I dialled it, then held the handset to his head. There was a pause before he said, "Gibbons, this is Matterson . . . my health is none of your damn' concern. Now, listen: get up to my place fast . . . there's been a killing." His head fell back on to the pillow and I replaced the handset.

I kept the shotgun centred on Lucy's middle. She was white and unnaturally calm, standing there with her arms straight down by her sides. A tic convulsed her right cheek every few seconds. Presently Matterson began to talk in a very low voice and I motioned the nurse nearer so that she could hear what he said. She had a pen and a notebook and scribbled in long-hand, but Bull wasn't speaking very fast so she had time to get it all down.

"Howard was envious of Frank," said the old man softly. "Young Frank was a good boy and he had everything—brains, strength, popularity—everything Howard lacked. He got good grades in college while Howard ploughed his tests; he got the girls who wouldn't look at Howard, and he looked like being the guy who was going to run the business when old John and I were out of the running, while Howard knew he wouldn't get a look-in. It wasn't that John Trinavant would favour his son against Howard—it was a case of the best man

227

getting the job. And Howard knew that if I got down to making a decision I'd choose Frank Trinavant, too."

He sighed. "So Howard killed Frank—and not only Frank. He killed John and his wife, too. He was only twenty-one and he was a triple killer." He gestured vaguely. "I don't think it was his idea, I think it was hers. Howard wouldn't have the guts to do a thing like that by himself. I reckon Lucy pushed him into it." He turned his head and looked at her. "Howard was a bit like me—not much, but a bit. She took after her mother." He turned back to me. "Did you know my wife committed suicide in a lunatic asylum?"

I shook my head, feeling very sorry for him. He was speaking of his son and daughter in the past tense as though they were already dead.

"Yes," he said heavily. "I think Lucy is mad—as crazy mad as her mother was towards the end. She saw that Howard had a problem and she solved it for him in her way—the mad way. Young Frank was an obstacle to Howard, so what could be simpler than to get rid of him? The fact that old John and his wife were killed was an incidental occurrence. John wasn't the target—*Frank was!*"

I felt a chill in that big, warm, centrally-heated room—the chill of horror as I looked across at Lucy Atherton who was standing with a blank look on her face as though the matter under discussion did not concern her a whit. It must have been also "a minor happening of no great consequence" that a hitch-hiker called Grant was also in the car.

Matterson sighed. "So Lucy talked Howard into it, and that wouldn't be too difficult, I guess. He was always weak and rotten even as a boy. They borrowed my Buick and trailed the Trinavants on the Edmonton road, and ran them off that cliff deliberately and in cold blood. I daresay they took advantage of the fact that John knew the car and knew them."

My lips were stiff as I asked, "Who was driving the car?"

"I don't know. Neither of them would ever say. The Buick got knocked around a bit and they couldn't hide that from me. I put two and two together and got Howard cornered and forced it out of him. He crumpled like a wet paper bag."

He was quiet for a long time, then he said, "What was I to do? These were my children!" In his voice was a plea for understanding. "Can a man turn in his own children for murder? So I became their accomplice." There was now a deep self-contempt in his voice. "I covered up for them, God help me. I built a wall around them with my money."

I said gently, "Was it you who sent the money to the hospital to help Grant?"

"I was pulled two ways—torn down the middle," he said. "I didn't want another death on my conscience. Yes, I sent the money—it was the least I could do. And I wanted to keep track of you. I knew you'd lost your memory and I was scared to death you'd get it back. I had a private investigator checking up on you but he lost you somehow. Must have been about the time you changed your name." His hands groped blindly on the coverlet as he looked into the black past. "And I was scared you'd start back-tracking in an attempt to find yourself. I had to do something about that and I did what I could. I had to get rid of the name of Trinavant—it's an odd name and sticks in a man's memory. John and his family were the only Trinavants left in Canada—barring Clare— and I knew if you bumped up against that name you'd get curious, so I tried to wipe it out. What put you on to it?"

"Trinavant Park," I said.

"Ah, yes," he chuckled. "I wanted to change that but I couldn't get it past that old bitch, Davenant. She's about the only person in Fort Farrell I couldn't scare hell out of. Independent income," he explained.

"Anyway, I went on building the company. God knows what for, but it seemed pretty important at the time. I felt lost without John—he was always the brains of the outfit— but then I got hold of Donner and we got going pretty good after that."

There was no regret for the way he had done it. He was still a tough, ruthless sonofabitch—but an honest sonofabitch by his lights, dim though they were. I heard a sound outside—the sound of a fast-driven car braking hard on the gravel. I looked at the nurse. "Have you got all that?"

She looked up with misery in her face. "Yes," she said flatly. "And I wish I hadn't."

"So do I, child," said Matterson. "I should have killed the pair of them with my own hands twelve years ago." His hand came out and plucked at my sleeve. "You must stop Howard. I know him—he'll go on killing until he's destroyed. He loses his head easily and makes terrible mistakes. He'll kill and kill, thinking he's finding a way out and not knowing he's getting in deeper."

I said, "I think we can leave that to Gibbons—he's the professional." I nodded to the nurse as a faint knocking sound echoed through the house. "You'd better let him in. I can't leave here with her around."

I still kept a close watch on Lucy whose face continued to twitch spasmodically. When the nurse had gone I said, "All right, Lucy: where are they? Where are Clare Trinavant and McDougall?"

A chill had settled on me. I was afraid for them, afraid this crazy woman had killed them. Matterson said bleakly, "Good Christ! Is there more?"

I ignored him. "Lucy, where are they?" I could have no pity for her and had no compunction in using any method to get the information from her. I pulled out the hunting knife. "If you don't tell me, Lucy, I'll carve you up just like I'd carve up a deer—with the difference that you'll feel every cut."

The old man said nothing but just breathed deeper. Lucy looked at me blankly.

I said, "All right, Lucy. You've asked for it." I had to get this over with fast before Gibbons came up. He wouldn't stand for what I was about to do.

Lucy giggled. It was a soft imbecile giggle that shook her whole body, and developed into a maniacal cackle. "All right," she yelled at me. "We put the sexy bitch in the cellar, and the old fool with her. I wanted to kill them both but Howard wouldn't let me, the damn' fool."

Gibbons heard that. He had opened the door as she began laughing and his face was white. I felt a wave of relief sweep over me and jerked my head at Gibbons. "The nurse say anything about this?"

"She said a little." He shook his head. "I can't believe it."

"You heard what this one said, though. She's got Clare Trinavant and old McDougall locked in a dungeon of this mausoleum. You'd better put cuffs on her, but watch it—she's homicidal."

I didn't take the shotgun off her until he had her safely handcuffed and then I tossed it to him. "The nurse will fill you in on everything," I said. "I'm going to find Clare and Mac." I paused and looked down at the old man. His eyes were closed and he was apparently sleeping peacefully. I looked at the nurse. "Maybe you'd better tend your patient first. I wouldn't want to lose him now."

I hurried out and down the staircase. In the hall I found a bewildered-looking man in a dressing-gown. He came over to me at a shuffle, and said in an English accent, "What's all the fuss? Why are the police here?"

"Who are you?" I asked.

He drew himself up. "I'm Mr. Matterson's butler."

"Okay, Jeeves; do you have any spare keys for the cellars."

"I don't know who you are, sir, but——"

"This is police business," I said impatiently. "The keys?"

"I have a complete set of all the house keys in my pantry."

"Go get them—and make it fast."

I followed him and he took a bunch of keys from a cabinet which contained enough to outfit a locksmith's shop. Then I took him at a run down to the cellars which were of a pattern with the house—too big and mostly unused. I shouted around for a while and at last was rewarded by a faint cry. "That's it," I said. "Open that door."

He checked a number stencilled on the door and slowly selected a key from the bunch while I dithered with impatience. The door creaked open and then Clare was in my arms. When we unlatched from each other I saw she was filthily dirty, but probably not more than I was. Her face was streaked with dirt and there were runnels down her cheeks where the tears ran. "Thank God!" I said. "Thank God you're alive."

She gave a little cry and turned. "Mac's bad," she said. "They didn't feed us. Howard came down sometimes but we haven't seen him for five days."

I turned to the butler who was standing with his mouth open. "Send for a doctor and an ambulance," I said. "And move, damn you."

He trotted off and I went in to see how bad Mac was. It figured, of course. Crazy Lucy wouldn't bother to feed people

231

she already regarded as dead. Clare said, "We've had no food or water for five days."

"We'll fix that," I said, and stooped down to Mac. His breathing was quick and shallow and the pulse was weak. I picked him up in my arms and he seemed to weigh no more than a baby. I carried him upstairs with Clare following and found the butler in the hall. "A bedroom," I said. "And then food for six people—a big pot of coffee and a gallon of water."

"Water, sir?"

"For Christ's sake, don't repeat what I say. Yes—water."

We got Mac settled in bed and by that time the butler had aroused the house. I had to caution Clare not to drink water too fast nor to drink too much, and she fell on cold cuts as though she hadn't eaten for five weeks instead of five days .I reflected that I hadn't lived too badly in the Kinoxi Valley, after all.

We left Mac in the care of a doctor and went to find Gibbons who was on the telephone trying to make someone believe the incredible. "Yes," he was saying. "He's loose in the Kinoxi Valley—got a shotgun with rifled slugs. Yes, I said Howard Matterson. That's right, Bull Matterson's son. Of course I'm sure; I got it from Bull himself." He looked up at me, then said, "I've got a guy here who was shot at by Howard." He sighed and then brightened as though the news had finally sunk in on the other end of the line. "Look, I'm going up to the Kinoxi myself right now, but it's unlikely that I'll find him—he could be anywhere. I'll need a back-up force —we might have to cordon off a stretch of the woods."

I smiled a little sadly at Clare. This was where I came in but this time I was on the other end of a manhunt—not the sharp end. Gibbons spoke a few more words into the mouthpiece, then said, "I'll ring you just before I leave with any more dope I can get." He put down the telephone. "This is goddam incredible."

"You don't have to tell me," I said tiredly, and sat down. "Did you really speak to Bull?"

Gibbons nodded and there was a kind of desperate awe in his face. "He gave me specific instructions," he said. "I'm to shoot and kill Howard on sight just as if he were a mad dog."

"Bull's not too far wrong," I said. "You've seen Lucy—she's crazy enough, isn't she?"

Gibbons shuddered slightly, then pulled himself together. "We don't do things like that, though," he said firmly. "I'll bring him in alive."

"Don't be too much the goddam hero," I advised. "He's got a shotgun—a five-shot automatic loaded with 12-gauge rifled slugs. He nearly cut Jimmy Waystrand in two with one shot." I shrugged. "But you're the professional. I suppose you know what you're doing."

Gibbons fingered some sheets of paper. "Is all this true? All this about them killing the Trinavants years ago?"

"It's a verbatim report of what old Matterson said. I'm witness to that."

"All right," he said. "I have a map here. Show me where you last saw Howard."

I bent over as he unfolded the map. "Right there," I said. "He took two shots at the helicopter as we were taking off. If you want to get up to the Kinoxi fast that helicopter is just outside the house, and there might even be a pilot, too. If he objects to going back to the Kinoxi tell him I said he was to go."

Gibbons looked at me closely. "I got a pretty garbled story from that nurse. I gather you've been on the run from Howard and a bunch of loggers for three weeks."

"An exaggeration," I said. "Less than two weeks."

"Why the hell didn't you come to me?" Gibbons demanded.

It was then I started to laugh. I laughed until the tears came to my eyes and my sides ached. I laughed myself into hysteria and they had to bring a doctor to calm me down. I was still chuckling when they put me to bed and I fell asleep.

2

I woke up fifteen hours later to find Clare at the bedside. I saw her face in profile and I've never seen anything so lovely. She became aware I was awake and turned. "Hello, Boyd," she said.

"Hi, Trinavant." I stretched luxuriously. "What time is it?"

"Just past midday." She looked at me critically. "You could do with a clean-up. Seen yourself lately?"

I rubbed my jaw. It no longer prickled because the hair had grown too long for that. I said, "Maybe I'll grow a beard."

"Just you dare." She pointed. "There's a bathroom through there, and I got you a razor."

"I trust I won't offend your maidenly modesty," I said as I threw back the sheets. I swung out of bed and walked into the bathroom. The face that stared at me from the big mirror was the face of a stranger—haggard and wild-looking. "My God!" I said. "No wonder that pilot was wetting his pants. I bet I could stop cows giving milk."

"It will come right with the application of soap and water," she said.

I filled the bath and splashed happily for half an hour, then shaved and dressed. Dressed in my own clothes, too. I said, "How did these get here?"

"I had them brought from Mac's cabin," said Clare.

Sudden remembrance hit me. "How is he?"

"He'll be all right," she said. "He's as tough as Bull. He seems to be bearing up under the strain, too."

"I want to get him in court to tell that story," I said grimly. "After that I don't care if he drops dead on the spot."

"Don't be too hard on him, Bob," said Clare seriously. "He had a hard decision to make."

I said no more about it. "Have you been filled in on all the details of this caper?" I asked.

"Mostly, I guess—except for what you have to tell me. But that can wait, darling. We have plenty of time." She looked at me straightly. "Have you decided who you are?"

I shrugged. "Does it matter? No, Clare; I'm no nearer finding out. I've been thinking about it, though. After the Matterson family a guy like Grant, a drug-pusher, is pretty small potatoes. What's a drug-peddler compared with a couple of multiple murderers? Maybe Grant wasn't such a bad guy, after all. Anyway—as I said—does it matter? As far as I'm concerned I'm just Bob Boyd."

"Oh, darling, I told you that," she said. We had a pretty passionate few minutes then, and after coming out of the clinch and wiping off the lipstick, I said, "I've just thought of

234

a funny thing. I used to have bad dreams—real shockers they were—and I'd wake up sweating and screaming. But you know what? When I was under *real* pressure in the Kinoxi with all those guys after my blood and Howard coming after me with his shotgun I didn't get too much sleep. But when I did sleep I didn't dream at all. I think that's strange."

She said, "Perhaps the fact you were in real danger destroyed the imaginary danger of the dream. What's past is past, Bob; a dream can't really hurt you. Let's hope they don't come back."

I grinned. "Any nightmares I have from now on are likely to be concerned with that automatic shotgun of Howard's. That really gave me the screaming meemies."

We went in to see McDougall. He was still under sedation but the doctor said he was going to be all right, and he had a pretty nurse to look after him. He was conscious enough to wink at me, though, and he said drowsily, "For a minute there, down in that cellar, I thought you were going to let me down, son."

I didn't see Bull Matterson because his doctor was with him, but I saw the night nurse. I said, "I'm sorry I busted in on you like that, Miss . . . er . . ."

"Smithson," she supplied. She smiled. "That's all right, Mr. Boyd."

"And I'm glad you turned out to be level-headed," I said. "A squawking woman rousing the house right then could have queered my pitch."

"Oh, I wouldn't have made a noise under any circumstances," said Miss Smithson primly. "It would have adversely affected Mr. Matterson's health."

I looked straight-facedly at Clare who was disposed to burst into a fit of the giggles and we took our departure of the Matterson residence. As we drove away in Clare's station-wagon I looked into the driving mirror at the over-bloated splendour of that fake castle and heartily wished I'd never see it again.

Clare said pensively, "Do you know how old Lucy was when she and Howard killed Uncle John, Aunt Anne and Frank?"

"No."

"She was eighteen years old—just eighteen. How could any body do anything like that at eighteen?"

I didn't know, so I said nothing and we drove in silenc through Fort Farrell and on to the road which led to Mac cabin. It was only just before the turn-off that I smote th driving wheel, and said, "My God, I must be nuts! I haven told anyone about the quick clay. I clean forgot."

I suppose it wasn't surprising that I had forgotten. I'd ha other things on my mind—such as preventing myself gettin killed—and Bull Matterson's revelations had also helped t drive it out of my head. I braked to a quick standstill an prepared to do a U-turn, then had second thoughts. "I'd bette go on up to the dam. The police should have a check-poir there to prevent anyone going up into the Kinoxi."

"Do you think they'll have caught Howard yet?"

"Not a chance," I said. "He'll be able to run rings roun them. For a while, at least." I put the car into gear. "I'll dro you at the cabin."

"No you won't," said Clare. "I'm coming up to the dam."

I took one look at her and sighed. She had her stubbor expression all set for instant use and I had no time to argu "All right," I said. "But stay out of trouble."

We made good time on the Kinoxi road—there were n trucks to hinder progress—but we were stopped by a patro man half a mile short of the power-house. He flagged us dow and walked over to the car. "This is as far as you go," he sai "No one goes beyond this point. We don't want any sigh seers."

"What's happening up there?"

"Nothing that would interest you," he said patiently. "Ju turn your car round and get going."

I said, "My name's Boyd—this is Miss Trinavant. I want see your boss."

He stared at me curiously. "You the Boyd that started a this ruckus?"

"Me!" I said indignantly. "What about Howard Matte son?"

"I guess it's all right," he said thoughtfully. "You'll want see Captain Crupper—he's up at the dam. If he's not the

236

you wait for him; we don't want anything going wrong in the Kinoxi."

"Then you haven't caught him yet," said Clare.

"Not that I know of," said the patrolman. He stood back and waved us on.

Work was still going on at the power-house and I could see a few miniscule figures on top of the sheer concrete wall of the dam. There was still the sea of mud at the bottom of the escarpment, a slick, slimy mess churned up by the wheels of trucks. It had been too much for a couple of trucks which were bogged down to their axles. A team of sweating men had anchored a power-winch on firm ground and was hauling one of them out bodily.

I pulled up next to a big car and found myself looking at Donner, who looked back at me expressionlessly, then got out of the car. I went to meet him with Clare close behind. "Donner, you're in trouble." I waved at the power-house and up at the dam.

"Trouble!" he said bitterly. "You think *this* is trouble?" For a reputedly bloodless and nerveless man he was showing a hell of a lot of emotion. "Those goddam crazy Mattersons," he burst out. "They've put me in one hell of a spot."

I knew what was wrong with him. He was one of those people who make bullets for others to shoot, but he'd never take responsibility for pulling the trigger himself; a perfect second-in-command for Bull Matterson but without Bull's guts. Now he found himself in charge of the Matterson Empire, if only temporarily, and the strain was telling. Particularly as the whole thing was about to fall apart. Nothing could now prevent the whole story coming into the open, especially the double-dealing with the Trinavant Trust, and it was easy to see that Donner would be hunting around for ways to unload the blame on to someone else.

It wouldn't be too hard—Bull Matterson was too sick to fight back and Howard, the murderer, was a perfect scapegoat. But it was a trying time for Donner. However, I wasn't interested in his troubles because a bigger danger was impending.

I said, "This is more trouble than you think. Did you read my report on the geology of the Kinoxi Valley?"

"That was Howard's baby," said Donner. "I'm just the accountant. I didn't see the report and I wouldn't have understood it if I had."

He was already weaselling out from under the chopper; he could see trouble coming and was disclaiming responsibility. Probably, on the balance of things, he really hadn't seen the report. Anyway, that didn't matter—what mattered was getting every construction man off the site as soon as possible.

I pointed up at the escarpment. "That hillside is in danger of caving in, Donner. It can go any tme. You've got to get your men out of here."

He looked at me incredulously. "Are you crazy? We've lost enough time already because that dumb bastard Howard pulled men away to look for you. Every day's delay is costing us thousands of dollars. We've lost enough time because of this mud, anyway."

"Donner, get it through your skull that you're in trouble. I really mean what I say. That bloody hillside is going to come down on you."

He swung his head and stared across at the solid slope of the escarpment, then gave me an odd look. "What the hell are you talking about? How can a hill cave in?"

"You should have read that report," I said. "I found quick clay deposits in the valley. For God's sake, didn't you do a geological survey of the foundations of the dam?"

"That was Howard's business—he looked after the technical side. What's this quick clay?"

"An apparently solid substance that turns liquid if given a sudden shock—and it doesn't need much of a shock. As near as I can check there's a bed of it running right under the dam." I grinned at him humourlessly. "Let's look on the bright side. If it goes, then a couple of million tons of topsoil is going to cover your power-house—the clay will liquefy and carry the topsoil with it. That's the best that can happen."

Clare touched my elbow. "And the worst?"

I nodded towards the dam. "It might jerk the foundation from under that hunk of concrete. If that happens, then all the water behind the dam will flow right over where we're standing now. How much water is backed up behind there, Donner?"

238

He didn't answer my question. Instead, he smiled thinly. "You tell a good story, Boyd. I like it very much, but I don't go for it. You have a good imagination—an earthquake laid on to order shows real creative thought." He scratched his chin. "The only thing I can't figure is what you reckon to gain by stopping construction now. I just can't figure your angle."

I gaped at him. McDougall had been right—this man figured every motive in dollars and cents. I drew a deep breath, and said, "You stupid, ignorant oaf!" I turned from him in disgust. "Where's the police captain who's supposed to be here?"

"Here he comes now," said Donner. "Coming out of the valley."

I looked up to the road that clung to the hillside above the dam. A car was coming down, trailing a dust plume behind it. "Captain Crupper hasn't the power to close down operations," said Donner. "I wish I knew what you were figuring, Boyd. Why don't you tell me what you're getting at?"

Clare said hotly, "Something you wouldn't understand, Donner. He just wants to save your life, although I'm damned if I know why. He also wants to save the lives of all those men, even though they were after his blood not long ago."

Donner smiled and shrugged. "Save those speeches for suckers, Miss Trinavant."

I said, "Donner, you're in trouble already—but not in real bad trouble because the worst that can happen to you is jail. But I'll tell you something: if anyone gets killed here because you've ignored a warning you'll have a lynch-mob after you and you'll be damned lucky not to be strung up to the nearest tree."

The police car rolled to a stop quite close and Captain Crupper got out and came over. "Mr. Donner, I asked you to meet me here, but apparently it is now unnecessary."

Donner said, "Captain Crupper, this is Mr. Boyd and Miss Trinavant."

Crupper switched hard eyes to me. "Hm—you stirred up something here, Boyd. I'm sorry it had to happen to you—and to you, Miss Trinavant." He looked at Donner. "It appears an investigation of the Matterson Corporation would be in order; running a private manhunt doesn't come under normal business procedures."

"That was Howard Matterson's affair," said Donner hastily "I knew nothing about it."

"You won't have to worry about him any more," said Crupper curtly. "We've got him."

"You got on to him fast," I said. "I'd have guessed it would take longer."

With grim humour Crupper said, "He's not as good in the woods as you, apparently." His lips tightened. "It cost us a good man."

"I'm sorry to hear that."

He slapped his gloves against his thigh. "Gibbons was shot in the knee. His leg was amputated this morning."

So Gibbons had to go and do the heroic bit after all. I said, "I warned him not to monkey around with Howard. But Matterson warned him, too."

"I know," said Crupper tiredly. "But we always try the pacific way first. We can't shoot on sight just on someone's say-so. There are laws in this country, Boyd."

I hadn't noticed the law around the Kinoxi Valley during the last couple of weeks, but I said nothing about that. "There's going to be a lot more good men lost if this idiot Donner doesn't pull them off this site."

Crupper reacted fast. He jerked his head round to look at the power-house, then speared me with a cold glance. "What do you mean by that?"

Donner said silkily, "Mr. Boyd has laid on an instant earthquake. He's been trying to make me believe that hillside is going to collapse."

"I'm a geologist," I said deliberately. "Tell me, Captain, what is the road like up in the Kinoxi? Wet or dry?"

He looked at me as though I had gone mad. "Pretty dry."

"I know," I said. "You were kicking up quite a cloud of dust coming down the hill. Now tell me, Captain: where the hell do you think all this mud is coming from?" I pointed to the greasy waste around the power-house.

Crupper stared at the mud, then looked at me thoughtfully. "All right. You tell me."

So I went into it again and finally said, "Clare, tell the Captain of the demonstration I showed you with the quick clay cores. Don't embroider it—just tell it straight."

She hesitated. "Well, Bob had some samples of earth—he'd taken them from up here before Howard ran him off. He took a piece and showed how it could bear a big weight. Then he took another piece and stirred it in a jug. It turned to thin mud. That's about all."

"Sounds like a conjuring trick," said the Captain. He sighed. "Now I have a thing like this dumped on me. Mr. Donner, what about pulling your men off pending an expert investigation of the site?"

"Now look here, Crupper," Donner expostulated. "We've had enough delay. I'm not going to waste thousands of dollars just on Boyd's word. He's been trying to stop this project all along and I'm not going to let him get away with any more."

Crupper was troubled. "There doesn't seem to be anything I can do, Mr. Boyd. If I stop work on the dam and nothing is wrong my neck will be on the block."

"You're damn' right," said Donner viciously.

Crupper looked at him with dislike. "However," he said firmly, "if I thought it in the public interest I'd stop construction right here and now."

I said, "You don't have to take my word for it. Ring the geology faculty at any university. Try to get hold of a soil mechanics specialist if you can, but any competent geologist will be able to confirm it."

Crupper said with decision, "Where's your telephone, Mr. Donner?"

"Now, wait a minute," cried Donner. "You're not going to grind this man's axe for him, are you, Crupper?"

Clare said suddenly, "Do you know why Bull Matterson had a heart-attack, Donner?"

He shrugged. "It was something about Boyd being Frank Trinavant. Now, there's a cock-and-bull story!"

"But what if it's true?" she said softly. "It will mean that Bob Boyd will be bossing the Matterson Corporation in the future. He'll be *your* boss, Donner! I'd think about that if I were you."

Donner gave her a startled glance, then looked at me. I grinned at Clare and said, "Check!" She was pulling a bluff but it was good enough to manipulate Donner, so I followed up quickly. "Do you pull the men off the site or not?"

Donner was bewildered; things were happening too fast for him. "No!" he said. "This is impossible. Things don't happen like this." He was a man who lived too far from nature, manipulating his money counters in drilled formations, unconscious of living in an artificial environment. He could not conceive of a situation he could not control.

Crupper said harshly, "Put up or shut up. Where's your site boss?"

"Over in the power-house," said Donner listlessly.

"Let's get over there." Crupper moved off through the mud.

I said to Clare, "Take the car and get out of here."

"I'll go when you go," she said firmly, and followed me to the power-house. There wasn't much I could do about that, short of spanking her, so I let it go. As we went along I sampled the mud, rubbing it between forefinger and thumb. It still had that slick, soapy feeling—the feeling of disaster.

I caught up with Crupper. "You'd better plan for the worst, Captain. Let's assume the dam goes and the lake busts through here. The flood should follow the course of the Kinoxi River pretty roughly. That area should be evacuated."

"Thank God this is an underpopulated country," he said. "There are only two families likely to be in trouble." He snapped his fingers. "And there's a new logging camp just been set up. Where's that goddam telephone?"

Donner came back just as Crupper finished his telephone conversation. Behind him was a big hulk of a man whom I had last seen closely when crashing a gun butt into his jaw.

It was Novak.

He stiffened when he saw me and his hands curled into fists. He shouldered Donner aside and strode over and instinctively I got ready for him, hoping that Crupper could break up the fight quickly. Without taking my eyes off him, I said to Clare, "Get away from me—fast."

Novak stood before me with an unsmiling face. "Boyd, you bastard," he whispered. His arm came up slowly and I was astonished to see, not a fist but an open hand extended in friendship. "Sorry about last week," he said. "But Howard Matterson had us all steamed up."

As I took his hand he grinned and rubbed his face. "You damn' near busted my jaw, you know."

"I did it without animosity," I said. "No hard feelings?"

242

"No hard feelings." He laughed. "But I'd like to take a friendly poke at you some time just to see if I could have licked you."

"All right," said Crupper testily. "This isn't old home week." He looked at Donner. "Do you tell him—or must I?"

Donner sagged and looked suddenly much smaller than he really was. He hesitated and said in a low voice, "Withdraw the men from the site."

Novak looked at him blankly. "Huh!"

"You heard him," said Crupper abruptly. "Pull out your men."

"Yeah, I heard him," said Novak. "But what the hell?" He tapped Donner on the chest. "You've been pushing to get this job finished; now you want us to stop. Is that right?"

"That's right," said Donner sourly.

"Okay!" Novak shrugged. "Just as long as I get it straight. I don't want any comeback."

I said, "Wait a minute; let's do this right. Come with me, Novak." We went outside and I looked up at the dam. "How many men have you got here?"

"About sixty."

"Where are they?"

Novak waved his hand. "About half are down here at the power-house; there are a few up at the dam and maybe a dozen scattered around I don't know where. This is a big site to keep track of everybody. What the hell's going on, anyway?"

I pointed up the escarpment to the dam. "You see that slope? I don't want anyone walking on it. So those guys up at he dam will have to take to the high ground on either side. See Captain Crupper about getting the boys away from the power-house. But remember—no one walks on that slope."

"I guess you know what you're doing," he said. "As long as Donner goes along with it, it's okay by me. Getting the guys off the dam will be easy—we have a phone line up to there."

"Another thing—have someone open the sluices up there before leaving." That was merely a gesture—it would take a long time for the new Lake Matterson to empty but whether the slope collapsed or not it would have to be done eventually and the job might as well be started as soon as possible.

Novak went back into the power-house but I waited a while

243

—maybe ten minutes—then I saw the small figures of men moving off the dam and away from the danger zone. Satisfied, I went inside to find Crupper organizing the evacuation of the power-house. "Just walk out of here and find high ground," he was saying. "Keep off the Fort Farrell road and away from the river—keep off the valley bottom altogether."

Someone shouted, "If you're expecting the dam to bust you're crazy."

"I know it's a good dam," said Crupper. "But something's come up and we're just taking precautions. Move, you guys, it's no skin off your nose because you're still on full pay." He grinned sardonically at Donner, then turned to me. "That means us, too—everyone gets out of here."

I was feeling easier. "Sure. Come on, Clare. This time you are leaving, and so am I."

Donner said in a high voice, "So everyone leaves—then what?"

"Then I have a closer look at the situation. I know the dangers and I'll walk on that slope as though on eggs."

"But what can you *do* about it?"

"It can be stabilized," I said. "Others will know more about that than I do. But in my opinion the only way will be to drain the lake and cap the clay outcrop. We can only hope the thing doesn't slip before then."

Novak said in sudden comprehension, "*Quick clay?*"

"That's right. What do you know about it?"

"I've been a construction man all my life," he said. "I'm not all that stupid."

Someone yelled across the room, "Novak, we can't find Skinner and Burke."

"What were they doing?"

"Taking out stumps below the dam."

Novak bellowed, "Johnson; where the hell's Johnson?" A burly man detached himself from the crowd and came across. "Did you send Skinner and Burke to dig stumps below the dam?"

Johnson said, "That's right. Aren't they around here?"

"Just how were they taking out those stumps?" asked Novak.

"They'd got most of 'em out," said Johnson. "But there

244

were three real back-breakers. Skinner has a blasting ticket so I gave him some gelignite."

Novak went very still and looked at me. "Christ!" I said. "They must be stopped." I could visualize the effect of that sharp jolt on the house-of-cards structure that was quick clay. There would be a sudden collapse, locally at first, but spreading in a chain reaction right across the hillside, just like one domino knocks down the next and the next and so on to the end of the line. Firm clay would be instantaneously transformed into liquid mud and the whole hillside would collapse.

I swung round. "Clare, get the hell out of here." She saw the expression on my face and turned away immediately. "Crupper get everyone out fast."

Novak plunged past me, heading for the door. "I know where they are." I followed him and we stood staring up at the dam while the power-house erupted like an ants' nest stirred with a stick. There was no movement on the escarpment—no movement at all. Just a confusion of shadows as the low sun struck on rocks and trees.

Novak said hoarsely, "I think they'll be up there—on the right, just under the dam."

"Come on," I said, and began to run. It was a long way to the dam and it was uphill and we were pounding up that damned escarpment. I grabbed Novak's arm. "Take it easy——we might start a slide ourselves." If the shear strength had fallen according to my estimates it wouldn't take much disturbance to initiate the chain reaction. The shear strength was probably under five hundred pounds a square foot by now—less than the pressure exerted by Novak's boot hitting the ground at a dead run.

We moved gently and as fast as we could up the escarpment and it took us nearly fifteen minutes to do that quarter-mile. Novak lifted his voice in a shout. "Skinner! Burke!" The echoes rebounded from the sheer concrete face of the dam which loomed over us.

Someone quite close said, "Yeah, what do you want?"

I turned. A man was squatting with his back to a boulder and looking up at us curiously. "Burke!" said Novak explosively. "Where's Skinner?"

Burke waved. "Over behind those rocks."

"What's he doing?"

"We're getting ready to blow that stump—that one, there."

It was a big stump, the remnant of a tall tree, and I could see the thin detonating wire leading away from it. "There's going to be no blasting," said Novak and walked quickly over to the stump.

"Hey!" said Burke in alarm. "Keep away from there. It's going to blow any second."

It was one of the bravest things I have seen. Novak calmly leaned over the stump and jerked the wire away, bringing the electrical detonator with it. He tossed it to the ground casually and walked back. "I said there'll be no blasting," he said. "Now, get the hell out of here, Burke." He pointed up to the road that clung to the hillside above the dam. "Go that way —not down to the power-house."

Burke shrugged. "Okay, you're the boss." He turned and walked off, then paused. "If you want the blasting stopped you'll have to hurry. Skinner's blowing three stumps all at once. That was only one of them."

"My God!" I said, and both Novak and I turned towards the jumble of rocks where Skinner was. But it was too late. There was a sharp popping sound in the distance, not very loud, and a nearer *crack* as the detonator Novak had pulled out exploded harmlessly. Two plumes of dust and smoke shot into the air about fifty yards away and hung for a moment before being dissipated by the breeze.

I held my breath and then slowly released it in a sigh. Novak grinned. "Looks like we got away with it that time," he said. He put his hand to his forehead then looked at the dampness on his fingers. "Sure makes a man sweat."

"We'd better get Skinner off here," I said. As I said it I heard a faint faraway sound like distant thunder—something more felt inside the head than heard with the ears—and there was an almost imperceptible quiver beneath my feet.

Novak stopped in mid-stride. "What's that?" He looked about him doubtfully.

The sound—if it was a sound—came again and the quiver of the earth was stronger. "Look!" I said, and pointed to a tall, spindly tree. The top was shivering like a grass stalk in a strong wind, and as we watched, the whole tree leaned sideways and fell to the earth. "The slide," I yelled. "It's started."

246

A figure came into sight across the hillside. "Skinner!" shouted Novak. "Get the hell out of there!"

The ground thrummed under my boots and the landscape seemed to change before my eyes. It wasn't anything one could pin down, there was no sudden alteration—just a brief, flickering change. Skinner came running across but he had not come half the distance when the change became catastrophic.

He disappeared. Where he had been was a jumble of moving boulders tossed like corks in a stream as the whole hillside *flowed.* The entire landscape seemed to slip sideways smoothly and there was a deafening noise, the like of which I had never heard before. It was like thunder, it was like the sound of a jet bomber from very close quarters, it was like the drum-roll of tympani in an orchestra magnified a thousand times—and yet it was like none of these. And underneath the clamour was another sound, a glutinous, sucking noise as you might make when pulling a boot out of mud—but this was a giant's boot.

Novak and I stood rooted for a moment helplessly looking at the place where Skinner had vanished. But it was no longer correct to call it a place because a *place* by its nature is a definite locality, a fixed point. Nothing was fixed on this escarpment and the "place" where Skinner had been ground between the boulders was already a hundred yards downhill and moving away rapidly.

I don't suppose we stood there for more than two or three seconds, although it seemed an eternity. I dragged myself out of this shocked trance and shouted above the racket, "Run for it, Novak. It's spreading this way."

We turned and plunged across the hillside, heading for the road which represented safety and life. But the chain reaction under our feet, flashing through the unstable clay thirty feet underground, moved faster than we did, and the seemingly solid ground rocked and slid under us, dipping and moving like an ocean.

We ran through a scattering of saplings which bent and swayed in all directions and one fell immediately in front of us, its roots tearing free from the moving ground. I vaulted it and ran on but was momentarily held by a half yell, half grunt from behind. I turned and saw Novak sprawled on the ground, held down by the branch of another toppled tree.

247

When I bent to examine him he seemed dazed and only half-conscious and I struggled violently to release him. Luckily it was only a sapling but it took all my strength to shift it. The continuous movement of the ground made me feel queasy and all the strength seemed to be leeched from my muscles. It was very hard to think consecutively, too, because of the tremendous noise—it was like being inside a monstrous drum beaten on by a giant.

But I got him free and only just in time. A big glacial boulder moved past, tossing like a cork on a stream, right over the place where he had been pinned. His eyes were open but glazed and he had a witless look about him. I slapped his face hard and a glimmer of intelligence came back. "Run," I shouted. "Run, goddam you!"

So we ran again, with Novak leaning heavily on my arm and I tried to steer a straight course to safety, something which was damn' near impossible because this was like crossing a swiftly flowing river and we were being swept downstream. In front of us a fountain of muddy water suddenly jetted fifteen feet into the air and soaked us. I knew what that was—the water was being squeezed out of the quick clay, millions of gallons of it. Already the ground beneath my feet was slippery with mud and we slithered and slid about helplessly as this handicap was added to the violent movements of the earth itself.

But we made it. As we came nearer the edge of the slide the movement became less and I finally let Novak slip to solid ground and sobbed for breath. Not very far away Burke was lying prone, his hands scrabbling into the soil as though to clutch the whole planet to himself. He was screaming at the top of his voice.

From the time the first tree went down to the time I dropped Novak in safety couldn't have been more than one minute—one long minute in which we had run a whole fifty yards. That was no record-breaking time but I don't think a champion sprinter could have bettered it.

I wanted to help Novak and Burke but something, call it professional interest, held my attention on this great catastrophe. The whole of the land was moving downhill at an ever-increasing speed. The front of the slide was just short of the power-house and whole trees were being tossed into the air like spillikins and boulders ground and clashed together with a noise like thunder. The front of the flow hit the power-house and the walls caved in, and the whole building seemed to fold and disappear under a river of moving earth.

The topsoil flowed away to the south and I thought it was never going to stop. Water, squeezed from the clay, spurted in fountains everywhere, and through the soles of my boots I could feel the vibrations of millions of tons of earth on the move.

But finally it did stop and everything lay quiet except for the occasional rumble here and there as strains were eased and pressures equalized. Not more than two minutes had elapsed since the blasting of the stumps and the slide was fully two thousand feet long and extended five hundred feet from hill-side to hillside. Ponds of muddy water lay everywhere. The clay had given up all its water in that awful cataclysm and there would be little danger of a further slide.

I looked down to where the power house had been and saw just a waste of torn earth. The slide had erased the power-house and had gone on to cut the Fort Farrell road. The little group of cars that had been parked on the road had vanished, and from the tip of the slide gushed a torrent of muddy water already carving a bed in the soft earth as it rushed to join the Kinoxi River. There was no other move-ment at all down there and I was painfully aware that Clare might be dead.

Novak got to his feet groggily and jerked his head quickly as though to shake his brains back into position. When he spoke he shouted, "How the hell . . .?" He looked at me in astonishment and began again more quietly. "How the hell did we get out of there?" He waved his hand at the slide.

"Sheer luck and strong legs," I replied.

Burke was still clutching the ground and his screams had not diminished. Novak swung round. "For God's sake, shut up!" he yelled. "You've survived." But Burke took no notice.

A car door slammed on the road above and I looked up to see a policeman staring at the scene as though he couldn't believe his eyes. "What happened?" he called.

"We used a mite too much gelignite," shouted Novak sardonically. He walked over to Burke, bent down and clouted him on the side of the head. Burke's screams suddenly stopped but he continued to sob raspingly.

The policeman scrambled down to us. "Where did you come from?" I asked.

"From up the Kinoxi Valley," he said. "I'm taking a prisoner into Fort Farrell." He clicked his tongue as he gazed down at the blocked road. "Looks as though I'll have to find another way round."

"Is that Howard Matterson you have up there?" When he nodded I said, "Keep tight hold of that bastard. But you'd better go on down there—you might find Captain Crupper, if he's still alive." I saw another policeman on the road. "How many are there in your car?"

"Four of us, plus Matterson."

"You'll be needed in rescue work," I said. "You'd better get moving."

He looked to where Novak was cradling Burke in his arms. "Will you be all right here?"

I was tempted to go with him to the bottom, but Burke was in no condition to move and Novak couldn't carry him unaided. "We'll be all right," I said.

He turned to climb up to the road and at that moment there was a great groan as of intense pain. At first I thought it was Burke but when the sound came again it was much louder and boomed right down the valley.

The dam was groaning under the pressure of water behind it and I knew what that meant. "Jesus!" I said.

Novak picked up Burke bodily and began to stumble up the hill. The policeman was climbing as if the devil was at his heels, and I ran across to help Novak. "Don't be a damn fool," he panted. "You can't help."

It was true; two men couldn't lug Burke up that slope any faster than one, but I hung around Novak in case he slipped. More noises were coming from the great concrete wall of the dam, strange creakings and sudden explosions. I looked over my shoulder and saw something incredible—water under pressure fountaining from *underneath* the dam. It jetted a hundred feet high and spray blew in my face.

"It's going," I yelled, and looped my arm around a tree, grabbing Novak's leather belt with the other hand.

250

There was a loud crash and a fissure appeared, zig-zagging down the concrete face from top to bottom. The quick clay had slipped from underneath the dam and the waters of Lake Matterson were blowing the foundations out, leaving nothing to bear the enormous weight.

Another crack appeared on the face of the dam and then the water pressure from behind became too much and the whole massive structure was pushed aside impatiently by a solid wall of water. A great chunk of reinforced concrete was thrown out from the dam; it weighed every ounce of five hundred tons, but it was thrown into the air and toppled in twisting flight until it crashed into the sea of mud below. In the next second it was overwhelmed and covered by the rush of lake water.

And so were we.

We just hadn't been able to go that extra few feet up the hill and the flood swirled in its first crest just above us. I had the sense to see what was coming and to fill my lungs with air before the water hit us so I didn't think I'd drown, but I thought I'd be torn in two as the fast water hit Novak and swung him off his feet.

With one hand grasping his belt I was holding the weight of two big men and I thought my arm would be sprung from its socket. The muscles in the other arm cracked as I desperately hung on to the tree and my lungs were bursting when I finally managed to gulp air.

That first great crest could not last long but while it did it filled the valley from side to side and was a hundred feet deep in that first great lunge to the south. But it dropped rapidly and I was thankful to find the strain taken from me as a policeman grabbed Novak.

He shook his head and gasped. "I couldn't help it," he cried desolately. "I couldn't hold him."

Burke was gone!

There was a new, although impermanent, river below us which had calmed down to a steady and remorseless multi-million-gallon flow that would ebb, hour by hour, until there would be no more Matterson Lake—just the little stream called the Kinoxi River that had flowed from this valley for the last fifteen thousand years. But it was still a raging torrent, three hundred feet wide and fifty feet deep, when I staggered

251

up and planted my boots firmly on that wonderful solid roa

I leaned on the side of the police car and shuddered vio
ently and then became aware that someone was watching m
In the back of the car, sandwiched between two policeme
was Howard Matterson, and his teeth were drawn back in
wolf-like grin. He looked totally mad.

Someone tapped me on the shoulder. "Get into the car—
we'll take you to the bottom."

I shook my head. "If I travel with that man you couldn
stop me killing him."

The policeman gave me an odd look and shrugged. "Su
yourself."

I walked slowly down the road towards the bottom of th
hill and desperately wondered if I would find Clare. I was gla
to see some survivors; they picked their way slowly down th
hillside and walked like somnambulists. I came across Donne
he was smeared with viscid mud from head to foot and wa
standing looking at the flood water as it streamed past. As
passed him I heard him muttering. Over and over again he wa
saying, "Millions of dollars; millions of dollars—all gone
Millions and millions."

"Bob! Oh, Bob!"

I swung round and the next moment Clare was in my arm
sobbing and laughing at the same time. "I thought you wer
dead," she said. "Oh, darling, I thought you were dead."

I managed a grin. "The Mattersons had a last crack at m
but I came through."

"Hey, Boyd!" It was Crupper, no longer neat and trim
uniformed but looking like a tramp. Any one of his own me
would have put him in jail just for looking like he did. H
stuck his hand out. "I never expected to see you again."

"I thought the same about you," I said. "How many wer
lost?"

"I know of five for certain," he said gravely. "We haven
finished checking yet—and God knows what is happenin
downstream. They didn't have much warning."

"You can make it seven for certain," I said. "Skinner an
Burke both bought it. Novak came through."

"There's a lot needs doing," said Crupper. "I'll get on wit
it."

I didn't volunteer for anything. I'd had a bellyful of troubl

nd all I wanted to do was to go away somewhere and be very
uiet. Clare took my arm. "Come," she said. "We'll go away
om here. If we climb the hill there we might be able to find
way round the flood."

So we made our way up the hill very slowly, and at the top
e rested a while and looked north over the Kinoxi Valley.
he waters of Matterson Lake would fall very quickly to
veal the jagged stumps of a raped land. But the trees still
ood in the north—the forest in which I had been hunted like
1 animal. I didn't hate the forest because I reckoned it had
ved my life in a way.

I thought I could see the green of the trees in the far
istance. Clare and I had lost four million dollars between us
ecause the Forestry Service would never allow a total cut
ow. Yet we were not displeased. The trees would stay and
row and be cut down in their season, and the deer would
rowse in their shade—and maybe I would have time to make
iends with brother Bruin after having made amends for the
are I gave him.

Clare took my hand and we walked slowly along the crest
f the hill. It was a long way home, but we'd make it.

Desmond Bagley

'Mr. Bagley is nowadays incomparable.' *Sunday Times*

The Snow Tiger

The Tightrope Men

The Freedom Trap

Running Blind

The Spoilers

Landslide

The Golden Keel

Wyatt's Hurricane

High Citadel

The Vivero Letter

 *Fontana Books*

Alistair MacLean

His first book, HMS *Ulysses*, published in 1955, was outstandingly successful. It led the way to a string of best-selling novels which have established Alistair MacLean as the most popular adventure writer of our time.

Breakheart Pass

Bear Island

Caravan to Vaccarès

The Dark Crusader

Fear is the Key

Force 10 from Navarone

The Golden Rendezvous

The Guns of Navarone

HMS *Ulysses*

Ice Station Zebra

The Last Frontier

Puppet on a Chain

The Satan Bug

South by Java Head

The Way to Dusty Death

When Eight Bells Toll

Where Eagles Dare

Night Without End

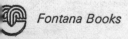 *Fontana Books*

Fontana Books

Fontana is a leading paperback publisher of fiction and non-fiction, with authors ranging from Alistair MacLean, Agatha Christie and Desmond Bagley to Solzhenitsyn and Pasternak, from Gerald Durrell and Joy Adamson to the famous Modern Masters series.

In addition to a wide-ranging collection of internationally popular writers of fiction, Fontana also has an outstanding reputation for history, natural history, military history, psychology, psychiatry, politics, economics, religion and the social sciences.

All Fontana books are available at your bookshop or newsagent; or can be ordered direct. Just fill in the form and list the titles you want.

FONTANA BOOKS, Cash Sales Department, G.P.O. Box 29, Douglas, Isle of Man, British Isles. Please send purchase price, plus 8p per book. Customers outside the U.K. send purchase price, plus 10p per book. Cheque, postal or money order. No currency.

NAME (Block letters)

ADDRESS
